BEAU'
THE

BY
LOIS FAYE DYER

AND

THEIR MIRACLE
TWINS

BY
NIKKI LOGAN

MILLS
BOON

Dear Reader,

Collaborating with friends Chris Flynn, Pat Kay and Allison Leigh to create our second HUNT FOR CINDERELLA mini-series ranks in my top-ten, most-fun-ever projects. We four had so much fun brainstorming these books. Billionaire Harry Hunt has turned his matchmaking focus on the four Fairchild sisters—and in my story, Frankie Fairchild is determined to foil his benevolent scheming. But when she enlists childhood crush Eli Wolf in a plan to stymie Harry, she gets far more than a co-conspirator—because Eli is the one man Frankie has never been able to resist. And unknown to Frankie, Eli's more than ready to convince her he's the one man she can trust with her heart.

I hope you enjoy Frankie and Eli's story—and that you'll return next month for *Meet Mr Prince* by Patricia Kay for the final installment in the HUNT FOR CINDERELLA series.

Happy reading!

Lois

BEAUTY AND THE WOLF

BY
LOIS FAYE DYER

All the characters in this book have no existence outside the imagination of the author, and have no relation whatsoever to anyone bearing the same name or names. They are not even distantly inspired by any individual known or unknown to the author, and all the incidents are pure invention.

First published in Great Britain 2012
by Mills & Boon, an imprint of Harlequin (UK) Limited,
Eton House, 18-24 Paradise Road, Richmond, Surrey TW9 1SR

© Lois Faye Dyer 2011

ISBN: 978 0 263 89398 4

23-0112

Harlequin (UK) policy is to use papers that are natural, renewable and recyclable products and made from wood grown in sustainable forests. The logging and manufacturing processes conform to the legal environmental regulations of the country of origin.

Printed and bound in Spain
by Blackprint CPI, Barcelona

Lois Faye Dyer lives in a small town on the shore of beautiful Puget Sound in the Pacific Northwest with her two eccentric and lovable cats, Chloe and Evie. She loves to hear from readers. You can write to her c/o Paperbacks Plus, 1618 Bay Street, Port Orchard, WA 98366. Visit her on the web at www.LoisDyer.com.

For Michael, Stefanie, Randall, Lilia and Ava—
you're the best family possible.

Chapter One

The living room of Harry Hunt's lakeside mansion in Seattle glowed with warm light. Two matching Tiffany chandeliers were suspended from the high ceiling at each end of the spacious room, their stained-glass flowers vibrant with color. Outside, the rain and wind of a Pacific Northwest storm picked up speed as it raced across Lake Washington to hammer against the window glass. Inside, the people gathered in the big room were warm and comfortable, thanks to the fire crackling in the hearth beneath the hand-carved cedar mantel.

Frankie Fairchild rose from an overstuffed armchair and crossed the room to the bar, leaving her mother, Cornelia, chatting animatedly with Lily Hunt. Several bottles were clustered on the gleaming mahogany surface, and Frankie chose one with a distinctive label. The tart white wine from the Chateau Ste. Michelle Winery just north of Seattle was a personal favorite. She tilted the bottle to refill her glass.

As she sipped from the stemmed crystal, her gaze drifted idly over the room, pausing at the sight of her cousin Justin's little daughter, Ava, hopping along the edge of the oriental wool carpet.

Harry's neighbor, local actress Madge Edgley, bent to speak to Ava as the child reached the quartet of people chatting together on the bright red and blue carpet.

Harry always invites the nicest mix of friends and interesting people to his get-togethers, Frankie thought with appreciation. She moved on, noting familiar faces in the groups of people scattered around the long room, until she reached the group of men standing in front of the fireplace. Her uncle Harry and his son Justin were deep in conversation with two other men. Frankie knew one of them—Nicholas Dean—only slightly. The fourth man she knew very well. Eli Wolf was tall and broadshouldered, with black hair and a rugged handsomeness that could make a woman's heart stutter if he smiled directly at her.

Eli looked up, snaring her with an intent look from smoky blue eyes. Frankie froze, unable to look away.

It wasn't until he turned to answer a question from Harry that Frankie realized she'd been holding her breath, caught by that enigmatic, very male stare.

She spun around to face the bar, topping off her wine with faintly trembling fingers.

What on earth is wrong with me?

Ever since Eli had given her a kiss at her last birthday party, she'd been thinking about him much too often. The kiss had sizzled, smoked, even though it was too short. In fact, the memory of his mouth on hers hadn't faded in the four months since; if she closed her eyes, she could still feel the heat. She'd actually conducted an experiment over the last couple of months, purposefully kissing three other very attractive men. Though all three were adept, practiced and assured at kissing, none of them had stirred one iota of serious interest, let alone lust. She'd felt nothing remotely resembling what she'd felt with Eli. Zero. Zip. Nada.

It was very annoying.

She couldn't decide what to do about it, if anything. And inaction was so unlike her that her inability to decisively resolve the issue and put it behind her was worrisome.

"Frankie." A friendly pat on her shoulder accompanied the greeting. "How are you, honey?"

She turned around, glad of the distraction from her thoughts, smiling with affection at the tall, lanky man who was her host. "I'm good, Uncle Harry." She glanced over his shoulder. "I thought you were busy talking business with Nicholas."

"I was." Harry's shrewd gaze went from Frankie's face and down the length of the room to the fireplace, where the owner of Dean Construction stood with Justin and Eli. "I must say I'm impressed with Nicholas. He's built his daddy's construction company into a solid corporation, despite strong competition. I'd bet money he'll triple his net worth in the next five years."

"You're rarely wrong about these things, so he must be an excellent businessman." Frankie sipped her white wine, her gaze following Harry's. There was no question Nicholas Dean's appearance backed up Harry's assessment of his potential for success; he fairly oozed self-confidence. He was tall, well built and had an air of easy, affable friendliness that was belied by his sharply intelligent eyes. His presence here tonight, at a gathering of Harry's family and personal friends, was significant. Frankie met Harry's eyes once again. "You're thinking of giving him the contract for building the new HuntCom campus in south Seattle, aren't you?" she guessed.

"I'm considering it." Harry nodded. "I've narrowed the list down to two—it's between him and Eli."

"Hmm." Frankie wasn't surprised. Elijah Wolf was the head of Wolf Construction and fiercely competitive. He and Justin were in their thirties now and remained close, although Justin was married, with a little girl, and Eli was still a bachelor.

"If Nicholas gets the contract, we'll be seeing a lot more of him," Harry told her.

"Mmm-hmm," Frankie murmured.

"Whoever gets the job will be working closely with my boys, of course," he went on, "but Eli's practically a member of the family already, while Nicholas isn't as well known to us."

"Wouldn't it be easier, then, if you awarded the contract to Eli and his brothers at Wolf Construction?"

Harry shrugged. "Maybe. But if I don't give Dean Construction fair consideration for the job, it smacks of nepotism."

Frankie choked on a sip of wine. Harry immediately clapped a big hand against her back, thumping her between her shoulder blades.

"Are you all right?" he asked with concern.

"I'm fine, Uncle Harry," she got out. She coughed to clear her throat and took another sip of wine. "It was the shock of hearing you mention nepotism as if it were a bad thing," she said, tongue in cheek.

"I don't practice nepotism," he growled defensively.

Frankie laughed, her amusement drawing a reluctant grin from Harry.

"All right," he said with a shrug. "Maybe I tend to take care of my family first, but is that a crime?"

Frankie gave him an impulsive hug, the familiar scent of his aftershave warming her with affectionate memories. "No, Uncle Harry, it's not."

"Well, then…" He wrapped an arm around her and gave her a quick hard hug in return. "Besides, you'll notice I'm not automatically giving Eli the contract. I'm seriously considering Dean Construction. That's why Nicholas is here tonight—to see how he fits in with our family and friends."

"He seems to be doing just fine," Frankie told him, knowing Harry considered business a family matter.

"Yes, he does." Harry's gaze rested on Nicholas for

a moment. "He'd make a good husband for some lucky woman," he commented guilelessly.

"Hmm," Frankie responded, distracted as Ava, Justin and Lily's daughter, ran across the room and threw herself at Eli. Eli laughed, swinging the little girl high in the air before settling her on his hip. Ava cupped his face in her little hands and gave him an enthusiastic kiss. Eli's eyes sparkled with amusement and his mouth curved in a grin, white teeth flashing in his tanned face. Distracted and charmed by the unabashed affection between the big, undeniably handsome man and the dainty, feminine little girl, it was a moment before Frankie registered Harry's last words. Her gaze snapped to his face. He was eyeing her with an all-too-familiar expression. She nearly groaned aloud. *Oh, no. Surely he's not matchmaking again—and with me and Nicholas Dean?*

She lowered her lashes and hoped her expression didn't give away her suspicions as her mind raced, considering the possibility that Harry had turned his penchant for meddling on her.

"Nicholas has what a woman should be looking for in a husband," Harry continued. "He's proven he's dedicated to business, so he'll be a good provider. Plus, he's young enough to have children but old enough to be a settled father."

Frankie blinked, staring at Harry. "You think that's all a woman wants in a husband? How did you arrive at this abbreviated list?"

Harry waved a hand dismissively. "I covered the essentials. If a woman wants romance, then I suppose

Nicholas qualifies in that department—he's not a bad-looking guy."

"Harry, you're astounding." Frankie leaned closer, gripping his lapel and staring into his eyes. "You left out something extremely important."

"What's that?" Harry's deep voice rumbled, his voice suspicious, as if he was bracing for a blistering lecture.

"You left out the all important x-factor."

His eyebrows lifted. "The x-factor? I've never heard of it."

"Some people call it chemistry. Some call it sexual attraction. I call it the x-factor." *And Eli has it in spades.* The thought flashed through her mind, startling her.

"And you think Nicholas doesn't have it?" Harry sounded skeptical.

"I don't know," Frankie admitted. "I've never been out with him. I was speaking in general terms about women and men."

"Then you're conceding you might be attracted to Nicholas Dean," Harry said shrewdly.

"No." Frankie let go of Harry's lapel and shook her head, exasperated. Over the last few months, she'd successfully ducked Harry's attempts to meddle in her love life, but her sisters Tommi and Bobbie hadn't been as lucky. Fortunately, they'd managed to meet and fall in love with wonderful men on their own, despite Harry's interference. There was no guarantee Frankie would be as lucky, however. She did *not* want Harry focused on finding a husband for her. The very thought was enough to make her shudder and break out in hives. "And we're not talking about Nicholas and me—there *is no* Nicholas and me," she stressed.

"But there could be," Harry insisted. "As soon as his company was shortlisted for HuntCom's south Seattle construction, I had the usual background check run. Which is why I know Dean Construction badly wants to win the contract. I'm dead sure Nicholas will cooperate in getting to know you—and you can find out if the two of you are attracted to each other."

"Harry," Frankie said with forced calm. "I am *not* going to date Nicholas Dean. I don't need my uncle's help in finding men."

"It's not as if I'm out there tracking down men for you, Frankie," Harry protested. "But—"

"Good," Frankie interrupted. "Because if I thought you were trolling Seattle looking for men you can coerce into dating me, I'd go hire a hit man and give him your address."

"Frankie!" Harry looked shocked, but his eyes twinkled. "That's a terrible thing to say. What would your mother think of her favorite daughter threatening my life?"

"She's used to you, Uncle Harry," Frankie said dryly. "She'd probably just ask me what you'd done this time to deserve it."

Harry threw back his head and roared with laughter.

Harry's booming laugh drew everyone's attention. Eli Wolf looked up, over the top of Ava's dark curls and across the room at Frankie Fairchild. She sipped white wine from a stemmed glass, her thick-lashed brown eyes fixed on Harry, an amused smile curving her lips. She was tall at five-eight, with long legs and curves that made a man's hands itch to stroke her. Caramel-blond hair fell to her shoulders in a sleek curtain, framing her beautiful face. The simple, clean-cut lines of a black cocktail dress clung to her body, the long sleeves ending at her wrists. The dress hem was just above her knees, drawing the eye to sleek calves and the delicate bones of her ankles above black pumps with impossibly high heels.

Eli wondered how women walked in those things.

He'd known Francesca Fairchild since she was a little girl. Also, her cousin Justin was his best friend. Unfortunately, those two facts meant Frankie was strictly off-limits for all the things he'd like to do with her—something he'd regretted more often than he cared to think about. Especially over the past four months—ever since that unforgettable kiss at her birthday party.

"Unca Eli?" Ava's small hand tugged his face around until she could meet his gaze. "Mommy says I can have a pet bunny, but first we have to get a cage for him. Will you make one for me? And can I come visit and help you hammer the nails and boards when you make it?"

Eli grinned, glad to be distracted from thoughts of Frankie and charmed as always by the little girl's green eyes and hopeful smile. "Sure, honey. Let's go ask your mom and dad when we can do that."

With Ava perched on his hip, Eli strode across the room to join her parents and settle into a leather armchair. The seat gave him an unobstructed view of Frankie and was placed at right angles to the sofa where Justin and Lily chatted with Cornelia Fairchild, Frankie's mother.

"Mommy." Ava's clear voice piped up. "Unca Eli's going to help me build a bunny house."

"That's wonderful, honey." Lily's rueful gaze met Eli's. "And how does Uncle Eli feel about this?"

"We have a plan," Eli told her with a grin. "And it includes Justin's barbecuing steaks for my granddad to pay my carpenter fee."

"What? How did I get caught up in this?" Justin demanded, his eyes amused.

"Hey, you're the dad," Eli told him with a shrug. "I'm just the uncle."

"I love you, Unca Eli." Ava wrapped her arms around his neck and gave him an enthusiastic kiss on the cheek.

"I love you, too." Eli barely had time to register the swell of affection that filled him before the little girl jumped off his lap and climbed onto her father's. Both Justin and Lily received hugs and kisses, the adults exchanging amused looks.

Ava launched into an excited description of plans for the rabbit hutch.

Only half-listening, Eli leaned back in the comfortable chair, his gaze going past the trio and across the room, drawn inexorably to Frankie once again.

The interplay between her and Harry as they conversed held the ease of comfortable familiarity. Frankie's smile was affectionate as she smiled up at Harry, whose black hair and shrewd eyes, hidden behind dark-framed glasses, belied his age. Eli knew Frankie's father had died when she was a child and if one could judge by appearances, it seemed Harry had stepped in to fill the role.

We have that in common, except it was my grandfather who took over my father's role, Eli mused. *And Frankie still has her mom while I lost both parents.*

Cornelia was a force to be reckoned with, Eli thought, glancing at the older woman's serene face as she listened to Ava describe her rabbit.

But then, so was Jack Wolf. Eli's grandfather had taken in Eli and his three brothers, Conner, Ethan and Matt, a short two hours after a car crash on Seattle's I-5 had taken their parents' lives. Already a widower, Jack became a substitute parent to the four grieving boys, and his fierce commitment and support had created a family to heal their shattered lives.

Frankie watched Eli and Ava cross the room to join Justin and Lily, the little girl waving her hands excitedly as she talked.

"Why are you so determined to fix me up with Nicholas?" she demanded in an attempt to distract Harry, gesturing with her glass. "What about Eli? He's single, he and his brothers own a successful construction company—isn't he on your list of potential suitors?"

Harry glanced over his shoulder. "I'd be happy if you dated Eli. I like the boy," he told her. "But he shows no signs of wanting to settle down. I suspect he's a confirmed bachelor—I doubt he'll ever marry."

"You felt the same way about Justin once," Frankie reminded him. "And look at him now—devoted father, loving husband. He's a contented, happy man since he married Lily."

"True," Harry conceded with a dismissive shrug. "But Eli's different than Justin. Justin hadn't dated for a year or more before he and Lily got back together. He clearly needed Lily and wanted a wife and family. But like I said, Eli's never given the slightest indication of being ready to settle down." He nodded in Nicholas's direction. "Now, you take Nicholas—he seems much more the type to marry and start a family."

Frankie only half listened as Harry continued to list Nicholas Dean's virtues. Unfortunately, she had to agree with Harry about Eli. He'd spent most of the last year recovering in stages after an accident on a construction site that snapped the bone in his lower left leg. Prior to that, however, if rumor was true, he'd been perfectly happy running his company and dating a variety of women. He'd been the poster boy for the quintessential bachelor before his accident, and Frankie assumed he'd returned to his active dating life now that he was recovered.

Wait a minute. Her eyes narrowed with sudden insight. The only way she could convince Harry to scratch her off his list of unmarried family members in need of his matchmaking assistance was if she could make him believe she was in a serious relationship.

But she wasn't dating anyone at the moment, let alone deeply involved. What she needed, she realized, was a man willing to conspire with her to foil Harry. A man who, like her, had something to gain from plotting against her uncle. And a man who had no interest in settling down.

Eli Wolf was *exactly* the kind of man she needed.

She glanced sideways at Harry, murmuring a noncommittal response as he listed the charities that Nicholas Dean had contributed to the prior year.

The question was, would Eli be willing to plot with her to trick Harry?

"…and Nicholas said his family has lived in Queen Anne for over a hundred years," Harry's deep voice recited.

"Interesting," Frankie murmured, catching only the end of Harry's comment.

"Both of his grandmothers are alive," Harry continued, "and live within a few blocks of each other on prime pieces of real estate."

Harry kept talking, but Frankie tuned him out as she considered Harry's matchmaking and how to stop him. She cherished her independence, loved her job as a research assistant and substitute English-literature professor at the University of Washington, and had no interest in changing her life. She was happy, content and did *not* want Harry nudging her toward marriage, no matter how well-intentioned his efforts.

Once again, her gaze went across the room, unerringly zeroing in on Eli. He and Ava were now seated with Lily and Cornelia, the little girl perched on his knee as she waved her hands and chattered enthusiastically to her mother.

Eli Wolf was the only man she knew who could stop Harry's plans. He was well liked by Harry; in fact, he was practically an adopted son. And his company would benefit by getting the contract for constructing the HuntCom campus, so he, too, would benefit from joining forces with her.

An hour later, Frankie was still mulling over the potential scheme as she drove home. It wasn't until she was in her pajamas and in bed, a book opened and then ignored on her lap, that she faced another, potentially more important, issue.

If Eli agreed to help her, they would have to spend time together pretending to be a couple. And maybe— just maybe—she would finally get over her long-ago crush on him.

She'd known Eli since she was eleven years old and her cousin Justin had brought his best friend to a party at Harry's house. When she was fifteen, he'd joined Justin in vetting and harassing her first boyfriends, all under the guise of being protective stand-in brothers.

At sixteen, she'd suffered through a major crush on Eli, who was then twenty-one. By the time she was nineteen, she'd believed her crush was behind her and was relieved she'd kept her feelings a secret. She hadn't even told her three sisters, Georgie, Tommi and Bobbie, about it.

She'd thought yearning after Eli Wolf was a part of her childish, romantic past, her feelings packed away with other high school memories. She'd gone on to date college boys and, later, a fellow professor at the University of Washington, a CPA and a lawyer or two.

She frowned at the blurred lines of type in the open book, not seeing the words.

Until he'd kissed her to wish her happy birthday, she'd been so sure she was over her crush. But the kissing experiment with three other men had raised serious questions.

Surely it couldn't be that Eli Wolf's kisses were addictive and had resurrected her schoolgirl infatuation—but if not, why did other men's lips taste bland and boring?

She needed an answer. She didn't date often, preferring instead to have a mixed circle of friends who attended events in a group. But in her admittedly limited experience, she'd never yet met a man who could hold her interest longer than a few dates. Surely the same thing would happen with Eli—and she'd permanently set aside her childish adoration for him and move on to happily date other men.

But what if she fell for him, rather than growing tired of him?

That won't happen, she scoffed silently as she closed her book, set it on the nightstand and snapped off the lamp. *I'm not foolish enough to fall in love with a commitment-phobic bachelor.*

But she'd have to be on guard, she thought sleepily. She liked her life just as it was. She didn't want to fall in love and surrender her independence or change the basics of her comfortable life. Though twenty years had passed since her father's death, she vividly remembered the following days and months and how devastated her mother had been. Watching her mother over those early years as she coped with grief, Frankie had come to believe that loving deeply carried the potential for even deeper hurt.

Because Cornelia, Frankie and her sisters had adored George Fairchild. It wasn't until after his death that they'd learned he'd had a gambling habit that left his grieving family nearly destitute.

She'd trusted her father with all the blind faith of a child. While she hadn't stopped loving him, as she grew older she'd sworn never to foolishly trust a man that deeply again.

She'd always been goal-oriented and focused, she thought, stifling a yawn. Surely she could be the same while dealing with Eli? She'd keep her eyes on the prize—derailing Harry's matchmaking intentions and putting to rest forever any remnants of her teenage crush.

Satisfied she'd fully considered and understood both the upside and downside of her plan, Frankie fell asleep.

She dreamed of a tall, broad-shouldered man with

black hair and smoky-blue eyes—he held out his arms and her dream self ran joyously toward him.

In her quiet bedroom, she tossed and turned, murmuring and tangling the blankets as she dreamed.

Chapter Two

Two days after dinner at Harry's house, Frankie left her office on the University of Washington campus midmorning and drove to Ballard. The Seattle community was twenty minutes west of the UW campus and an equal distance northwest of downtown Seattle. Wolf Construction's business office was located in the industrial section near the Ballard Locks. Except for a diesel pickup truck with a Wolf Construction logo on the door, the parking lot on the south side of the building was empty.

When she entered the outer office, the reception area was quiet and empty, the two secretarial desks vacant.

"Hello?" No one answered her call, and she frowned. Surely the office's outer door would have been locked if no one was here?

The silence was broken by a loud thump somewhere deeper in the building, followed by a male voice muttering what sounded like swearing. Frankie peered past the desks and down the hallway beyond, where several doors stood open into offices.

"Hello?" she called again. When no one appeared, Frankie waited another moment before determinedly rounding the desk and marching down the hall.

"Damn it," a male voice rumbled with annoyance. "Where the hell did Connor put those plans?"

Frankie followed the deep voice, stepping into an office. She halted just inside. Eli stood across the room, his back to her as he pulled open a drawer and shuffled through the papers inside. He wore heavy black work boots, jeans and a black T-shirt. He bent over the drawer, and faded denim pulled tight over his rear. Beneath the snug clothes, sculpted muscles shifted and bunched as he stretched to reach the back of the drawer. Frankie stared, riveted, her body heating as her gaze followed the movements of his powerful body.

He straightened, shoving the drawer closed and opening the next one with an impatient jerk.

The noise snapped Frankie out of the spell that held her, and she gathered her composure, taking a deep, calming breath. "Hello, Eli."

He stiffened and quickly swung around, his eyes flaring with surprise just before his mouth curved in a grin.

"Frankie? What are you doing here?"

Now that she was actually about to propose her

plan to Eli, Frankie was suddenly nervous. Her fingers gripped the leather strap of her black Coach purse a bit tighter.

"I need to talk to you about something. Do you have a few minutes?"

Clearly surprised, he cocked his head to the side, considering her for a brief moment. "Sure." He tossed a roll of blueprints into the open drawer, pushed it closed and moved away from the cabinet. "Come on in. Have a seat." He gestured at the two leather armchairs facing the desk. "I'd offer you something to drink, but the office staff has the day off and the coffee is probably cold sludge left over from yesterday."

"Thanks, but I'm fine." Frankie crossed to the chair and sat, perching on the edge of the comfortable seat.

Eli half sat on the edge of the desk facing her. The position had him much too close to her. She had to look up to meet his gaze. At eye level, the worn denim of his jeans stretched across powerful thighs. Determinedly, she kept her gaze on his face.

"So, tell me," he prompted when she hesitated. "What brings you to Ballard this morning?"

Now that she was here, faced with explaining her plan to Eli, Frankie was reluctant to begin the conversation.

"What were you looking for when I came in?" she asked, not answering his question. "You sounded frustrated."

Eli glanced over his shoulder at the cabinet. "Frustrated isn't a strong enough word," he said, his gaze swinging back to meet hers. "My brother Connor told his secretary to send the blueprints down to the job site, but she sent the wrong ones. I came back to pick them up, but I'll be damned if I can find them." He jerked a thumb over his shoulder at the cabinet with its long drawers. "They're not in the project drawer." He sounded thoroughly disgusted.

"Can you call him on his cell and ask him?" Frankie suggested.

"I tried that," he told her. "He's not answering."

"I'm sorry," she said with sympathy. "I know how disturbing it can be to have a project stopped. I hate wasting time while I wait for someone to respond before I can move forward."

He nodded, his blue eyes warming. "It's bloody annoying," he agreed.

Eli studied Frankie through narrowed eyes.

She's nervous, he thought with surprise. Making small talk about his search for the blueprints was only a ruse to delay telling him why she was here.

When he'd swung around and saw her framed in the office doorway, he'd been slammed with the same jolt of awareness that had plagued him ever since they'd shared a kiss at her birthday party four months earlier. Though it was meant to be casual, he hadn't been able to forget the feel and taste of Frankie's soft, lush mouth under his.

She'd featured prominently in more than one hot, sweaty dream ever since, leaving him sleep deprived and cranky the next morning.

He raked his fingers through his hair and shifted, forcing himself to remember the beautiful blonde sitting in the chair facing him was Justin's cousin and, therefore, off-limits. "Come on, Frankie," he coaxed. "Tell me why you're here."

She shifted in her chair, slim fingers tucking a strand of hair behind one small ear. She sat primly, feet aligned on the floor, hands now resting quietly on her lap. "I've known you a long time, Eli," she began. "And more importantly, you've known my uncle Harry since you were a teenager. I'm sure you're aware of Harry's scheme to force his sons to marry, and how Justin fell in love with Lily in spite of Harry's interference."

"Of course." Eli nodded. "Justin told me before the wedding."

"What you might not be aware of," Frankie went on, "is that Harry seems to think that since his scheming to force his sons to marry turned out so well, he's decided to become a matchmaker for the Fairchilds. All four of us—including me."

Eli was stunned. "You're kidding" was all he could manage to get out. He shook his head in disbelief, but Frankie's face didn't look as if this was a joke. "That doesn't make any sense. He damn near ruined all four of his sons' chances at marrying the women they wanted."

"I know!" Frankie leaned forward. "And he almost did the same with Tommi and Bobbie! Apparently, he thinks he's successful, however, because he's turned his sights on me."

"What the hell?" Eli felt as if he'd been punched in the gut. "Who does Harry want you to marry?"

"Nicholas Dean."

Oh, hell no! Eli's rejection of the possibility that Frankie would marry Nicholas Dean was visceral and immediate. Somehow, he kept himself from snarling aloud. "Why did he pick Dean?" he asked, aware his voice was deeper, rougher than it had been only moments before.

Frankie waved one small, graceful hand. "Who knows? I think he picked Nicholas because Dean Construction was on Harry's radar. Harry told me he'd run the usual background check on the company when it was shortlisted for the contract to build HuntCom's new building in south Seattle. Evidently, Harry was impressed with Nicholas's work ethic, plus the fact that he's single, so Harry decided he should encourage Nicholas to ask me out."

"And you're not on board with the plan?"

"No!" Frankie frowned at him, her brown eyes sparking with gold. "I'm not."

"I see." Relief flooded Eli, the corners of his mouth lifting in a grin. "And you want me to tell Harry you're not interested in dating Nicholas?" he guessed.

"I've already told Uncle Harry I'm not interested," she informed him. "It didn't faze him, and I suspect he's working on a scheme to push me and Nicholas together even as we speak."

Eli's smile disappeared.

"I've watched Uncle Harry interfere in Tommi's

and Bobbie's love lives," Frankie went on. "And I'm convinced the only way to stop his matchmaking is to convince him that I'm taken. That's where you come in."

Eli blinked. "That's where I come in?" he repeated.

She nodded decisively. "I have zero interest in getting married—and the general consensus of opinion in the family is that you don't, either. Which makes you the perfect person for my plan."

Eli narrowed his eyes over her thoughtfully. "I'm not sure I'm following you. Maybe you should give me the abbreviated version."

Frankie waved her hands expressively, her expression wry. "I'm sorry—let me back up. The other night at Harry's house when he was telling me all the reasons I should want to date and perhaps marry Nicholas Dean, you were standing across the room holding Ava. I'm afraid I used you to distract Harry and asked him why he didn't suggest you as a potential husband. He told me he doubted you would marry. He said you seemed perfectly happy with your life as it was. Well…". She shrugged. "The moment Harry said that, I realized you were the perfect person for me to date, because neither of us wants to get married. When Harry kept droning on about all of Nicholas's good qualities, I had a brainstorm."

"A brainstorm," Eli repeated. He realized belatedly that he kept repeating her statements and told himself to stop.

"Yes, exactly." She leaned forward, her brown eyes

gleaming with determination. "Which brings me to the reason I came to see you today. I need to convince Harry I'm madly in love and deeply committed to someone so he'll stop trying to pair me up with single men. But I'm not in love, and there's no one on my horizon. So I need someone to *pretend* to be involved with, while you," she continued, pointing at him, "would like Wolf Construction to win the contract for the new HuntCom building. So...my proposal is that we team up. If you'll pretend to be involved with me, I can almost guarantee Uncle Harry will move Wolf Construction to the top of the list for the contract. He's already narrowed it down to you and Nicholas, and he as good as admitted to me that he's inclined to award contracts to family or close family friends."

"You want me to date you in order to get Harry to give my company a contract?" Eli asked, his tone neutral.

"Not exactly," she told him. "I'm only suggesting that we both have something to gain—and frankly, I need a pretend-date/boyfriend as fast as possible. Harry, my mother and sisters already know and adore you, so they won't bat an eye if it's you I claim to have fallen madly in love with. If I introduce someone new, they're going to be more skeptical. I want Harry off my back. Heaven knows what trouble he can stir up for me." She shuddered.

Eli stared at her for a long moment. He didn't want her believing he was the kind of man who would use her to gain a lucrative construction contract. On the other hand, there was no way he'd let her be courted by Nicholas Dean.

Not that Dean was a bad guy. He was, in fact, everything Harry thought he was—smart, successful and played a mean game of pool. Just the kind of man a woman could easily fall in love with.

Which was why there was no way in hell Eli was going to let him near Frankie, not if he could help it. He knew he was being territorial, but he couldn't seem to help it.

Probably because I want to be the one burning up the sheets with Frankie, he thought. In fact, he realized with a start, he'd felt that way for months.

And it was time he did something about it.

"Well," she said expectantly, interrupting his thoughts. "Will you do it?"

"Yeah," he said with a slow drawl. "I will." He stood, bending to cup her elbow and lift her from the chair. "Let's go get some coffee and talk about the details."

He hustled her out of the office and down the street to Zena's Café before she had time to change her mind.

"So," he said when they were seated in a booth with steaming mugs in front of them, "how do you envision going forward with this campaign to fool Harry?"

"I thought we'd keep it simple," Frankie told him. "We can work out a list of events Harry is likely to attend. Then we can appear together and pretend to be in love while Harry's watching. Hopefully, it won't take long to convince him. Once he accepts that, he can cross me off his matchmaking list and sign your company contract for the new HuntCom campus, and we can go back to our normal lives."

"Harry's pretty shrewd—I'm not sure he's going to be as easy to convince as you seem to think," Eli told her. "He didn't get his reputation as a shark in the financial world by being dense."

"But that's business." Frankie propped her forearms on the polished wood tabletop and leaned forward. "When it comes to personal relationships, Harry can be amazingly unaware. Look at the women he married—disasters, every one of them."

"You've got a point." Eli shrugged. "It's hard to argue with his marital record. The only good thing about Harry's ex-wives is that he stopped getting married after making four bad choices."

"Exactly." Frankie nodded decisively. "I truly anticipate he'll accept our romantic smoke screen as fact. I don't think he'll look deeper."

"Nevertheless," Eli told her. "If we're going to do this, let's do it right. Remember," he cautioned her, "it's not just Harry we have to convince. Your mother or sisters are likely to be attending the same functions as Harry. If we're not believable, they'll never buy it. Cornelia's not going to be easy to fool—especially when it comes to one of her daughters. And if Cornelia knows we're faking, she's likely to tell Harry."

Frankie frowned, unconsciously winding a lock of hair around her forefinger in a gesture Eli had noticed her make before when she was deep in thought.

"You're right," she murmured. She looked up at Eli,

her brown eyes alive with bright determination, gold flecks swimming in the chocolate-brown depths. "So we can't let her know we're pretending. Think you can pull it off?"

Her tone matched the challenge in the quick curve of her lips.

"Absolutely." He lifted a brow, tossing the challenge back at her with a slow smile. "The question is, can you?"

She laughed, shrugging in a quick, elegant shift of her shoulders beneath the tailored blue suit jacket. "A woman learns to fake being interested in a guy before she's out of junior high school. It's a rite of passage."

"Yeah?" Startled and intrigued, Eli lifted an eyebrow in inquiry. "Why in junior high?"

"Because at my school, that was the first year of boy-girl dances, and every girl wanted a date. Unfortunately, the girls outnumbered the boys two-to-one. Which meant there was a lot of competition for invitations to the school functions."

Eli swept a slow, appreciative gaze over her face, hair, down her throat and the swell of her breasts beneath the cream blouse she wore under her suit jacket. The table edge prevented him from going lower, and he returned to meet her eyes. "I bet you never had to compete for a date. I'm guessing the boys were lined up next to your school locker, waiting for you to choose."

She threw back her head and laughed, the throaty musical sound stroking over Eli as if she'd touched him.

"Not hardly," she said when she stopped chuckling,

her eyes dancing. "When I was thirteen, I wore braces, was skinny—straight up and down without a curve in sight—spent most of my time with my nose buried in a book, and last but not least, I was taller than any boy in my class. So, no...I wasn't exactly the most desirable date on anyone's list." She lifted her cup and sipped, eyeing him with amusement.

"No kidding?" Bemused, he stared at her. "I'm trying to imagine you as a skinny thirteen-year-old with crooked teeth, and it just doesn't compute."

"I'll show you one of my seventh-grade class pictures sometime. Trust me—I'm not lying. In fact..." She considered for a moment. "It's entirely possible that the reality of my thirteen-year-old nerdiness was much worse than I'm describing."

Eli laughed, charmed by her candid comments. "Why don't I remember you at thirteen?" he asked.

"Because you and Justin were freshmen in college that year and really busy—I hardly saw Justin that year, except for dinner on Christmas Day," Frankie told him.

"That's right," Eli mused, thinking back. "First year at the UW was crazy busy. Now I wish I'd taken time to visit at Christmas. If I had, I could have seen you in braces."

"You didn't miss much," she said dryly. "How about you? I'm guessing you weren't a skinny nerd with braces when you were thirteen."

Eli considered. "You'd have to ask the girls in my class whether they thought I was a nerd," he told her. "I didn't have braces, but I earned good grades and I was certainly a lot skinnier than I am now."

"I bet you were cute." She sighed. "If you'd been in my class, I'm sure you would have had girls lined up outside your locker." She eyed him with curiosity. "And I bet you have girls lined up outside your condo now. It just occurred to me to wonder—do you have a lady friend who's going to be upset with our pretend love affair?"

He shook his head. "No. If I did, I wouldn't have agreed."

She sipped her coffee and eyed him over the rim. "I know it's none of my business, but after listening to the occasional comment from Justin, I've always assumed you're usually dating someone. I'm glad you're currently available, because it certainly makes my plan to fool Uncle Harry much easier, but why are you unattached?"

Eli didn't want to tell her that even if he'd been dating someone, he would have untangled himself immediately. There was no way he'd let Harry maneuver her into dating and maybe marrying Nicholas Dean. He didn't want to look too closely at the reasons he felt so strongly about Frankie dating Dean, but he accepted that he did.

"I suppose the truth is, I haven't had time to think about dating lately. I've only been back at work full-time for a couple of months."

"Oh, that's right." Her brown eyes warmed with sympathy. "I knew you were hurt at work last year, but I hadn't realized you'd only recently recovered."

"It took a while," he said. "I fell off a scaffold on a construction site and broke my left leg." He shrugged. "It was a clean break, but there were complications requiring two more surgeries—I was housebound and unable to work most of the year. Plus, I was in physical therapy off and on for months. The end result was that I was rarely in the office—or anywhere else, for that matter," he added. "Practically the only social function I went to that year was your birthday party at Harry's house. I was between surgeries that month."

Her lashes lowered, screening her eyes, and faint color tinted her fair skin. "No wonder you aren't involved with someone at the moment," she said, lifting her gaze to his once more. "You haven't had time."

"No." He pretended not to notice she'd avoided commenting about her birthday party but knew from the color in her cheeks that she hadn't forgotten that kiss any more than he had. "The worst part was the boredom. I have no patience with sitting around. A guy can only watch so many cable-TV sports events without a break. Thank God I'm fully recovered and back at work, because, trust me—my grandfather and brothers were about ready to throw me into Puget Sound and let me drown."

She laughed, her eyes sparkling with amusement. "I'm sure you couldn't have been that difficult."

"According to them, I was worse," he assured her. "I'm not a good patient—in fact, I'm lousy at it." Maybe that was the reason he was so eager to take up Frankie's plan to foil Harry, Eli thought. Maybe the memory of those long, boring months had made him susceptible to any pretty woman with an interesting scheme. "Your plan to outmaneuver Harry at his own game is perfect timing for me," he told her, although he suspected Frankie was the most compelling element. "It's just intriguing enough to distract me and make me forget those never-ending months of being stuck at home with my leg in a cast."

"Whatever it is that made you agree, I'm just thankful you've said yes." Frankie smiled at him and slid the tip of her tongue over the plump curve of her lower lip, licking away a drop of creamy coffee. Eli nearly groaned out loud, his body tensing.

He saw women drinking coffee nearly every morning when he stopped at the local Starbucks on his way to work. He didn't have this reaction to any of them, he realized with a flash of awareness. Only Frankie managed to turn him on with one glimpse of the tip of her tongue sliding slowly over her bottom lip.

No, it's not just any woman I want. It's Frankie.

Chapter Three

Frankie glanced up just in time to see Eli's lashes lower, his eyes going dark as he stared at her mouth.

She'd certainly seen desire on a man's face before. But Eli's intent, focused stare sent heat shivering through her belly. She felt her cheeks warming and knew her face must be flushing with pink color.

She was speechless, unable to respond as she watched Eli's dark gaze flick upward to hers, awareness arcing between them in a palpable hum.

Fortunately, he apparently took pity on her frozen vocal chords. His mouth curved in a warm smile.

"When do you want to start our scam?" he asked mildly, with no trace of the heat that had flared between them. "Soon?"

"The sooner the better," she told him, happy to set

aside contemplation of that moment between them until she was alone. "Especially if you're right about Harry not being convinced quickly or easily."

"This is one time when I hope I'm wrong, but knowing Harry, I doubt it," Eli said wryly. "That only makes the challenge more interesting, though." He winked at her, a gleam of anticipation in his blue eyes. "Do you have a plan?"

"I thought we'd start with a simple, first-date kind of thing. Mom has tickets to a fundraiser for the Children's Hospital on Saturday night—she said a group of her friends are going together, including Harry."

"Sounds good. What time shall I pick you up?"

"Around eight—and it's black tie," she added.

"I think Connor mentioned he's taking someone," Eli commented. "It's a dinner dance, right?"

Frankie nodded.

"Do you think Cornelia can wangle seats for us at her table? I'm assuming Harry will be sitting with her."

"He almost always does if they're at the same function. I'll ask her to pull strings so we can join them." Frankie glanced at her wristwatch and gasped. "Oh, no. Look at the time. I'm going to be late for my next class." She caught up her purse and slid out of the booth, only to find Eli already standing.

He pulled a handful of bills out of his pocket and peeled off several, dropping them on the table before cupping her elbow in his warm palm. "Let's go."

They moved quickly down the sidewalk and back to the Wolf Construction parking lot; Eli tucked a card with his home and cell-phone numbers into her jacket pocket as they walked. Frankie recited her home address and phone numbers, impressed when he didn't need to write them down.

At five-eight, Frankie had never considered herself dainty but walking next to Eli made her feel delicate and very feminine. He was not only much taller, he was broader, bulkier and outweighed her by what must surely be at least a hundred pounds. Additionally, he exuded a protectiveness that made her feel safe. Cherished.

He handed her into her car, bending to say he'd see her on Saturday night. As she drove away from the lot, she glanced in her rearview mirror. He stood motionless, hands shoved into the front pockets of his jeans, the faint breeze ruffling his dark hair as he watched her leave.

She wondered briefly if she'd made a mistake. She wanted to put a stop to Harry's matchmaking so she could go on with her life, unimpeded by marriage-minded suitors. She'd purposely picked Eli because she was convinced he had as little interest in matrimony as she did.

But after spending more than an hour in his company, she was having second thoughts.

Not about Eli—about herself. She was definitely attracted to him. Could she keep that attraction from complicating their plan to distract Harry?

She narrowed her eyes thoughtfully as she left Ballard and headed back to the university campus.

Of course I can, she concluded after several moments.

Granted, Eli Wolf has the power to send my hormones crazy, but that doesn't mean I have to act on the feeling.

She'd remain levelheaded and keep the end goal in mind, she decided firmly. Eli would only become a problem for her if she allowed him to distract her. She just had to remember that he wasn't a man interested in a long-term relationship—that irrefutable fact should be enough to keep her from falling foolishly in love with him.

Braking for a stoplight, she used her cell phone's speaker feature. "Mom? I'm so glad I caught you—can you get me two tickets for the fundraiser on Saturday night? And can we join your table?" She paused. "Yes, Mom, I'm bringing a date. Oops, have to go—I'm driving back to campus and the light just changed. See you Saturday!"

Later that evening after showering and donning pajama bottoms and a pink tank top, Frankie brewed a cup of green tea and climbed into bed. She loved her bedroom—it was her favorite room in her Queen Anne condo. Aided by her sisters, she'd painted three of the walls in a buttery cream color, but the fourth was a warm shade of red-gold pumpkin. Her bedstead was antique mahogany and had a matching nightstand. After months of searching, she'd found a tall chest of drawers that nearly matched the bed at an antique shop in Greenwood.

The lamp on her nightstand was a rare antique Tiffany,

a Christmas gift from Uncle Harry, while the fluffy white comforter that covered the bed's wide mattress had been a birthday gift from her mother.

In a corner near the window, a huge Boston fern sat atop a tall wicker floor stand, just to the left of a low base holding a medium-sized TV, its plasma screen now dark.

Frankie plumped the pillows and tucked them against the headboard behind her, then picked up the remote control and switched on the television. The eleven o'clock news was airing video of local trash collectors' union members marching outside city hall with picket signs. The mayor's comments on the status of union negotiations accompanied the video.

Frankie leaned back and sipped her tea as her thoughts drifted to her meeting with Eli that morning.

After spending time alone with him, she certainly understood how he'd earned a reputation as a man adored by women. No wonder he was reputed to date a lot. He was undeniably handsome, but there was something else, some indefinable element that made a woman feel as if she were the only female in the room. When he'd stared at her mouth, his eyes going dark, she'd felt the intensity of his gaze as if he'd reached out and touched her.

She shivered. This morning's encounter with Eli had erased any doubts—she was still attracted to him. And that scared her.

Frowning, she sipped her tea and pondered why that should be. She'd dated off and on since she was sixteen;

she'd known Eli longer than that. She wasn't afraid of him in any rational way.

And yet, she was wary on some deep, primal level.

But wouldn't any reasonable woman be cautious of a man who could break her heart?

No. She instantly rejected the possibility he could break her heart. *I had a schoolgirl crush on him. That's the only reason I'm feeling this way. I can't possibly be in love with him, therefore, he can't break my heart.*

She was twenty-nine years old, not sixteen, she told herself. And she was eminently practical and well educated, having earned a doctorate in English lit, a master's degree in mathematics and a second master's degree in science. She was light-years away from that foolish sixteen-year-old who had dreamed about Eli Wolf.

But maybe the timing was wrong back then, a small voice said. And maybe now, with Eli unattached and you available, too, the stars are aligned and the time is right.

Frankie ignored the voice, burying it under a determined analysis of the details of the plan to fool Harry.

Yes, she thought firmly, *this will work. I just have to remember we're both playing a part, pretending to be attracted to each other.*

Unbidden, the memory of his eyes staring at her mouth swept over her.

Pretending to be attracted to Eli wasn't going to be the problem, Frankie realized. The real problem might very well be convincing herself *not* to truly fall for him.

* * *

Saturday dawned wet and chilly. The sky over Seattle was gray and lowering, the clouds seeming to hover around the top of the Space Needle. Rain fell intermittently, but the weather cleared late in the afternoon, giving Frankie hope that the evening might be nicer.

Before heading for the shower prior to her date with Eli, Frankie selected a small emerald green envelope purse from a chest drawer. She tucked the two tickets to tonight's fundraiser, a condo key, lipstick, a twenty-dollar bill for emergencies and several tissues into the bag. Then she slid her favorite evening coat from its padded hanger in her bedroom closet and carried both items into the living room, dropping the purse onto the seat of an upholstered wing chair and draping the coat over the back. The long black coat reached almost to her ankles and, with its round collar and loose sleeves, was perfect for protecting an evening gown from the winter wind and rain.

Back in her bedroom, she laid out underwear and chose a pair of black stiletto heels to pair with her gown. A half hour later, fresh from her shower, she smoothed scented lotion over her skin and slipped into a lacy strapless bra with matching celery-green bikini panties and garter belt.

Justin's wife, Lily, was a lingerie designer and kept Frankie in fabulous underwear. Everything feminine within her delighted in the silk and lace creations—in fact, walking into Lily's shop, Princess Lily's Boutique, in Ballard, never failed to make her smile with delight.

She sat on the edge of the bed to carefully don sheer, delicate stockings before stepping into her dress. The emerald-green satin gown was strapless, with a zipper up the back. The bodice was snug, fitted to closely follow the outward curve of her breasts and inward curve of the narrow waist. A wide band of crystal beading in glittering jet black covered the upper edge of the bodice.

Frankie slipped into her shoes, fastening the narrow black straps around her ankles, and rose to cross to the antique mirror standing next to the closet doors. She twisted to look at the zipper closure, checking to ensure it was fastened, then took jet black drop earrings with their matching necklace and bracelet from the jewelry case atop the high chest. It was the work of a few moments to fasten the earrings and bracelet, but the necklace clasp was difficult. After several tries, Frankie left the room with the gold-set jet beads cradled in one hand, switching on the bedside lamp as she went.

The doorbell rang just as she entered the living room, and a quick glance out the peephole revealed Eli in the hallway outside. He wore a classic black tuxedo, the white collar of his shirt a sharp contrast against the tanned skin of his throat. He stood with casual ease, his hands tucked into the pockets of his slacks.

The quick little zing of anticipation that sent her heart racing wasn't quite as startling this time. Maybe she was simply growing accustomed to the increase in heartbeat and the adrenaline rush she felt each time she saw him, she thought. She slipped the dead bolt free and pulled the door open.

"Hi, Eli. Come in—I'll just be a moment."

"Hey," he said lazily, his gaze slowly moving over her face, hair, and lower to her toes before returning to meet hers once again. Male appreciation heated his blue eyes. "You look great. I like the dress."

Frankie's toes curled in her black stilettos, and the heat that arced between them had her lowering her eyes from his and turning away to a small oval mirror. The glass hung on the wall next to the coat closet, only feet from the door.

"Thank you. I won't be long—I just have to fasten my necklace." She frowned at the clasp. It wasn't the usual hook and cye, nor did it have a sliding lock. The mechanism was one Frankie hadn't seen before.

"Problems?" Eli asked, walking closer.

"I'm not sure how to close this clasp." She held up the necklace, narrowing her eyes over it. "It belonged to my great-aunt Francine. This is the first time I've worn it, and I've never seen a fastening quite like this."

"May I?" He held out his hand, and Frankie dropped the web of gold-set jet beads into his palm.

He lifted the necklace, the delicate feminine settings dangling from his calloused fingers as he inspected the lock.

"I think I've got it. Turn around and hold up your hair."

Frankie obeyed, waiting until he draped the necklace

around her throat before she bent her head and lifted her hair up and away from her nape. The mirror on the wall allowed her to see his frown of concentration as he bent his head. The backs of his fingers brushed against her skin as he fastened the intricate clasp. Each warm touch heightened her senses, making her vividly aware of his taller, broader body only inches from hers. Her heart beat faster, her breathing shallower and more swift.

"Done," he said with satisfaction. He looked up, his gaze unerringly finding hers in the mirror's reflection.

Frankie caught her breath. For one long moment, time slowed.

Heat flared in his eyes, the curve of his mouth suddenly sensual, fuller. Frankie's heart fluttered wildly. She was suddenly unsure how she would react if he turned her into his arms and kissed her as he had in her dreams.

Then his thick lashes lowered, effectively screening his eyes. He stepped back, and the spell was broken as he turned to lift her coat from the nearby chair.

He held the black evening wrap, and, wordlessly, she slipped her arms into the sleeves. His hands rested lightly on her shoulders for a brief, electric moment before he handed her the tiny green purse from the chair's cushion.

"Got everything?" he asked as she turned toward the door.

"Yes." She smiled up at him, determined to match his cool calm.

They left the condo, chatting about the weather as they rode downstairs in the elevator to the quiet lobby.

A long, black limousine stood at the curb, and Frankie had barely cleared the lobby's doorway when the driver appeared to pull open the back door.

Eli cupped her elbow and hurried her across the sidewalk to tuck her into the backseat, sliding in behind her. The door closed smoothly, sealing them into the warm, dry, leather-scented interior.

"How lovely to have curb service," Frankie said with appreciation. "Especially since it's started raining again."

"Not to mention the driver is the one who'll have to negotiate the traffic downtown," Eli added dryly.

"Yes, that, too." Frankie nodded. "Very wise of you not to drive tonight."

Eli stretched out his long legs. "I would have driven, but my Porsche is in the shop and I didn't want to pick you up in my work truck." He grinned, amusement in his eyes. "I'd hate to get grease on that pretty dress you're wearing."

"Good call." Her voice was dry. "You should have told me about your car. I would have been happy to pick you up."

He lifted an eyebrow in pretend shock. "And risk having my grandfather find out I'd made a date and had the lady drive me?" He shuddered. "I'd rather be caught running naked on Denny Way. He'd never let me forget it."

Frankie laughed. "Your grandfather sounds like fun."

"He is," Eli answered promptly. "Don't get me wrong—I love the old guy. If he hadn't taken me and my brothers in after our folks were killed, we might have been split up and sent into foster homes. But he still thinks he should meddle in our lives, just like he did when we were kids."

"And you can't tell him to butt out, because you love him and don't want to hurt his feelings," Frankie guessed aloud.

"Exactly." Eli looked at her, his gaze searching her face. "How did you know?"

"Because that's how I feel about Uncle Harry," she replied. "I adore him, but he's got to stop interfering in my life." She shrugged. "Oh, I know we're both adults and I could just tell him to stop. I could be blunt and tell him I hate knowing he's actively trying to dragoon men into dating me, as if no guy would ever think of asking me out unless Harry strong-armed them." She lifted her hands in frustration, then let them drop to her lap. "But I know he'd be hurt, so I don't say the words. Which is why I came up with this scheme." She gestured between Eli and herself. "You and me."

"If Harry finds out you're trying to trick him, he'll be hurt anyway," Eli cautioned her.

"I know." Her mouth drooped. She glanced sideways and found him watching her with an oddly tender expression. "Which is why we have to be very convincing," she said firmly.

"Agreed." The car slowed, and he glanced out the window. "Here's the hotel—put on your best I'm-so-in-love acting face, honey, because the curtain is about to go up."

Chapter Four

The Grand Sylvania's portico roof shielded the car from the rain as Eli stepped out and turned to take Frankie's hand. The well-lit area did nothing to hold the wind at bay, however, and the two hurried into the hotel lobby, joining other guests to ride an escalator to the second floor. The muted rumble of crowd laughter and conversation underlaid an orchestra's rendition of a Broadway tune as they stepped off the moving stairs and neared an open ballroom door.

A hotel employee greeted them, taking Frankie's coat before passing it on to a young woman in a white evening gown, a Children's Hospital ribbon pinned to her bodice.

"May I have your tickets, please?"

Frankie quickly located the lavender cards in her small evening purse and handed them over.

"Ah, yes. This way, please."

"Thank you." Frankie smiled at their hostess and followed her. Close behind her, Eli's hand rested on the curve of her waist, his palm and long fingers warm and faintly possessive. Frankie was vibrantly aware of his broad bulk at her back; the very air separating them seemed alive with electricity.

They wound their way between tables toward the front of the big room. Frankie scanned the guests, locating Cornelia seated with Harry and another couple at a table for six on the edge of the polished dance floor.

Cornelia looked up, her lips curving in a welcoming smile as she raised a hand to beckon with a wave. Then her gaze moved past Frankie, her eyes widening as she saw Eli. She quickly looked back at Frankie, her eyebrows lifting in silent query just as the two reached the table.

"Hello, Mother." Frankie bent to kiss Cornelia's cheek and paused to say hello to Marcia Adkins.

Harry and Jonathon Adkins stood, greeting Frankie and Eli as he drew out a chair for her. She murmured her thanks, smoothing her skirts as Eli settled into the chair next to her.

"I didn't know you were bringing Eli," Cornelia said with a smile. "But I'm glad you did. It's lovely to see you, Eli. I hardly got to say more than hello to you the other evening at Harry's house."

"I'm sorry, Cornelia. Justin and Lily promised Ava

she could have a pet rabbit for her birthday. We spent most of the evening discussing the proper size of the hutch we're going to build." Eli's eyes twinkled.

"That's my Ava," Harry said with a fond pride. "You'll notice she went straight to a professional builder," he said to Jonathon.

"Not to mention choosing a man most likely to give her whatever she wants," Eli said dryly, earning him a soft, approving smile from Cornelia.

"You've got competition for the title," Harry told him. "From her dad, me and her three uncles."

Eli laughed. "True. She's a charmer, that little girl." He turned to speak with a waiter, and Cornelia leaned close to murmur in Frankie's ear.

"You didn't tell me Eli was your date for tonight."

"It was a last-minute thing," Frankie whispered back.

"I didn't realize you two were dating." Cornelia's comment held a question.

"We've seen each other a few times," Frankie said. It wasn't really a lie, she told herself. She and Eli *had* seen each other recently—once at Harry's house and then again at his office. That qualified as seeing each other, didn't it?

Cornelia's expression was intrigued, but before she could question Frankie further, two waiters arrived with bottles of champagne and began pouring.

"Oh, how wonderful. I love champagne," Frankie said with delight, accepting a flute from Eli. "How did you know?"

"You had champagne at your last birthday party."

His gaze met hers, and Frankie's heart skipped a beat. The memory of her birthday party and the kiss they'd shared was in his eyes, and Frankie was suddenly back there, his mouth on hers, his arms warm and hard, wrapping her tight against the powerful muscles of his chest and thighs....

"How nice that you remembered."

Cornelia's warm voice broke the spell that held Frankie, and she tore her gaze from Eli's, looking down at the bubbles rising in the gold liquid filling her flute.

Eli relaxed in his chair, a glass in one hand, the other arm stretched out along the back of Frankie's chair. His fingers brushed the bare curve of her shoulder before closing warmly, lightly, over the nape of her neck.

"I remember everything about Frankie." His voice was deeper, huskier.

Frankie glanced sideways, and their gazes meshed. She tried to remember he was only playing a role. But his blue eyes were darker, smokier, and the heat within seemed so real Frankie felt herself melting, her body unconsciously softening, easing toward his.

"I don't recall seeing you at Frankie's last birthday party," Harry said.

Frankie glanced up, alerted by Harry's tone, and saw his eyes narrow over Eli.

"I wasn't there long," Eli said without missing a beat. "I'd barely recovered from a second leg surgery and stopped in for a few minutes, looking for Justin. I didn't know you were having a party until I got there and only stayed long enough to say hello and toast the birthday girl before leaving."

"Ah, that must be why I don't remember—I probably didn't see you in the crowd," Harry mused.

"There were a lot of people at the house," Eli agreed.

His fingertips absently stroked the curve of Frankie's shoulder, almost as if he was savoring the tactile pleasure of her skin against his. Despite knowing he was only touching her because Harry and Cornelia were watching, Frankie still shivered inwardly, her skin heating beneath his touch.

"Oh, Jonathon," Marcia exclaimed, her eyes lighting as the orchestra played the opening notes of a classic Burt Bacharach tune. "I love this song—come dance with me." She held out her hand to her husband.

"Excuse us, folks," Jonathon said as he rose and took his wife's hand.

Eli leaned closer, his lips brushing Frankie's earlobe.

"Let's dance."

She nodded silently, and he stood, pulling back her chair.

"Harry, you should dance with Mom," she said as Eli took her hand, threading her fingers through his.

"I think we'll sit this one out and finish our champagne," Harry replied.

Frankie thought she caught a fleeting frown cross

her mother's features before Eli tugged her gently out onto the gleaming floor.

He turned her into his arms, tucking her close. Her temple rested against his cheek, and each breath she took drew in the subtle scent of his aftershave, warmed by body heat. She loved that smell, she thought, leaning closer.

"Did you see Harry's face?" Eli's voice was a low rumble. He chuckled, his breath ghosting against her ear. "He can't decide whether to demand we tell him why we're here together or pretend it's not happening."

Frankie laughed, "I'd give anything to hear what he's saying to Mom right now."

Eli's arms tightened around Frankie. "Heads up," he whispered in her ear. "Harry and your mom are heading this way."

Frankie tilted her head back and looked up at him. "Do we have a plan?" she asked, even as she reveled in the muscled strength of his arm at her waist, his warm fingers threaded through hers and the press of her increasingly sensitized body as it lay against his from breast to thigh.

His lashes lowered, his eyes going darker as the moment stretched. Then he swung her in a slow circle, his steps sure as he swept her into a secluded corner, behind a tall column with baskets of ferns and flowers widening its base.

Her skirts swirled around his legs as he stopped, easing her backward against the column's support.

His gaze didn't leave hers as he bent his head and brushed his mouth against hers.

It was like touching a live electrical wire. Frankie started, her hands curling into fists over his lapels as she caught her breath.

"Shh," he murmured against her lips. Then his mouth fitted carefully over hers, changing the angle of the kiss as it lengthened, stealing the oxygen from her lungs until he breathed for her.

Frankie forgot that a roomful of people danced and laughed only feet away from where she stood, locked in Eli's arms, concealed behind the column. The world faded away, narrowing to hold only Eli.

When at last he lifted his head, she was breathless. If she hadn't been supported against his solid strength, she knew she would have wobbled, her knees weak.

Eli's hooded gaze searched hers, his breath coming too fast. His fingertips moved reflexively against the bare skin of her back above the low-cut gown as if unable to keep from stroking, and a muscle ticked along the line of his jaw. Whatever he saw in her eyes had his lips curving upward in a slow, sensual half smile that made Frankie yearn for the feel of his mouth on hers again. Then he wrapped her closer and swept her out from behind the column, back into the crowd, the music a slow swirl of sound around them. Frankie let him guide her, her feet automatically moving to the rhythm as she struggled to clear her head.

She was every bit as shaken now as she'd been by that first kiss all those months ago at her birthday party. No question about it, she thought with faint dismay, when she'd felt the earth move during that first kiss, it hadn't been the result of drinking too much champagne on an empty stomach.

Because it had just happened again.

Harry and Cornelia, with half the dance floor now separating them from Eli and Frankie, were each trying to digest and interpret what they'd just seen.

"I haven't purposely spied on any of my daughters since they were teenagers," Cornelia told Harry. "I feel guilty."

"We didn't spy on them on purpose," Harry protested. "We just happened to be dancing near them when he pulled her behind that column. It's not as if we were using binoculars."

Cornelia leaned back against his arm and looked up at him. "Even you can't believe that excuse, Harry," she admonished him, shaking her head. "You know very well you asked me to dance solely to keep an eye on Frankie and Eli."

"All right," he admitted. "It's true. But in my defense, I'm having a hard time believing she's suddenly interested in Eli. They've known each other for years, and I've never seen a hint of anything romantic between them."

"Maybe that's precisely why," Cornelia pointed out. "Sometimes two people can be too close and not realize they're perfect for each other."

"I find that hard to believe," Harry scoffed, dismissing the concept. "If a man and a woman are thrown together often enough, sooner or later they'll realize they're attracted. Probably happen sooner rather than later," he added.

"Perhaps," Cornelia conceded. "But some people are *so* obtuse, they wouldn't see the perfect partner if they tripped over them."

Her voice held an underlying snap, but Harry didn't notice.

"Well, I still think Nicholas would make the perfect man for Frankie."

Cornelia's eyes widened, then narrowed over Harry's face. "Please tell me you're not matchmaking again, Harry."

Her voice held an ominous tone. Harry winced. "Now, Cornelia," he said persuasively, "what makes you think I'd do that?"

Cornelia wasn't entirely convinced but let the subject drop as the orchestra left the bandstand for a break and they returned to their table.

Three hours later, after dinner followed by more champagne and dancing, Eli handed Frankie into the back of the limousine once more.

The car moved smoothly away from the hotel portico. Outside the tinted windows, the glow of downtown Seattle's neon signs, bright car headlights and red taillights blurred into rivers of moving color in the rain.

Frankie sighed and relaxed, turning her head against the buttery soft leather seat to look at Eli. "I think we were a success tonight. Harry was clearly surprised to see you with me, although I'm not sure he's convinced yet that we're a couple. What do you think?"

"I suspect it's going to take more than one appearance to make Harry believe we're involved. He needs to be convinced you're crazy about me and unlikely to be interested in someone else if he's going to stop trying to hook you up with Nicholas." Eli's half smile was wry. "Harry's like a dog with a bone. Once he gets an idea in his head, it takes major evidence to get him to change his mind. He's stubborn."

"Then we'll just have to be even more determined—and outlast him. Are you up for that?"

Eli shrugged, his eyes glinting at the challenge. "I told you when we first talked about this that I didn't expect Harry to be easily convinced." He shrugged. "Tonight was just the opening salvo in a campaign—but in the end, we'll win."

Frankie stared at him, arrested. "You sound like a character out of the *Godfather* movies. I suppose next you'll be telling me we need to go to the mattresses."

He laughed out loud. "We might reach that point, knowing Harry."

"I know," Frankie murmured, distracted by the flash of his smile in the shadowy interior of the limo. "I confess, when I came up with this plan, I thought we could be seen together a couple of times and Harry would abandon his matchmaking schemes. I should have known he wouldn't give up so easily."

"Not to worry." Eli picked up her hand, threading her fingers through his before resting their joined hands on his thigh. "We're partners, right? The two of us together are a match for Harry."

The car slowed, pulling to the curb and stopping. Eli glanced out the window. "We're home." Before their driver could exit to open their door, Eli stepped out and opened an umbrella as he turned to lend Frankie a hand.

Rain pattered on the umbrella, but beneath it Frankie was warm and dry, tucked into the curve of Eli's side, his hand at her waist. They hurried up the sidewalk to the shelter of the condo building's wide overhang. The lobby was empty and quiet when they entered, the elevator and third-floor hallway equally hushed.

Frankie unlocked her door and turned, her shoulder brushing against Eli's black tux jacket. "I'll call you as soon as I talk to Mom and find out where we might run into Harry again," she told him.

"Sounds good." He leaned in and brushed a kiss against her mouth. "Good night," he murmured, his blue eyes darkened between half-lowered lashes.

"Good night," Frankie managed to respond before slipping inside and closing the door. She leaned back against the panels, hearing the sound of the elevator's ping announcing its arrival, then silence. She hurried across her living room and peered out through the blinds at the street below. Short moments later, Eli moved across the sidewalk and ducked into the waiting limo. Then the car pulled away from the curb and disappeared around the corner at the end of her street.

She left the window and moved slowly into her

bedroom, stripping off her coat and hanging it away in the closet before unzipping her gown and stepping out of it.

She couldn't stop thinking about Eli as she finished undressing, removing her bracelet. To her relief, the necklace clasp opened easily, and she tucked it and the bracelet into her jewelry box. But when she took off the matching earrings, she discovered one of them was missing. Despite searching the carpet and shaking out the green gown and evening coat, she didn't find the one-of-a-kind heirloom. With sinking heart, she added the single earring to the lacquered jewelry box and closed the lid.

I can't imagine how I'll find a jeweler to create a matching earring, she thought as she slipped into pink flannel pajama bottoms and a cotton tank top.

The troubling loss of her earring was soon set aside as she returned to thoughts of Eli. So far, her plan to erase unrealistic romantic notions left over from her teenage years was failing miserably. Eli Wolf was even more charming than she'd expected.

And kissing him could prove to be addictive, she thought as she settled under the comforter and turned out the lamp.

She still believed her plan to make Harry cease his matchmaking by convincing him she was madly in love with Eli would work.

But she wasn't nearly as positive that spending more time with Eli would cure her of her high school crush. In fact, she suspected it just might do the opposite.

Chapter Five

On Sunday afternoon following the fundraiser for the Children's Hospital, Frankie drove to her mother's house. She was sure Cornelia would question her about Eli, but her mother didn't raise the subject as they chatted about the success of the event while brewing a pot of tea in the kitchen. While Frankie loaded a tray with the Wedgwood teapot and cups, Cornelia carried napkins and a plate of shortbread biscuits out to the front porch just as a white pickup with a Wolf Construction logo on the doors pulled to a stop at the curb.

"Frankie," Cornelia called, peering out a tall window as the driver stepped out of the pickup. "Isn't that Eli? Were you expecting him?"

Frankie stepped out onto the porch, carrying the tea

tray. She set the heavy silver tray on the low table in front of her mother and looked out the window.

There was no mistaking the tall, broad-shouldered man strolling up the walk—and no denying the swift surge of pleased surprise the sight of him elicited in Frankie.

"It *is* Eli—but I have no idea why he's here."

Cornelia had renovated the porch of her beautifully restored Queen Anne home and enclosed the wide space with waist-high windows. Now it was an extension of the living room, a wide glassed-in entry room that ran the length of the front of the house. Lazily turning wooden fans were suspended from the high ceiling; the floor was painted a glossy gray, and area rugs dotted the gleaming wood boards. Chairs and sofas of white wicker with colorful pillows were grouped in comfortable seating areas down the length of the room. At the moment, Cornelia sat in an armchair, its soft cushions covered in bright cotton with a coral and green floral pattern. Frankie took a seat on the padded white wooden swing, within reach of the low wicker table where she'd set the tea tray.

Eli glanced up as he neared, his gaze meeting Frankie's through the glass. He smiled, his stride quickening as he loped up the three shallow steps to the door.

"Come in, Eli," Cornelia called.

"Hello, ladies."

Frankie felt the room shrink as he stepped inside and closed the door, his presence seeming to suck up the oxygen. He wore faded jeans, black boots, and a pale blue polo shirt under a worn brown bomber jacket. Raindrops glistened in his black hair as he shrugged out of his jacket and hung the damp leather over the back of a nearby rocking chair.

She drew a deep breath and patted the cushion beside her. "I didn't expect to see you today—how did you know I was here?"

"I stopped by Justin and Lily's place to deliver the plans for Ava's rabbit hutch—which has turned into a rabbit-condo-castle," he said with a wry grin. "Lily told me you'd mentioned spending the afternoon with your mom, so I thought I'd drop by on my way home." He shoved one hand into his jeans pocket and pulled out a glittering jet and gold earring. "You lost this in the car last night. I thought you might be worried about it."

"Oh, you found it! Thank goodness." Frankie held out her cupped hand, and Eli dropped the earring into her palm.

He settled onto the swing, one arm stretched out along the seat back behind her.

"I was so upset—I was afraid I'd lost it forever." Impulsively, she leaned sideways into Eli and kissed his cheek. "Thank you!"

"You're welcome." His eyes smiled at her. "Feel free to lose jewelry in my car anytime. I like the way you say thank you."

Frankie felt heat move up her cheeks and knew her face was no doubt pink. She shot a quick glance at her mother from beneath lowered lashes. An amused, indulgent smile played about Cornelia's lips. Apparently, her mother approved of Eli's charm.

"I hope I don't lose track of any more family heirlooms in the future, but if I do, it's nice to know you'll find them for me." She patted his cheek with easy familiarity and shifted back, away from the hard curve of his body. Pretending she didn't miss the sheer pleasure she felt in leaning against his warm strength, she leaned forward and picked up the Wedgwood teapot. "Mom and I are having Earl Grey—would you like a cup?"

She poured and handed Cornelia a delicate cup and saucer before glancing inquiringly at Eli.

"Tea?" He winced. "Honey, you know I don't do tea."

She couldn't help laughing at his apologetic but pained expression. "I'm sure Mom has something else to drink."

"Actually, I just had hot chocolate with Ava, so I'm good."

"Did you drink it out of a mug or a thimble-sized toy china teacup?" Frankie asked, stirring sugar into her own tea before sitting back on the swing, cup in hand, one foot tucked beneath her so she could face Eli.

"Today we sat at the kitchen-island counter and had normal size mugs," Eli told her. He shook his head. "Thank God. I can hardly pick up those tiny cups of hers. Not to mention, sitting at that little-girl table scares me. I'm constantly worrying the chair won't hold me and I'll break it."

Frankie and Cornelia smiled with sympathy. Frankie

had a swift mental image of Eli's tall, broad body perched on one of Ava's child-sized chairs. The picture was endearing.

"Do you see a lot of Ava?" she asked, sipping her tea.

"Not as much as I'd like—Justin has to spend quite a bit of time on his ranch in Idaho." He leaned forward, taking a shortbread biscuit from the plate on the tea tray. "But when they're in Seattle, we get together fairly often." He glanced at Frankie, the tiny smile lines at the corners of his eyes crinkling. "I'm her honorary uncle, and apparently Ava thinks that requires certain duties."

"One of which is having tea with her dolls?" Frankie guessed.

"Yeah, that's one of them." He pretended to shudder, but the fond smile barely curving his lips told her he didn't really mind playing tea party with the little girl.

Rain pattered against the glass. Frankie sighed and eyed the wet world outside with gloom. "I think I'll cancel tonight. The thought of standing around in the rain at a campus rally for world peace doesn't appeal."

Eli gave her disbelieving look. "You were going to join a bunch of college kids, in the rain, to listen to a freshman lecture everyone about solving the world's ills?"

"How did you know the scheduled speaker is a freshman?" she asked, intrigued.

He shrugged. "They're always freshmen—by their second year in college, students are more cynical." He lowered his voice. "Rumor has it, the change is due to the amount of beer consumed at all those freshman frat parties."

Cornelia laughed. "I think you may be right, Eli."

"He could be." Frankie tried to hold back a smile but failed. "I bet you formed this opinion through first-hand experience," she said dryly.

"I have to confess I helped lower the beer level in a few kegs during my freshman year at college," he confirmed. "But I never picked up a bullhorn and lectured the student population on a solution for world peace."

"Did you rally for any good causes?" Cornelia asked him.

Curled next to him on the cushioned wooden bench seat, Frankie sipped her tea and listened as Eli bantered back and forth with her mother about his activities in college. He'd been a part of their extended group of family friends for a long time through his friendship with Justin. She knew he'd attended the University of Washington by combining scholarships and working at Wolf Construction. By the time he'd earned an engineering degree, Wolf Construction's business had taken off under his leadership and become a major contender for commercial building in Seattle and the surrounding area.

Everything Harry had told her about Nicholas Dean's success could be said of Eli, she thought, feeling a surge of pride at his accomplishments.

Eli glanced sideways at her, his gaze warming.

"Come to the movies with me tonight, Frankie," he

said easily. "We'll be inside a theater, we'll be dry and I'll buy you buttered popcorn."

"What movie are you going to see?" she asked, aware of her mother listening.

"An action adventure based on a book by one of my favorite authors."

"Sounds like fun."

He eyed her. "You like those kinds of books, too?"

"Why wouldn't I?"

His blue eyes gleamed with approval. "I'll be damned. I keep learning things about you that amaze me."

Frankie huffed. "Lots of women read suspense novels."

"I know, but you have a PhD in English literature. Somehow, I didn't expect you to like action-adventure fiction."

"I'd be just as interested if there was a new film based on one of Jane Austen's titles," Frankie said firmly. "But I'm not a snob about books—I like all different kinds. I'd love to see the movie tonight."

"Great." Eli looked at Cornelia. "How about you, Cornelia? Would you like to come with us?"

"Oh, no." Cornelia waved a hand. "My favorite mystery series is on PBS tonight, and I've been looking forward to the next installment. I'm going to curl up in my jammies in front of the TV with a bowl of ice cream."

"All right, but you know you're welcome to join us if you change your mind," Eli told her. He looked at Frankie. "I'll pick you up at seven?"

She nodded. "I'll be ready. What theater are we going to?"

"Pacific Place downtown." He stood, the swing dipping and swaying on the heavy chains suspending the seat. "I'd better get going. I need to run by a construction site and check with the security guard."

"Is there a problem?" Frankie felt a swift stab of concern.

"Only with water—we've had a lot of rain the last couple of days. I want to make sure there's no flooding." He took his jacket from the back of the chair and shrugged into it.

Cornelia rose, collecting the tea tray. "It was lovely to see you, Eli—stop by again soon."

"I will, Cornelia, thank you."

Her slim figure disappeared into the front hall.

Eli held out his hand, and Frankie put her fingers in his, letting him pull her to her feet. He slung an arm over her shoulders, tucking her against his side, and walked her toward the outside door.

"I hope you don't mind my dropping by without calling. But when Justin told me you were spending the afternoon with your mom, I thought it was a perfect opportunity to return your earring and spend a little time reinforcing Cornelia's belief that we're a couple."

"I don't mind at all—I'm glad you stopped by. I confess I don't like keeping the truth from Mom. The only thing that makes me feel okay about deceiving her is that I know she'd be the first to join us if she knew Harry was meddling again."

"I suspect you're right about Cornelia. But the more people who know about our plan, the more difficult it would be to keep it a secret from Harry, I'm afraid."

Frankie sighed. "I'm sure you're right."

He stopped at the door, turning to face her, his back to the screen and glass and the gray rain outside.

"You don't have to take me to the movie tonight, Eli. Mom will never know."

He lifted an eyebrow. "Are you kidding? Hanging out with you is one of the perks of this scam. Besides, it's always more fun to watch a movie with someone. Then later you can go over the good parts, or, if it's a bad film, you can commiserate and complain about all the lousy acting and special effects."

"Ah, I see. So it's not that you want my company," she teased, inordinately pleased that she'd see him later, "it's that you want someone to compare opinions with after the credits roll."

He laughed. "You've caught me, that's part of it." He bent his head to whisper in her ear. "Your mom is standing at the kitchen sink. If she looks sideways, she can see us. Want to give her something to tell Harry?"

"Okay." Frankie nodded, her heartbeat beginning to race as his mouth curved in a slow smile at her assent.

He slipped his arms around her waist and eased her nearer, lifting her up on her toes as his head bent.

Warm, seductive, his mouth coaxed hers to respond. Frankie clutched his biceps, her head spinning as the world narrowed to the hard body she leaned against and Eli's lips on hers.

The kiss only lasted a moment. Too soon, Eli lifted his head, easing her back off her toes.

"I'll pick you up at seven," he murmured, blue eyes darkened to navy.

She nodded, unable to gather her wits and form a sentence.

He bent, his lips brushing against the sensitive shell of her ear. "And, Frankie, kissing you is one of the best parts of this scheme."

Frankie felt her eyes widen. Then he shoved the door open behind him and, with a quick grin, left her. The door closed on his back as he loped down the sidewalk. Moments later, his pickup truck accelerated away from the curb.

He's right, she thought, still faintly dazed. *Kissing is definitely one of the perks of having Eli pretend to be my boyfriend.*

Eli arrived at Frankie's condo that evening and within a short half hour, they'd reached the Pacific Place and were settled into comfortable seats in a row near the back of the theater. He held her coat while she slipped out of it before handing her the container of popcorn.

"This is a lot of popcorn for only two people," she said, eyeing the bucket dubiously.

"I like popcorn. Trust me." He winked at her. "It won't last long."

Frankie laughed and took a handful of the salty kernels. As she ate, she glanced around the theater. The lights were still on and local business advertisements played with minimal sound on the wide screen up front.

"This reminds me of going to the movies with Mom and my sisters when we were little," she said. "I love rainy Sundays at the theater."

"Granddad used to drop off me and my brothers at the theater in Ballard on Saturday or Sunday afternoons," Eli told her. "I suspect it gave him a much-needed break."

"I'm sure Mom enjoyed the peace and quiet when we all were focused on the screen, too," Frankie replied. "Parenting looks like a tough job when there are two people, but being a single parent must be beyond difficult."

"I agree." Eli nodded. "Watching Justin and Lily with Ava has been a real eye-opener. Don't get me wrong," he added hastily. "I think she's great, but, man, she wears me out."

"I know what you mean. Ava has nonstop energy." Frankie smiled with affection as she sipped her water. "I have a play date scheduled with her on Saturday morning and I'm wondering if I should increase my vitamin intake and start lifting weights to build my endurance."

Eli grinned at her. "Might not be a bad idea. Aren't you a little old to have play dates?"

"Absolutely not," Frankie said emphatically. "I adore Ava and every third Saturday, we get together to go to the park or the zoo or a children's exhibition at the Seattle Center. Of course," she added with a twinkle,

"I call it bonding, but Ava insists we're having play dates."

"Ah." Eli nodded. "Makes sense. So what else did you do when you were a child?" Eli asked. "Besides go to movies on Sunday afternoons."

"Skipped rope, rode bikes, played Monopoly with my sisters, and—" Frankie paused to sip her water "—volunteered at a horse rescue barn in Arlington."

Arrested, Eli stopped eating popcorn, one eyebrow rising in query. "I didn't know you were interested in horses. I thought you were a city girl, through and through."

"I suppose I am to a certain extent," Frankie agreed. "But I love animals, especially horses. When I celebrated my eighth birthday, Mom told me it was time for me to pick a cause to donate my time to and I chose abused horses."

"Good choice." Eli nodded, his eyes gleaming with approval. "When Granddad told us we were old enough to start giving back to the community, I picked Habitat for Humanity."

"That's a wonderful cause," Frankie enthused. "I've considered signing up, but I don't know anything about carpentry."

"A lot of volunteers don't when they start. Join my group," he said. "I'll make sure you learn how to swing a hammer and saw a board."

"I doubt it's that easy," she said with a shake of her head.

He shrugged. "It's not complicated—and professional

carpenters team with new volunteers to supervise them."

"If you promise to teach me enough about carpentry so my contribution doesn't result in a house falling down, I'll sign up," she told him.

He laughed. "You couldn't make a house fall down. Don't worry about it."

Before Frankie could respond, the house lights dimmed and the previews for upcoming movies began.

When the popcorn container was empty and napkins had wiped away any traces of salt and butter, Eli caught her hand in his, threading her fingers between his own. Startled, she glanced sideways at him, but he was focused on the screen, his profile lit by the flickering light from the movie.

There was something nice about sitting in the dark theater, Eli's warm, callused palm pressed to hers, the hard strength of his shoulder against hers.

Frankie turned back toward the screen, deciding to enjoy the moment and not worry about what it might mean that her heart stuttered each time his thumb smoothed over the back of her hand.

Since they both had to rise early for work the following morning, Eli dropped her off just after ten-thirty, saying good-night with another kiss that left her breathless. Forty minutes later, as she climbed into bed and switched off the lamp, Frankie realized she hadn't spent such a relaxing, thoroughly enjoyable evening in a very long time.

And it was entirely due to Eli's company.

Part of her loved the thought—while another part dealt with the niggling worry that she liked his company far too much.

A wise woman wouldn't tempt fate, she thought drowsily.

Chapter Six

On Wednesday morning, Frankie was in her office at Liberty Hall on the University of Washington campus. Since completing work on a museum exhibit in December, she'd been reassigned from her usual duties as a research assistant. She was now temporarily filling in for an English Literature professor who'd gone on emergency leave. Much as she loved the variety of her research work, Frankie welcomed the opportunity to teach in a classroom. The new responsibility challenged her creativity and gave her one-on-one contact with students, which wasn't usually the case.

Since her next lecture wasn't for another forty-five minutes, she planned to make good use of the time to catch up on a few non-classroom duties.

Her desk was littered with data reports, printouts of

class grading curves and miscellaneous information. Deep in thought, she contemplated a possible change in her syllabus notes for the current lecture series on classic British authors of the twentieth century.

"Hey, Professor." The deep male voice was soft, just above a murmur, but Frankie jumped nonetheless, startled, her gaze flying to the doorway.

Eli leaned against the doorjamb, one broad shoulder propped against the walnut edge. He was dressed for work in a blue-and-white plaid flannel shirt that hung unbuttoned over a white T-shirt tucked into the waistband of snug faded jeans. A black leather belt was threaded through the belt loops of the jeans, and dusty black boots covered his feet.

"Hey," she responded faintly.

"Sorry I startled you." He shoved away from the doorjamb and walked toward her, his stride easy. "I had to stop at a job site near here, and when I picked up coffee, I thought about you, probably stuck in your office, slaving away. So I brought you a latte—double shot, vanilla, right?" He held up two take-out Starbucks cups with lids.

Frankie beamed at him, delighted. "You remembered." She took the cup and sipped, closing her eyes in pleasure. "I owe you."

"And I'll collect," he shot back, grinning when her eyes opened and she studied him with suspicion. He picked up a straightback wooden chair and spun it around, straddling it, his forearms resting along the top of the polished oak back. "Any new thoughts about our next move against Harry?"

Frankie leaned back in her swivel chair, propping her stockinged feet atop the open bottom desk drawer, ankles crossed. "Believe it or not, Harry called this morning. He's having a group of people over for dinner on Friday night to welcome a visiting software mogul from London. He asked if I'd like to join them." She looked at Eli from beneath lowered lashes. "I told him yes, providing I could bring a date."

"And what did Harry say?" Eli drawled, lifting his cup to sip, his blue eyes watching her over the rim.

"He asked me if my date was Nicholas Dean."

Eli stiffened, his eyes narrowing over her. "He's still pushing Dean at you."

Frankie nodded. "Apparently."

"Has Dean called you?" Eli asked, his voice neutral.

"Interestingly enough, no, he hasn't." Frankie tucked her hair behind her ear.

Eli's gaze tracked her fingers' movement, lingering over her hair before fastening on her face once again. "So Harry must not be giving Dean the same kind of verbal nudging he's giving you," he guessed.

"I suspect not." Frankie frowned, considering. "Has Harry tried to grill you about me?"

"Not yet." Eli shrugged. "But we have a meeting tomorrow to discuss the Wolf Construction proposal for the south Seattle project. Maybe he's waiting until then." He sipped his coffee once again. "Harry's cagey—I wouldn't put anything past him, and if he's not nudging Nicholas about asking you out, he must have a reason."

"Or maybe Nicholas refused to get involved in Harry's schemes," Frankie said. "And if he did, then our plan isn't really necessary."

Eli's eyes glinted. "If you believe that, then you don't know Harry as well as I thought you did."

"What makes you say that?" Frankie hoped Eli had a really good answer, because she was enjoying seeing him and didn't want their dates to end.

"Harry always has a bigger view of his projects, and if fixing you up with Nicholas didn't work out, he would go to plan B."

"And what's plan B?" Frankie asked.

"Not what—*who*. I have no idea who Harry would pick out to be the next candidate, but I'm sure he has another name on his list as a backup for Nicholas."

"Of course." Frankie sighed, tense muscles relaxing. "You're right. Harry always has a plan. Mom said that's the reason he was always so good at chess."

"That sounds like Harry." Eli glanced at his watch. "Time for me to go—I have an appointment in fifteen minutes." He stood, swinging the chair back into its original position. "What time do you want me to pick you up on Friday?"

"How about seven?"

"I'll see you then." His gaze flicked to her mouth, lingered, before returning to her eyes. "Have a good afternoon," he murmured, his deep voice a rumble.

And he was gone, before Frankie could gather her wits after that hot, focused stare.

Several minutes later, she was still sitting motionless, staring blankly at the notes on her desk when, for the second time in a half hour, knuckles rapped against her open office door. She looked up to find her friend and coworker, assistant professor Sharon Katz, standing on the threshold. Before Frankie could say hello, Sharon spoke.

"Wow, Frankie, who was that guy?" she asked, curiosity lighting her face. "He's gorgeous."

Frankie laughed at her friend's expression. "He's a friend of my cousin Justin."

"And he's visiting you…why?"

"He brought me a latte." Frankie lifted the Starbucks cup and saluted Sharon with it before drinking.

"Nice." Sharon leaned against the doorjamb, arms crossed, a sheaf of papers in one hand. "Come on, fess up. Are you dating him?"

"I am." Frankie grinned when Sharon rolled her eyes and fanned herself with the papers.

"Way to go, Professor." She straightened, glancing over her shoulder. "Darn, students are already filing into my lecture hall. I have to go—let's have lunch tomorrow, and you can fill me in on all the details, okay?"

"Okay." Frankie turned back to the half-completed report on her desk as Sharon disappeared, the quick tap of her heels fading away down the hall.

Anticipation buoyed Frankie over the next day. But Friday morning brought disappointing news. Her department head emailed to tell her attendance was mandatory at an impromptu after-work cocktail party. She suspected her boss wanted to impress his superiors with the presence of the entire department.

Disappointed that she had to cancel her plans with Eli that evening, Frankie dialed his cell phone several times, but each time the call went immediately to his answering service. As the morning flew by and became afternoon, she grew more concerned that she wouldn't be able to catch him before he left the house to pick her up at her condo.

She tried reaching him at the office, but when the message center picked up, she remembered Eli telling her that he'd given the secretaries the afternoon off. She left a message with the answering service but the operator couldn't guarantee Eli would get it before Monday morning when the office staff returned and picked up messages.

Frankie hated the thought that Eli might think she'd stood him up but couldn't think of another way to reach him.

Unless she could catch him on a job site, she thought with sudden inspiration.

She collected her purse and left her office in Liberty Hall. She was fairly certain she knew the address of the Wolf Construction site not far from campus. She had no idea whether Eli would be there or not, but she hoped to find someone who could tell her how to contact him. Within ten minutes, after a wrong turn that had her backing out of a dead-end street, she found the site.

The skeleton of what would become an upscale, five-story condo building rose in the air above her as she turned off the street and onto the bumpy dirt lot. Puddles of water left by the early morning downpour dotted the ground, and Frankie avoided them as best she could. Still, she knew her just-washed BMW would need another bath, and soon.

A contractor's trailer stood at the end of the lot, and several pickup trucks were parked in front of it, two of which had Wolf Construction logos on their doors. Frankie hoped that meant Eli was in the trailer, and she mentally crossed her fingers as she parked next to one of the trucks and got out.

Skirting a muddy puddle, she climbed the two wooden steps and knocked on the metal trailer door.

"Come in."

Frankie didn't recognize the deep male voice, but nevertheless she pushed the door open and stepped inside, halting abruptly.

Three men stood at a drafting table that was littered with blueprints and notes. A fourth man, his eyes bright blue in a lined face below a shock of white hair, sat in a battered office chair, one foot propped on the opposite knee as he leaned back.

None of the four were Eli. All of them were big, broad and dressed alike in faded jeans, plaid flannel shirts and muddy work boots. And all of them watched her with alert male gazes.

Frankie returned their interested stares with a friendly but reserved glance. She'd never met Eli's brothers or his grandfather, but the resemblance was unmistakable. These four had to be related to him.

"Hello. I'm looking for Eli Wolf."

"I'm his brother Connor," one of three men at the table drawled. "You're too pretty for Eli, honey. I'd be happy to help you—with whatever you need."

Taken aback, Frankie was speechless for only a second before the twinkle in Connor's eye reassured her. She smiled. "Sorry—honey—but it's Eli I need to find."

"Smart woman."

The deep, amused voice came from her left, and before Frankie could fully turn, Eli slipped an arm around her waist and bent to brush a quick kiss against her cheek.

"Hi, Frankie. What are you doing here?"

"I've been trying to reach you, but you didn't answer your cell phone," she told him. "I have to go to a faculty cocktail party right after work, so I can't make dinner at Harry's tonight. I'm sorry to cancel so late, but my boss just informed me attendance is mandatory. Apparently, the department head wants to impress the university president with our show of support." She grimaced. "I'd rather spend an hour or two being tortured by cannibals, but I can't get out of it."

"Sounds pretty bad," he said with sympathy. "Did you let your mom know we won't be able to join her at Harry's?"

She nodded. "Mom said she'd apologize to Harry for me." She looked up at him. "You should go, anyway—

everyone has to eat, right? And maybe you could pin Harry down about the contract."

He shook his head. "No, thanks—I think I'll pass." He smiled, a slow curve of his lips that made her breath hitch. "Just wouldn't be the same without you."

"I hate to interrupt you two," Connor broke in. "But don't you think you should introduce us to the lady, Eli?"

Frankie had been so focused on Eli that she'd all but forgotten the presence of the other four men. Now she realized they were all watching her and Eli with interest and curiosity. Even the older man had a curious gleam in his eye.

"Sorry," Eli said easily, clearly not the slightest bit concerned at Connor's inference he'd been lacking in manners. "Frankie Fairchild, these are my brothers— Connor, Ethan and Matthew. And the gentleman in the chair there is our grandfather, Jack." He bent to whisper in her ear, loud enough that the others could hear. "All of them are disreputable and untrustworthy, and they cheat at cards—so watch out if you ever get in a poker game with them."

"Good afternoon," Frankie said, her amused gaze meeting each of theirs. Eli's three brothers were as tall, brawny and as handsome—each in his own way—as Eli. They all had coal-black hair and blue eyes and an air of assured male strength. In fact, she thought dazedly, the amount of testosterone filling the air was palpable. She glanced at Jack and found him watching her shrewdly. She felt her cheeks warm under his knowing gaze.

"They're kind of overwhelming, all in one room, aren't they, missy?" he asked, his blue eyes warming. "Just like their grandpa, they have to beat women off with a stick."

"Geez, Granddad," Matt groaned, giving Frankie an apologetic look. "Sorry, Frankie. We can dress him up but can't take him out—not anywhere in polite company, at least."

"Hmmph," the older man snorted. "Who'd have guessed I'd run into polite company in a construction trailer? Usually it's just you four, and you don't qualify as polite."

Frankie laughed out loud. She could easily see the affection between the four brothers and their grandfather and was charmed. "I'd better get going." Frankie looked up at Eli and found him watching her, his blue eyes half concealed by thick lashes as he looked down at her. "I'm keeping you from your work, and I have a class in—" she glanced at her wristwatch "—twenty-five minutes. I'll leave and let you all get back to what you were doing." She waved a hand at the drafting table with its unrolled stack of blueprints held flat by a large rock sitting on each corner.

"You're not keeping us from work," Eli told her.

"Not at all," Ethan added, his voice a slow, deep drawl.

"We were all tired of looking at these damn blueprints," Connor added.

"Nevertheless, I'd better get back to campus." Frankie turned, and Eli was there before her, opening the door and holding it for her. "It was nice to meet you," she told the four Wolf men.

They echoed a chorus of goodbyes, and Frankie stepped outside, followed by Eli, who pulled the door shut.

"Where are you parked?" He frowned at the wet ground.

"Just over there." Frankie pointed at her car, just beyond the big dual-wheeled white pickup.

Eli took her elbow, scanning the ground between the steps and her car before walking beside her. "You're not wearing the right kind of boots for this weather. I'll get you a pair of rubber mud boots to keep in your car."

Frankie felt inordinately pleased that he seemed to expect her to visit again. "That would be nice," she murmured.

They reached her BMW, and he pulled open the door.

"How long do you think you'll have to stay at the cocktail party tonight?" he asked, leaning on the open door to look down at her as she turned the ignition key.

"Not too long, I hope," she told him. "I'm planning to slip out as soon as possible and head home. It's been a long week—I think I'll curl up in front of the TV and watch something mindless."

He chuckled. "Sounds like a good plan. Drive carefully." He stood back, closing the door with a quiet thunk.

As Frankie negotiated the bumps and puddles of the

lot and turned onto the smoothly paved street, she could see Eli in the rearview mirror. He stood, hands thrust in jeans pockets, the sun glinting off his black hair, watching her drive away.

She'd been looking forward to seeing him this evening, and having to cancel their dinner date made the prospect of the boring cocktail party seem even more dull.

She turned a corner and could no longer see Eli nor the construction site.

No doubt about it, she thought with a sigh. She was much more interested in spending an evening with Eli than schmoozing at a cocktail party with her boss and coworkers.

Apparently, she wasn't immune to the lure of a tall, dark and handsome man. Especially not when the man was Eli.

Eli watched Frankie's car disappear into traffic before he turned and reentered the work trailer.

"Pretty woman, Eli. Where'd you meet her?" Connor asked.

"Does she have a sister?" Matt asked, grinning when Eli shot him a quick glare as he crossed to the kitchenette and poured a mug of coffee.

"Yes, she has sisters, and no, I'm not going to introduce you," Eli said as Matt's eyes lit with interest. "And I've known her since she was just a kid."

"Yeah?" Ethan frowned at him. "I don't remember a girl named Frankie."

"Francesca Fairchild—she's Justin's cousin."

"I still don't remember her," Connor said.

"She must be Cornelia Fairchild's daughter," Jack said with a decisive nod. "Cornelia's the widow of Harry Hunt's original partner—I heard the families stayed close after Cornelia's husband died, and the girls consider Harry their uncle and his boys their cousins."

"That's right." Eli carried his mug to the drafting table and set it on the ledge above the blueprints. "Frankie's closer to Justin than any of his brothers. I met her through Justin when she was still in grade school."

"Was she gorgeous in grade school, too?" Matt asked.

"She's always been pretty," Eli answered shortly. He leveled a lethal glare at Matt. "And she's off-limits."

"Whoa." Matt took a step back, lifting his hands in mock defense, palms out. "Sorry, big brother. Didn't know you'd already staked a claim."

Ethan laughed, Jack's chuckle joining him.

"You must be blind, Matt," Connor said. "Nobody could have missed that whole she's-mine-touch-her-you-die thing Eli had going on a few minutes ago."

Matt's deep laugh joined the other three, and Eli threw them a disgusted glare.

"Can we move past this and get back to work?"

"Sure," Matt said, his eyes twinkling as he clapped Eli on the shoulder. "It's nice to see you getting irritated with us over a woman, Eli. Must mean you're finally recovered from the accident and back to normal."

Eli growled a noncommittal response, and the conversation returned to finding a solution for a glitch in the design of the second-floor balcony supports.

Later, when his brothers and Jack left the trailer and he was alone, Eli's thoughts returned to Frankie.

Where the hell had that surge of possessiveness come from when she'd stepped into the trailer and met his brothers? The Wolf men had hammered out an unwritten rule while in their teens—none of them ever poached each other's dates. He had no reason to worry that Matt, Ethan or Connor would do more than flirt harmlessly with Frankie as long as he was dating her.

He'd never before felt the urge to threaten his brothers over a woman. So, why now—and why Frankie?

"The protective thing must be left over from Justin and me vetting her boyfriends when she was a teenager," he muttered aloud, frowning unseeingly at the drawings taped on the wall.

Of course that was it, he thought with relief. He'd known Frankie a long time—it was only natural he'd feel protective. No doubt if he'd had a sister, he'd feel the same way.

A small voice in his head uttered a loud *hah!*

Eli ignored it, grabbed his hardhat and left the trailer to purposely stay busy so he wouldn't have time to ponder all the reasons why he might feel so strongly about Frankie and other men.

Even if the other men were his brothers.

Even if he knew she was perfectly safe with them.

It was going to be a long afternoon, he thought with resignation.

It was nearly seven o'clock before Frankie reached home that evening. The afternoon sunshine had given way to dark skies and sheets of rain that drenched her as she ran from her car. She shrugged out of her raincoat, hanging it on a hook beside the door, then toed off her wet pumps the moment she closed and locked the condo door behind her. Bending to pick them up, she walked in damp-stockinged feet into her bedroom. She dropped her purse and leather briefcase onto the bed, set her shoes next to the floor heat vent and stripped off her jacket, blouse, skirt and hose.

She flipped on lights as she went, turning on the shower and letting it run to heat up the space while she shed bra and panties, dropping them into the hamper before she stepped into the shower.

The water pulsed against her skin, and she turned her face into the spray, relishing its heat for several moments before she shampooed and scrubbed.

She felt a thousand times better when she left the bathroom. She'd towel-dried her hair then run a brush through the tangles until it lay sleek and smooth before donning a clean black bra, panties and gray University of Washington sweatpants. She drew on a matching gray UW hoodie, zipping the front closed to a few inches below her collarbones.

Her stomach growled as she walked barefoot into

the living room, pausing to switch on the television to a cable twenty-four-hour news channel before heading for the kitchen. She shifted items on the refrigerator shelves, but nothing appealed. She was just contemplating calling a local Chinese restaurant to order delivery when the doorbell rang.

Sighing, she padded out of the kitchen, across the living room to the tiny entryway. *I bet it's Mrs. Ankiewicz,* she thought. Her eighty-year-old neighbor often dropped in on a Friday evening if Frankie was home. Much as she adored the feisty old lady and enjoyed their conversations, however, she was more interested in food at the moment.

One glance through her front door's small glass viewer, however, had Frankie catching her breath.

Eli stood in the hall outside.

The sense of disappointment she'd felt since leaving him at the work site lifted, instantly replaced by a surge of delight.

Oh, no! Her fingers tightened on the doorknob. She leaned her forehead against the solid wood door panel, nearly groaning in disbelief.

What happened to her determination not to give in to her attraction to him? She knew he was dangerous for her heart—she did *not* want to take any of this too seriously.

She lifted her head, narrowing her eyes at her reflection in the mirror.

We're just two people conspiring to teach Uncle Harry a lesson, she told her reflection sternly. Eli isn't really interested in me—I'm not his girlfriend and he's not my boyfriend.

Not really. She repeated the words in her mind but she couldn't ignore the mirror's reflection of the anticipation that flushed her cheeks and sparkled in her eyes.

She turned away from the mirror and its too-revealing image, drawing a deep breath and straightening her lips in an attempt to erase the smile.

Then she pulled open the door.

Chapter Seven

"Hi." Unfortunately, she suspected her expression told him exactly how happy she was to see him, but she couldn't bring herself to care. "I wasn't expecting you tonight."

"I thought you might be hungry, so I picked up a pizza—unless the food at the party was good…?" He lifted a square box in one hand; his other held a six-pack of imported beer.

"The food was awful, actually. Come in." She caught his arm and pulled him inside, closing the door to lead him to the kitchen. "You're drenched. It must be raining harder than it was when I came home." She drew in a deep breath when he set the pizza box down on the table and lifted the top. "That smells like heaven." With perfect timing, her stomach let out a low rumble.

"I'm guessing that means you *are* hungry?" A smile curved his lips as he shrugged out of his damp jacket and hung it over the back of a chair. He wore faded, well-worn jeans and a light blue polo shirt, the fabric stretching snugly over the hard, defined muscles of chest and thighs.

"That means I'm starving!" She laughed and opened cabinet doors to take out plates. "Why don't you take off your boots and set them on the floor grate over there." She pointed at the scrollwork vent under the window. "I use the vents for my shoes all the time—works like a charm."

Eli nodded and pulled off his boots, padding in stockinged feet to set them on the grate.

"Will you grab some napkins out of the drawer next to the sink?" Frankie plied a wheeled cutter with quick efficiency, cutting the pizza into slices.

They carried loaded plates and napkins into the living room, Eli balancing two bottles of beer and a single glass for Frankie.

"Are you sure you don't want a glass?" she asked, curling one leg beneath her as she sat on the sofa, balancing her plate on her lap.

"Positive." Eli set his plate on the coffee table while he removed bottle caps, pouring a glass for Frankie and setting it on the lamp table next to her at the end of the sofa. "Real men drink beer straight from the bottle."

Frankie rolled her eyes at him. "I'll let that pass," she said magnanimously. "I'm feeling kindly toward you since you knocked on my door bearing edible gifts." She lifted her slice of pizza. "Mmm."

Moments passed while they concentrated on their pizza.

"So, how boring was the cocktail party?" Eli asked after he'd finished his first slice.

"Deadly."

"That bad, huh?"

Frankie pursed her lips, considering. "On the scale of really bad, it was somewhere between the torture of sitting through an hour lecture on the conception process of boll weevils and the Spanish Inquisition."

"Whoa." He held up his hands in surrender. "I'm not even going to tell you about the most boring work party I was ever forced to attend. You win."

She smiled sunnily, the last remnants of weary annoyance from a long day fading away. "Sometimes parties at work aren't boring—I think this one wasn't enjoyable because it was last-minute on a Friday night. Plus I was annoyed that it forced me to change our plans."

"I know what you mean." He nodded and picked up another pizza slice. They ate in companionable silence.

Frankie finished her second piece with a sigh of contentment, set her plate on the coffee table and picked up the remote.

"Is there anything you want to watch?"

"ESPN."

"No."

"Oh, come on," he coaxed. "I brought you pizza—and there's a Knicks game on tonight."

"How about a compromise? I won't make you watch a chick flick if you don't make me watch a ball game."

He tipped his bottle and eyed her over the rim. "How about a guy movie?"

She narrowed her eyes suspiciously. "What, exactly, are we talking about here?"

"Cruise through the channel listings and I'll show you."

"Okay." Frankie thumbed the remote and brought up the channel log. "See anything interesting?"

They finally settled on an action film starring Will Smith.

As the opening credits began to roll, rain hammered against the windows outside. January in Seattle often brought winter storms roaring in off the Pacific to pound the city with wind and rain. Tonight was clearly no exception.

Inside, Frankie curled her legs under her. Eli stretched his long legs out in front of him, propping his feet on the coffee table, ankles crossed.

The wind whistled around the corner of the building. Frankie looked at the windows, where the shadowy shapes of tree branches, tossing in the wind, were visible in the faint glow from streetlights.

"Brr." She shivered, clutching a throw pillow against her middle. "I'm glad we're not at Harry's. We'd have to drive home in this."

"It's nasty out there," Eli agreed. He looked sideways

at her. "Come here." He reached out and wrapped one arm around her shoulders, toppling her sideways against him. Her head rested on his shoulder, his arm cradling her. Startled, she twisted to look up at him, but he gently pushed her head back down on his shoulder. "This is more comfortable," he told her before pointing at the screen. "Shh, the movie's starting."

He's right, Frankie thought as she wriggled slightly and stretched out her legs on the sofa cushions. *This is very comfortable.* His chest was warm and solid against her side, his arm draped around her enclosed her in a warm cocoon of male heat and his shoulder was the perfect cushion for her head.

"You still have freckles," he murmured a few moments later, trailing a fingertip over the bridge of her nose.

She tilted her head back to look up and found him watching her instead of the television screen. "You noticed I had freckles?" she asked, surprised.

"Of course." He looked faintly insulted. "You were a cute little kid with a little spray of freckles just over your nose and your cheekbones."

His head lowered, and he brushed soft, tasting kisses over her face, following the arch of her cheekbone. Frankie's breath caught.

"I've wanted to do that for a while," he murmured as he drew back a few inches.

"Have you?" she whispered. His thick, dark lashes were half lowered as he cupped her chin in his palm and stroked his thumb over her cheek. She shivered.

The faintly rough pad of his thumb moved against her sensitive skin, stirring heat in her midsection. His lashes lifted, his gaze leaving her mouth and lifting to meet hers. Desire, hot and alive, lit his eyes. Her skin warmed, flushing under his stare.

"Eli, I don't want to mistake what's happening here." Her voice was a soft murmur. "We agreed to pretend we're attracted to each other to fool Harry—but at the moment, he's not here. It's just the two of us."

"Frankie," he muttered, his fingertips trailing down her throat. "Just so we're clear—this has nothing to do with Harry." His gaze flicked to the base of her throat, where his thumb stroked over the fast race of her pulse. "I want you."

His blunt words widened Frankie's eyes and sent heat flooding through her body. "Eli, I don't—"

He stopped her with a fingertip across her lips. "I'm not saying I want out of our deal to fool Harry. I just want you to know that if I'm kissing you—" he paused, his eyes going hotter "—or anything else physical, I'm not acting."

Frankie's gaze searched his face but found only sincere, focused intent. Much as she was tempted to tell him she wanted him, too, she was scared to death of opening that door. Desire warred with a deep conviction that she needed to protect her heart.

But if she wanted to move past her schoolgirl crush, maybe she needed to be a little more daring. Perhaps limited lovemaking with Eli would inoculate her against another full-blown crush, she thought.

Or maybe she was rationalizing because she desperately wanted more of his kisses. Whatever it was, Frankie decided to take a chance.

"Okay," she murmured. He didn't move, his gaze fixed on hers. Although his thumb continued to stroke seductively against her throat, he clearly waited for her to respond further. She'd never had a conversation quite like this with any man she'd dated but decided to be equally blunt with him. "I'm not ready to sleep with you yet."

"All right."

His body had tensed with her words, his restraint palpable as he waited.

She slipped her arms around his neck, her fingers testing the heavy silk of his dark hair. "Just so we're clear, when we're alone, I'm not pretending, either. And I'm sure I'm ready for more kissing." His muscles tightened against hers. "Maybe some serious fooling around?" she ventured.

A half smile tilted his lips. "I'll take whatever I can get," he murmured before he lifted her, settling her across his lap, and his mouth took hers.

When Eli left Frankie's condo several hours later, he was aroused and hungry, but he'd managed to keep his vow to honor Frankie's decision not to make love.

How the hell he'd kept from seducing her on the sofa, or the carpet or any other available flat surface, he had no idea. He couldn't remember the last time he'd wanted a woman this badly, nor when he'd been so turned on just by kissing.

He drove home and went to bed, but his dreams were hot and vividly sexual.

And all of them featured making love with Frankie.

After one last sizzling good-night kiss, Frankie closed the door behind Eli and slumped against the wood panels. When she straightened, she caught a glimpse of herself in the mirror. Her hair was disheveled and tumbled to her shoulders; her mouth was deeply pink and faintly swollen from the pressure of Eli's lips; her eyes were heavy-lidded and her skin flushed.

She'd barely managed to keep from begging him to make love to her, and if he'd pushed, she wasn't sure she could have said no.

Which meant she needed to decide how she felt about him while he wasn't in the same room, because she obviously lost the ability to think clearly when he was kissing her.

She needed to talk to her sisters, badly.

Frankie picked up the phone and tapped in half the numbers for Tommi before she remembered to look at the clock.

Ten-thirty. On a Friday night. She couldn't call her sister this late. Tommi was five months' pregnant, probably exhausted from a long day at her thriving restaurant and, if she was lucky, her guy was rubbing her feet and feeding her chocolates right about now.

Since Max adored Tommi, Frankie was pretty sure

he was taking good care of her sister, and she didn't want to disrupt their time together. Tommi deserved to be cherished and coddled.

She'd talked to Georgie at work earlier that day and knew she had plans to go out that evening.

And that left Bobbie—but Frankie suspected her younger sister and her new husband were also probably engaged in newlywed bliss at the moment.

Where are the Fairchild women when I need them? She sighed and returned the phone to its base. Her two younger sisters were dizzy with happiness, partnered with men who adored them. Frankie couldn't be happier for them.

But having her sisters busy left Frankie with no one to confide in.

Sighing, she walked into the bathroom. A few moments later, she'd changed into pajamas and climbed into bed, switching off the lamp to stare at the dark ceiling.

Suddenly, she sat bolt upright.

Lily, she realized with delight. She could talk to Lily about Eli. Not only had Lily gone through turmoil before she and Justin had worked out their difficulties to happily marry, but she also knew Eli very well.

She was scheduled to have a playdate with Ava the following morning. They'd arranged to meet at Lily's boutique in Ballard—she could arrive early and, hopefully, have a private conversation with Lily before Justin dropped off Ava.

Relieved that she had a plan, Frankie closed her eyes. Her evening with Eli continued to replay itself behind her lowered eyelids, however, and it was some time before she finally fell asleep.

Chapter Eight

The following morning, she drove to Princess Lily's Boutique a full hour before the time she'd agreed to meet Ava, stopping at a Starbucks in downtown Ballard on her way.

She breathed a sigh of relief when Lily's assistant told her Lily was in the workroom on the second floor. Frankie climbed the stairs and knocked on the open door of the big workspace.

Dressed in slim black slacks, ballet flats and a loose, chic black-and-white patterned top, Lily leaned over the wide table, shears moving swiftly and smoothly as she cut fabric. She glanced over her shoulder at Frankie's knock, a smile lighting her face.

"Frankie! You're here—come in."

"I hope I'm not interrupting you."

"Not at all." Lily's dark hair brushed her shoulders as she shook her head. "I'm glad you could come by early—it seems as if we hardly ever get to chat. We can catch up while we're waiting for Justin to drop off Ava."

"What an excellent idea." Frankie handed Lily a take-out Starbucks cup. "It's green tea," she assured her when Lily lifted a questioning eyebrow. "I thought we'd switch to tea for a while. I considered chai tea," she said, perching on a stool next to Lily's, one of several ranged along the edges of the long worktable that filled the center of the room, "but wasn't sure if you liked the black pepper and spices."

"I'm not a big fan," Lily said. "But I love green tea— so thanks for thinking of me." She leaned a hip against the wide cutting table where a roll of apricot silk snuggled against a half-unrolled bolt of cobalt blue. "I had the distinct impression when you called this morning that this wasn't a spur-of-the-moment visit."

"No," Frankie admitted. "I need a woman's perspective about something, and I can't talk to my sisters about it."

Lily's eyes widened. "And you came to me?" She pulled a stool closer and perched on it, her expression pleased. "I'm all ears." She glanced at her watch. "And we have at least an hour before Justin drops off Ava for your playdate."

"It's about Eli—and me."

"Ahh." Lily nodded sagely. "I heard you two have been dating."

"Yes—we have," Frankie confirmed. She was silent for a moment, tugging on the end of her ponytail.

"And?" Lily prompted when the silence stretched.

"Well…" Frankie drew a deep breath. "Here's the thing. When we started dating, we agreed that it would be…uncomplicated." She was having a difficult time finding the words to make Lily understand without confessing the entire scheme to trick Harry.

"Uncomplicated? As in—you were just friends?" Lily asked.

"Yes, sort of." Frankie sipped her tea and frowned.

"And that's become a problem?" Lily nudged.

"Exactly." Frankie rubbed her fingertips against her temple. "Will you promise not to tell Justin about this?"

"Of course," Lily said firmly.

"Good," Frankie said with relief. "Because he and Eli are such good friends, and I don't want him telling Eli about our conversation."

"I totally understand," Lily assured her.

"So, here's the thing. Since Eli and I have been dating, I'm finding it increasingly difficult to say no to him. It's not that other men haven't wanted to go to bed with me, but…this is *Eli*." Frankie spread her hands expressively, the take-out cup of tea tilting precariously in one hand. "He's practically part of my extended family. If I sleep with him and things don't work out, it's not as if I can just walk away. I'll keep running into him at family gatherings. I'll hear about him in casual conversation from Justin or Uncle Harry."

"I see your problem," Lily said slowly, sipping her tea.

"Not to mention the fact that he hasn't said a word about where he thinks our relationship is going," Frankie added.

Lily's sable eyebrows lifted. "Do you want it to go somewhere? Permanently, I mean?"

Frankie's mouth drooped. "I don't know. I've never wanted a permanent relationship." She slipped off the stool and paced across the room to stare out the bank of tall windows that looked out on Ballard Avenue. Traffic hummed along the brick street below. "But with Eli, I find myself wondering if having a man in my life for the long haul might not be a bad thing."

"Are you saying you've thought marriage was a bad thing up until now?" Lily asked, her voice gentle.

"Maybe not bad," Frankie told her. "Just…not something I could see myself choosing."

"You mean, before Eli?"

"I never thought about it before Eli."

"Ah." Lily nodded and sipped her tea.

"Has it been worth it for you? I mean—" Frankie waved her hand to encompass the high-ceilinged, well-appointed workroom with its bright bolts of silk, mannequins and lingerie-design sketches tacked on the white-painted walls "—you were a successful designer before you met Justin and had Ava. It must have been difficult to readjust your life to include a husband and child."

"Oh, yes." Lily's face softened, her eyes warm as her

gaze met Frankie's. "But their presence in my life has made me a better designer. And even more importantly, a happier, more contented, more fulfilled person."

"Hmm," Frankie murmured, considering Lily's words.

"You and Eli haven't had any conversations, even a few comments, about where your relationship is going?" Lily asked.

Frankie shook her head. "No. We've only been seeing each other for a short time." She paced away from her abandoned stool and Lily, then turned to pace back, too restless to be still. "That's one of the things that bothers me. How can I feel so strongly about him after only a few weeks—days, really," she amended.

"But haven't you known him a long time?"

"Yes, since I was a little girl," Frankie conceded. "But still…" She stopped, leaned a hip against the worktable, and eyed Lily. "Eli Wolf is handsome, charming and kisses like the devil himself. I'm incredibly attracted to him. But he has a reputation for serial dating. He scares me—and I don't know what to do about him."

Lily smiled a mischievous, impish grin. "I swear, I felt the same way about Justin. And I never admitted it to a living soul. Kudos to you, Frankie, for being so honest."

"I don't know what good it does me," Frankie grumbled. "It's not making me feel better. I hate not having answers. I'm a woman who treasures a rational, reasonable approach to life. My sisters tell me I'm too brainy and value logic over emotion, but the truth is, I've never found a situation I couldn't resolve through research and rational thinking." She threw up her hands and paced away once more. "And this situation is filled with emotion and too little logic. He's making me crazy. And on top of everything else about him that's so incredibly attractive, he doesn't appear to be the slightest bit intimidated that I have a PhD in English Lit and two master's degrees. I've never dated a man who didn't ultimately resent me for having a double master's in math and science. It's as if men are offended by a female who likes math or science, but Eli doesn't seem to care in the slightest."

"So, you're saying Eli sees you as a woman, not a brain?"

Frankie thought for a moment, eyes narrowed, before nodding abruptly. "I suppose I am."

Lily's laugh was infectious. "Frankie, do you realize you have the opposite problem from most pretty women—and you are *definitely* pretty," she said firmly. "In any event—" she waved a hand before continuing "—women are more likely to complain that men notice their face and body first, while ignoring their brain. You, on the other hand, appreciate Eli because he sees past your brain to the wonderful woman you are."

"I suppose you're right," Frankie murmured, considering Lily's words.

"I know I'm right," Lily said firmly. "And how terrific is it that Eli appreciates your emotional, physical self and accepts the cerebral, brilliant side of you as well?"

"I think that's part of why I'm so drawn to him," Frankie admitted.

Clear childish tones sounded in the stairwell, answered by a deep male voice as footsteps clattered on the stairs.

"I think Ava's arrived," Lily told her.

The little dark-haired girl burst through the doorway, followed by Justin. Lily's smile held warm affection as she bent to swing Ava up for a hug. The glance she exchanged with Justin as he bent and brushed a kiss against her mouth was filled with love. A twist of wistful envy swept Frankie.

Could she have that with Eli? Was it possible?

"Hi, cousin." Justin threw an arm around her shoulders and gave her a quick, hard hug. "How's everything?"

"Fine, Justin, just fine. How are you?"

He gave her a wry grin. "I've just spent an hour eating pancakes with Ava at Vera's Restaurant. My ears hurt from all the chattering."

Frankie laughed. "That's what you get for having a bright, precocious daughter. When are you going to have a little boy so your family balances the male-female ratio?"

Justin looked at Lily, lifting an eyebrow. "I'll let Lily field that question," he said dryly.

"And Lily's not talking," his wife said with a laugh.

"Good for you," Frankie told them. "Don't cave in to peer pressure. Have a baby when you're ready."

"I'm ready," Ava piped up. "I want a baby brother."

The adults blinked before exchanging glances and laughing.

A half hour later, Frankie and Ava left Lily and Justin in the design room above the boutique to drive to the park for an hour of play.

"Cousin Frankie, can we ride our bikes over there?" Ava pointed at open space in the parking lot behind them.

"Well, we could," Frankie acknowledged. "But if we follow the path around the park, we can stop and get hot chocolate at the coffee stand halfway around."

"Ooh." Ava's eyes lit with anticipation. "Let's go on the path."

"Yes, let's." Frankie unloaded their bikes from the back of the SUV she'd borrowed from Lily. She tucked the keys into the pocket of her black fleece jacket and pushed her bike beside Ava's little pink and white bicycle with its two-toned training wheels as they set off down the path that wound through the Ballard green space. The park was geared toward family activities, and even on this chilly January day, with a brisk breeze tangling hair and turning cheeks pink, the space was thronged. Parents accompanied children as they rode bicycles, tricycles and scooters along the paths, slid down slides or glided high on swings. Bundled up in boots, jeans, fleeces zipped to just beneath their chins, with gloves on their hands and earmuffs to keep their ears warm, Ava and Frankie joined the other children and adults on the wide, paved bike path.

Ava concentrated on pedaling and keeping her wheels

straight, the tip of her pink tongue just visible between her teeth as she focused. The loquacious little girl couldn't be silent for long, however.

"Cousin Frankie, you have to come to my house and see my bunny."

"I heard you have a new rabbit," Frankie told her. "What color is he?"

"He's white with brown spots." Ava wobbled to a stop and looked up, her eyes sparkling. "And he has brown ears!"

"Wow, brown ears? He sounds beautiful," Frankie said gravely.

"And he's really a big bunny," Ava confided. "Daddy says he's a flop-ear."

"Flop-ear?" Frankie repeated, nonplussed. "Oh, you mean a lop-ear?"

"Yes, and he has floppy ears, so I call him flop-ear." Ava beamed.

"Is that his name?"

"No, his name is Mr. Bunny."

"That sounds like a perfect name for a rabbit," Frankie said, hiding a smile.

"I think so, too." Ava nodded emphatically. She pushed determinedly on the pedals, struggling to set the bicycle in motion.

"Can I give you a push?" Frankie asked. "Just till you get going," she added hastily, well aware Ava was currently passionately committed to doing all things by herself, with no adult assistance.

"I guess that's okay." Her little legs pumped when

Frankie moved the bike forward, and once again they were on their way. "Riding bikes is hard," she confided to Frankie. "But now that I'm a big girl, I can steer really good."

"Yes," Frankie agreed solemnly. "I can see that."

"Look!" Ava stopped pedaling and pointed down the path. "It's Unca Eli."

Frankie's gaze followed the direction indicated by Ava's chubby little index finger. Sure enough, Eli was strolling toward them. He wore faded jeans, tennis shoes and a dark blue pullover fleece over a white T-shirt. The breeze tousled his black hair; his cheeks were pink from the cool air. As he drew nearer, his lips curved in a smile, and Frankie felt her heart soar as he reached them.

"Hi, Unca Eli." Ava grinned up at him, and he tousled her hair.

"Nice earmuffs, Ava," he told her, eyeing the hot pink headware.

"Thanks." She beamed and pointed at Frankie. "Cousin Frankie has some just like mine. We match."

"I see." Eli's gaze skimmed over Frankie's hair and met her gaze. "Nice earmuffs, Frankie." His words were so unconnected to the heated message she saw in his eyes that Frankie didn't react for a moment.

"Umm, thanks," she murmured. She glanced sideways at Ava, and the dizzying swirl of mental images, memories of being in his arms last night, dissipated. "What are you doing in the park this morning?" she asked, her voice perfectly steady and normal once more.

"I talked to Justin earlier, and he said you were riding bikes with Ava, so I thought I'd join you," he replied, his eyes lit with amused acknowledgment.

"But you don't have a bike," she pointed out reasonably.

"True." He glanced at Ava. "I'll have to jog to keep up with you. Unless you're training for the Olympics this morning—are you racing this morning, kid?"

The little girl giggled. "No!"

"Whew." He pretended to wipe sweat from his brow with his forearm. "That's a relief. Because if you were racing, I wouldn't have a prayer of keeping up with you—since you're a speed demon!"

He snatched the little girl up and held her suspended over his head as she giggled and squealed. Just as swiftly as he'd picked her up, he planted a smacking kiss on her cheek and lowered her back onto the bike seat.

"I'm ready to jog," he said to Frankie, as if the quick, noisy moment with Ava had never happened.

"I doubt you'll need to run to keep up," she said dryly, bending to give Ava a little push to set her bike wheels in motion. "We're taking it slow and enjoying the moment, aren't we, Ava?"

"Yup." Ava veered sideways before laboriously straightening her handlebars and forging slowly ahead.

Frankie walked beside Eli, pushing her bike as they followed a few steps behind Ava.

"We're stopping for hot chocolate at the refreshment stand just at the halfway point," Frankie told him, pointing at the cream-and-blue wooden building just visible over the heads of a group of teenagers on bikes.

"Do they have coffee?" Eli asked, his expression hopeful.

"Yes, I'm sure they do." Frankie saw his face lighten and laughed. "Not enough caffeine yet this morning?"

"Not enough caffeine since I went to a job site at 4:00 a.m.," he told her.

"Ouch, that's early." She winced in sympathy. "More problems with flooding?"

"Not yet, but I'm worried there might be." Eli briefly explained there was an unstable slope caused by clear-cutting the timber above his construction site. "We're all praying the retaining wall is finished before there's any serious flooding."

"Can't the owner of the lot above yours fix this?" Frankie frowned. "It seems unfair for you and your brothers to suffer damages for his negligence."

Eli shrugged. "That's life in the construction business."

"It still doesn't sound reasonable," Frankie said.

He caught the end of her ponytail and tugged gently, his smile warm. "You're probably right."

"Cousin Frankie," Ava piped up, interrupting them. "Time for hot chocolate."

Frankie realized they'd reached the Blue Hat coffee stand.

"Yes, it is," she agreed. They wheeled their bikes off the path.

Eli plucked Ava off her pink vinyl seat and settled

her on his shoulders. Frankie left her bike next to Ava's, and they joined the line in front of the window.

"What are you doing tonight?" Eli asked her as they waited.

"I'm taking my mom to the Pops symphony at Benaroya Hall. I bought the tickets last fall when they first went on sale."

"Sounds like fun," Eli said. He quirked an eyebrow at her. "Is that your favorite kind of music?"

"Not my favorite, but I like going to the symphony. What's your favorite music?" She eyed him. "Let me guess—some heavy-metal rock band."

"Nah, I like classic rock, like the Stones and Leonard Cohen."

They compared artists they liked, finding they agreed more than they disagreed as the line moved forward until it was their turn to place their order. Moments later, they carried hot take-out cups to a nearby picnic table.

"Come on, Ava-wave-a, time to get off." Eli set his cup down and swung the little girl off his shoulders, depositing her on the bench seat.

"Thanks." She beamed up at him when he handed her a cup of chocolate. "Want to know what my bunny did last night?" she asked, clearly expecting him to say yes.

Eli shot a quick, amused smile at Frankie as he slid onto the bench opposite her and Ava before answering. "Absolutely," he told her.

"Well…" Ava launched into a description of her father

and mother chasing the bunny around the house after he'd escaped when she'd left the cage door open. "Mama says she's going to have you put a lock on the bunny-castle door, Unca Eli. With a key and everything." Her rosebud lips drooped. "But Daddy says he's going to keep the key."

"I see." Eli coughed and covered his mouth.

Frankie was sure he was covering a laugh. *He's so good with her,* she thought. Ava clearly adored him, and, just as clearly, she'd spent a lot of time with him, because she treated him with all the ease and comfort of family.

He'd make a wonderful father. Startled by the thought, she coughed and lifted her cup, sipping the hot chocolate to clear her throat. *Where did that come from?*

It was nearly lunchtime when the three completed the loop of the park and reached the SUV and the parking lot once more.

Eli loaded the two bikes into the back of the SUV while Frankie snapped the latches to secure Ava in her car seat.

"Bye, Ava." He leaned in and gave her a kiss, accepting a chocolate-flavored smack on his cheek in return. He tapped his forefinger against the end of the little girl's nose and closed the door.

"Have fun tonight," he said, holding the door while Frankie slid behind the wheel.

"I will. What are you doing this evening—do you have plans?" she asked, latching her seat belt.

"I'm supposed to have dinner with a college friend, but he hasn't called to confirm, so I might not." He shrugged. "Maybe I'll rent a DVD and order in."

"I wish I had another ticket—you could join us at the symphony," she said.

"Thanks, but you two will enjoy it more without a critic along. Drive carefully." He stepped back and closed the door, waving as they drove away.

Much as Frankie had looked forward to this evening, she couldn't help wishing Eli would be there, too. Activities seemed infused with a certain energy and heightened interest when he was present.

Eli drove away from the park, heading back to the job site. He figured he probably didn't need to double-check the slope again, since it was barely one o'clock and the weather had been clear and cold with no rain since five that morning. Nevertheless, it was second nature for him to be cautious, especially when Wolf Construction had so much time, effort and money invested in the project.

As he'd hoped, the work site was wet from last night's rain, but no further damage had occurred. Eli headed across I-5, on his way to Ballard and his grandfather's home.

"Hey, Granddad," Eli called, rapping his knuckles on the back door as he stepped through it and into the kitchen. He'd grown up in the rambling old house on Sixty-fifth Street, blocks away from historic Larson's Bakery in Ballard. When their parents were killed in an accident, Jack Wolf had taken his four grandsons into his home. Now the big house was once more occupied only by the veteran carpenter, since Eli and his brothers each lived in their own place.

"Is that you, Eli?" Jack's gravelly voice grew louder and he entered the kitchen from the living room. He beamed. "Haven't seen much of you lately. Where you been keepin' yourself?" He waved a gnarled hand at the kitchen table with its red plaid oilcloth cover. "Sit down, I just made a pot of coffee."

"Coffee sounds great, Granddad." Eli deposited the bag of chocolate-covered donuts on the table and shrugged out of his jacket, hanging it on the back of an oak chair. He pulled the chair out and sat, stretching his long legs out to cross them at the ankles.

Jack carried two mugs to the table, his eyes lighting when he saw the bag. "You stopped at Larson's Bakery? I always knew I liked you the best of my four grandsons."

Eli chuckled. "You say the same thing to whichever one of us brings you donuts from Larson's."

"Well, yeah, I do." Jack set a mug in front of Eli and took the seat across the table. "But then, whoever brings me something from Larson's, that's the boy I like the best. At least for the moment," he added with a twinkle in his eyes.

Eli opened the bag, took out a donut and passed the bag to Jack. "Then I suppose I'll enjoy my favorite-grandson status, for the moment."

"Wise of you." Jack accepted the bag and squinted

into it before grunting his approval and removing a chocolate-covered donut. "What are you doing at my house on a Saturday afternoon?" he asked before taking a bite.

"I had to check a job site for flooding, and since I had to drive by the bakery, I stopped to pick up donuts."

"The condo building over by the university?" Jack asked, his eyes narrowing.

Eli nodded. "Yeah, that's the one. The owner clear-cut the trees off the slope above it, so every time it rains, there's the potential for trouble."

"You're putting in drains to take care of the problem long-term, aren't you?"

"Yeah, but they aren't finished, and until they are, I'm keeping a close eye on the site."

Jack nodded. "Good call. I once lost a whole six-story building, just days away from completion, when a bad storm soaked the slope above it. Four big cedar trees uprooted and slid down the hill, taking everything on the slope with them. That landslide slammed into the retaining wall, took out the back of the building and destabilized the whole shebang." Jack shook his head at the memory. "What a waste. We had to tear down the building and get the ground stabilized before we could rebuild. Your dad was mad as a hornet over that one."

"I bet the insurance company wasn't happy, either," Eli commented.

"Nope, they weren't." Jack finished his donut and took another from the sack. "That was a pretty woman who came looking for you the other day."

Eli glanced sideways to find Jack eyeing him, curiosity gleaming in his blue eyes.

"Yes," he agreed. "She's pretty."

"You two been keeping company for a while?"

"Not too long."

"You met her folks yet?"

Eli shot a sharp glance at his grandfather, but Jack only stared back, an innocent expression on his features.

"Justin introduced me to her mother years ago, and her father died when Frankie was young."

"Hmm." Jack narrowed his eyes thoughtfully. "Seems to me I remember you mentioning Justin Hunt being kinda protective of his cousin Frankie."

"Yeah, so?"

"So how does your best friend feel about you dating his favorite cousin?"

Eli shrugged. "I don't know. We haven't talked about it."

"Seems to me you better have an answer. Justin ran wild in this house when you two were kids, so I'm thinking I know him pretty well. He's likely to demand to know your intentions toward her. You'd better be ready with the right answer, or there's likely to be trouble."

"Justin's not going to go off half-cocked," Eli growled, shooting a frown at his grandfather. "He knows me better than that."

"Huh." Jack snorted. "He knows you've never had a permanent woman in your life, that's what he knows."

"What's that got to do with it?" Eli demanded.

"You and Justin were bachelors for a long time, so you know each other's habits well. He's not going to want you sleeping with his cousin for a while, then moving on to the next female," Jack said bluntly.

"Damn, Granddad." Insulted, Eli stared at him. "You think I'm not capable of having anything more than a temporary connection with a woman?"

"No. Hell, no." Jack shook his head emphatically. "I'm just sayin' that up until now, you haven't had anything close to permanent. That's all."

Eli stared moodily at his coffee mug, turning it in slow circles on the red and white oilcloth. "Yeah, well… maybe that's changed."

"Yeah?" Jack's eyebrows rose in surprise. "If that's true, I'm glad to hear it. Up until now, none of you boys have showed any signs you might be considering settling down. I'd be happy if you were thinking about something permanent with Frankie."

"I'm not saying I am, and I'm not saying I'm not," Eli told him.

"What *are* you sayin'?" Jack asked testily.

Eli looked up and met his grandfather's blue eyes, fierce beneath lowered white brows.

"If I were looking to settle down, Frankie's the kind of woman I'd be looking for." Eli saw the old man's eyebrows shoot upward and his eyes light with glee. "But I'm not looking for a woman to settle down with."

"Hmph." Jack snorted and grabbed another donut. "You don't make any sense."

Eli wasn't sure he was making sense, either, but he'd

be damned if he'd tell his granddad. "Yeah, well, I'm only thirty-five. Statistics say lots of men in today's world don't get married until they're forty. They're busy building careers first."

Jack's hmph of disgust clearly conveyed his opinion of the statistics and the reasoning behind them. "Your daddy and mama were married when they were barely twenty years old, both of them. And your daddy had a family while we were both busy building the company." Jack leveled a finger at Eli. "And don't tell me you're not glad we kept Wolf Construction afloat during those early hard years, 'cause I know you like running it. And if we could both juggle families and working, you and your brothers could, too." He nodded emphatically and reached for another donut.

"You're right. I like running Wolf Construction." Eli didn't think it would help to tell his granddad that he'd spent a couple of hours in the park with Frankie and Ava earlier. Nor that watching her with Ava had made him wonder what it would be like if the little girl were their child.

Frankie would make a wonderful mother. She was great with Ava, affectionate and warm but firm when needed.

The sudden mental image of a little girl with Frankie's blond hair and brown eyes, one that called him daddy, had stunned him. He hadn't been able to get that image out of his mind.

But damned if he was going to confess that to Jack.

The old man would never give him any peace if he knew he was imagining having children with Frankie.

"I'm starting to wonder if any of you boys will ever get married and give me great-grandchildren to take fishing," Jack growled.

"What?" Startled, Eli's attention snapped back to his grandfather. Had the old man been reading his mind?

"I'd like some kids in this family," Jack told him bluntly. "It's been too long since we've had little ones around."

"Justin's dad felt that way and tried to force his sons to marry and have kids," Eli reminded him. "Don't take a page from Harry's playbook—he's lucky his sons are still speaking to him after he threatened to sell HuntCom."

"Wouldn't work with you and your brothers," Jack said regretfully. "You've already inherited your dad's sixty percent of Wolf Construction." He eyed Eli speculatively. "I suppose I could threaten to sell my forty percent to an outside party if you four don't get married soon and have some babies."

"Don't even think about it," Eli said mildly, sipping his coffee.

Jack laughed. "Might be worth it, just to make you all a little crazy." His eyes twinkled.

"Connor might have a heart attack," Eli told him. "Just remember—" he pointed his index finger at Jack "—paybacks are hell."

"That's true." Jack heaved a loud sigh and took another doughnut from the bag.

"Damned straight." Eli nodded emphatically. He wondered why the thought of getting married and having kids didn't seem as inconceivable as usual.

He doubted it was coincidence that listening to Jack talk about marriage and babies led directly to Technicolor mental images of Frankie.

Eli could handle lusting after her. Any healthy male with a libido would react the same to the beautiful blonde.

No, what shook him were the unfamiliar feelings of possessiveness and the gut-deep need to claim and protect.

He'd never felt this level of emotion for a woman before. If he were a man who believed in fate, he'd suspect he'd met his match in Frankie Fairchild and life as he knew it had been changed forever.

Chapter Nine

On Sunday afternoon, the day after biking in the park with Eli and Ava, Frankie met two of her sisters to shop at Pacific Place in downtown Seattle. Tommi was busy with Max and couldn't join them, but Bobbie, Georgie and Frankie happily browsed racks of sweaters, slacks and jeans, then tried on shoes before gathering for lunch at one of their favorite spots, the Nordstrom café.

"It looks like Bobbie has the most bags," Frankie said, stowing her single bag containing a lime-green cashmere sweater with matching hat and gloves under her chair.

"I found shoes on sale," Bobbie replied, delighted. "Fabulous prices—I couldn't resist."

"I bought a pair of black heels," Georgie put in. "I'm

looking forward to shopping in New York and didn't plan to buy a thing today but I couldn't resist them."

"I also hit the lingerie section." Bobbie swung a light bag from one finger, her smile slightly wicked. "Gabe is going to love what I bought."

"Show us," Frankie demanded, knowing her sister's smile meant she planned to seduce her fiancé.

Bobbie opened the bag and tugged out just enough black lace over cream satin to make her sisters ooh and ah before tucking the bag beneath her chair with her purse.

The waiter arrived with their order, placed earlier at the long counter in the entry room, and it was several moments before conversation resumed.

"Can you believe Mom?" Frankie asked, stirring a teaspoonful of sugar into her tea. "I wonder if she's serious about the golf pro at the club?"

"I doubt it." Georgie shook her head.

Frankie wasn't so sure. She noted the unconvinced expression on Bobbie's face and looked back at Georgie. "Why don't you think this might be serious—is it because he's so much younger than her?"

"That—and I can't see Mom remarrying," Georgie said. "Look how long she's been single." She took a bite of her club sandwich.

"I don't know," Bobbie put in. "I'm a firm believer in a woman's right to change her mind about living alone. Tommi and I did."

"Yes, but you're a lot younger than Mom," Georgie pointed out.

"True," Bobbie conceded.

"But Mom looks and acts so much younger than her real age," Frankie argued. "I swear, she seems younger than most fifty-year-olds."

"Which is probably why Greg is so taken with her," Bobbie pointed out.

"I wonder if Mom realizes she's now doing what she always told Harry he *shouldn't* do when he dated younger women," Frankie said with a grin, filled with amusement that sixty-six-year-old Cornelia was dating a man of forty-nine.

"I'm not brave enough to tell her." Bobbie's eyes twinkled as she sipped her green tea.

"Me, either!" Frankie said promptly, her words immediately echoed by Georgie.

"Speaking of dating," Georgie said, fixing Frankie with a curious look. "I hear you went out with Eli Wolf."

Frankie nodded, well aware that Bobbie had stopped eating and was staring at her with surprise.

"I didn't know you were going out with Eli," Bobbie told her. "When did this happen?"

"We went to the Children's Hospital fundraiser last Saturday," Frankie said.

"Are you seeing him again?" Bobbie asked.

"Tomorrow night," Frankie responded. "He's taking me to his favorite bar to meet his brothers and have dinner."

"It sounds as if the two of you are spending a lot of time together," Georgie commented.

Frankie shrugged. "Just a few dates. I won't see him the rest of the week because he and his brother Connor are flying to Las Vegas for a business conference on Tuesday and won't be back till late Sunday night."

She didn't miss the significant glance Bobbie exchanged with Georgie.

"What?" she demanded.

"For someone who's had only 'a few dates,' it certainly sounds as if the two of you are an item," Georgie said.

Bobbie leaned forward, fixing her with a sober stare. "What about the physical side? Are you compatible?"

"He's an incredible kisser." Frankie's gaze went slightly unfocused as she remembered their heated kisses. "I haven't slept with him," she said bluntly, "but I'm guessing it would just as amazing."

"You haven't slept with him?" Georgie's eyes went wide.

"No." Frankie shook her head. "Why do you sound so surprised?"

"Because you've apparently been seeing quite a bit of each other and rumor has it, Eli never dates women just for their conversation."

"Hmm." Frankie had heard those same rumors. "I'm not likely to get involved with a man who'll break my heart," she told them. "Not to worry."

Bobbie and Georgie looked unconvinced but didn't protest when Frankie asked Georgie a question about her upcoming assignment that would take her to New York City for several months.

She was relieved when the conversation turned away from her and Eli. Because the truth was, she had to admit Eli Wolf was much more than she'd anticipated—more attractive, more charming, more seductive. Added to that, she was finding she simply liked the man he was.

And that was perhaps the most dangerous thing of all.

The following Monday evening, Eli picked up Frankie and drove to Killoran's Pub in Ballard. Tucked into a brick side street off Ballard Avenue, the pub had been the Wolf brothers' favorite place to play pool, listen to live music, drink beer and grab a hot sandwich or pizza since they'd turned twenty-one.

"I can't stay too late," Frankie told Eli as he held the heavy door for her. "I have an early class in the morning."

"I'll have you home before ten," he promised.

They stepped inside and paused, met with a wave of conversation and laughter. The yeasty smell of beer and bread mixed with the scent of pizza in the walnut-paneled room.

"Hey, Eli, back here," Connor yelled from a table halfway to the rear of the long, narrow room.

Eli lifted a hand in acknowledgment and tucked Frankie under his arm. Together they wound their way between crowded tables toward his brothers.

Several times they were stopped when someone

caught Eli's arm, halting him to say hello and exchange a few words before they could move on.

"You know lots of people here," Frankie said, leaning up to speak close to his ear so he could hear her over the noise.

He nodded. "I've been coming here after work for years. A lot of these guys have worked on jobs with me."

At last, they reached the table. Eli pulled out chairs for them, seating Frankie before dropping into the chair next to her.

"Man, it's crowded in here tonight," he commented, holding Frankie's black raincoat as she shrugged out of the sleeves.

"Michael O'Shea is playing later," Ethan told him. "He has a lot of fans."

"Yeah, and they're all crammed into this room," Matt added dryly. He lifted a pitcher and poured a glass of beer, passing it to Frankie before filling another for Eli. "Have you two eaten yet?"

"No. I wanted Frankie to try the grilled Italian sandwich on ciabatta bread."

"Good call." Connor leaned forward to nod. "The pizza is good, too."

"What do you say, Frankie—sandwich or pizza?" Eli asked, stretching his arm along the back of her chair and leaning in so she could hear him over the noise.

"What are you having?" she asked. Her lips brushed his ear as she spoke, and he turned his head to look at her, blue eyes heating. Electricity arced between them, and Frankie caught her breath.

"Sandwich," he murmured against her ear.

Frankie shivered with awareness, his breath stirring the tendrils of hair at her nape. Earlier, she'd pulled her hair up into a ponytail, donned a black cashmere sweater over pencil-thin jeans with boots and slipped gold hoops into her earlobes. The ponytail left her nape bare, and when Eli stroked his thumb over the back of her neck, she realized how very vulnerable she was to his touch.

"How about you?" he asked.

Belatedly, Frankie realized he was waiting for her to answer.

"Oh, me, too," she said. "Whatever you're having."

His lips curved in a brief smile, and Frankie suddenly wished they were alone. She badly wanted his mouth on hers.

On the stage behind them, the microphone screeched. The noise yanked Frankie back to awareness of her surroundings, and she sat forward, reaching for control as she moved away from Eli's disturbing touch. She picked up her glass and sipped her beer, leaning her elbows on the table as Eli stopped a waiter to recite their order and she listened to his brothers arguing.

"...and I'm telling you there's no way that specific gaming software will run as fast as it should on your computer," Ethan said vehemently. "You need more hard-drive capacity."

Frankie blinked. "Your brother is a techno guy?"

she murmured to Eli. "Does he know anything about programming cell phones?"

"Probably," Eli told her. "You have a problem with yours?"

She nodded. "I have a new phone and haven't had time to figure out how to transfer all my numbers and info from my old phone," she explained. "So I'm carrying both of them, because my address book, email addresses, et cetera, are all stored in the original phone. I'd love to get rid of it and just have one."

"I can fix it," Matt put in before Eli could respond. "I'm good with cell phones."

"I'm better," Connor declared. "Besides, I just did that with my new cell. It'll be a piece of cake."

"Don't let either of them touch your phone," Ethan warned her with a slow smile. "They'll break it."

"I'll do it for you," Eli told her. "If you let any of them have your phone, God knows what they'll do to it."

"Oh, come on, Eli," Matt protested. "I programmed all the work cell phones a few months ago, and they all work fine."

"Yeah," Eli said, his voice dry. "And the ring tones were annoying as hell."

Matt grinned at Frankie. "He's just mad because his ringtone was 'Macarena.'"

Frankie sputtered, nearly choking on a mouthful of her drink. Eyes wide, she looked at Eli to find him watching her, a lazy smile on his handsome face. Within moments, though, she joined his brothers, laughing at Eli's disgruntled expression.

"I'm better than my brothers with technical equip-ment, Frankie. You'd better let me fix your phone," Ethan repeated.

"No." Eli's voice held finality. "I'll do it."

"All right." Frankie opened her purse, shifting through the contents until she found the two cell phones. "Here you are." She handed them to Eli as she dropped her purse at her feet once more. "The new one is the hot-pink one. The old one is the silver."

"Hot pink?" Eli lifted his eyebrows in disbelief. "You have a hot-pink phone? Geez." Eli clearly was speechless. Nonetheless, he started scrolling through her menu.

As Eli concentrated on her phones, the three younger Wolf brothers regaled her with stories of the hours they'd spent in the bar and the musicians who'd appeared on the small stage—some already famous, some who had gone on to become famous. They took turns teasing each other about the women they'd met, won and lost within the four walls.

The waiter interrupted them to slide plates of sand-wiches with pickles and chips on the table in front of Frankie and Eli. He deposited a large pizza, loaded with cheese, meat and veggies, in the middle of the table and set plates in front of Ethan, Connor and Matt.

Eli handed Frankie her phones.

"Are you done already?" she asked, startled.

"Yeah," he told her. "I'll explain how I did it later."

"Great." She smiled at him with delight. "Thanks so much. I have no idea when I would have had time to sit down and figure out how to transfer everything. I owe you."

The slow curve of his lips set her heart pounding.

"I'll think of a way for you to pay me," he murmured so only she could hear.

Flushing, Frankie darted a quick look at the others around the table as his smile widened, his eyes gleaming with amusement at her reaction to his flirting. Thankfully, the others were busy loading pizza onto plates.

"Hey, Frankie, do you have any sisters?" Matt asked, his expression hopeful.

"Yes, I do." She sipped her drink, making him wait. "Three, to be exact. But one just got married, the other is in a relationship, and only the third is single. Unfortunately—" she picked up a chip and nibbled "—she's moving to New York City soon."

Matt's face fell. "Damn."

Frankie glanced at Eli. The amusement in his blue eyes echoed her own and when he winked, she laughed.

The evening flew, Eli looking on indulgently as his brothers tried to coax Frankie to introduce them to her friends, teasing her when she demurred and arguing over which one of them should be allowed to take Eli's place and drive her home.

Time flew and all too soon, it was after nine-thirty.

As promised, Eli led Frankie out of the pub early and drove her home.

"I'd love to ask you to come in," she told him after

unlocking her condo door. "But if I do, I won't want you to leave."

"I make a mean omelet," he told her, bracketing her against the closed door panels by planting his palms on each side of her shoulders and leaning close. He brushed a kiss against the corner of her mouth. "And great coffee. I'll feed you breakfast in bed before you leave for work."

Frankie closed her eyes, tilting her head back to give his warm, seductive lips better access to her throat.

"Tempting," she managed to get out. He nudged her coat collar aside and explored the juncture where throat met shoulder. She shivered with longing but planted her palms against the soft fleece covering the hard muscles of his chest, keeping him from pulling her into his arms. "But I really do have to be at work early in the morning."

"I'll drive you to work early," he murmured, lifting his head to look down at her. His eyes were heavy-lidded, the blue irises darkened to navy.

"If you come in and stay, neither one of us will get any sleep tonight," she told him, smiling at the reluctant acceptance she read on his features.

He drew a deep breath, expelling it in a rough sigh.

"You're right. Kiss me, and I'll go home," he growled, pulling her close.

Lips curved in a smile, Frankie wound her arms around his neck and went up on her toes, meeting his mouth with hers, quickly swept away by the passion that flared between them.

When he set her back on her heels, she was dazed,
her knees like jelly.

He tucked her hair behind her ear. "Connor and I
have an early flight in the morning, but I'll call you
from Vegas. The conference lasts through Friday, but
we're staying to play a little blackjack and flying home
late Sunday."

"I'll miss you," she told him. "Be safe."

"I'll miss you, too. Don't run off with any other guy
while I'm gone," he teased. Then he took her mouth in
one more swift, hard kiss before he pushed open the
door behind her and gently shoved her inside. "Lock
the door," he ordered softly as he pulled the door shut.

Frankie twisted the deadbolt closed and slid the
chain into its slot. Listening, she didn't hear Eli walk
away until after the locks snicked closed. Smiling at his
protective patience, she turned and strolled toward her
bedroom, dreamily reliving those heartstopping kisses
while she got ready for bed.

And when she fell asleep, she dreamed of Eli.

Eli and Connor flew out of Sea-Tac the following
morning to attend the contractor's conference in Las
Vegas. Although he called Frankie each night, he missed
seeing her. Months earlier, when they'd booked the conference, he and Connor had planned to spend the weekend in Vegas after the conference ended on Friday. He
wasn't slated to fly back to Seattle until Sunday evening,
but on Friday he changed his flight and flew home on

the red-eye, reaching home in Seattle just after two in the morning.

The following morning, he was awake by nine, but Frankie didn't answer her cell phone when he called. Fortunately, he reached her sister Tommi at her restaurant and learned Frankie had driven to Arlington, north of Seattle, to spend the day volunteering at a rescue horse stable.

Eli scribbled the directions Tommi gave him on a napkin and headed north up I-5, toward the farm.

He remembered Frankie had briefly mentioned her volunteer work at the barn while telling him anecdotes about her childhood with Cornelia and her sisters. Cornelia had sat Frankie down on her eighth birthday, discussed the responsibility of individuals to contribute to the larger community and asked her to pick a cause to which she would commit her time and energy. Frankie loved horses and had chosen an organization that rescued abused and damaged horses.

That early exposure had become a lifelong devotion to the rescue operation in Arlington. Tommi had told him earlier that Frankie usually left her cell phone in her car when she was at the barns. While disappointed that he couldn't reach her, Eli decided that surprising her in person would be even better.

He left the freeway just past Arlington, turning onto a two-lane road that wound through the countryside, where rolling acres of green pastures held horses and the occasional cow. After twenty minutes of driving past farms and fields, he reached a complex of big barns and fenced pastures. He turned into the wide lane, jolting over bumps and avoiding holes in the graveled road before parking in a large dirt lot.

A huge wooden barn, a round pen with green metal pole fencing and a long low stable were set in a semi-circle around the dirt parking lot.

Eli left his car and walked to the open barn doors, following the sound of voices as he stepped inside. To his left, a flight of stairs led upward, and, hearing voices, he climbed the steps to the second floor. But the office there was empty, as were the bleacher seats that lined the outer walls. He peered over the waist-high divider and down into a huge arena with a soft dirt floor. An older woman in boots and jeans stood in the center of the arena, directing a young girl wearing a riding helmet and snug pants tucked into high boots. She sat atop a rangy thoroughbred that looked too tall and much too big for the small girl. Nevertheless, she handled him with easy confidence.

Eli retraced his steps down the stairs and turned left, following a hallway until it turned sharply right. Ahead of him stretched a wide alley with stalls opening off each side. He started down the alley, stopping to stroke his palm over muzzles as horses looked out over the top of open half doors to nicker and call.

"Back up, Daisy. Stop being so stubborn. You know you can't go outside."

Frankie's annoyed voice reached Eli's ears. He searched the barn ahead of him but didn't see her. A side alley opened to the left just two stalls ahead, and several thuds and bumps sounded as if the noise came from there. Hoping to surprise her, his stride lengthened and he rounded the corner.

Frankie stood at an open stall door only feet away, a halter rope in one hand while the other hand and one shoulder pushed against the side of a massive draft horse.

The huge horse was clearly winning the argument as she took a step forward, her hooves big as dinner plates and planted too close to Frankie's boots.

Cold fear iced Eli's heart. He reached Frankie in three long strides, lifting her out of the way with an arm around her waist.

"W-what on earth…!" Frankie sputtered in surprise.

Busy muscling the big draft horse back into the stall, Eli didn't look at Frankie until he'd slammed the door on the massive horse. Then he turned to face her.

"What the hell do you think you're doing?" he roared.

She stiffened, surprise giving way to anger that flushed her delicate features with color, her brown eyes snapping. "My job," she said succinctly. "What are you doing?"

"Saving your pretty butt," he snapped. "Did you not notice that horse outweighs you by a thousand pounds?"

"More than that," she shot back. "And I fail to see what concern that is of yours."

"Are you crazy? You were about to get stepped on."

Frankie waved a hand at the big horse, who watched them with interested brown eyes from her stall. "I was *not*. Daisy has never stepped on anyone in all the years she's been here. She tries to get out into the paddock whenever someone opens her stall door, but she's perfectly docile. She's never hurt anyone in her life."

"She's so big she wouldn't know if she hurt you," Eli told her, his voice just barely below a roar. "You could have been killed or badly hurt. You're too little—you can't handle a horse that big."

"You don't have the right to tell me what I can or can't do," she told him, fingers curled into fists at her sides.

"Well, someone has to. You clearly don't have sense enough to know you're too damned small to muscle around a horse that's twenty times your size and weight," he growled, anger fueled by the terrifying sight of her pitting her fragile frame against the huge horse.

Her brown eyes shot sparks. "I've been making my own decisions since I was eighteen," she informed him, her voice dripping ice. "And if I was going to give someone permission to interfere in my choices, it would *not* be you. Especially since you clearly know *nothing* about horses," she snarled.

"I don't need to know anything about horses to know this horse—" he jerked a thumb over his shoulder at the stall "—is too damned big for you to push around."

"It's got nothing to do with her size," Frankie yelled, planting her fists on her hips, the air fairly sizzling around her. "She's a Clydesdale and so gentle Ava could handle her. Oh, what's the use? You're impossible." She threw up her hands and turned on her heel.

"Where are you going?" Eli yelled after her.

"Home," she shot over her shoulder as she strode away, her boots kicking up puffs of dust. She stopped abruptly and spun around to glare at him. "And don't follow me. I don't want to talk to you. Not until you realize what an ass you've been and are ready to apologize— and maybe not even then." She spun on her heel once more and stalked off.

Fuming silently, Eli watched her until she disappeared through the door at the end of the alley lined with stalls. He didn't care how mad she was; he was right about this. *And it'll be a cold day in hell before I apologize for trying to keep her safe.*

Thoroughly disgusted and out of sorts, he left the barn. Frankie was nowhere to be seen when he reached the parking lot and drove away.

I should have stayed in Vegas, he told himself as he headed back to Seattle. *I could be sitting at a blackjack table, enjoying myself, instead of wasting my time trying to reason with an irrational woman.*

The first drops of rain hit his windshield. Eli looked at the sky and realized that while he'd been in the barn, the sunny morning had turned dark and cloudy.

"Great," he muttered. "Just great."

Frankie dashed away tears of anger as she drove south toward Seattle. The fact that she was tearing up infuriated her. She'd missed Eli more than she'd thought possible over the last few days and had looked forward to seeing him when he returned.

Then he'd stalked into the barn and like a typical domineering male, assumed she was acting foolishly and set out to save her from her own stupidity.

"Arrogant jerk," she muttered, fingers tightening on the steering wheel.

He hadn't even bothered to ask her—no, he'd all but *told* her she was an idiot for handling Daisy.

"As if I didn't know how big Daisy is," she grumbled to herself. "As if I haven't been shoving Daisy around since she was three months old. But did he ask me anything about her? No, he did not," she answered her own question. "Men," she snarled, eyes narrowing at the windshield. "They're impossible."

A few fat raindrops splatted against the windshield.

Frankie switched on the wipers. *Perfect,* she thought, *just what I needed.*

Traffic slowed with the sudden downpour, taillights winking red as drivers braked.

Frankie groaned and wished she were home, impatient with the delay that gave her far too much time to contemplate how much she wished she'd taken more time to tell Eli Wolf how wrong he was about her ability to handle Daisy. And she should have added how annoying she found it when someone prejudged a situation without first asking questions and gathering facts.

And men think women act irrationally, she thought with a humph of disbelief.

She refused to think about how much she'd been

looking forward to his return from Las Vegas—and how disappointed she felt that anticipation had turned into anger.

With a quick twist, she turned on the radio, filling the car's interior with the sound of upbeat bluegrass music.

The bright music failed to lift the leaden weight that pressed on her chest but she ignored it, determined not to mope because she and Eli had argued.

Chapter Ten

The rain continued all weekend, and Monday brought more gray skies and wet weather.

Tuesday night, Eli drove home from work, parked his truck in the garage and entered his condo through the utility room. He paused to take off his wet, muddy boots and left them on the mat next to the washing machine. Then he shucked off his jeans, soaked and splattered with mud from hem to knees, and dropped them into the empty washer, following them with his wet flannel shirt and socks. Wearing only a white T-shirt and navy boxers, he padded in bare feet into the kitchen, stopping to set the containers of take-out Chinese food he'd bought earlier on the counter before heading upstairs to the bathroom.

Three days had passed since he and Frankie had

argued at the horse barn, and he'd been in a foul mood ever since. His brothers were threatening to ban him from the work trailer.

It's the rain, he told himself. *Anybody would be in a bad mood with three days of gray skies and downpour.*

He turned on the shower, letting the steam warm the tiled area as he stripped out of his boxers and T-shirt.

When he finally stepped into the stall, the enclosure was heated, the pulse of the showerhead hitting him with enough force to make him groan with relief. He shampooed and scrubbed, then let the hot spray of water sluice the suds away. He propped his palms on the tiled wall and let the water beat a rhythm against aching back muscles until it began to cool before he got out.

Drying off, he walked naked into the bedroom to pull on clean boxers, a pair of worn jeans and a soft T-shirt.

His hair was still damp when he went back downstairs, pausing in the living room to switch on the television. In the kitchen, he collected a fork and the thermal containers of takeout, then grabbed a beer from the fridge and returned to the living room.

Outside, the wind howled as the storm continued to dump rain on Seattle. It reminded Eli of the evening he'd spent in Frankie's apartment, curled up next to her on the sofa. He wished he was back there.

Damn. He stared at the TV without seeing it. He missed the hell out of being with Frankie.

He liked his condo, liked his independent life. Since

he'd started seeing Frankie, however, he'd realized that just spending time with her, even if they were only sharing a pizza and watching a movie, felt right—maybe more right than being alone.

It was almost as if a missing piece of his life had fallen into place.

Before dating Frankie, he hadn't even known there *was* a piece of his life missing.

He'd dated a lot of women and enjoyed their company, but dates had always been a precursor to sex. He couldn't remember a time since puberty when just being in a woman's company was enough.

Not that he didn't want to sleep with Frankie. In fact, he suspected he was damned near obsessed with the thought of taking her to bed. He prided himself on his self-control, but he had to admit it was growing increasingly more difficult to stop at kisses and fooling around. Especially since she seemed to find him just as irresistible as he found her.

But he still sensed a certain hesitancy, a kind of wariness in her. With any other woman, he would have tried to charm and seduce her out of whatever was making her hold back. But with Frankie, it was strangely imperative that she choose to come to him willingly, wholeheartedly.

Why it was so, he didn't know. Maybe simply because this was Frankie, and he'd known her since she was a girl. Maybe it was because she was Justin's favorite cousin. Whatever it was, what was happening between

Frankie and him was different from any relationship he'd had with a woman before.

Not that there was anything happening between him and Frankie at the moment, he thought, frowning. She hadn't called him, and he hadn't called her, either. He'd told himself it was because she'd made herself clear before she stalked away from him and out of the barn. She'd said she didn't want to talk to him. He was only being cooperative, giving her time to calm down.

Yeah, right. The real reason he wasn't calling Frankie was because she'd scared the hell out of him at the barn. Seeing the big Clydesdale horse looming over her had made his blood run cold.

I overreacted when I yelled at her. But, damn, what was I supposed to think?

And Frankie was too independent to let him get away with ordering her around. In fact, he doubted she'd ever let anyone tell her what to do—not unless there was a logical reason. And then a person would be wise to suggest, not order or demand.

Hell. He scrubbed his hand down his face and sighed, a deep, gusty sound of frustration. He wasn't very good at taking orders himself. Fate must be howling with laughter. He'd found the one woman he couldn't—didn't—want to live without, and she was just as bloody stubborn and independent as he was.

Stunned, he considered what he'd just thought.

Was he in falling in love with Frankie? Was that what the sleepless nights and foul temper were all about?

He didn't even want to think about it.

Determinedly, he took a bite of chow mein and switched the channel to a basketball game on ESPN.

He couldn't be falling in love.

And even if he was, he thought with a frown, he was damned if he'd keep thinking about it nonstop.

After several hours of slamming pots and pans, then cleaning her condo from top to bottom while listening to Sugarland and Jon Bon Jovi CDs on Saturday afternoon, Frankie's temper settled into a slow simmer.

She'd suspected Eli seemed too perfect to be true, she reflected on Sunday afternoon as she jogged around Green Lake. And sure enough, he'd revealed he was human on Saturday at the barn.

No, not that he's human, she thought with a flash of anger, *that he's a jerk who thinks I'm incapable of making sensible decisions about my safety.*

She jogged faster, pumping her arms, the steady downpour of rain soaking the shoulders of her all-weather jacket. She'd stuffed her hair up under a bright blue wool stocking hat that matched her coat. The hat was damp and so were the black leggings that covered her long legs. Her toes squished inside her running shoes.

It was a measure of how restless and unsettled she was that she'd chosen to face the rain and elements rather than run on the treadmill at home.

After circling the lake twice, she left the wide tarmac path and drove to her mom's house.

"Mom? Are you home?" she called as she stepped

into the glassed-in porch. She toed off her shoes, leaving them to drip on the mat, and padded across the painted board floor to the inner door. Her damp socks left footprints on the flooring.

"Frankie? I'm in the kitchen," Cornelia called.

Frankie hopped on first one foot, then the other, to tug off her wet socks before walking across the beautiful Oriental wool rug and into the kitchen. Cornelia stood at the counter next to the stove, pouring water from a steaming kettle into a china teapot.

"Hi, Mom. Tommi, I didn't see your car outside." She was glad to see her sister. Tommi was perched on a stool at the island in the center of the big kitchen, a bright red maternity smock stretched over her burgeoning tummy.

"Max dropped me off—he's coming back to pick me up in an hour." Tommi's eyes twinkled. "You'd think no other woman had ever been pregnant before. He insists on driving me everywhere—at least, everywhere I'll let him." She grinned, clearly enjoying the coddling.

"For heaven's sake, Frankie," Cornelia looked up from the Wedgwood teapot and returned the kettle to the stove. "You're drenched. What have you been doing?" She threw the question over her shoulder as she disappeared into the half bath just off the kitchen.

"Jogging at Green Lake," Frankie responded.

"Couldn't you have stayed in and used the treadmill?" Tommi asked as Cornelia reappeared with a thick towel.

"Yes, why didn't you?" Cornelia asked, handing over

the towel and taking Frankie's drenched coat. "I'm going to toss this in the dryer," she said, leaving the room again.

Frankie plucked the soggy hat off her head and dropped it on the tile counter next to the sink. "I'm tired of being stuck in the house," she said. "And I'm not made of sugar—I won't melt in the rain."

"Yes, but you might catch your death of cold," Cornelia said, coming back into the room. "Dry off. I've got vitamin C and zinc tablets here."

Frankie and Tommi exchanged a fond glance.

"Thanks, Mom." Frankie knew from experience that it was easier to let Cornelia mother her. She rubbed her face dry and blotted her hair before joining Tommi at the counter, taking a stool directly across from her. "How's everything at the restaurant?"

"Wonderful." Tommi fairly glowed as she brought Frankie up to date on the latest innovations.

Frankie listened, murmuring encouragement to keep Tommi talking. She loved seeing her sister so clearly happy, deeply in love with Max, excited about the baby and the success of her restaurant.

Cornelia joined them at the tiled island and poured herbal tea into mugs, setting one in front of Frankie with several tablets.

"Thanks, Mom." Frankie spooned honey into her tea.

"Enough about me." Tommi lifted her mug to sip. "What's new with you, Frankie? I've hardly seen you over the last few weeks."

"I've been busy at work." Frankie met Cornelia and Tommi's gazes and decided to be blunt. She needed to vent, and who better than family to understand? "And I've been seeing a lot of Eli."

Tommi's eyes widened. "Eli Wolf? Justin's friend?"

Frankie nodded, taking a brownie off the plate in the center of the island. The chocolate square had sinfully decadent, rich fudge frosting.

She glanced up to see Cornelia and Tommi exchanging glances.

"You didn't tell her we were at the fundraiser with you and Harry, Mom?"

Cornelia shook her head. "No, I didn't. To be honest, Frankie, I thought you and Eli were just together on a casual date. Much as I like Eli, he doesn't appear to be someone you'd ever get serious about, despite his being handsome, very charming and undeniably interested in you."

"Why didn't you think I might be seriously drawn to Eli?" Surprised, Frankie stared at her mother.

"I suppose because the men you've dated in the past have been more intellectually oriented, less…physical than Eli."

Frankie's eyes narrowed as she considered her mother's words. "It's true I've spent more time with men who earn their living in white-collar jobs, and Eli's definitely a blue-collar guy. But one of the things I like about Eli is that he's not intimidated by my job, or my college degrees. In fact, the subject never even comes up. Actually," she added slowly, thoughtfully, "he challenges me, makes me laugh, and I never feel as if I'm marking time with him until I can do something more interesting." She swept Cornelia and Tommi with a glance that surely reflected her surprise. "I hadn't realized that until just now. It's probably irrelevant after what happened Saturday."

"Why?" Tommi asked.

"What happened?" Cornelia's question melded with Tommi's.

Frankie quickly gave them an abbreviated version, ending with the last words she'd yelled at Eli, telling him she didn't want to talk to him until he was ready to apologize.

When she finished, Cornelia set her mug down with a snap. "Men," she muttered. "They can be so stubborn."

"Exactly," Frankie said with an abrupt nod of agreement.

"I always thought Eli was smooth with women—at least that's his reputation," Tommi added when Frankie glared at her. "But he certainly screwed up with you." She pursed her lips, her gaze considering. "I wonder why?"

"Because he's impossible, that's why." Frankie took a bite of chocolate brownie. Her eyes closed in sheer bliss. "Mom, these are amazing."

"Thank you. It's a new recipe," Cornelia said, distracted from what were clearly deep thoughts.

"If Max had done something like that," Tommi continued, undeterred, "I'd suspect it was because he was scared silly and terrified I'd be hurt. Nothing seems to shake Max, but since he loves me, he'd freak out if I was in danger."

"But I wasn't in danger," Frankie pointed out. "And Eli doesn't love me—we've only been dating for a couple of weeks or so."

"Time doesn't necessarily matter—not if it's the right person," Cornelia put in.

"And Eli didn't know you weren't in any real danger," Tommi pointed out.

"Which is why he should have asked me!" Frankie declared, angry all over again at how unreasonable Eli had been. "If he'd asked, I would have explained Daisy is as docile as a lamb."

"I don't think men can wait if they believe someone they love is in danger," Tommi told her. "They automatically shift into protection mode and ask questions later."

Frankie looked at her mother. Cornelia nodded in confirmation.

"Tommi's right," Cornelia said. "At least, that's been my observation. Even Harry, although he went about it in his usual bumbling way, tried very hard to protect all of us after your father died. If I'd allowed it, Harry would have wrapped us all in cotton wool, installed us in his mansion and hired nannies to care for you girls and a maid to wait on me."

"Yes, but that's Uncle Harry," Frankie pointed out reasonably. "He tends to bulldoze his way through life, unaware he's making people who love him crazy."

Cornelia rolled her eyes. "I can't deny that's a perfect description of Harry."

"You must have been a very determined woman to stand up to him all those years when we were growing up," Frankie told her.

Tommi laughed, amusement gleaming in her eyes. "That's an understatement. Uncle Harry still hasn't stopped trying to arrange our lives—look what he did with Bobbie and me."

"True." Frankie wished she could tell them Harry had set his sights on her. She'd love to confide the details of her and Eli's plan to thwart Harry's matchmaking scheme and get their perspective. "I wish he'd turn his attention elsewhere."

"So do I." Cornelia's mouth firmed, her eyes snapping militantly. "I'm getting tired of dealing with him—and being his last-minute date for functions. In fact, the golf pro at the club asked me out, and I said yes. Maybe Harry will stop taking us all for granted if we're not so available whenever he calls."

"Mom!" Frankie was speechless and suspected her shock was written on her face. She glanced at Tommi to see the same stunned surprise on her sister's face. "I've never heard you complain about Uncle Harry before."

"Well, you're hearing it now," Cornelia's cheeks pinkened, her eyes bright with annoyance beneath the smooth sleek chignon that swept her blond hair up and away from her face, exposing the clean lines of beautiful bone structure. "I've dealt with Harry for years, and frankly, I'm fed up."

Frankie couldn't imagine her mother staying angry at Harry. Cornelia had argued with Harry over the years, most often when he'd wanted to lavish her daughters with extravagant gifts. But the two had been friends since they were children.

Much as she wanted Harry to stop trying to fix her up with eligible men, she didn't want to see friction between him and her mother.

And Cornelia sounded as if she were upset with Harry on a personal level.

Surely Cornelia would soon calm, forgive Harry, and things would go on as usual. Wouldn't they?

Sharing tea, chatting and laughing with her mother and Tommi was just what she'd needed, Frankie reflected later as she drove home.

The phone rang just as she unlocked her condo door and she hurried inside, relocking the door behind her before walking quickly across the living room. She dropped her car keys and purse on the sofa and picked up the phone. "Hello?"

"Hi, Frankie, this is Harry."

Her anticipation deflated and she realized she'd hoped the caller was Eli.

"Hi, Uncle Harry." Phone tucked between shoulder and ear, she shrugged out of her coat and went to hang it up. "What are you up to?" she asked, curious.

"I've been working on a new software program that has the potential to revolutionize the future of robotics. But that's not why I called," he said abruptly. "I want to ask you about something, but I don't want you to tell your mother."

Frankie's eyebrows lifted. "All right. Unless it's something I think she needs to know about," she added hastily. This was, after all, Harry Hunt. Who knew what he was up to?

"Your mother told me the other night that she couldn't go to a function with me because she already had a date. I want to know who she's seeing."

His blunt request for information left Frankie speechless.

"Harry, I think you should ask Mom this question. If she wants you to know, she'll tell you."

"I can't ask Cornelia," Harry said impatiently. "She'd probably tell me to go take a flying leap."

Yes, she very well might, Frankie thought with a grin. "Nevertheless, I'm a little uncomfortable answering you, Uncle Harry, especially if you think Mom wouldn't want you to know."

"I didn't say I thought she doesn't want me to know," Harry growled. "I just said she'd make me suffer before she told me."

She couldn't hold back the laugh that bubbled up. "And you'd rather skip the suffering and just get the information?"

"Of course. Who wouldn't?" Harry sounded put out. "I can't believe Cornelia is dating someone else. Why would she do that?"

Frankie rolled her eyes. "Why wouldn't she, Uncle

Harry? She's an attractive, single woman. Why shouldn't she enjoy an active social life?"

"Because up until now, her social life has included me and apparently she's decided to change the rules, that's why." Harry's deep voice roared over the line.

Frankie winced and held the phone away from her ear.

"I'm sorry I yelled," he said immediately, frustration apparent in his voice. "But I don't understand why you're reluctant to tell me what I need to know."

"All right." Frankie made a swift decision. "Mom's been dating the golf pro at her club."

"Greg?" Harry's voice was incredulous. "He's too young for her."

"I suspect the same could be said about the women you've dated in the past," Frankie told him evenly. "And I don't see why Mom shouldn't go out with Greg if she wants. I think she's having fun."

"Fun." Harry's voice was totally without expression.

"Yes, fun," Frankie said firmly. "I wouldn't be surprised if their relationship develops into something deeper," she added thoughtfully. "He's very nice to her."

"He's nice to her." Again, Harry repeated her words with no inflection whatsoever.

"Very nice," Frankie said.

"Well…" Silence spun out. "Thanks," he said abruptly. And he hung up.

Frankie shook her head, exasperated. Sometimes,

Harry took abruptness to a whole new level, she thought as she headed for the shower.

The brief conversation had distracted her and lifted her spirits, but thoughts of Eli intruded as Frankie showered and dressed in comfortable flannel pajama bottoms and a cotton knit top.

She refused to keep thinking about him, however, and managed to stay busy, writing copy for the volunteers' section of the horse barn's website, until bedtime.

Once she fell asleep, however, she couldn't force thoughts of Eli to the back of her mind and he returned full force, featuring prominently in dreams filled with arguments that ended with the two of them in bed.

Chapter Eleven

Late Sunday afternoon brought a respite from the downpour of rain with weak sunshine that continued through Monday. But by Tuesday, another winter storm had blown in off the Pacific, bringing with it more rain and dark skies.

Eli sent the work crew home early, and by five-thirty he'd showered, donned dry clothes and driven to Justin's house for dinner. Ava was in the kitchen with Lily, happily tearing up lettuce for salad and "helping" her mother with other cooking chores. Eli joined Justin in the game room, where they relaxed with a friendly game of pool.

"What's going on with you and Frankie?"

"What do you mean?" Bent over the pool table, cue in hand, Eli didn't need to look at Justin to know his friend's expression was as casual as his voice. He also knew Justin's question wasn't the slightest bit casual.

"Dad tells me you two are dating."

"We've been out a few times," Eli conceded. He tapped the four ball into a side pocket and stood to walk around the table, considering his next shot.

"Lily says Cornelia saw you two kissing at a fundraiser."

"Did she?"

"Apparently, Cornelia said it wasn't just a friendly kiss on the cheek."

"Hmm." Eli grunted a noncommittal reply and bent over to line up his cue stick.

"And since you're refusing to talk about her," Justin went on, his voice mild, "I can only assume you're trying to seduce my cousin."

Eli jerked upright. "I am *not* trying to seduce Frankie," he ground out. Justin smiled and lifted an eyebrow. "Oh, hell." Eli tossed the cue stick onto the table, scattering the remaining balls, and stalked to the sideboard. He poured himself a shot of whiskey and downed it, scowling at Justin. "And I'm not sleeping with her, if that's what you're asking."

"Are you saying you don't want to?"

"Hell, no!" Eli thrust his fingers through his hair and slammed the shot glass down on the glossy mahogany bar. "She's a beautiful woman. Any sane man would want to sleep with her. But I'm not." He glared at Justin.

Justin leaned his cue against the wall and joined Eli

at the bar. He took a bottle of imported beer from the refrigerator concealed behind a mahogany panel and pried off the cap with an opener.

"But you'd like to," Justin nudged, tipping the bottle to drink.

"That's a helluva question for you to be asking about your favorite cousin," Eli growled.

"Not really." Justin shrugged. "Frankie's a grown woman. She's smart, able to make her own choices."

"If you think that, then why are you asking me about her?" Eli said.

"Because ever since her last birthday, I've noticed you watching her when you thought she wasn't looking."

"So?" Eli spun the empty shot glass on the bar, turning it in slow circles.

"So I recognize the look in your eyes. Damned if you don't remind me of myself, before Lily agreed to marry me."

Eli's head lifted, his eyes narrowing over Justin's half smile. "What the hell does that mean?"

"It means, friend, that I think my pretty cousin has you tagged and bagged."

Eli snorted. "In your dreams. This isn't hunting season, and I'm not somebody's trophy."

"No, you're not." Justin smiled and shook his head. "I remember fighting the inevitable myself, for as long as I could. But looking back, I wish I hadn't wasted so much time—I could have been with Lily and Ava from the beginning."

Eli stared at his friend. He remembered too well how

grim Justin had been during those months when he'd been separated from Lily. He also remembered telling Justin he was a bloody idiot after he'd confessed he'd left the woman he loved because he'd been convinced he couldn't be a good husband—or father.

"Me and Frankie—our situation isn't anything like yours with Lily," he growled finally.

"Not the little details," Justin conceded. "But for a guy, the core reason women like Lily and Frankie scare us to death is because we know they could clip our wings for good." Justin retrieved his pool cue and strolled to the table. "Men are hunters—we don't settle down easily."

Eli knew having Frankie in his life permanently had been figuring prominently in his dreams lately. So he only grunted noncommittally and picked up his own cue off the green felt tabletop. He took a seat on one of the tall stools at the old-fashioned bar and observed as Justin walked around the table, gauging potential shots with a critical eye.

"You seem happy enough," he said.

Justin glanced up. "I am." He leaned forward, lined up the shot and tapped the six ball into a side pocket. He rose, gave a faint grunt of satisfaction and chalked the end of his cue. "Lily's the best thing that ever happened to me. And Ava." He smiled fondly. "She's the icing on the cake."

"Think you'll have more kids?" Eli asked idly.

"We both would like at least one more." Justin set down the chalk on the edge of the table and eyed the

position of the seven ball. "But the timing's up to Lily—
she's got a lot on her plate right now at work."

"Do you ever worry about her?"

Justin looked up, frowning. "Worry? In what way?"

Eli shrugged. "Her safety—does she do things that
scare the hell out of you?"

Justin squinted, considering the question. "Not so
far—but she's pretty independent, so I wouldn't be surprised if she might, someday. Why?"

"Just wondering."

"What did Frankie do?" Justin asked with shrewd
insight.

"Tried to push a horse several dozen times her
weight into a barn stall." Just thinking about it made
Eli scowl.

"You were up at the horse barn with Frankie?" Justin
sounded surprised.

"Not with her, exactly. I drove up to Arlington to surprise her when I came home early from Vegas. Scared
the hell out of me when I saw her with that mountain
of a horse."

Justin let his pool cue slide through his fingers until
it hit the floor, butt-end first. "And what did you do?"
he asked.

"Same thing any guy would do—I moved her out of
the way and put the horse in the stall."

Justin stared at him for a long, silent moment. "And
what did she do?"

"She yelled at me." Eli thrust his fingers through his

hair. "Told me I was being an ass. That was right before she told me she didn't want to talk to me again."

"Damn, Eli, that's harsh."

"Tell me about it," he growled. "All I was doing was making sure she was safe. You should have seen the size of that horse—it was huge."

"I'm guessing Frankie didn't see it your way." Justin's smile was wry. "She's been volunteering at that stable since she was a kid, probably worked with that particular horse more than once."

"That's what I got from what she said," Eli admitted. "Which I didn't realize when I caught sight of her with that huge mare."

"Would it have made a difference?" Justin asked.

"Probably not," Eli admitted. "I acted on instinct."

"Something Frankie's not likely to accept as an excuse," Justin told him. "She's pretty independent."

"No kidding," Eli muttered.

"Frankie's usually willing to listen to a reasonable argument, though," Justin said. "Have you explained to her why you did what you did?"

"No. I sent her flowers, but I haven't talked to her."

"Did you at least put a note in the flowers saying you're sorry?"

"No," Eli growled. "Because I'm damned sure I'd do it all over again, given the circumstances."

Justin grinned, white teeth flashing in his tanned face. "You've got it bad, Eli. You're in love."

"I'm not in love," Eli said stubbornly. "Just because I

worry that she might get hurt doesn't mean I'm in love with her."

Justin shrugged and laughed out loud. "Have it your way, but it sure sounds like love to me."

His cell phone rang before Eli could reply. Justin took the silver phone from his pocket and flipped it open, glancing at the number before answering.

"Hey, Frankie, what's up?"

Eli stiffened, going more tense as Justin's grin was quickly replaced with a frown.

"No problem. I'll have Lily put dinner on hold and be right there. Wait in the car, I won't be long." He listened a moment. "Don't worry about it. Sit tight and I'll be there in about fifteen minutes."

"What's wrong?" Eli demanded when Justin shoved the phone back in his pocket.

"Frankie worked late, and when she went out to the parking lot to go home, her car wouldn't start."

"I'll go." Eli slid his pool cue back into the wall cabinet and turned to the door.

"Are you sure? I thought you weren't talking to her."

Eli flicked his friend a glance over his shoulder. "You take care of Lily. I'll make sure Frankie's okay."

Justin's chuckle of amusement followed Eli down the hall as he collected his coat and left the house.

Frankie tucked her chin into the collar of her coat and crossed her arms over her chest. The temperature outside her car was hovering around forty degrees, but the damp air and cold rain pounding her windshield made it feel colder. The university parking lot was nearly empty, with only a few vehicles spaced around the big tarmac area.

She wished she hadn't picked tonight to work late. Or that her car hadn't chosen tonight to stop running. If she'd left her office at the usual time, she could have caught a ride home with a friend and called the repair garage from the warmth of her condo.

Sighing, she pulled her purse nearer and searched through it for a granola bar. Then she remembered she'd eaten it at lunch. Her stomach growled, and she pressed her palm against her abdomen.

Working late after eating only a granola bar and a container of yogurt for lunch hadn't been a wise choice, she thought wryly.

The only sound was the rain, hammering on the metal roof of her car. Frankie had a swift, mental image of being curled up with Eli on her sofa while the rain pounded down outside the windows.

Stop thinking about Eli, she ordered herself.

She still didn't know what to do about him. Tommi's observation that Eli had reacted the same way her Max would have had made Frankie wonder if there was any possibility Eli felt more than lust for her.

While she was vacillating, unable to make up her mind, she'd arrived home Monday to find a bouquet of bright spring flowers in front of her door. The card had only the initial *E,* the black script decisive and dark. She knew instantly it was from Eli.

She loved the flowers, and something about the gesture eased the faint ache in her heart. But he hadn't called, and three days had passed. She'd started to wonder if the flowers were his way of saying goodbye.

A vehicle turned into the parking lot and drew nearer, the headlights arcing over her car as the truck pulled up and parked next to her. Frankie had expected Justin's Porsche, but it took only a second of confusion before she recognized the driver.

What on earth is Eli doing here? she thought as her heart beat faster.

He stepped out of the truck, hunching his shoulders against the rain as he jogged to her car and tapped on the window. Frankie rolled the glass down, just far enough to talk to him. Even that small opening let wind-blown rain inside.

"Hi." She was so glad to see him she could have hugged him. "Where's Justin?"

"He's home having dinner. Let's get you in my truck. You might as well stay warm while I check out your car."

She nodded and pushed open the door. Eli pulled open the passenger door of his truck, and before she could climb in, he caught her around the waist and lifted her onto the high seat. Frankie caught her breath. Even through the layers of raincoat and the cashmere sweater she wore beneath, his touch made her breathing falter.

"Thanks," she murmured as he tucked her coat hem inside.

"No problem. Turn up the heater if you're cold. I'll only be a minute."

The interior of the truck cab was wonderfully warm. Frankie stretched out her legs to let the air from the heater vent warm her cold toes. Through the rain-streaked truck window, she could see Eli as he raised the hood of her car and fiddled with something on the engine.

Then he slid behind the wheel. She thought he turned the key but couldn't see clearly before he exited, slammed the hood down, and jogged around the truck. When he opened the door and slid behind the wheel, he brought the scent of rain and fresh air with him.

"Did you fix it?" she asked.

"No. I think the battery's dead." He shifted the truck into gear, and they left the parking lot. "I'll take you home and come back in the morning with jumper cables. I usually carry a set in the truck, but Matt borrowed them last week and didn't return them." His deep voice was reserved, carefully polite.

She hesitated a moment. "I can't thank you enough for doing this, Eli. I hope you know how much I appreciate it."

"No problem." He flicked a hooded glance over to her before looking out the windshield again. "Have you had dinner?"

"No. But I'm sure there's something at home in the fridge I can warm up." She eyed him with curiosity. "How did you happen to get stuck rescuing me in the rain?"

"Justin and I were playing pool at his house when he talked to you. I volunteered to come get you."

"I see." Frankie wanted to ask him why he'd offered to come out in the downpour to help her, especially since the last time she'd seen him, she'd told him she didn't want to talk to him.

They stopped at a red light. Eli picked up his cell phone from the seat divider, dialing from memory. While they waited for the light to turn green, he placed an order for take-out Thai food.

"You missed dinner with Justin and Lily in order to come get me, didn't you?" she asked as the traffic light changed from amber to green and Eli accelerated down the street.

He shrugged. "I'll see them next week—Justin's barbecuing steaks for Granddad on Saturday."

"Nevertheless, I'm sorry you had to miss dinner tonight because of me."

"Trust me, it's not a problem." He glanced sideways, a brief smile curving his mouth. "I can have dinner at Justin's anytime. Rescuing a pretty woman is more important—especially if she'll agree to share Thai takeout with me."

His smile eased the uncomfortable, faintly unsettled tension in Frankie, and she smiled back at him. "I have a bottle of wine that would be perfect with Thai food."

"Sounds good."

Eli braked, slotting the truck into an empty space in front of a Thai restaurant at the foot of Queen Anne.

"I'll be right back." He left the truck's engine running,

the heater continuing to blow warm air on Frankie's damp feet. The windshield wipers swished rhythmically as he jogged through the rain and disappeared inside the restaurant. Moments later, he returned. The two brown bags he tucked behind the seat filled the cab's interior with mouthwatering smells.

"What kept you at work so late?" he asked as he pulled out of the parking slot and headed for her condo building.

"A department staff meeting," she told him. "Even though I'm subbing in English Lit, I'm still technically a part of the research department. In order to stay involved with decisions on future projects, I have to attend staff meetings."

"Isn't it unusual to have someone in research lecturing in the classroom?" Eli asked, curious.

"I suppose it is," she replied. "But the circumstances were unique. The English department needed someone immediately, and not only was I temporarily unassigned, since I'd just completed a project, but I have a doctorate in English Lit and I'm qualified to teach." She shrugged. "It was an easy fix."

"Do you enjoy the change?" He glanced sideways at her. "Or are you counting the days until you're back on your regular schedule?"

"I'm enjoying it," she told him with a smile. "But then, I love my job in research, too."

"When will you go back to it—next quarter?"

"I'm not sure. The return date for the professor on emergency leave is open-ended."

A few moments of silence passed until they reached Frankie's building. Eli parked and got out, jogging around the truck to open her door; together, they ran through the rain to the lobby.

Inside Frankie's condo, she slipped out of her raincoat and tugged off her boots.

"You can leave your wet things here," she told Eli as she picked up her purse and briefcase. She dropped them on the seat cushion of an armchair as she passed it on her way into the kitchen.

He shrugged out of his jacket and pulled off his boots before following her. "Where's the bottle of wine?"

"In the cabinet below the coffeemaker." She lifted plates down from an upper cupboard while Eli set the bags of Thai takeout on the table and located the wine.

Frankie went up on tiptoe to reach stemmed wine glasses on a higher shelf, but they were just barely beyond her fingertips.

"Here, let me." Eli stretched above her, his chest pressing against her back as he easily lifted two glasses and set them on the countertop.

His body radiated heat; she felt it from her shoulders to her knees, his chest lightly touching her back, his thighs barely brushing hers. Her eyes closed, and she drew in a deep breath.

Eli stilled. Then his palms settled on the countertop on each side of her, his big body bracketing hers. His head bent, and she felt him brush his face against her hair.

"Frankie," his deep voice murmured in her ear. "I'm sorry I upset you the other day at the barn. I didn't mean to insult your intelligence. I saw you with a horse as big as a mountain and instinct took over. I only wanted to protect you."

Frankie turned, looking up into his face as she searched his eyes. She found only sincerity.

"I'd like to swear I'd never do that again, but I can't lie to you." His face hardened. "If I thought you were in danger, I'd probably act on instinct and try to protect you."

Any remaining anger leached away, receding behind a warm swell of emotion and leaving Frankie amused at his expression. Eli was braced, clearly expecting her to be angry at him.

"As far as apologies go, that's just about the worst one I've ever heard," she told him, sliding her hands up the fine wool sleeves covering his forearms, over the swell of biceps under his black V-neck sweater, until her fingers curled over the slope of his shoulders. "You're sorry but you'd do it again?" She laughed at the chagrined look on his face. "Couldn't you have stopped at 'I'm sorry'?"

"I should have," he agreed, the taut line of his mouth easing into a slow, sexy grin. "But I didn't think lying was a good plan."

"Will you at least promise to ask me if I know what I'm doing the next time, and if I want or need help before you barge in and save me?" she asked, enjoying the sense of leashed power beneath her fingers and palms.

"I promise I'll try." He bent his head, resting his forehead against hers. "You scared the hell out of me, Frankie. Compared to the size of that horse, you're tiny."

"I suppose I am," she conceded. "And since you hadn't seen Daisy before, you had no way of knowing she's as harmless as a friendly puppy. But still…" She eyed him, wanting to make her point. "You need to ask me next time."

A frown drew his dark brows down, and he leaned back to search her features. "Just for the record—are you doing anything else dangerous on a regular basis?"

"Oh, no." Frankie smiled up at him, laughing aloud when relief erased the worry lines. She lifted on her toes, pressing an impulsive, affectionate kiss on his mouth.

Eli immediately caught her close, taking over as he ravaged her mouth with a possessive, claiming kiss. When he lowered her back on her heels, she was breathless.

"Maybe we should eat," he suggested, deep voice rasping.

"Yes," she said, her own voice husky with arousal. "That's a great idea."

"In here at the table—or in the living room?" he asked.

"Living room, I think. We can turn on the news or a movie."

"Sounds good." Eli poured wine into the glasses and carried them into the living room, returning to carry off the plates, utensils and napkins as Frankie set them on the counter.

Frankie joined him with the two take-out bags, which she immediately unloaded onto the low coffee table. Eli opened the first few white boxes, and the aroma of spicy food reminded them both that they were ravenous.

"That was delicious," Frankie said after emptying her plate. She curled her feet under her and settled back on the sofa, a glass of wine cradled in her hands.

Eli set his glass on the coffee table and, in one easy move, tugged her feet across the sofa cushion and propped them on his thigh. Startled, Frankie was about to protest when he ran his thumb down the arch of her right foot and pressed.

"Ohh," she groaned, half closing her eyes. "That feels so wonderful."

"Good."

She lifted her lashes to find him watching her, a slow smile curving his mouth, his eyes that smoky, darker blue she loved.

He shrugged, his hands continuing to massage her foot. "Just part of my attempt to seduce you, ma'am," he drawled.

She laughed. "Where did you get the cowboy accent?" she asked.

"It's part of the seduction," he told her. "Women love cowboys, don't they?"

"Let me think. Except for Justin, the only cowboys

I've seen are ones in the movies. Definitely a lot to love there, so, yes, I suppose women do love cowboys."

"See? The cowboy vibe works. That's where the 'ma'am' came from." He winked at her. "Throw in foot massage, Thai food and flowers and a guy has a chance with a lady."

Frankie rolled her eyes in disbelief. "Does this line actually work with the women you date?"

"Sometimes." He shrugged. "Sometimes they just say thank you for the foot rub and tell me to go home." He picked up her other foot and rubbed her arch.

She nearly groaned aloud again. "I won't tell you to go home," she murmured.

He shot her a look from beneath his lashes, his eyes flashing blue. "Does that mean I can stay the night?"

Frankie knew the seemingly casual question was anything but—Eli had made no secret that he wanted her. She loved his bluntness because it freed her from the usual games men played. Was she ready to sleep with him? She wanted him, but the wariness that demanded she protect her heart still told her to wait. She wasn't sure what she was waiting for, exactly. She'd long since moved past believing she was seeing Eli only as part of a scheme to distract Harry. And she knew her love of independence was fast taking second place to the sheer pleasure of sharing time with Eli. But Frankie believed in listening to her instincts and those instincts were whispering wait. Reluctantly, she heeded the warning.

"I don't think so," she said. "Not yet."

"At least you didn't say never," he told her with a wry

grin. "I'll just have to keep trying." He lifted her bare
feet from his thigh and set them on the cushion. "We
need music," he declared, pushing to his feet.

"Why?" Taken by surprise, she looked up at him.

"Because dancing is the next item on the seduction
list," he told her, his gaze flicking over the room, stopping on the radio and CD player on the shelf below the
television set. He knelt on one knee to switch off the
audio on the TV and turn on the radio. Instantly, the
room was filled with a slow, bluesy tune from Seattle's
jazz station.

"Nice music." He rose and walked to the sofa. "Dance
with me, Frankie."

Lifting the glass from her hand, he set it on the table
and caught her fingers in his to draw her up from the
soft cushions.

He tucked her close with his hands at her waist, and
she wrapped her arms around his neck, her fingers testing the silky black hair at his nape as his arms hugged
her closer. They moved slowly in time to the music,
bodies swaying in the lamplit room.

Eli's arms tightened, his hands smoothing over the
soft strip of bare skin in the space between the hem of
her sweater and the waistband of her skirt.

"Should I worry about losing my head and being
seduced?" Frankie murmured against his throat.

She felt his lips curve against her temple. "Not unless
you want to be. Of course," he drawled, his powerful
thighs moving against hers as they swayed to the music,
"any time you want to lure me into your bed, feel free.

I'm just a poor innocent country boy, so you could probably have your way with me before I knew what you were up to."

Frankie tilted her head back, laughing as she met his gaze. "You're an innocent country boy? Is this part of the cowboy-vibe thing?"

"Yup. Be gentle with me."

Frankie was laughing when he kissed her. His warm lips curved in a smile as they settled over hers.

"I missed you," she sighed when his head lifted and she tucked her face against the strong, warm column of his throat. Each breath she took drew in the subtle tang of his aftershave and, beneath it, the elusive male scent she'd come to associate with Eli. "Let's not fight anymore."

His arms tightened reflexively, pressing her closer.

"No," he rasped in agreement. "Let's not fight."

Their bodies moved together, the very air thickening with heat.

"I missed you, too."

Frankie's heart slammed in her throat. "Did you?" she whispered.

He nodded, his cheek, faintly rough with beard stubble, moving against her hair. "Too much." His voice was deeper, rougher. He stopped dancing, his mouth claiming hers with unmistakable desire.

Chapter Twelve

Frankie felt surrounded by Eli as he swung her off her feet and carried her to the sofa. His much bigger frame crowded hers on the wide cushions, but Frankie didn't care. She was swept up in the heat that exploded between them.

This was what she'd always wanted, needed, and had never found in any man she'd dated before. The passion that roared out of control between them was irresistible, and Frankie didn't try to fight it. Confident in his willingness to stop if she said no, she let desire pull her under, reveling in the shudder that shook his big frame when she slid her hands under his sweater and stroked her palms up the length of his bare back.

Eli tugged at her sweater, his hand flattening over the bare skin of her ribcage above her waistband.

When his fingers brushed over the soft swell of her breast above her bra, Frankie murmured against his mouth, shifting beneath the heavy thigh covering her own.

Long heated moments passed before Eli gradually eased them back from the edge, his kisses soothing rather than stoking the fire between them. At last, he lifted his head and looked down at her.

"Honey, if you're not going to ask me to stay for breakfast, we'd better go back to watching TV."

Dazed, Frankie stared up at him, struggling to process the switch from passion to practicality.

"I…"

The phone rang, startling both of them.

"Do you need to answer that?" Eli asked.

"I suppose I should."

He lifted away from her, stretched across the sofa and grabbed the phone from the end table and handed it to her. Frankie sat upright and slid her feet to the floor.

"Hello?" She frowned slightly. "Yes, this is Frankie Fairchild." Her eyes widened. "Oh, hello, Nicholas. How nice to hear from you."

Beside her, Eli's big body tensed. She glanced at him to find him watching her, eyes narrowed, his face inscrutable.

She paused, listening. "Much as I'd love to, I'm afraid I'm busy on Saturday. I'm so sorry."

Frankie exchanged a few more polite comments with Nicholas, then rushed to end the call, clearly impatient—and mad. "I'm so sorry, Nicholas, but my date just arrived. I'm afraid I have to ring off—lovely to hear from you. Yes, I'll tell Mom hello for you. Bye."

She switched the phone off and looked at Eli.

"That was Nicholas Dean," she said unnecessarily. "He told me he ran into Harry and Mom this afternoon and they mentioned how much I've been wanting to see the new musical at the Pantages. And since he has tickets, he thought we could go together."

"I bet he did," Eli said, his voice a growl.

"Harry's still matchmaking—and with Nicholas." Frankie could hardly believe it. "He *knows* you and I have been dating. And so does Mom. Why on earth would she have gone along with Harry nudging Nicholas to ask me out?"

"I don't know. I thought she liked me," Eli commented, a muscle flexing along his jawline. He stood, raking his hair back. "Maybe she likes the idea of you paired with Nicholas better."

"Oh, no, Eli. I'm sure that's not true." Frankie rose to slide her arms around his waist, and Eli instantly slipped his arms around her, tugging her forward until she rested against his hard length. "It's far more likely that Harry was not so subtly encouraging Nicholas to call me and Mom wasn't able to stop him. You know how Harry is when he gets an idea fixed in his head— he's like a bulldozer with no brakes."

"That's true." Eli nodded, his hands smoothing over her waist. "And apparently he's still fixated on getting you and Nicholas together." He looked down at her. "You're sure you're not interested in him?"

She shook her head.

"Thank God." He narrowed his eyes over her. "I've always liked Nicholas, but I'm not sure we'd stay friends if you went out with him."

"Are you saying you might be unfriendly if you ran into him?" Frankie asked.

"I'm saying I'm not normally a violent man, but I'm making no promises if you start dating other men."

"Just so we're clear," she said slowly, suppressing a smile. "Are you saying you want us to be exclusive and not date other people?"

"That's exactly what I'm saying, and you know it," he told her, eyes gleaming with amusement.

"I just wanted to be clear. And to be even more clear, you're asking me, not telling me, correct?"

He nodded. "Absolutely. I would never order an intelligent, independent woman such as yourself not to date other men. I'm sure you'd call me a neanderthal if I did."

"Yes," she told him primly. "I certainly would."

"Then I can count myself lucky we're in agreement." He picked her up, her feet dangling in the air, and kissed her.

The kiss was hot, carnal and a fierce declaration of possession, branding Frankie as surely as if he'd marked her. When he lowered her feet to the floor, she had to clutch his arms to keep from staggering.

"Since you won't let me stay for breakfast, I think it's time for me to leave, while I can still tear myself away."

Much to her satisfaction, Eli's breathing was as ragged as hers.

He wrapped an arm around her shoulders, and they walked to the door.

Moments later, after he'd donned jacket and boots and they'd shared another kiss that left her feeling dazed and hot, he left.

As Frankie turned out her bedside lamp later, she vowed to have a talk with Harry and her mother. She was certain Cornelia must have been an innocent bystander to Harry's machinations.

But Harry better be prepared to explain why he's continuing to interfere in my love life when it's clear Eli and I are involved, she thought with determination.

Frankie called Cornelia the following morning and, after chatting for a few moments, learned her mother was meeting Harry at his house that evening after work.

"Why don't you join us, Frankie?" Cornelia said. "We're going over the applications for the HuntCom college scholarship program. I'd love to have your input, and I know Harry would, too."

"What time?" Frankie asked, listening as Cornelia gave her the details. When she hung up, she'd promised to join them for an hour.

And she planned to use most of that hour grilling Harry about his matchmaking efforts, she thought with determination.

When she pulled into Harry's driveway that evening, Cornelia's Volvo was parked next to a long, black town car. Frankie slotted her BMW in beside the limo and walked quickly down the walk. She glanced at the sky over the lake, thankful that the Pacific Northwest was enjoying a beautiful clear day although the sun was already low on the horizon, sinking behind the Seattle skyline.

"Good evening, Sonja," she said as Harry's longtime maid opened the door. "I'm meeting my mother here—is she in the library with Harry?"

"Yes, miss." Sonja took her coat. "Will you be staying for dinner?"

Frankie shook her head. "I doubt it, not tonight."

In fact, she thought as she left the maid and walked through the house to reach the library, she might not be staying more than a few minutes. It all depended on whether Harry agreed to cease his attempts to fix her up with Nicholas Dean.

She'd long since grown accustomed to the opulent home Harry had built with the fortune he'd made from HuntCom, the computer software corporation he'd built through sheer genius and hard work. Cornelia and her husband had grown up with Harry; the two men had been partners when HuntCom was a fledgling firm operated out of Harry's garage. When Frankie's father died suddenly, leaving little money for his widow and daughters, Harry had tried to convince Cornelia to let him take care of her and the girls. But Cornelia had refused, stubbornly determined to make her own way. She'd sold their big house and moved her daughters back to her family home in Queen Anne, then taken a job working at a private school to fund their education. Through sheer determination and shrewd acumen, Cornelia had managed to raise her girls with only minimal interference from Harry. She'd accepted his offer of educational traveling during school vacations, however, and reluctantly agreed when he gave them each a large sum of money upon high school graduation.

Frankie had used Harry's graduation gift to pay her tuition while she earned two master's degrees and a PhD.

Much as she adored her uncle Harry, however, she was determined to take a firm stand on the issue of his matchmaking. He'd simply stepped beyond what any self-respecting woman could accept, she thought as she entered the library.

"There you are, Frankie," Cornelia greeted her with a welcoming smile. She and Harry were seated at a cherrywood library table halfway down the long room.

At the far end of the room, facing a wall of windows and French doors that led to a patio, was Harry's massive mahogany desk. The room provided a fabulous view of Lake Washington and the Seattle skyline beyond.

Frankie's heels tapped on the polished wooden floors, grew muffled as she crossed a deep-piled oriental carpet, then clicked on bare flooring once more.

"Hello, Mom, Harry." Frankie set her purse on the table and took the chair on Harry's right. He sat at the end of the table, Cornelia on his left, several stacks of papers arranged on the glossy surface. Both he and Cornelia had sheets of paper and a small group of scholarship applications on the table in front of them. A coffee-service tray took up space just beyond Cornelia.

"I'm so glad you could make it," Cornelia said. "I'd love your input on several of the applications. We've narrowed down the number, as you can see." She gestured at the smaller stacks.

"I'm happy to help, Mom," Frankie replied, her back ramrod straight and several inches away from the back of her chair. "But first, I need to talk to you and Harry."

"Oh?" Cornelia glanced from her to Harry, a puzzled frown pleating her brow. "What about?"

"I had a phone call last night—from Nicholas Dean."

The brief flash of guilt that flickered across Harry's features confirmed Frankie's suspicions that he'd instigated the call.

"Uncle Harry, I specifically told you the night we were all here for dinner that I wasn't interested in Nicholas," she told him. "And yet you're apparently trying to push the two of us together."

"Harry!" Cornelia's expression was appalled, her dismay echoed in her voice. "Please tell me you haven't been meddling in Frankie's love life."

"Now, just a minute," Harry blustered, his cheeks flushed. "I wouldn't call it meddling."

"What *would* you call it?" Frankie demanded.

"Well," he grumbled. "I only mentioned that you'd been wanting to see the new musical at the Pantages, that's all."

"And?" Frankie prompted when he paused.

"All right," he admitted. "I might have suggested Nicholas should phone you."

Frankie groaned. "Why do you keep doing this?" she asked, genuinely perplexed. "First with your own sons, then with Tommi and Bobbie—and now me! You've got to stop interfering in our lives."

"My sons are all happily married, and Tommi and Bobbie appear very happy, so how is that a bad thing?" Harry asked.

"You were lucky, Uncle Harry—what if your sons or my sisters had ended up brokenhearted, or divorced?"

"But they didn't," he insisted with stubborn logic.

"But you couldn't have known how things would turn out when you started throwing people together," Frankie pointed out. "And it could have been a disaster."

"I only wanted you and your sisters to be as happy as my boys," Harry said. "Even your mother thought Nicholas was right for you."

Frankie's eyes widened. "Mom, please tell me you didn't know Harry was doing this. I assumed you were an innocent bystander when Harry cornered Nicholas and told him to phone me." The sense of betrayal was sharp. Surely her mother wouldn't have gone along with Harry's crazy scheme?

"I had nothing to do with that," Cornelia said firmly. She frowned at Harry, her eyes accusing. "I admit we discussed how much we liked Nicholas the night of the Children's Hospital fundraiser. I may even have commented that he seemed more of a match for you than

Eli, but I *never* told Harry to interfere and set you up with Nicholas."

"Of course she didn't," Harry put in abruptly. "But there's no ignoring the facts. You're twenty-nine, Frankie. You need to marry soon—or you'll miss your best childbearing years."

"My best childbearing years?" Frankie seethed. "You make it sound as if I'm a brood mare, Harry."

"No, no, that's not what I meant," he said quickly, looking harried. "I only meant having younger people in my life as I get older—my sons, you and your sisters, my granddaughter, Ava—is one of the greatest joys I know. But I wasn't aware it would be so when I was your age." He gestured at Cornelia. "And your mother would make a wonderful grandmother, not to mention how much she'd love having grandchildren."

"Harry." Cornelia was clearly restraining herself. "I have the urge to rap you over the head with my umbrella. How on earth can you be so dense about people?"

Harry looked bewildered. "I only wanted you to know the joy of having little ones in the family again, Cornelia. At our age, it's a wonderful thing." His jaw firmed, and he straightened. "And you must admit, if Frankie continues as she has for the last several years, she'll probably have earned more university degrees by the time she's forty, but she won't have children."

"If you're suggesting that I'm too bookish to have sex, Uncle Harry," Frankie said with deadly calm, "then you don't know me at all." She pushed back her chair and stood. "Eli and I have been sleeping together for ages," she declared with dramatic flair. "And if hot, sweaty, amazingly fabulous sex is a guarantee of pregnancy, then I'm probably pregnant already." She was lying through her teeth, but Harry didn't know that, and her rashly impulsive claim was worth the guilt she might feel later, Frankie thought as Harry's eyes widened and his face grew even redder. She glanced at Cornelia and saw her mother's eyebrows raise with surprise. Much to her relief, she also saw a spark of amusement as Cornelia glanced at Harry and then back at Frankie.

Frankie picked up her purse. "I'm sorry I can't stay and help with the applications. Perhaps I can go over them later in the week at your house, Mom?"

"Of course, dear." Cornelia smiled benignly at her.

But as Frankie turned to leave, she saw her mother turn to face Harry, her expression threatening.

"Harry, explain yourself." Cornelia's demand held an ominous tone even Harry couldn't ignore, Frankie thought as she swept out of the library and then out of the house.

She hadn't wanted to confront Harry about his match-making, because she was well aware he had good intentions and meant well. But sometimes, she told herself as she drove home, there was no other recourse than to be blunt and forceful.

Which pretty much described how Cornelia was probably dealing with him at the moment, she thought with a grin.

* * *

"Harry Hunt, I cannot believe you're doing this again."

"Now, Cornelia, you know we discussed how much Frankie and Nicholas have in common," Harry said, trying to placate her. "And how great it would be if they got together."

"That doesn't mean I wanted you to blatantly suggest Nicholas should call and ask her out." Cornelia was livid, her eyes snapping with frustration. "For heaven's sake, Harry, how many times do you have to be told to stop interfering in our children's lives? First your sons—and that came much too close to being disastrous," she said. "And now my girls? You've got to stop this. No more!"

"My boys are all happily married," he pointed out in an attempt to reason with her. "And if I hadn't given them an ultimatum, God knows whether they ever would have considered marriage."

"We'll have to agree to disagree on the subject of your sons," Cornelia told him. "But as for my daughters…" She stood, picked up her purse, and pointed her index finger at him. "Leave my girls alone, Harry. Period."

And with that, Cornelia turned on her heel and marched regally out of the library, leaving Harry to mumble and mutter and stare morosely at the closed door.

He'd really angered Cornelia this time, he thought,

and Frankie, too. Much as he hated to give in, he supposed he'd have to abandon his efforts to get Frankie and Nicholas together.

Too bad, he mused. They had so much in common.

Harry frowned, thinking about Frankie's stunning declaration.

If Eli's sleeping with Frankie, Harry decided grimly, *he'd better have marriage in mind.*

I think I'll have a talk with him. Harry shoved away from the table and stood to stride out of the library, his steps purposeful.

Chapter Thirteen

Harry's black limo pulled into the Wolf Construction building site near the university campus late the following afternoon. The long car bumped and rolled over the rough dirt-and-gravel surface, its tires splashing through muddy puddles left from predawn showers.

The driver slotted the big car into an area in front of the work trailer. The pickups and cars of the work crew had long since left the lot, but Eli's work truck was still parked in front of the trailer. Harry exited the vehicle, his long, black overcoat flapping in the breeze as he climbed the wooden steps and knocked on the door. No one answered. He turned, scanning the scaffolding of the building under construction on his left.

"Harry," Eli called as he stepped between the studs

of a first-floor garage and strode across the lot toward him. "What brings you out here so late?"

"I was hoping to talk to you. Have you got a few minutes?"

"Sure. Let's go inside." Eli led the way into the portable office. "Have a seat, Harry. Want something to drink?" he asked over his shoulder as he took a mug off the pegs on the wall above the coffeemaker.

"I could use a cup of coffee, black," Harry replied, hands shoved in his coat pockets as he inspected the blueprints taped on the wall next to the drafting table.

"Here you are." Eli handed Harry a steaming mug and leaned his hips against the drafting table, muddy work boots crossed at the ankle. "So, what can I do for you, Harry?"

"Frankie came by the house last night," Harry said. "And after what she told her mother and me, I decided to look you up and ask you point-blank..." He fixed Eli with a steely gaze. "What are your intentions toward my niece?"

Eli blinked once and set his mug down on the counter. "Exactly what did Frankie tell you?" he asked, curious.

"Nothing you don't already know," Harry growled.

"Humor me," Eli said, his gaze holding Harry's.

"She said the two of you have not only been dating— you've been sleeping together."

"Did she?"

"Yes, she did," Harry said. "In fact, I believe she said it was hot, sweaty and fabulous. Then she said she might be pregnant already, given how often the two of you have been going at it. Which is why I'm asking you—what the hell do you intend to do about Frankie?"

Stunned, Eli stared at Harry for a full minute as he tried to absorb the surprising information. Then a slow smile curved his lips. "Harry, I can guarantee you I don't plan to do anything that would harm Frankie, nor anything she doesn't want me to do."

"That didn't answer my question." Harry's brows lowered.

"No, it didn't." Eli unbuckled his tool belt and slung it on the counter behind him. "And with all due respect for your concern about Frankie, and your long relationship as her adopted uncle, I'm not going to answer it." He shrugged out of his safety vest and hung it on the high back of the drafter's stool.

"Wolf Construction and Dean Construction are the final two companies being considered to build the Hunt-Com campus," Harry said. "Whether or not you plan to marry Frankie could make a big difference as to who's awarded the contract."

Eli stiffened, anger roaring through his veins.

"Harry, I've known you a long time, and I've always had the greatest respect for you." His voice turned colder. "But if you think you can make Frankie a part of some business deal, you're dead wrong. Give the contract to Dean Construction—I don't want it."

He turned on his heel and in two long strides, reached the door.

"Well, I'll be damned." Harry's mellow tones held amazed delight. "You love her."

Eli froze, hand on the door latch. He looked over his shoulder, frowning at Harry. "I never said I love Frankie."

"You don't have to." Harry's grin lit his entire face. "I've known you since you were a kid, and over the years I've watched you build your father and grandfather's company into a powerhouse. There's no way you'd turn down a contract like HuntCom's unless you had a powerful incentive. And that's love," he added, beaming.

Eli shook his head at Harry's insistence. Over the last few days, he'd privately acknowledged to himself that he was in love with Frankie. But he'd be damned if he told Harry before he bared his heart to her. "Believe what you like, Harry, but leave Frankie alone. And don't encourage Nicholas again." His voice was a low, threatening growl.

"Of course I won't," Harry replied with alacrity. "She's obviously taken." He rubbed his hands together, clearly relishing what he thought was a match between Eli and Frankie.

Eli could have groaned aloud. He bit off a hot retort about the older man's interference in Frankie's life. "Think what you like, Harry, but stop looking for men to send after Frankie."

And with that, Eli shoved open the door and left the trailer, loping down the wooden steps to his truck. As he backed out of his parking slot and left the lot, he saw Harry exit the trailer, standing on the wooden steps with the evening breeze lifting his black hair, a satisfied smile on his face as he watched Eli depart.

Eli wanted to drive straight to Frankie's condo and talk to her, but he knew she was having dinner with her mother tonight. Besides, he was muddy after a day spent on the job site, so he reined in his impatience and instead went home, where he showered, shaved and changed clothes before driving to Queen Anne. He made a stop at Ballard Blossom to pick up a bouquet of flowers.

It was barely seven-thirty when he knocked on her door.

"Eli." Frankie opened the door, surprise and pleasure easily readable on her features. "I didn't know you were coming over tonight. I thought you had a meeting."

"I did—but I decided not to go." Eli hadn't given the meeting another thought after Harry told him about Frankie's declaration. He stepped inside, closing the door as he held out the flowers.

"Oh, Eli, they're lovely." Frankie cradled the bouquet, dropping her head to inhale, her lashes lowering. "They smell marvelous—just like spring." Her brown eyes were soft as she looked up at him. "How did you know I was wishing for winter to go away today?"

"I didn't. I just wanted to see you smile, and since you love flowers, I figured these would do it."

Her lush mouth curved, her brown eyes warm as she met his gaze. "You were right," she murmured. She waved her hand toward the living room. "Why don't you have a seat? I'll put these in water."

Eli followed her into the kitchen, leaning against the

doorjamb to watch as she went up on her toes to reach a shelf above the sink.

She wore a pair of dark green knit pants with a tie at the waist. As she stretched to reach a crystal vase on an upper shelf, her short-sleeve white knit top rode up to reveal a strip of soft pale skin and the delicate indentation of her navel above the waistband of the green pants. Her blond hair was loose, brushing against her shoulders as she turned her head to look at him.

"Have you had dinner?" she asked, casting a sideways glance at him before running tap water into the vase.

"I grabbed a sandwich at home." He didn't tell her he'd eaten it in three bites while he stripped off muddy clothes before showering.

"If you're still hungry, Mom sent beef Stroganoff and pineapple cheesecake home with me."

Eli was tempted. But other things were uppermost in his mind, so he shook his head. "Thanks, but I'm good."

Finished with arranging the fragrant blue, pink and white blooms, Frankie picked up the vase and walked past him into the living room. Eli followed her, tensing as she bent to set the vase on the coffee table, the soft green knit pulling tight over the curve of her bottom as she did so.

"I'm glad you're here, Eli, I have something I wanted to talk to you about and didn't want to do it over the phone." She turned and found Eli so close that she effectively stepped into his arms. "Oh." Startled, she clutched his biceps.

He settled his hands at her waist, steadying her.

"I had a visit from Harry today," he told her, watching intently for her reaction.

Frankie groaned and closed her eyes, then opened them to look up at him. "I'm afraid to ask why," she said.

"He wanted to know my intentions."

"Your intentions? About what?" She frowned at him, puzzled.

"You," Eli said succinctly.

She stared at him, still clearly puzzled, before understanding dawned. She flushed, color moving up her throat to stain her cheeks a deeper pink. "I'm going to kill him," she muttered. "I suppose he told you about my conversation with him and Mom last night?"

"Part of it," Eli confirmed.

"I was afraid of that," she told him. "That's what I wanted to talk to you about tonight, Eli. I'm afraid I lost my temper with Harry and told him we're sleeping together."

"That's what he said." Eli tugged her forward until her thighs rested against his. "He also said you thought it was hot, sweaty and fabulous."

Frankie's face turned pinker, but her brown gaze remained on his. "Yes, that's what I said. But, Eli, I lost my temper," she repeated. "Not that it's an excuse for lying," she added hastily. "Harry had just finished telling Mom I was likely to have more university degrees by the time I was forty but not children." Her eyes sparked with anger. "He all but said I was too much of a bookish nerd to attract a man."

"Harry's an idiot." Eli was dumbfounded. "Where did he get the idea you couldn't get a man? You're beautiful and sexy as hell. You must have men following you around with their tongues hanging out."

Startled, Frankie laughed with delight. She slipped her arms around his neck. "You're such a charmer, Eli."

"No, I'm just stating the obvious." He urged her closer. "I'm glad you told Harry and your mom we're sleeping together. Because it gave me hope. I don't think you would have said that in front of your mother if you weren't ready for it to be true."

Her eyes widened. "I'm not sure I—"

Eli bent his head and stopped her protests by covering her mouth with his. The soft curves of her body already rested trustingly against the harder angles of his, and she murmured with pleasure when he stroked one hand up her spine to cup the back of her head. Her hair was pale silk against his fingers, her soft curves willing as he urged her closer.

"Honey," he said, reluctantly releasing her mouth to lift his head and look down at her. Only inches separated them. Her thick-lashed brown eyes were dazed, eyelids heavy, and her soft mouth was faintly swollen from the pressure of his. "Take me to bed." He stroked his tongue over the lush fullness of her lower lip, tasting her, and she shuddered.

"Yes," she murmured against his lips.

She slipped her hands from his neck, catching his hand to tug him with her into her bedroom. She stopped next to her bed and began unbuttoning his shirt, slipping the buttons through the holes with slow concentration. She tugged the shirttails out of his jeans and pushed the white cotton off his shoulders.

Eli grabbed the white T-shirt he wore underneath and yanked it up and off over his head, tossing it behind him on the floor. Frankie murmured, a soft hum of approval. He shuddered when she flattened her palms on his abdomen, tracing the swell of muscles.

The fascination on her face was arousing as hell. Eli stood it as long as he could, loving the feel of her hands on him, before he bent and took her mouth with his in a quick, hard kiss. He slipped his hands under the hem of her cotton T-shirt and pulled it up, her hair drawn upward to expose the arch of her throat and nape, then tumbling to her shoulders when he tugged the shirt off over her head. Beneath it, she wore a pale green lace and satin bra. Pretty though it was, Eli wanted her naked.

He wrapped his arms around her and a moment later, tugged the bra free and slid the straps down her arms. He froze, hands on her waist, and stared.

Frankie was awash in pleasure. It took her a moment to realize Eli had gone still. She swept her tumbled hair behind one ear and looked up to find his eyes heavy-lidded and intent, smoky with arousal.

"You're so beautiful," he muttered, his voice rasping, deeper than a moment before.

His hands stroked upward from her waist, tracing

over her rib cage. He eased her closer, his thumbs brushing the lower curve of her breasts. Then one arm swept around her waist, bending her backward as his mouth took hers and one hand cupped her breast. Frankie shuddered when his thumb stroked over the sensitive, taut nipple, and she strained closer, pushing against him, wanting more contact.

Eli groaned, his lips tasting the underside of her chin, the curve of her throat and upper swell of her breast before his mouth closed over the tip. Frankie twisted against him, shivering with pleasure, her arms holding him closer. The heat between them rose higher.

Impatient, Eli shoved the knit pants down her legs and hooked his thumbs under the lace-covered bikini panties over her hips. He eased them down her legs and off before tumbling her backward onto the bed. She held out her arms, waiting as he shoved his jeans and boxers off before joining her.

The hard angles of his body settled against hers, and Frankie welcomed his solid weight. Her breasts were crushed softly against the powerful muscles of his chest; Frankie twisted, loving the slide of his skin against the sensitive tips.

Eli took her mouth, nudging her knees apart with his thigh. Frankie shuddered, wanting him even closer, and wrapped her legs around his waist. Groaning, he flexed his hips and with a powerful surge, joined them. She cried out, arching beneath him, and the world narrowed to the man above her, heat raging out of control until they both shuddered, falling over the edge together.

* * *

"Good morning, sunshine."

Frankie muttered and burrowed deeper into her pillow.

"Time to wake up."

She could swear her dream had somehow added aromas to its visual and audio dimensions. She frowned, half awake.

Eli's lips brushed over her temple. "Honey, are you always like this in the morning?" His deep voice held amusement, layered with affection.

Frankie opened one eye. Eli was sprawled across his side of the bed, his head propped on one hand. The smile on his face was sinfully sexy—and he held a mug of steaming coffee a few inches from her nose.

"You brought me coffee?"

"It's yours if you'll sit up," he told her, his smile widening.

Sighing, Frankie levered upright, clutching the sheet to her chest, and shoved her pillow behind her against the headboard.

"I'm up." She yawned, covering her mouth with one hand, and considered him through half-open eyes.

He caught her hand, curled her fingers around the mug and grinned at her. "You're cute when you're comatose."

"You brought me coffee. Therefore, I'll let you get away with that." She yawned again, settling back against the pillow and smiling sleepily. "I could get used to this," she told him.

"Uh-huh." He bunched up his pillow against the headboard and stretched out beside her, his big frame taking up more than his share of the bed. He leaned sideways, gathered her up and shifted her closer, bracing her back against his chest, his arms wrapped around her waist.

"Hey," she protested. "You could have spilled my coffee."

"But I didn't." He nuzzled the back of her neck, moving her hair aside until his lips found the sensitive skin of her neck.

Frankie closed her eyes, smiling contentedly. "This is a very nice way to wake up." Her voice was throaty, bemused.

"Yeah, isn't it?" His lips trailed down the curve of her throat to her shoulder, and she tipped her head to give him better access. He tugged the sheet lower, his hands replacing the soft cotton as he cupped her breasts. "I like it. A lot."

The alarm on the bedside table went off, and the radio came on, the voice of the morning announcer bright and cheery.

"Darn." Frankie stirred, lifting her head. "I have a breakfast meeting this morning," she said regretfully.

"Skip it." Eli brushed a kiss against the soft, vulnerable skin just beneath her ear.

Frankie closed her eyes as the world began to slowly spin. "I can't," she got out. "I have to give a report."

"Damn." Reluctantly, Eli released her.

She turned her head, her lips meeting his. The kiss

was sweet and long, and Frankie was reluctant to end it. But at last she sat up to deposit her mug on the bedside table before slipping out of bed.

"Want some help showering?" Eli asked as she entered the bathroom.

A quick glance over her shoulder told her he'd watched her walk naked out of the room. She flushed. "No, thanks. If you help, I'll take twice as long, and I'll miss my meeting."

"Yeah, but you'll have twice as much fun."

"Sorry, but no." She laughed at his disappointed expression and closed the bathroom door.

They left her apartment together, Eli opening Frankie's car door and kissing her breathless before he walked away. His truck was parked on the street, and as she left the condo's parking garage, she waved. He lifted a hand in reply, his handsome face creasing in a smile as he watched her drive away.

Frankie realized she was smiling, happiness bubbling up from inside. She was in love. She wanted to tell the world.

So why hadn't she told Eli?

A better question was: If he felt the same, why hadn't he told her?

Last night had been wonderful. Making love with Eli was everything she'd hoped and dreamed it would be. She no longer had any doubts about her feelings for him, but she was uncharacteristically reluctant to tell him how she felt. Not until she had some indication he felt the same.

She didn't like being unsure of herself.

This is one of the reasons I never wanted to fall in love, she thought with a sigh. *I'm uncomfortably vulnerable and unsure of him. Why didn't I just ask him?*

She knew why—but she hated to admit it, even to herself.

Because she knew, she would have been devastated if Eli had told her he didn't love her in return.

Chapter Fourteen

Frankie set aside her worries over Eli's long-term intentions, instead focusing on the amazing night she'd spent in his arms. Happiness bubbled through her veins, and she had the urge to call Tommi and Bobbie to tell them she totally understood why they seemed to glow. Falling in love did that for a woman, she thought.

She had only two morning classes. When she left the lecture hall and hurried back to her office, she was still walking on air. Planning to visit Lily's boutique and buy new lingerie, she grabbed her purse and raincoat and left the hall to hurry to her car. She'd just tossed her purse onto the passenger seat and switched on the engine when her cell phone rang.

"Hello?" Her brain was fully occupied with wondering whether Eli liked black lingerie or if he preferred

red. Distracted, she didn't catch the first words the caller spoke. "I'm sorry, who is this?" she asked, holding the phone to her ear with her left hand while her right fitted the key into the ignition.

"This is Matt, Eli's brother."

"Hi, Matt." Wondering why Eli's brother would be calling her, Frankie switched on the engine.

"Connor thought I should call and let you know there's been an accident. Eli's fine, but we thought he might want you to know."

Frankie froze, her heart seeming to stop beating.

"Where is he?"

"He's in the ER at Harborview."

"Harborview?" Frankie's veins turned to ice. She knew serious trauma cases were taken directly to Harborview. "How badly is he hurt?"

"The doc isn't sure. They're still running tests."

"What happened?" Her fingers gripped the steering wheel, knuckles whitening.

"That damned slope above the job site slid on the east side." Matt's voice was taut with anger and disgust. "Took out a big fir just past the work trailer and caught Eli's truck. He was running to move it out of the way when one of the big tree limbs caught him."

"Oh, my God." Frankie caught her breath.

"The doc's running an MRI now. I'll call you back when we hear the results, okay?"

"Yes," Frankie managed to get out. "Okay."

She dropped her phone into her purse and waited a moment, willing her fingers to stop trembling. Then she left the parking lot, heading across town to the hospital.

The parking at Harborview was nonexistent. Frankie drove through the stacked levels of the huge garage twice before finally finding a spot. She breathed a sigh of relief and quickly nosed her car into the open space before hurrying toward the elevator, her heels tapping quickly on the cement as she ran.

When she left the elevator, it took her fifteen minutes to find her way through the maze of hallways. Harborview was Seattle's general hospital, and not only were serious trauma and accident patients seen there, but also those folks without insurance. Consequently, the halls were thronged with a variety of people, from the homeless to well-dressed businessmen to middle-income housewives.

At last, Frankie reached the emergency area and found the waiting room. But none of Eli's brothers were there—she didn't recognize any of the people seated in the chairs or ranged on the two sofas.

Terrified, she left the waiting room and stopped a nurse in green scrubs just outside.

"I'm looking for an accident patient. He's supposed to be in the ER—his name is Eli Wolf."

The nurse eyed her shrewdly. "Are you a family member?"

"He's my fiancé." Frankie lied without a shred of regret.

"Then I'm sure it's okay for you to go in. This way." The nurse held open the heavy door and led Frankie into a big room sectioned off with curtains that slid on overhead transoms. Several of the curtains were open, the beds within their semicircles empty.

The nurse led her across the room. Just as she pulled back a section of the heavy drape, masculine laughter rang out.

"He's in here," the nurse told her, standing back to let Frankie pass.

Frankie stepped quickly through the opening and stopped abruptly, her eyes filling with tears.

Eli was propped up in the raised hospital bed, his chest bare above the white sheet bunched at his waist. Red scrapes marred the left side of his chest, and bruises left faint blue marks. But he'd been laughing, a smile still curving his mouth and lighting his eyes.

Ethan and Connor sat in plastic chairs, long legs stretched out, while Matt stood at the foot of the bed.

They all looked up when she stepped into the room.

Frankie's frantic gaze tracked over what she could see of Eli's body. She was relieved to find nothing worse than scrapes and bruises. The tight knot squeezing her chest and sitting like lead just below her collarbone eased, but the tears streaming down her face didn't stop.

She brushed at them with trembling fingertips while she stared at Eli, unable to speak.

"Frankie," his deep voice rumbled. "Honey, I'm all right."

She didn't speak, and the tears wouldn't stop falling.

Her feet wouldn't move; they felt cemented to the floor.

"I'll see you guys later," Eli said without taking his eyes from Frankie. "Thanks for coming down."

"Yeah, no problem." Metal chair legs scraped against the linoleum-covered floor as Ethan and Connor stood. Matt joined them, and the three filed out, each pausing to awkwardly pat Frankie's shoulder as they passed.

"Come here, honey." Eli opened his arms. The words lifted the paralysis that held her. At last, Frankie could move.

She ran across the waxed floor. Eli caught her hand and tugged her down onto the hospital bed, facing him. And when he wrapped his arms around her, she willingly let him tuck her close, her face pressed against the strong column of his throat, his pulse beating with rhythmic thuds against her cheek.

"You scared me." She ran her hands over him, searching for breaks. Remembering the scrapes on his side, she carefully backed away from him, although he didn't let her go far. The raw places on his ribs looked like rug burns, and she winced as she barely skimmed her fingertips over one. "This looks sore."

He shrugged, the hard muscles of his chest shifting under her hand. "They're just a few little scrapes."

"What caused them?"

"I don't remember exactly, but I think it was the branches of the fir tree." He shook his head in disgust. "I knew that slope was going to slide sooner or later. We're just lucky it only gave way on one end."

"Did you have to be standing there when it did?" she demanded, smoothing her fingertips over the bruise on his cheekbone before cupping his cheek.

"I didn't exactly plan it that way," he told her, a small, endearing smile lifting the corners of his mouth. "If I'd had a choice, trust me, I would have been on the other side of the lot with Connor."

"Humph." Frankie wasn't mollified. She continued to stroke her fingers over the warm, satiny skin of his chest, the feel of his hard muscles and the lift of his chest as he breathed soothing the terror that had shaken her. Suddenly, she stiffened and sat up. "Eli, you're bruised on your left side. Did the tree damage your left leg—the one you broke last year?"

"No." He pulled her back, tucking her head beneath his chin. "That's why the doctor scheduled me for an MRI. Well, that and the general beating I got all over from the tree," he conceded. "But the leg is fine. I'm sure I'll be stiff and sore tomorrow, and probably for a few days to come, but ultimately I was incredibly lucky. No serious damage."

"Thank goodness." Frankie hugged him tighter before instantly loosening her grip. "Sorry, I didn't mean to hurt you."

His arms pressed her close once again. "You didn't hurt me." He brushed a kiss against her hair. "The accident was a wake-up call for me, Frankie. I could have died this afternoon without telling you how much I love you. I should have told you last night—or this morning. I don't know why I didn't. Yes, I do," he said with a shake of his head. "I chickened out because I was afraid you weren't ready to hear it." His arms tightened, pressing her closer, and his voice rumbled. "I couldn't stop thinking about you after we kissed at your birthday party. If you hadn't walked into the office and asked me to help you, I would have called and asked you out. I wasn't just pretending to be interested in you—I wanted to spend time with you and this was the perfect opportunity." He paused, his voice deeper when he continued. "We hadn't been dating for more than a week when I knew I was in deep trouble. You weren't just another beautiful woman. I didn't want to admit it, even to myself, but I'd fallen in love with you."

"Eli," she breathed, tilting her head back to look up at him. "I love you, too. I wanted to tell you last night, but I wasn't sure you felt the same way about me."

His eyes flared, hot with blue fire, and he bent his head and kissed her. The warm pressure of his mouth reaffirmed he was safe, his injuries minor, and her earlier terror that she'd lost him melted away.

When he lifted his head, his blue eyes were heavy-lidded and darkened. "Harry asked me yesterday what my intentions were toward you, Frankie. I want to spend my life with you. I want to wake up in the morning with you in my arms and go to bed at night with you beside me. I want you to marry me. I want us to have a little girl who looks just like you and makes me sit on little chairs to play at tea parties." He stroked his thumb over the faintly swollen fullness of her lower lip. "But most of all, I want you to love me the way I love you. I wasn't sure that was possible, but when you walked in here, I began to hope."

"Oh, Eli." Frankie's eyes filled, and tears spilled down her cheeks. "I love you so much it scares me."

"Scares you?" He frowned. "Why?"

"Because loving someone this much is a scary thing for me. I was very young when my father died, but I remember watching my mother grieve and thinking I never wanted to love someone that much, and I've never let myself fall in love. Until now—I can't control how I feel about you. It's as if you're the other half of me, as if I didn't even realize I needed you until we started dating." She shook her head. "Like I said, loving you is scary. I've never done it before. I'm in uncharted territory."

He smiled slowly. "If it helps, honey, you're not alone."

"Really?" She searched his face. "You've never been in love like this before, either?"

"No."

"Good," she said firmly. "Then we can muddle through together."

"I'm game for anything we can do together, honey," he said. "How soon do you think we can spring me from this place?"

"I don't know. Certainly not until the doctor has run all the tests he needs to be sure you're all right."

"I'm fine. And I'll be better as soon as we're home." He lifted a questioning brow. "My place or yours? I don't care which, just pick one. But you're spending tonight with me."

"Only if the doctor says it's okay," she warned him.

"Honey, I'm not asking the doc if I can make love to you tonight," he told her with a slow grin. "It wouldn't matter if he told me yes or no. But if you'll go find him, we can get me released and out of this place. Unless you want to climb under the sheet with me and get creative?"

Frankie laughed and slipped off the bed. "You're incorrigible. I'll see if I can find a nurse."

Once again, family and friends gathered at Harry's lakeside mansion. This time to celebrate Eli's release from the hospital and his engagement to Frankie.

The panel of doors between the living room and an adjacent family room were thrown open, and the space was crowded with guests. Harry had spared no expense—tables groaning under the weight of catered food and champagne fountains flowing.

At the end of the room, standing near the ebony grand piano with the Seattle skyline visible through the floor-to-ceiling windows behind them, Harry and Cornelia stood apart, savoring a moment alone.

"Well, Harry—" Cornelia lifted her champagne glass, sipping as she eyed his tall, lanky figure and the smile wreathing his features "—all has turned out well. I've never seen Frankie so happy. She absolutely glows."

"And Eli looks pretty happy, too," Harry agreed. He lifted his glass, touching it to Cornelia's with a small click of congratulations. "Here's to another wedding in the family."

"I'll drink to that." Cornelia sipped once more, sighing contentedly as she looked about the room. "It was lovely of you to volunteer to hold Frankie's engagement party here, Harry. We could have had it at my house, but I'm not sure we would have all fit."

"It's my pleasure." Harry's eyes gleamed, his gaze intent on Cornelia as she smiled and waved at Tommi, standing with Max, Bobbie and Gabriel across the room.

Their moment of quiet conversation was all too short, and soon Cornelia was called away by a group of Frankie's high school friends. Harry let her go and moved through the crowd, visiting with friends and greeting some guests he hadn't met before. One of those was Eli's grandfather, Jack, who accepted with alacrity Harry's offer of whisky instead of champagne.

"Nice of you to throw this party for Eli," Jack told Harry.

The two older men stood at the end of the long living room, heavy lead crystal glasses containing a few inches of whisky in their hands.

"Glad to do it," Harry said expansively. "He's been practically a member of the family for years." He nodded at the newly engaged couple holding court near the fireplace halfway down the room. "And now that he's engaged to my niece, he'll be making it official. Seems like a natural next step."

"Does that mean Wolf Construction gets the contract

to build HuntCom's new campus?" Jack asked casually, his blue eyes shrewd as he looked at Harry.

"Of course." Harry's eyes twinkled. "Can't have my niece's fiancé out of work."

Jack chuckled. "Good to know my grandson is marrying into a family that understands taking care of its own."

"There will be other opportunities, too, of course," Harry told him. "HuntCom has facilities outside Seattle, some overseas."

"I'd just as soon the boys worked closer to home, especially now that Eli's going to be married," Jack told him. "It's hard to keep a wife happy and be a good dad from half a world away."

"True." Harry nodded his agreement.

Jack's deep laugh was clearly audible over the murmur of conversation. Frankie looked at Eli's grandfather, finding him in deep conversation with Harry, and felt a niggle of foreboding. Arm hooked through Eli's, she leaned against his side and went up on tiptoe to reach him. He bent his head.

"Eli, your grandfather and Harry look like they're plotting," she whispered in his ear. "Should we be worried?"

He glanced up and across the room, covering her hand with his where it rested on his sleeve. "No," he reassured her. "Harry's a cagey guy, but Granddad can run him a close second. They're probably telling each other stories about the business deals they've wangled, trying to top each other."

"You know," Frankie said slowly, watching the two older men and the ease they seemed to feel with each other. "I'm wondering if we made a mistake getting those two together. Jack Wolf might be the only man I ever met who can match Harry's willingness to tell his family members what to do."

Eli laughed and bent to brush a kiss against her cheek. "How did you figure that out about Granddad so quickly?"

"I've had a couple of conversations with him over the last few days," she told him. "And he doesn't pull his punches. He wants us to have a baby—soon."

"He told you that?" Eli demanded, a frown growing.

"Yes, but don't be angry with him." Frankie smoothed her fingertip over the frown lines, easing them away. "I told him Harry had already informed me that I'm soon going to be past my best childbearing years and I'd duly noted the information."

"Damn, Frankie." Eli's voice held admiration. "I think Granddad finally met his match in you."

Her mouth curved in a small smile. "That's what he said."

Eli hugged her, laughter rumbling as he did.

"Are you sure we shouldn't warn Georgie about Harry?" Frankie said, still concerned. "It's not like Harry to abandon a project, and he seems obsessed with matchmaking."

"No, I don't think so. After all," Eli said, "look how well his meddling worked out for us."

"But we got together while trying to avoid Harry's scheming," she reminded him.

"But the end result was the same. Harry meddled in your love life, and, in the end, you and I are together." Eli tipped up her chin, his eyes a deep, smoky blue behind half-lowered lashes.

"That's true," Frankie agreed. "And how amazingly wonderful is that?"

"Pretty damned incredible," Eli said fervently. He bent his head, his mouth covering hers.

Yes, she thought as the kiss swept her under. She adored him more than she'd ever thought possible, more than her long-ago crush. And even more astounding, he loved her, too.

Life stretched before her, filled with infinite happy possibilities. Frankie wrapped her arms around his neck and kissed him back, unaware that the roomful of guests was cheering with delight.

* * * * *

THEIR MIRACLE
TWINS

BY
NIKKI LOGAN

First published in Great Britain 2012
by Mills & Boon, an imprint of Harlequin (UK) Limited,
Eton House, 18-24 Paradise Road, Richmond, Surrey TW9 1SR

© Nikki Logan 2012

ISBN: 978 0 263 89398 4

23-0112

Harlequin (UK) policy is to use papers that are natural, renewable and
recyclable products and made from wood grown in sustainable forests. The
logging and manufacturing processes conform to the legal environmental
regulations of the country of origin.

Printed and bound in Spain
by Blackprint CPI, Barcelona

Dear Reader,

In 2009, when writing my book *Their Newborn Gift,* I wanted to explore the idea of a young woman who takes on her (dead) sister's unborn embryos rather than see them lost to her family forever. But that book was part of a series and—generally speaking—killing off another author's characters is frowned upon, and so I put the idea on ice (pun very much intended) for a future book where no-one but my own characters are involved.

Their Miracle Twins is that book.

There are obvious ethical issues for IVF patients around which box to tick to instruct the laboratory regarding any unused embryos—"donate" or "destroy". But the idea of an unmarried heroine fighting in the courts to make sure they are donated to her is ethically complex, too. Will fixating on the children stop her from grieving properly? Will a single mother living in a tiny flat in Chelsea make a good mother? Will they have as good a life as a more established, supportive married couple could give them?

And more importantly…what happens if there's two?

Belinda Rochester fights like a lioness for her sister's unborn children, but she soon finds out that her family is not the only one affected. And that being able to *fight* for custody is not the same as being *right* for it.

I hope you take pleasure in meeting Bel and Flynn and experiencing the beautiful life they forge for themselves high in the tablelands of Australia.

Enjoy,

xx

Nikki Logan

Nikki Logan lives next to a string of protected wetlands in Western Australia, with her long-suffering partner and a menagerie of furred, feathered and scaly mates. She studied film and theatre at university, and worked for years in advertising and film distribution before finally settling down in the wildlife industry. Her romance with nature goes way back, and she considers her life charmed, given she works with wildlife by day and writes fiction by night—the perfect way to combine her two loves. Nikki believes that the passion and risk of falling in love are perfectly mirrored in the danger and beauty of wild places. Every romance she writes contains an element of nature, and if readers catch a waft of rich earth or the spray of wild ocean between the pages she knows her job is done.

For Mel & Jase

CHAPTER ONE

London, England

THE sterile double doors of the hospital whispered open as Bel Rochester approached, wiping her free hand on her jeans and gripping her overnight case like a sweaty lifeline in the other. It wasn't every day you walked into a hospital a single woman but walked out a single mother.

Pregnant with your sister's babies.

Lucky the whole thing had happened so fast—barely six hours had elapsed from the moment the clinic called to say her levels were optimum to her stepping out of the black taxi on Chelsea Bridge Road. The crazy chaos meant she hadn't had time to get nervous. To indulge in second thoughts. Anyway, she wasn't a woman to second-guess herself once she'd made a decision, and she'd done enough thinking for a lifetime.

She made her way to the busy admissions desk and waited patiently while the woman behind the desk finished directing phone calls. Her eyes strayed down a long corridor—a corridor she'd walked a few weeks ago when the hormone treatments first began—and she wondered which of the hospital's dozen labs currently housed Gwen and Drew's two remaining IVF embryos.

Her niece or nephew.

Her future children.

'Sorry, love. Can I help you?'

She snapped her attention back to the woman behind the desk. 'Belinda Rochester—' she smiled, sliding her appointment letter onto the counter '—I'm being admitted today for an embryo transfer.'

No, that wasn't weird to say. *At all.*

The woman consulted the flat screen monitor on her desk and checked the letter before absently returning it. Then she nodded and confirmed, 'Dr Cabanallo? Fertility department?'

Stupidly, the word 'fertility' still made her blush even though what was about to happen to her was about as *un*-sexy as anything possibly could be. Induced uterine preparation, assisted implantation, fostered maturation. Hardly the stuff of romance.

Not that she had much to compare it to.

She cleared her throat. 'That's right.'

The admissions clerk nodded. Then she looked discreetly at the large empty space around Bel and smiled kindly. 'No one with you, love? For support?'

Would she need a support team? It hadn't occurred to her. She'd become so accustomed to doing things solo. Gwen would normally have been her support of choice, but her sister's death two years before was the whole reason Bel was here now. When she and Drew had gone down with the ferry while travelling through south-east Asia, they'd left behind no instructions regarding the remaining IVF embryos they had on ice. And, although there was a tick in the box next to *donate* on the clinic's signed consent form that determined what happened to any unused embryos, Bel had fought all the way to the High Court to make sure that they were donated—*to her.*

It was worth every sleepless night, every invasive question and every last pound of her grandmother's inheritance to secure custody and keep the babies together. There was no way they were going to someone else while she breathed.

They were Rochesters.

Renewed purpose pushed the momentary uncertainty out

of the way. She lifted her chin and smiled breezily. 'Nope. It's just me.'

Exactly why the court case had been so fiddly. She'd had to convince three consecutive magistrates not only that she had a familial right of first preference to her sister's embryos but also that she was fit to be their parent. Despite being technically unemployed. Despite being, for all intents and purposes, estranged from her own parents. Despite being single.

Did she have support?

Nope. Not a whit.

She would have said whatever it took to make sure Gwen's embryos didn't go to strangers. Or into a furnace. The law was a hard blue line and she'd balanced precariously right on top of it.

'Fill this out, please.'

The clerk slid a clipboard across the stylish countertop for her admission details, her eyes already sliding away to the next client.

Instinct made Bel turn as the smell of fresh earth reached her on a slap of cold London air. The whisper-quiet hospital doors had admitted a man—broad-shouldered, lean-hipped. He strode towards them, pushing fingers through damp brown hair, his scuffed work boots squeaking on the polished hospital floor. He was the complete cowboy cliché, only missing the Stetson.

Who got around like that in London?

Bel's eyes drifted down long demin-clad legs to those boots. They'd genuinely seen time out in the fields and were unmistakably the source of the *eau d'earth* since the rest of him was straight-from-the-shower spotless. The familiar scent gave her flagging spirits the tiniest boost.

Outdoors. Her favourite place in the world.

Not that she'd be getting out of her flat and into the wilds much once she was heavy with child. Another sacrifice she'd willingly make to raise her sister's children. Though not without some sorrow.

As she lifted her eyes, she realised he'd tracked her glance down to his mud-crusted boots. She quickly returned to her paperwork as he spoke to the admissions clerk.

'Russel Ives is expecting me.'

Every hair on Bel's neck stood on end and she sucked in a breath as painful as the coldest blast of Thames-chilled air.

Australian. Not American.

She hadn't heard the Aussie accent for two years, since they'd lost Drew. To hear it now, on a stranger, on this day of all days… She blinked rapidly past the unexpected sting in her eyes.

'Legal dep—?'

Tanned fingers shot out into mid air to halt the clerk's speech. Her mouth snapped shut with an audible click. Bel felt heat on her bent head and glanced up from her mountain of admissions paperwork to meet two male eyes. They should have been pretty—the ash of the tempestuous skies outside and with lashes to rival her own—but they were flat and…lifeless. And they were staring right at her.

'Do you mind?' His voice was as empty as his eyes.

Bel stiffened immediately at the presumption. She gave him her best *up yours* smile. 'Not at all. Say whatever you want.'

His silent glare was all the answer she got.

God, he even looked a bit like Drew—in the heavy-lidded shape of his eyes, the furrowed brow. Who knew, maybe all Australian men looked a little bit alike? Colonial origins, small founding gene pool and all that. But this man's arrogant manner was nothing like the charming Aussie her sister had fallen in love with, even if the single eyebrow lift was straight out of Drew's playbook.

Her stomach curled. His *former* playbook.

Sobriety brought her back to the whole purpose of today's visit. This wasn't a day to be messing with the minds of egotistical foreigners. But it galled her to concede even something as simple as an admissions desk, so she took just a tiny bit longer than necessary pulling her papers together and tugging the loaned clipboard to her chest, then she stepped quietly away and crossed to one of the comfortable waiting room couches to finish the forms.

Maybe his wife's in here somewhere, dying of cancer? Reasonable Bel forced her way forward to try and justify the man's appalling manners. *Maybe he's dying of something himself?* Her eyes flicked up briefly and assessed the back view of him. Fit, strong, excellent carriage. Amazing in jeans. No, that body wasn't the slightest bit ill. And as he ran his agitated left hand through his freshly washed hair, she confirmed something else, too.

No wife.

Just a jerk then. The simplest solution was often the best. Wasn't that what Gwen used to say? Thinking of her sister helped take her mind off the unsettling feelings that being treated like crap engendered. If she wanted to be treated like dirt she could go home to her parents.

She got it free there!

It was part of the reason she'd made the decision to raise her sister's babies as her own. A chance to have someone look at her as if she meant something. Something she'd not had for over two years since losing the people closest to her. She slid her hand low on her flat belly. In a couple of hours she was going to have two lives nestled in there—Gwen and Drew's DNA but her *children*. And Rochesters. Just a bunch of frozen cells right now, not even human in the eyes of the law, but *family* in the eyes of their biological aunt.

Their about-to-be mother.

Bel's heart tripped and thumped hard in its recovery. Even thinking the word was a huge adjustment. What did she know about mothering? But the alternatives were purely unthinkable. Disposal, donation or eternity suspended in ice. Either

way, that was her *blood* being banished from the family. And
Bel was determined that no more Rochesters would feel the
sting of not being wanted.

Her loud sigh achieved the unimaginable and drew the admission clerk's gaze off the man in front of her. Mr Personality
had finally finished his long discussion and now leaned on the
admissions counter, waiting, as she had. Refusing to yield an
inch more to some overly decorative tourist, she pushed to her
feet and returned her forms to the desk, clattering the clipboard
down noisily right next to his elbow.

The clerk gave Bel her full attention now, her attempts at
engaging the man visibly fruitless. 'The doctor will see you
now. You know the way?'

Bel smiled. 'Thank you. *Have a nice day.*' It was directed to
the clerk but purely for the benefit of the Wonder from Down
Under. A little lesson in etiquette for him.

Heh.

The clerk reached out and squeezed her hand. 'Good luck,
yeah?'

Bel nodded, but as she turned towards the corridor her gaze
collided with a pair of male eyes, still flat but harbouring a
strange new quality.

Was that a hint of…regret? Was he *possibly* embarrassed
by his dreadful manners earlier? She glanced at the rugged,
closed face and doubted it, then she pulled her overnight bag
up into a death grip, turned towards the corridor and let her
long legs carry her off.

She was halfway to the ward before it dawned on her that
she was no longer the slightest bit nervous.

'Is it too late to vote for drugs?' Bel asked with less quaver in
her voice than she felt.

She looked at the array of probes, tubes and long, long nee-
dles laid out beside her and asked herself—again—whether
staying conscious was the right decision. But if there was no

conception to be around for, then the transfer was as close as she was going to get to the moment Gwen's embryos became hers. Besides, her specialist had elected to go in through her belly button rather than up the birth canal given her…status… and that made it possible to watch the procedure with only a local anaesthetic.

The nurse added a nasty-looking hypodermic to the tray.

'Far too late.' Dr Cabanallo smiled at her.

'But going up has to be easier, surely. Isn't that what it's designed for?'

A nurse chuckled but the specialist's eyes widened in horror. 'And risk ruining my first ever miracle birth? Surely you jest.'

Ah, yes…Apparently the virgin jokes just never got old. Though the jury was still out on which Dr Cabanallo thought was more miraculous—a virgin having a baby in the first place, or a girl from Chelsea still being…intact…at twenty-three. It wasn't the first time she'd faced that silent scepticism.

'Right,' she said lightly. 'I forgot this was all about you.'

'Well, of course it is, Belinda—did you not read your agreement before you signed it?'

Despite the banter, she and Marco Cabanallo got on brilliantly. She'd shopped three IVF clinics until she'd met and clicked with the man now fiddling around with her midsection.

'Okay,' he said, lifting his head from a brief inspection in a microscopic device across the room. 'Let's get this party started…'

Somewhere down the hall voices were raised. One nurse turned to frown towards the unusual interruption as the other attended the specialist. The voices continued and drew closer. Dr Cabanallo lifted his head. So did both nurses. So, finally, did Bel.

'What the hell…?' He stripped off his gloves and stormed from the theatre as two suited men, one security guard and one ominously familiar face appeared on the other side of the observation glass.

The Wonder from Down Under.

His eyes widened and his brow formed more lines than a topographical map as he saw her propped up on the table. But the surprise quickly turned dark as she stared back at him. Bel glanced down at her gown to make sure everything important was covered now that there was a room full of strangers along for the ride. With the exception of an iodine stained square of her flat belly visible through the window cut in her blue gown, it was.

Dr Cabanallo's heated entry into the viewing room muted immediately as he spoke in a low tone to the men in suits. He glanced up at Bel, then back at the two men and shook his head, his waving hands testament to his Italian origins. Bel frowned, then looked back at the stranger, whose eyes had not left hers. As if he was studying her for the slightest reaction. Or trying to figure something out.

Dr Cabanallo's entire body language shifted. Became defensive. He pulled his face mask down around his throat and shrugged, shaking his head.

Bel could make out a few recognisable shapes on his lips. *No.* Then, *too late.* There was more furious discussion and then some hand waving from one of the suits. The Australian still did not take his eyes off her but he didn't say a word to anyone on his side of the glass, either.

She turned to him and frowned in query.

Without so much as blinking, he drew a sheet of paper from his pocket, unfolded it carefully, stepped forward to the glass nearest her and slapped it hard up against the window so she could read it.

Bel had to tip her head at an angle to see it and the text was too small to make out from this distance, but she recognised the crown letterhead immediately, and the formatting of the

document which matched that of her court approval to proceed
with the embryo transfer…

Her stomach tightened.

…and the big, fat, bold word centred at the top of the page.

Injunction.

Her whole body heaved as the air rushed out of it. Then she
lifted her eyes back to the twin bullets peering at her over the
top of the court notice.

Hate-filled. Pitiless.

Then she burst into tears.

CHAPTER TWO

RIGHT up until then…

Right up until the moment that Belinda Rochester's picture-perfect face had crumpled and folded in on itself in a flood of anguished tears, Flynn Bradley figured he had her nailed. A spoilt princess used to getting her own way. A younger version of her upper class sister.

But then she'd spread her hands across her face as if she could possibly hide from them all. From the truth. Except they weren't tantrum tears. They were genuine, one hundred per cent pure devastation. The same tears his mother had cried when they were notified about Drew's death. By the authorities, not by the high-and-mighty Rochesters, who'd never so much as sent a text message to offer condolences.

Now, the medical staff worked hard to help calm Gwen's little sister down. One of them muttered something about the hormones she was pumped full of—but it seemed to be more for Belinda's reassurance than for his—and slowly, awkwardly, she managed to regain some composure. The Italian was livid, ranting and roaming around the theatre in his surgical scrubs between bouts of staring obsessively at the clock. The security guard was tense, ready for anything. The hospital legals were—typically—remaining calm and quiet and waiting for all the histrionics to die down.

And he…

He was almost weak-kneed with relief. It was only the Bradley iron will that had him still upright.

But he'd made it in time.

Ten thousand miles and a three-hour sprint by car and he'd walked in here just as they were beginning. He'd been insane to take himself on a brisk circuit of the neighbouring gardens to settle his nerves, but he'd really needed to feel earth instead of pavement beneath his feet. Getting the injunction was the first win; it gave him enough time to appeal against this ludicrous court order. He'd picked it up from an out-of-hours bailiff on the way from Heathrow and he'd headed straight to the hospital to slap it on their legal department.

When he'd discovered the transfer procedure was happening right now, while he sat in a room full of hospital lawyers... That had nearly broken him. They'd practically chased him down the warren of corridors to this theatre.

He looked at Gwen's sister again. All geared up in her hospital gown, looking all of sixteen with her flame-coloured hair piled high on her head and her face free of make-up. So horribly close to being ready.

'Would someone *please* tell me what is going on?'

Belinda Rochester's tiny voice matched her appearance perfectly. He'd been floored when he realised she was the same woman from the hospital foyer—she of the forever legs and the provocative knee-high suede boots. Her snipe was the only thing to even vaguely slap him out of the pressure-induced dark place he'd been in since getting word of the approval of the injunction.

The flash of haughty disdain in her blue eyes as she looked at his muddy boots had managed to bring him back to the real world. Just a little bit. He should have guessed then that she was a Rochester.

No wonder Drew had loved it in London so much. Where cultured manners reigned.

'Miss Rochester...' One of the legals stepped in to bring

her up to speed. Her red-rimmed eyes widened and kept on widening as she discovered why he was here. 'It's simply an unacceptable level of risk for the hospital. I'm sorry.'

She turned her confusion to Flynn. 'Appealing the custody award? Why? On what grounds?'

'On the grounds that my family wasn't consulted,' he bit out.

'Wh… What family?'

'The Bradley family. Drew's family.'

Blue eyes narrowed. 'But…Drew's family were contacted. They made no petition.'

He shrugged. 'The letter was delayed.' Actually, not entirely true but close enough.

That seemed to fire her up. A single strand of phoenix-red hair fell down over her face. She brushed it away savagely. 'You're kidding me—you're playing the "we didn't get the letter" card? It's been ten months!'

He shrugged again. They had, in fact, received the letter. But some bureaucratic bungle saw it addressed *to* Drew by mistake, and his still-grieving mother had buried it amongst his other belongings, unable to face one more reminder of his death or—worse—one more demand for death taxes. As if losing him once wasn't bad enough… It was only luck that saw Flynn find the legal-looking letter when going through his brother's things the month before.

He'd nearly killed himself driving the three hours to Sydney at top speed to get the best lawyer his savings could buy.

Belinda swung her legs over the edge of the table to sit up straighter. He'd thought they were long back out in the foyer. Here, they went on eternally. Her sister hadn't been that tall. He dragged his eyes back up to her blazing ones.

So, she was a fast rebounder.

'Regardless, I'm the closest living relative.'

He snorted. 'In what universe?'

'Gwen was my sister. Biologically, I'm the closest relative to these children.'

'And Drew was my brother. That makes me just as close, genetically, to the *embryos*.' Damned if he was going to let her emotionalise this any further by acting as if two living, breathing kids stood in the room with them.

She reeled back. 'Drew didn't have a brother.'

Flynn sucked back the knives. Why that, particularly, should have hurt so badly after everything that had gone down between him and Drew... But to effectively disown him... 'I have a birth certificate that says otherwise.'

She frowned. 'Gwen wouldn't keep something like that a secret.'

Had Drew been so under the Rochester spell he'd denied his family's existence? His brother's? Old hurts fuelled his anger. 'Well, the fact remains Drew and I were brothers and I have a court injunction to prove it.'

The cornflower eyes blazed with bewilderment and fear. 'What do you want?'

'I want to stop the transfer.'

'Why?'

'Because your right to the embryos is no longer absolute. I have an equal right under the law.'

She frowned and pressed slim, perfectly manicured fingers to her temples. Every other person in the room was silent. 'You want to raise the babies?'

'I want the question of custody revisited,' he hedged. He sure as hell didn't want the only thing left of Drew being lost to his family. This was something concrete he could do. Something positive.

'But... There's no time...' She turned her pained face to the doctor. 'Is there, Marco?'

All focus shifted to the doctor. He'd tell her—that what started on ice could stay on ice indefinitely. Certainly long enough for him to get custody of Drew's biological material for his family. Not hers.

'Actually, no, there's not.'

Flynn's head snapped around. *What?* 'But the implantation hasn't started.'

'The embryos are prepared for transfer. They're human DNA, Mr Bradley. You can't simply re-freeze them like a pound of sausages if you change your mind.'

Belinda's blue eyes flared. 'They need to go in!'

The doctor nodded. 'Yes. They do.'

One of the hospital attorneys chimed in, drawing Belinda's focus with a snap. 'They're not going in.'

'But they'll die!' She dragged her eyes back to his, glittering blue again, but this time with fear. 'Please! You'll kill them.'

Tight claws skidded down his spine. That DNA was the only tiny part of Drew the fates had left behind when that Thai ferry sank. It was the gift of life none of his family had known a thing about. A second chance. He didn't want those cells anywhere near the Rochesters, let alone *in* one of them, but letting them die was absolutely not going to happen.

He turned to the attorneys. 'What are our options?'

The Italian cut in. 'How many verdant, prepared wombs do you see in this room, Mr Bradley?'

He looked around desperately and his eyes landed on one of the nursing staff.

She snorted and crossed her arms across an ample chest and barked at him disapprovingly in her broad accent, 'Don't you look at me, sunshine!'

He snapped his gaze back to the suits. 'There must be another option. Somewhere else to store the embryos…'

'It needs to happen now,' the doctor snapped. 'Every minute we waste is potentially destroying them. We're right on the edge of the viable time as it is because of how long it took Bel to get to the hospital.'

His thumping heart dragged his head back to hers. Every

resentment he'd ever had for the Rochesters and their influence on his brother bubbled up and spilled out at the vulnerable woman perched nervously on the edge of the table. 'Needed a pedicure first, princess?'

Her lips pressed into a tight, pained line and her hands twisted and untwisted in the hospital gown. But she didn't bite. Instead, her eyes implored him—*Please!*—and he got the feeling she was not a woman accustomed to begging.

And in that moment the balance of power shifted.

To him.

Belinda Rochester was every bit as desperate as he was. And desperate people did desperate things. A savage plan began to take shape.

'Possession is nine-tenths of the law.'

She shook her head. 'What?'

'There's not a court in the world that will grant me custody of those children after they've been gestating in your body.' He looked at the lawyers. 'Right?'

They both looked as if they wished they'd called in sick today. But they nodded. 'Almost certainly,' the only brave one amongst them said.

'Mr Bradley, please…' The Italian flattened both hands towards the ticking clock.

Flynn kept his eyes locked on Belinda's. 'If I let this happen, what's to stop you disappearing with them?'

She threw her hands up. 'The law?'

'The law hasn't done me any favours so far.'

'It gave you an injunction.'

'Which I had to fight for.'

She glanced at the doctor, who was looking plenty pensive, and hissed out a breath. 'I'll give you my word.'

His laugh was more of a bark. 'A Rochester's word? Worthless.'

'Then what do you want? We don't have time for this.'

'You come with me.'

More fiery strands fell free of her hairclip as she shook her head. 'What? Where?'

'Back to Australia. With me.'

'Are you insane? My life's here.'

And mine's on that tray over there. He was so close to saying it. He had so much to make up to his brother. His parents. He thought he'd lost the chance for ever. 'You want these kids or not? Either you come with me or their use-by date will expire while you watch.'

'Oh, my God. This is the worst kind of blackmail.'

'Whatever it takes, honey. The only way I'm going to know you haven't skipped the country with our *shared* property is if I keep you with me at all times. Until the case is decided. Until they're born.'

'Then what?' She threw her hands in the air. Presumably to make damned sure he knew she wasn't actually considering it.

'Then we abide by the court's decision. On equal ground.'

'It won't be equal. You said yourself the courts are going to favour me—'

His eyes shot to the lawyers, specifically the one who'd been brave enough to open his mouth and commit to something earlier. 'What will level out the playing field under UK law?'

The two of them conferred quietly, but then the sister's quiet voice drew his attention.

'Playing field? This is not a game. Were talking about lives here.'

He held her serious gaze and murmured, 'Tell me about it,' before facing the two suited men once again. 'Well?'

The taller one laughed but it was tight and high. 'Short of marrying her, not a lot.'

Even the nurses gasped and his eyes flicked back around in time to see Belinda Rochester's coral lips fall open. He stared her down, his mind racing through what precious few options he had. Then he shrugged. His life was going roundly down the gurgler anyway…

'It's just a formality—' he started, but she barely took a breath before squeaking her refusal.

'Are you insane?'

'No, I'm desperate. And so are you. Do you want this implantation or not?'

'You know I do. These babies mean everything to me.' She blazed fire and ice and brimstone and Flynn got a momentary glimpse of the protective mother she was going to be. And it wasn't unattractive.

'Then no price is too great, right?'

Not a single person in the room breathed. The clock on the wall ticked unnaturally loud.

'Bel…' The Italian finally broke the silence and looked meaningfully at the snap-frozen straws that must have held the embryos. They almost glowed with nearly wasted life.

She swung bleak eyes back to him, nostrils flaring. 'This is temporary. And a marriage on paper only. I'll break any part of you that so much as touches me.'

It was insane to laugh at a moment like this, but the idea of those birdlike bones doing anything more than bouncing ineffectively off a son of the outback was ludicrous.

'Absolutely.' Whatever it took. Belinda Rochester would incubate his brother's babies and, when the time came, he'd smile as he took them out of her arms and nudged her back onto a plane for Old Blighty.

She stared at him, round-eyed and loathing, and then swung those long legs back up onto the table and lay down, eyes fixed on the fluorescent lighting above, without so much as a word of acquiescence.

The hospital legal team looked at him for direction.

He took a deep, painful breath and spoke.

'Do it. Put them in.'

CHAPTER THREE

New South Wales tablelands, Australia

'WELCOME to Oberon.'

Bel tucked her arms around her light shirt as she stepped out of Flynn's purring ute. After their three-hour drive from Sydney—into the mountains and out the other side—warmth shimmered off its bonnet. Infinitely warmer than the air around her. And the silent man beside her.

She leaned against the toasty car and grumbled, 'I thought Australia was supposed to be hot?'

He took a deep breath, either annoyed that the first real words out of her mouth in twenty-four hours was a complaint, or relieved she'd finally broken the stony silence they'd both endured much of the way from Heathrow. Not that they hadn't spoken at all. Some speech was a practical necessity. He'd had to tell her his name—*Flynn*, ridiculously Australian—and she'd had to ask him several times to unfold himself out of his aisle seat so she could use the bathroom. Her own fault for choosing to sit by the window, but staring out at the vast, inky blackness was infinitely preferable to making polite small talk with a man who was practically kidnapping her.

She'd almost chickened out, waiting at the departure lounge. She had a passport, a fully cleared credit card, packed suitcases, full womb, and all the reason in the world to want to run.

But she'd made a few promises to Gwen in the tiny hours of the morning she'd been due at the hospital for the transfer, and honouring the one about giving those babies the best life she could—a better life than she'd had—meant something to her. Enough to see her striding, stiff-backed, down the gangway and onto the flight to hell.

'This is the high country,' Flynn said. 'The tablelands of the Blue Mountains. We're eleven hundred metres above the heat. I hope you brought some warmer clothes.'

She let her eyes drift around them.

'Not what you imagined...?'

She frowned, surprised by the miracle of conversation with Mr Strong-Silent-Type. 'Its name sounded a lot more...magical.'

Oberon. She'd had visions of Shakespeare and forests filled with Faeries. But while this little mountain town might not have horned folk and showering petals, it certainly wasn't without charm. Very Australian—particularly since it was the only part of Australia outside of Sydney's airport that she'd actually seen in anything other than a passing blur—and rather pretty.

'You live in town?'

'Nope. About ten kilometres back towards Jenolan. A place called Bunyip's Reach.'

'Why have we stopped here?'

'I figured you might like a break. And we could use the time to get our stories straight.'

She looked at him. 'We've had nothing but time for the past twenty-four hours.'

'You didn't seem—' He searched for the right word.

Approachable? No, probably not. She'd had the airline music pounding in her ears and her eyes glued to her e-reader pretty much the whole way. As though she was seated next to a total stranger. Actually, she might have tried to strike up a conversation with a total stranger...

'—ready to talk,' he finished.

Talk? With the man who hadn't managed more than fifty words to her since forcing her hand in the hospital? Bel took a deep breath of cold mountain air. The cleanest air she'd ever tasted. Then she tucked her arms more tightly around herself. 'What do you mean, get our stories straight?'

He glanced behind him. 'Let's get a hot drink. You're freezing. You seriously are going to have to dress warmer up here.'

The too familiar slice of his judgement stung. Was this how it would go? Him alternating between hostility and blatant condescension?

'I've been dressing myself successfully since I was four, Flynn. I'm sure I'll manage.' Now that she knew how unexpectedly like home the highlands were.

They walked a couple of blocks to a coffee house in awkward silence.

He spoke to several people on the way into the café, lots of nodding and curious glances and exchanges of *'mate'*. He was popular with the locals; that didn't bode particularly well for the quality of everyone else in the town, if an arrogant jerk was on the favoured-sons list.

It was only when they were seated with a herbal tea for Bel and a coffee for Flynn that he started speaking to her again, his eyes hard and determined. 'So, I wanted to set some ground rules.'

She lifted her eyebrows. 'Really?' *You and what army?*

'There are things that my family doesn't need to know just yet. But obviously they'll have questions…'

'You're coming home with a bride-to-be, pregnant with their other son's baby. I should think so.'

His lips tightened and his eyes flicked evasively out to the beautiful bush view.

'They do know about the embryos?' she asked. Because he surely would have told her something this important before now if they didn't. *Surely.*

His lips didn't loosen. Her mouth dropped open. 'They don't know?'

'No one knows. I'm the only one who's seen the letter.'

'Are you serious?' Her squeal drew curious eyes from the other patrons. 'How are you planning on explaining—' she waved her hands between them '—*this*, then?'

'We'll tell them I'm the father.'

She needed a second to gather her wits, which were scattered like straws around her. 'Really? And—what?—you met me on the outward flight to London, we got busy in the inflight loos and then you popped a ring on my finger? Fast work, Bradley.'

'No.' He expelled a frustrated breath slowly. 'They won't buy that for a minute. They know me.'

Finally! The voice of reason...

'I'm thinking we met in Melbourne last year,' he fabricated, 'where you were finishing your gap year...'

'I've never been to Melbourne. And I never had a gap year.' Not that he'd asked.

'And then we bumped into each other in London. Went out a few times, for old times' sake. One thing led to another.'

She frowned. 'And then you proposed?'

He shrugged. 'What can I say? I'm a passionate guy.'

'Uh-huh. And you never mentioned me to your family, this wonderful girl you met in Melbourne that drove you to such acts of passion? They won't find that strange?'

'Actually, I did meet a girl in Melbourne last year. Just not you. But they won't know that.'

That shut her up. How stupid was she not to have considered he might have a girlfriend tucked away somewhere? A girlfriend who would be crushed when her man came home with a pregnant bride in tow. God, could this get any more complicated?

'Oh, no... Will she—'

He waved away the concern. 'She's history.'

Literally? Or only now, since he unexpectedly had other

plans? But if he wasn't the type to join the Mile High Club, then hopefully he wasn't the type to so carelessly dispose of a human being. Despite what he'd threatened back in the hospital.

She took a head-clearing breath. 'So Melbourne, then. Last year. Party? Football? Pub?'

'I'm thinking somewhere more suitable for a woman of your…breeding.' Somehow he made the word more of an insult. 'Flemington. The Melbourne Cup. The races seems more credible, don't you think?' His lip almost curled.

Bel frowned. 'I have no idea. I've never been.'

His eyes narrowed. 'You've never been to a horse race?'

'Barbaric sport.'

'But you're a Chelsea girl.'

She shrugged. 'So?'

'Polo?'

A polo match, she *had* attended. But only one. 'Polo's vaguely more humane. But rather dull.'

'So I guess fox-hunting is out of the question? Steeplechase?'

She gave him *the look*. 'Okay this isn't getting us anywhere. How about we just rule out the animal-based sports altogether? Won't your family find it difficult to believe that both their sons should happen to meet a Rochester? In a country this size?'

He studied her closely. 'Which is why we won't be using your real name. What's your middle name?'

'Ah, no. Not going to happen.'

He leaned forward. Scenting a kill. 'Why not?'

'Because I don't like it. Can't I just make something up?'

'No. What is it?'

'None of your business.' Of course she could just lie and he wouldn't be any the wiser but there was something about his serious grey regard. The way he just…stared. He lifted one eyebrow.

'Oh, fine. It's Belaqua.'

He stared at her. 'Belinda Belaqua…'

'You see my concern?'

He frowned. 'Sounds like a porn star.'

She was too stunned that he'd cracked a joke to be seriously offended. 'Thank you so much.'

'You'll have to pick something else.'

She searched around in her subconscious. 'Depp?'

'Be serious.'

'Pitt.'

'Belinda…'

She wasn't prepared for the kick-in-the-ribs that her name on his lips would bring. And she couldn't blame Drew for this one—he'd only ever called her Bel. How did someone as disagreeable as Flynn manage to make seven letters sound so… gorgeous? She smiled overly brightly. 'Clooney, then.'

His eyes narrowed. 'Belinda Clooney. Okay, that sounds vaguely possible. But only because my parents live in a Country'n'Western bubble and barely go to the movies. And we'll spell it with a "u".'

There it went again… Her heart, tumbling like a pair of knickers in the dryer just because of the way he said her first name. She fought it valiantly with her weapon of choice—flippancy. 'You have a bit of the George about you, actually.'

'Uh huh.'

'Mostly in the forehead. Your smile. Though you have your brother's eyes…' The moment the words were out she regretted them. They caused such a deep sorrow in his expression, she yearned for the flat, dead look to return.

He cleared his throat. 'If you want to get specific, we both have my nan's eyes.'

The sorrow was replaced with patent affection. It made him seem more human. Just marginally. 'Will I meet her? Your nan?'

'You'll do more than meet her. You'll be living with her for the first while, at least until we can get hitched.'

Bel froze. 'You're offloading me on your grandmother?' After dragging her all this way?

The look he gave her then was strange. Sad and baffled at the same time. 'Drew really didn't tell you anything about us, huh?'

'Maybe Gwen didn't want him to. We'll never know.' She pointlessly stirred her coffee. Just for something to occupy her suddenly weak fingers.

'I live with Nan and Pop and my parents on Bunyip's Reach.'

Bel frowned. 'What? Like a commune?'

His laugh then was immediate and, for once, entirely sarcasm free. 'It's not a commune. It's called a family. And the Reach is one hundred and seventy acres.'

Her frown continued. 'You all live together?' In her family that was inconceivable. She'd left home at seventeen. Moved into the tiny flat her grandmother had left her as part of an inheritance.

'Well, no. I have my own place in a private croft. It's only small but it was built for Drew and I to share when we got older. You'll be staying with my family.'

'But they're complete strangers!' Except that they were also going to be the grandparents and great-grandparents of the babies she carried… Her hand slipped to her belly.

'So am I.'

That was true enough. Yet somehow he seemed so…not. Was it because he reminded her of Drew? 'Better the devil you know and all that. Why can't I just move straight in with you?'

He turned both hands upwards as though it was the most evident thing in the world. 'Because we're not married.'

She blinked at him. 'They're going to find out soon enough that I'm pregnant. I think they'll know we've been sleeping together.'

Fictionally… *Fictionally.*

His eyes grew cold again. 'Assuming you are pregnant. We

won't marry until we have absolute confirmation of that. What would be the point?'

Right. Because, if she wasn't, then warp technology wouldn't get her out of here quick enough. On that they were both agreed.

She shifted forwards in her seat. 'So, let me just clarify… I lie about my name. I lie about how and when I met you. I lie about how I got up the duff. I lie about marrying you. And then, later, when the court case is resolved, I just confess all to your family and trust they'll have a good laugh?'

His lips tightened again. 'It's not like I thought this through. If you recall, my hand was rather forced by circumstance.'

She gaped. '*You* were forced? I didn't see anyone holding the lives of two small babies to ransom to get *you* to comply. Give me one good reason why I shouldn't march into your family's house and tell them exactly who I am and exactly why I've come?'

He leaned in closer. 'Because my family hates yours. You wouldn't be welcome.'

That took her aback. 'What?'

'My family does not have the fondest feelings for the Rochesters.'

'But they've never met us. They've only met—' Instantly, her hackles rose. *They didn't like Gwen.* Her beautiful, courageous sister. The desire to defend was overwhelming. 'So that's where you get your judgemental bent from—your parents?'

'Judgemental?' he snorted. 'This coming from the woman who looked at me like I was filthier than the mud on my boots back in the hospital.'

She stumbled again. She could hardly tell him that the earth on his boots was the only reason she hadn't given him *both* barrels of what-for. She fought the conversation back on track.

'So they won't like me, big deal. Although lying is just one more thing for them to hate me for later.' His glance was steady and a tiny little lightbulb came on somewhere far back in her mind. She narrowed her eyes. 'But you don't care about that, do you?'

He pushed his lower lip out and paused. Was he debating whether to tell her the truth or not? 'Not particularly, no. You'll be back in England, so what does it matter?'

'Then why on earth do you imagine I'll play along with this ridiculous charade?'

'Because you lost your sister the way my mother lost her favourite son. And because finding out that son had children that she could never hold would be like ripping her heart out all over again.'

Bel had truly loved her brother-in-law—despite the secrets Drew had apparently been keeping. He'd been everything she could have wished for her sister, and the sort of man she secretly wished for herself. It was hard not to sympathise with a mother so deeply wounded by the loss of such a man.

'So if the court ruled in your favour, what would you do?' she asked.

'*When* the court rules in my favour I'll tell my parents the truth.'

'And *when* it doesn't?'

'Then I'll tell them nothing. You and I will just break up and you'll head back to England.'

There was no way she knew him well enough to even begin asking this kind of question but she asked him anyway. 'What makes you think losing your children would hurt them less than losing Drew's?'

His eyes held steady, though they grew guarded and he considered her for an age before finally answering. 'Past experience.' But then they flicked away and when they returned they'd gone back to carefully neutral. 'You can send photos every birthday. Which is more than we got from Drew.'

She hissed out a controlled breath. 'Okay, enough with the surly hinting. If there's something you want to say about—'

Her words were interrupted by the shrill call of his mobile

phone. He flipped it open without apology. 'Hey.' He took a
deep breath and listened. 'Yep. We'll be there shortly.' Whoever
was on the other end asked a question. He lifted his eyes and
looked at Bel. 'Yes, "we". I'll explain when I see you. Can
you check that the guest room is clear of Dad's fishing stuff?
Thanks, Mum.' Another pause. 'Love you.'

He muttered that last one on a half-turn away from her.
So the man loved his mother. No big news there—look at the
lengths he was going to protect her from further hurt. But that
didn't make him a saint. Unless the definition had changed
considerably.

'So do we have an agreement?' His eyes were uncompromising again.

'Agreement implies there was a negotiation. So far all you've
done is outline all the lies I'm expected to tell.'

'I've already agreed to your terms.'

'What terms?'

'I won't be touching you. On pain of dismemberment.'

'That was to get me to come here, not to lie shockingly to
the people putting me up. Besides, you've just finished telling me how much you loathe the Rochesters. I'm not feeling
at particular risk of sudden and erupting passion on your part.
The no-touching rule is nowhere near a decent trade.'

'What do you want, then?'

She considered him.

One year. That was what he was asking. Less if the court
case was settled quickly or the babies didn't take. Not a lifetime. Not forever. This was the gap year down under she'd
never had. With free room and board. Far from all the friends
and family who would take issue with what she'd decided to do
about Gwen and Drew's embryos. Ironically, he was offering
her a haven until the damage—as her parents would undoubt-
edly see it—was well and truly done. When she flew home it
would be with living human beings in tow, the most done of
done-deals. Non-commutable.

Or she could fly home with no one if things didn't go her way. More alone than ever.

She had her posse of lawyers working hard for her back in the UK—there was nothing she needed to do that they couldn't ask her via email. Her job was to get these two little beings past the first trimester successfully. And she could do that anywhere—might as well be on a commune in the Australian alps. Regardless of how many strings were attached.

She settled more comfortably in her seat. A total act. 'As soon as I work out what I want I'll let you know. For now, you'll just have to owe me one.'

He laughed, but it wasn't happy. 'Why would I agree to something that unspecified?'

'Because you have more to lose than me. I don't know your family. Hurting them wouldn't really hurt me at all.'

Brutal, but true.

He stared at her, knowing when he was snookered. 'I can see why you and my brother got on so well.' He leaned in closer and nailed her with steely eyes. 'When you come calling for that favour, Belinda, make it count. It's the only one you're going to get.'

No doubt. Flynn might have the same inherent personal charisma as his brother but it was nowhere like Drew's charming, comfortable likeableness. He had this whole intense, surly, younger brother thing going on. It would be interesting to discover which of them was the black sheep. For her own sake, and the sake of the babies she hoped were taking root deep inside her, Bel really hoped it was Flynn—that *comfortable* and *likeable* were dominant Bradley traits. If she was putting herself—and her sister's children—into the hands of people more like her own parents, then everything she'd fought for had no purpose.

The babies would have been better off going to strangers.

She sat up straight in her chair and pushed the half-drunk tea to one side. 'Fine. I'll play Belinda Cluney-with-a-u, frequenter of horse races and forgetter of birth control. Long enough for us to determine whether there's any need to continue this farce.' Then she lowered her voice. 'But don't for one moment think I don't realise that this handy string of lies you want me to spout also conveniently gets you out of confessing your ugly part in this charade. The court case, the threats, the blackmail. How wounded would your family be if I told them that?'

His stormy eyes clouded over as he pushed his chair back and stood. 'I'm sure they'd expect nothing less of me. Don't imagine you've got valuable ammunition there.'

I'm sure they'd expect nothing less.

That flash of pain suggested maybe everything wasn't quite as happy-family as she'd imagined over at the Bradley homestead. And while she should have been worrying about what she was walking into, for no good reason it actually made her feel fractionally better to know she wasn't the only outcast in the world.

And that she wouldn't be the only one working hard to fit in.

Fractionally enough that when Flynn slowed to let her exit the café ahead of him she didn't flinch at his warm hand low on her back as they stepped back out into the fresh, vital air.

CHAPTER FOUR

IT WAS still awkward four hours later as the entire Bradley family sat down for their evening meal and Bel slid into the empty place next to Flynn's grandmother, Alice. Given they were a family of five and this tree-slab table had been built for six, Bel knew exactly whose spot she was in. Sitting in what must have been Drew's seat gave her a welcome and surprising shot of comfort. Almost as if he was behind her, hands on her shoulders, backing her up silently.

'Well, isn't this nice?' Denise Bradley said on a bright smile by way of breaking the awkward silence that had descended. 'Belinda, what time does your body think it is right now?'

She glanced at the clock over the kitchen bench and did a quick burst of mental arithmetic and answered Flynn's mother. 'Actually, it's not too bad—at home it would be just before lunch. So eating now feels quite normal.'

Flynn reached over from across the long table and helped himself to a healthy serving of everything, as did everyone else, but Bel held back. It would be tempting to blame the babies for her lack of appetite, but it was more related to her level of unease at being so far from her comfort zone—and the rapidly amassing pile of manure she was feeding these people. They'd welcomed her as though she was a long-anticipated and greatly-looked-forward-to guest, not a last minute, unheralded blow-in.

Lying to their faces *in fact* was much harder than lying to them *in theory*.

'Do you come from a large family, dear?' This from the older woman next to her.

'Uh…no, just me and my—' At the last second she realised she had no idea whether she was supposed to manufacture an entire family dynamic or not. She coughed to cover the verbal stumble and took a sip of water to buy herself some thinking time. But in that stolen moment she knew that Flynn could do all he wanted to pretend his brother didn't exist but she wasn't about to deny her sister. 'There's just two of us girls and my parents.'

In truth it had often just been the two girls while their parents had either been at some social soirée or out dining with the moneyed set.

She glanced up at Flynn, at the white grip of his knuckles as he spooned a large helping of mashed potato onto his plate, and realised how unhappy he was that they'd already stumbled into such dangerous territory.

Not that he was doing anything to help matters.

'So tell me about the name of your property, Bill,' she said, turning quickly to Flynn's father. 'Does it mean something?'

'The Bunyip is one of Australia's most legendary mythical beasts—' Bill Bradley started in his deep Aussie accent and she could tell immediately that he was the story-teller in the family. Out of nowhere she had an image of him with a pair of small boys on his knees, making up wild stories about Bunyips and bush rangers.

'What a load of rot,' Flynn's grandfather cut in, obviously a regular occurrence judging by the way no one reacted. 'It's for the tourists.'

'You're a tourist operation?'

'We have chalets over the far side of the ridge,' Bill continued. 'Trout fishing. Mountain hikes. Wildlife tours. That sort of thing.'

She lifted her eyebrows and looked sweetly at Flynn. 'Chalets. Really?'

Oh, he was a dead man. She was enduring the ice-breaker from hell when she could be curling up in front of a fireplace and watching a movie in peace and quiet across the ridge.

'They're all full this time of year,' Flynn threw in quickly by way of covering his butt.

The whole table suddenly seemed to pick up on the tension between the two of them. She rushed in to move things on while he still did nothing to intervene. 'Well, that explains the wonderful hospitality. Thank you, you've made me feel very welcome.'

'You *are* welcome, Belinda. Just unexpected.' Denise turned a pointed look to her son, who only dug in harder to the meal on his plate.

She jumped in again rather than have more awkwardness. 'Please, call me Bel. Everyone does.'

'Flynn doesn't.'

Bel swivelled around to look at Alice, who continued, 'He calls you Belinda.'

And in that moment Bel realised who was the true matriarch of the Bradley family because, where Flynn had only rewarded his mother's subtle prods with silence, he immediately answered his grandmother's, gently and respectfully. And fraudulently.

'It's because everyone else calls her Bel that I've chosen not to.'

Alice smiled. 'I see. That's lovely. Special.'

His lips thinned. 'It's not *special*, Nan. It just is.'

Alice turned to her left. 'Do you have a nickname for Flynn, dear?'

Bel's eyes came up in the same moment Flynn's did.

The opportunity for revenge—albeit petty, albeit passive aggressive, albeit intensely juvenile—was way too good to pass up. She took a carefully staged sip of water and then said brightly, 'Well, I started out calling him the Thunder from Down Under—' Flynn practically choked on his peas '—but he didn't seem to like that. So then we worked our way through Flynn-the-Maudlin, Errol, and finally I settled on Hunky-buns.'

A stunned silence filled the room. Then, like a shared consciousness, two generations of Bradleys burst into inappropriately loud laughter. Tiny flecks of potato launched into the atmosphere from the direction of Bill Bradley and Denise slapped her husband hard on the arm with one hand while her other hand covered her mouth to prevent her from doing exactly the same thing.

It was disgusting.

It was wonderful.

Bel couldn't remember laughter at her own dining-room table growing up. Only her sister's barely suppressed giggles when they'd been sent to their rooms for not behaving. And if someone made any kind of mess, a maid spirited out of somewhere and cleaned it discreetly up.

She sat back in Drew's seat and grinned at Flynn—utterly triumphant.

He was the only one at the table not smiling.

But when he spoke it was deep and measured, and still obscenely sexy. He met her eyes head-on and it caused a wave of flutters in her belly.

'You aren't eating, Belinda.'

Exactly as he intended, that immediately switched the focus back to her as both older women launched straight into mother-mode, plying her with spoonfuls of vegetables and slices of roast lamb and oversized chunks of home-baked bread. She protested in vain that she wasn't hungry and, as her plate grew and she swung her eyes around the table from Alice at her right to Denise across the table, she caught the first glimpse of a smile from Flynn since they'd left England.

Tiny.

Barely deserving the name.

But most definitely there.

So that was how he wanted to play this? Fine. She let all the defiance and competitiveness she'd had nagged out of her as a child have its head. The little burst of adrenalin that came from besting someone gave her a much needed energy spike.

Game on, Hunky-buns.

'Excuse me,' Flynn said, pushing back his chair and standing. He'd barely lowered his fork after cleaning his plate of its contents, but he couldn't risk Bel finishing first, possibly coming with him. He needed space and he needed it fast. 'I'm just going to go and check on the platypus.'

He strode straight out of the kitchen with the slightest of touches for his mother as he passed.

'Did he say platypus?' he heard Belinda ask in her uptight British accent as he left the room.

'It's an animal, dear,' his nan said. 'Have you not heard of it?'

He crossed through the kitchen, heading for the nearest outside door.

'I have,' she said, 'but I thought it was like your Bunyip—mythological.'

His traitorous family laughed and his father answered. 'No, the platypus is very real. Although just as strange…'

He let the kitchen door slam shut behind him, locking in all the mirth and Belinda's rounded vowels, which mocked him without even trying. She sounded just like her sister. How could none of them pick it up?

He'd expected them to cool towards her the moment she'd opened her mouth. But they were practically gushing over her. She had them totally snowed, even acting all coarse to get them more on side and laughing loudly at Pop's lame jokes. A thousand miles from her sister's permanent aloof smile the single time she'd visited.

When his father had sprayed the table with half-chewed food

his heart had practically shrivelled into a tight, mortified fist. Then he'd wanted to slap himself senseless for giving a toss. This was Oberon, Australia. Country home, country rules. If she didn't like it, too bad.

Except that she wasn't showing any signs of not liking it. On the contrary. She seemed every bit as taken with them as they were with her. And despite her obvious nerves she was sliding pretty easily into his family.

Which absolutely could not be real.

He marched resolutely down a well-worn track towards the string of trees lining a stream that branched across his parents' lower paddock, memory guiding his way, the sliver of moon helping little.

Belinda Rochester had no place in his family. It half killed him to watch her sit in Drew's chair, knowing how they'd lost him to the Rochesters long before they'd lost him from life. Never mind that he had triggered Drew's long journey away from them himself, the Rochesters had consumed him, just like they consumed cars and flash houses and copious amounts of liquor at their society bashes. A man like Drew was a waiting meal for people like that. If he wasn't he never would have stayed away so long. Moved away.

Drifted away.

He'd fawned over Belinda's petite sister that time they'd come to visit, not long after their surprise wedding on holiday in Corfu, after they'd robbed his mother of her opportunity to see her oldest boy—her favourite—get married. She'd hidden her heartbreak well but ten minutes in the company of Gwen Rochester and things were already strained. His brother said the quickie wedding was to keep things simple but Flynn had his suspicions—like his parents did—that Drew had been keen to avoid bringing the two sides of the family together. As if they couldn't possibly mesh.

Yet here was a Rochester doing a bang-up job of ingratiating herself in the Bradley camp. How ironic.

Flynn slowed his steps thirty metres from the stream and gentled his breathing. Their sensitive bills wouldn't miss the surge of electromagnetism that was him approaching, but platypus were touchy at the best of times, they really didn't need him worked up and pumping out sparks like a neon sign.

And they brought him such peace, which he could use a whole heap of right now.

He sagged down onto the bank and closed his eyes, letting the silence resolve itself into the burbling stream, his steady breathing and the occasional shriek of a foraging bat overhead.

Lying because it was necessary was one thing. Turning it into a sport was quite another. And glittering with such glee… Well, that was altogether not on.

He'd never seen someone come alive like she had. The Belinda he knew was silent and pale and dead-eyed, in the hospital then a week later on the plane. To see her now with her hair freshly washed and flaming out behind her, touches of freshly applied colour on her lashes and lips, eyes sparkling and smile beaming…He'd been shocked at his own physical response at the dinner table when she'd teased him with alleged nicknames, stirred by the blatant challenge in her deep blue eyes. The snapping jaws of attraction came out of nowhere until he wrestled them to heel—made himself remember who she was—hence his haste in getting the hell out of the cosy family moment back in the dining room.

As if his family needed any more encouragement to meddle.

What moon there was showed itself from behind a shifting bank of cloud and illuminated the stream a little more. Enough that Flynn was able to make out the small sleek creature wiggling its way through the shallows upstream. This platypus and its mate nested just off the property but they foraged nightly within the rich pickings of Bunyip Reach's streams. Because they ran ever-hungry trout in the Reach's bigger waterways it meant the smaller ones were extra abundant with small fish, worms, glassy six-legged wrigglers, and all manner of aquatic or mud-loving bugs. A platypus smorgasbord.

Which was good, because there were precious few places left in this country where the little brown fellows could eke out a decent existence.

'Hey.'

The animal shot away faster than something with legs that short should be able to as Belinda appeared out of nowhere, waggling a large torch to light her way. So much for peace and quiet.

'Your grandmother suggested I come down. See the platypus.'

Of course she did.

His nan had been beside herself when she realised the woman he'd appeared with wasn't a lost tourist or an opportunistic chalet booking. She had a terrible poker face and her wide-eyed nonchalance was fooling no-one. Except possibly Belinda. She'd been pushing him for years to find a nice girl and settle down. And, because they didn't know otherwise, Nan would be working on a plan right now to make sure he settled down with Belinda. The girl who laughed at Arthur Bradley's corny, decades-old jokes would get a big fat tick in the *perfect granddaughter-in-law* box. Even on five minutes' acquaintance.

Until she learned the truth, anyway. His conscience muttered, but he shoved it down deep the way he'd learned years before. It could complain all it wanted down there; he'd never hear it.

'I think they just want to give us some alone time,' Bel said.

'No doubt.'

Silence descended.

After a few moments Bel said, 'I was thinking that maybe we should create our own alone time. That way we can control it, rather than having it thrust upon us.'

An annoyingly good idea. He didn't want her to be sensible

and quick to see things. He wanted her to be thoughtless and reactive and stupid. And he sure as heck didn't want to spend much time alone with her.

'You can come down to my place. Hang out down there when I'm out working. They'll assume we're together.'

'Is there not something I can do—to be helpful?'

'You can stay out of the way. That's helpful.'

She took it on the chin, flicking her eyes out to the still-empty waterway before bringing them, carefully schooled, back to him. 'I'm going to get bored with nothing to do. And when I'm bored I get restless. And when I'm restless I get annoying.'

She smiled brightly. The threat was implied. He could so imagine a 'restless' Belinda. And 'annoying' he'd already seen. It killed him that he wanted to echo her smile, but he managed to keep his face neutral. 'I would have thought doing nothing would be a Rochester specialty.'

Her eyes narrowed and hardened, even in the dim gloom as the clouds moved back over the moon. But she didn't bite. 'Why? Didn't Gwen help out when she was here?'

'Nope. And she kept Drew busy so he wasn't much use either.'

She frowned. 'It's not surprising. They were practically on their honeymoon.'

'So are we. Technically.'

'Ha ha. There must be something I can help with. I don't like to freeload.'

'You don't have a job.'

'Because I don't need one to live on. That doesn't mean I don't make a contribution. Or want to.'

'Helping out on a farm isn't the same as knitting quilt-squares for Africa or...' he searched his limited knowledge of what rich people did to pass the time '...hosting fund-raisers.'

She looked at him as if he were mad. Which he must be

to have started all of this in the first place. 'Lucky. Because I can't knit and I loathe crowds.'

He sighed. 'Have a word with Nan. She's always got something happening. I'm sure she'd be delighted to have more opportunities to grill you on the finer details of our acquaintance.'

'Oh. Well, that's not a good idea, is it?'

He shrugged. 'You seemed to enjoy it tonight.'

She stared at him. 'You deserved tonight. Leaving me to swing in the breeze like you did. If I didn't know any better, I'd say you want me to fail abysmally.'

She shot straight. Just like Drew. But it didn't appeal to him any more now than when Golden Boy used to do it when they were kids. 'I don't want you to fail. But I don't want any games either.'

She considered him. 'Then don't make it such fun. Honestly, sitting there looking like a giant black thundercloud. How are they going to buy for a moment that you care enough about me to marry me when all you do is glare?'

Something occurred to him. 'You seem very comfortable with putting on an act. Almost a natural at it.'

She shrugged. 'Practice makes perfect.'

'What does that mean?'

She glanced at her hands while she composed her thoughts. 'My family was in the veneer business. The glossier and happier the better. How many glossy, happy teenagers do you know? I learned early how to create it on demand.'

Didn't she think this moment demanded it? The poorly hidden sorrow on her face hit him low in his chest. He knew all about faking it. He'd been doing it for years. 'Your sister, too?'

She frowned. 'Gwen was different. She fitted the mould better. She didn't need to try so hard.'

Was she finally admitting Gwen really was the society heiress they'd met? 'I'm surprised you two got along, if you were that different,' he said. Although the jury was still out on how different they truly were. Belinda still had debutante written all over her, regardless of how many fights with Mummy and Daddy she'd had.

'It was Gwen or no one. But she was easy to love. I think that was why Drew and I got on so well together. We had that in common.'

Easy for them, maybe. 'And now?'

She stared into the tumbling stream. Then glanced down at her belly. 'And now I have the next generation of Rochesters to worry about. If I can bring them up to be the same sort of people as their parents then I'll be really happy with that.'

Assuming she got to bring them up at all. Which was a big call now she had some competition. 'In their image, not in your own?'

She lifted her head. 'Never in my image. That's not what this is about.'

He turned more fully towards her. 'What is it about, Belinda? Why are you doing this?'

'Because they have a right to stay in the family. To stay together. They're Rochesters.'

'And Bradleys.'

Her face creased. 'Yes. But until a week ago I had no idea what that meant. As far as we knew, Drew was estranged from his family.'

Flynn shifted uncomfortably. He pressed his lips together.

'What happened with you guys?' she risked. 'Why would he just…opt out?'

'Because of your sister.' The answer came way too easily. Way too loaded. He flexed his clenched fingers.

'But she met him in London. He'd already left here.'

Left you. She might as well have said it. 'There's not a lot of calling for merchant bankers in Oberon.'

'Sydney's not that far away. Why go to the other side of the planet?'

'Spirit of adventure?'

'Maybe. But there had to be more to it. Gwen was a wonderful person but she wasn't the sort of girl you give up a kingdom for.'

'Kingdom?'

She looked around her. At the green, rolling fields. The tumbling brook. 'All of this. Your family.'

Was that what she equated a loving family with? Riches? He battled the hint of softening deep inside. 'Maybe you didn't see her the way others did?'

'I looked at your family tonight and I couldn't imagine them not accepting her. What did she do that was so awful?'

'She took him from us.'

'Everyone grows up. Leaves home.'

'Not everyone wipes their family from existence. As soon as he entered your family he exited mine. It was like we barely existed. His trip home with your sister was like a farewell tour.'

Her brows folded down over eyes that wanted to understand. 'And you blame Gwen?'

'We blame all of you. The lifestyle that your family offered. The connections you represented. The money. Everything our family couldn't offer.'

She frowned again. 'But look at what your family does offer, Flynn. I've never had a meal like it.'

The image of his father's god-awful food spray filled his vision. He hoped she wasn't actually expecting him to buy that she'd enjoyed it. 'I'll bet.'

'It would have been foreign to Gwen, but I can't imagine her not embracing it. They're good people.'

What could he say to that? They absolutely were. Which was why what Drew did stank so much.

'That makes it even harder to do what you've asked me,' she went on. 'Can we not change our approach? Tell them? Your mother has heaps of support. She'll get through.'

'You weren't here. You didn't see what she was like. How low she sank. Drew was the light of her life.'.

Yet he'd still rejected her and the whole family in favour of his own life.

Both their heads snapped around as two platypus emerged onto the rocks a few metres from where they sat quietly talking.

'Oh, my goodness...' Belinda managed to scream in whisper. That took some talent. 'Look at them! They're amazing...' She scrunched forward and wrapped her arms around her knees, as if making herself smaller would make them larger.

'It's like someone swept up all the bits left over from nature's workshop floor and said, *Waste not, want not...*' she said, laughing.

Duck's bill, beaver's tail, otter's body, cat's paws, living in the water but laying eggs like a bird. 'Yeah, Frankenstein's pet.'

'Oh, I'm definitely going to send a photo home. The centre will want to see this.'

He dragged his eyes off the stream entertainment. 'Centre?'

She wasn't shifting her focus for anything and her wide-eyed wonder made her look more like she had on that hospital table. Young. Naïve. Hopelessly out of her depth.

'I work for SOS Hedgehog. Helping out.'

'You're kidding!' She was a volunteer? And a wildlife volunteer, at that. Possibly the last thing he'd expected to discover. No, correction, *exactly* the last thing he'd expected. 'Why hedgehogs?'

It pained her to drag her eyes away from the animals in front of her, but she did—briefly. 'Why not hedgehogs? They're as special as any other creature. We rehabilitate nearly six thousand a year. I was worried about leaving them, about missing them, but...' her smile broadened as she turned her face back to the stream '...I think I'm going to be just fine. These guys are going to be very good hedgehog substitutes.'

He stared at her beaming smile. What kind of a life did she have back in England—she'd left her city and family and friends and the only things she was going to miss were a few hedgehogs?

It was hard enough reconciling her physical appearance with being a Rochester—Belinda's Amazonian redhead to Gwen's diminutive blonde—but then to discover she'd give up her youth and her body to save two unborn children, and that her family background wasn't everything the Internet had led him to believe, and that instead of being a latte-drinking, trust fund debutante she gave up most of her week to help wipe hedgehog backsides...

'You're nothing like your sister, you know.'

That brought her attention back around. 'Screw you, too.'

His breath caught. 'You're as touchy as her, though. I meant that as a compliment.'

Dark eyes held his. 'I spent most of my childhood trying to be more like her. Failing abysmally. Being unlike her is *not* a compliment.'

'Depends on your perspective.'

Almost as though they sensed the growing tension on the bank and wanted to ease it, the two platypus increased their activity to fever pitch in his peripheral vision, splashing and wriggling in the shallows as they foraged, racing each other and galloping across the fallen stones as fast as those little swimming legs could take them. But if they'd tap danced across the log bridge it wouldn't have drawn his attention away from her.

Her eyes blazed. 'You're nothing like Drew, either.'

The man who blew off his family? 'Thank you.'

She shook her head. 'It's like we knew different people. My Drew and Gwen were wonderful, happy, talented people who were excited about starting a family. Yours were thoughtless, narcissistic miseries. How can they both have existed?'

The million-dollar question. 'Maybe it depends where you're starting from on the perspective continuum.'

Her whole body stiffened and she stood slowly, one eye on

the flighty platypus. 'You assume a lot, Flynn.' She looked down on him. 'Yet you really know nothing about me.'

That was true enough. All he knew was how much he obviously didn't know. Because a very bright mind ticked away behind those cornflower-blue eyes, too. A bright and captivating mind.

He pushed that thought away.

Roughly.

'Change of plan. Go and see Pop about helping out if you're so determined not to freeload.' *Like your sister.* 'Tell him about your hedgehogs. See what he can find for you to do for a few hours a day.'

His grandfather would definitely be able to use some help with the rescue animals if she had rehab experience.

She switched on her torch and kept it low, away from the stream. 'Thank you.'

'Might as well get as much exposure to Australia's wildlife as you can. This could all be over in a week.'

If she wasn't pregnant, she wasn't staying.

Then again, if she wasn't pregnant all she'd have would be these memories. And so far they hadn't stacked up to much.

Belinda nodded, took one long last look at the frolicking platypus and then turned for the house, her face drawn, leaving Flynn with all the peace and quiet he could ask for.

CHAPTER FIVE

SHE was pregnant. And she did stay.

Bel found herself slipping comfortably into Bunyip Reach's daily routine. Into the Bradley family. She let the 'guest' stuff go on for three days before gently starting to earn her way. She did her own laundry. Helped in the kitchen. Cleaned things as needed. And not just because it was such a novelty actually fitting in somewhere. She was happy to have busy hands because it stopped her mind from getting busy—thinking, worrying, wondering—as the deadline for her first assessment drew closer.

But then the two week test results had come in and, though a positive result was everything she'd wished for, there'd been little enough reason to celebrate. The embryos holding just meant that she and Flynn had to ramp up the legal fight for the little lives incubating deep inside her.

And had to kick into a whole new level of deception.

Her lawyers knew where she was and pumped her relentlessly for information they could use to weaken Flynn's case. But all she could tell them was how idyllic this place would be for a child, how loved one would be, how cherished. They soon stopped asking.

At the back of her mind, she knew Flynn's counsel would be doing the same. That every conversation she had might feed their case. He knew she was isolated, unemployed, had an unhappy childhood. She was sure he wouldn't be telling them about her conservation volunteering, or the fact she owned her own home outright. Even if it was small and grannyish.

She knew all of that, but found herself telling him things anyway. There had to be *someone* here that she wasn't lying to. Besides, she'd laid her situation open for all to see during the first legal petition—more or less—so there were few secrets left for anyone who cared to look.

In the afternoons she hung out with Flynn's grandfather and his terrible sense of humour and learned from a man who'd been working with Australian wildlife for the best part of six decades. He wasn't as perceptive as his wife—or if he was he didn't act on it—and for those few hours of the day it was possible for Bel to just be herself. Enjoy the animals. Enjoy the Australian outdoors.

Not that being someone else wasn't strangely liberating. How long had she wished she could become someone else? Fit better.

When she'd left home a few months ahead of her eighteenth birthday her parents had clearly received the signals she'd been sending and only engaged with her when she contacted them, which wasn't often. Bel considered they were just happy to be free of the problem child in the family, possibly congratulating themselves on how it had all worked out. Though they'd winced when Gwen had followed not long after. But Bel had what, ultimately, she'd wanted.

Her own life.

Away from the compulsory university studies they'd had lined up for her. Away from the damning self-talk they somehow birthed in her. Away from their parties and the drinking and the substances and apparently empty friendships.

Thank God her parents had found each other because who else would have had them? Even in the ridiculously moneyed set.

'Can you bring a sack over, Bel?' Arthur called from across the little fenced yard where the wallaby joeys lived. Each one had a sheepskin sewed up the side, turned inside out and folded into a proxy pouch where they spent the many hours when they weren't being hand fed, toileted or weighed. There were only three in residence—a good year on the roads according to Arthur—but there was room for a dozen more.

Her chest squeezed as Arthur withdrew the smallest of the three from its fake pouch and lowered it carefully into the sack she gave him. It was so young its fur was only just starting to come through and so it was all joints and gangly limbs and veins through translucent skin. Arthur hung the whole sack on an old-fashioned butcher's scales to weigh it. The needle barely travelled before swinging to a stop.

Poor little mite.

Had she always been this clucky? Or was it only since coming to Australia? Since being implanted? It was still such a surreal concept that at least one life was busy growing away deep inside her. In its own liquid pouch. She couldn't begin to imagine how her body would…adapt…for getting it out again and mostly she tried not to think about it, but since women had been doing it for millennia she had to assume that it *could* happen.

The wallabies had the right idea, born the size of a rice-grain and all their growing done externally.

That sounded infinitely more sensible.

'Good growth,' Arthur mumbled happily as he moved the tiny creature back into its usual abode.

Bel pottered around after Arthur, watching what he did and learning what to do herself. The road injured echidnas were similar enough to her hedgehogs to make her feel all warm and fuzzy towards them but different enough to have her shaking her head and smiling. It was a wonderful way to pass every afternoon and, as soon as she was past the vulnerable first trimester and she knew she'd be staying, she'd offer to help him with some of the rest of his jobs. The midnight feeds, the intensive care. The harder tasks.

It would be good training for nine months from now.

She bent to tip out the dregs of water from a ceramic bowl
for a refill and as she stood a wave of weakness washed over
her and she stumbled into the fence and grabbed it for stabil-
ity, letting the bowl slip from her fingers back down to the
rich earth. Its thud drew Arthur's eye to her before she could
straighten and compose herself and he was by her side in a
moment.

'Belinda…' His hands went under her elbows and took her
weight.

'Wow…' His strength freed her hands up to rub over her
face and eyes, scrubbing away the dizziness.

'Are you okay?'

'I'm…' She couldn't say what she was. 'Maybe it's the
Australian heat finally getting to me.' And maybe morning
sickness didn't have to be in the morning. 'I'll be fine in a moment, Arthur. Please don't worry.'

'I'll call Flynn.'

'No!'

The joeys lurched in their pouches at the vehemence in her
tone. Flynn's keen-eyed scrutiny was the last thing she needed.
He was constantly on the watch for any sign that things weren't
going well. He'd probably start looking up flights for the UK.
One way.

'He'll only tell me to stop helping you. And it's not necessary, I'm feeling better already. See?' She stood on her own
and only wobbled a little bit, quite proud of that.

'Well, at least go in to Alice, then. Make yourself a cool
drink and sit for a bit.'

Oh, heaven. 'Yes. I'll do that. Thank you, Arthur.'

She wobbled her way inside and waited until she was much
more recovered before emerging into the kitchen where Flynn's
nan was pickling onions. Within a heartbeat she went from
dizzy and nauseous to fixated on what Alice was doing.

She'd *kill* for a decent pickled onion.

Oh, Lord, was she going to be one of those pregnant women—licking blackboards and scarfing daisies when no one was looking? The thought brought a smile to her face just as Alice looked up.

'You look peaky. Sit down and I'll get you a drink.'

'I can get it, Alice.'

'Of course you can, but I'm right by the fridge. Just set yourself down.'

She did, and closed her eyes for a moment and when she re-opened them Alice placed chilled water with a twist of lemon in front of her and a plate with a selection of home-jarred goodies on it. A blob of chutney, some dried strip meat, cheese and a strange dark sphere. She leaned closer and examined it.

'It's a pickled egg. Bill makes them.'

Bel picked it up and studied the awful looking thing as closely as Alice was watching her. 'Why?'

'Everyone has different tastes,' she chuckled. 'He loves them.'

And then, for no good reason, Bel suddenly had the impulse to experience this new cuisine. Whole. She shoved the entire shelled egg into her mouth and her eyes drifted shut.

Heaven.

'Did you know I was a midwife when I was younger, Bel?' Alice mentioned casually after a moment.

Speaking around an entire boiled egg wasn't easy and so Bel didn't have a prayer of being able to respond. She just lifted both her eyebrows with polite enquiry and kept chewing, her hand discreetly in front of her mouth.

'Growing up out here, lots of women had to learn the essentials of childbirth,' she continued easily. She nodded to the jar of blackened eggs in the larder. 'Those were popular amongst the pregnant ladies. Anything pickled, really.'

Bel froze, but then realised how suspicious that would look and so kept chewing slowly, doing her best to appear normal.

Finally she swallowed it down. 'Interesting flavour,' she said, super-casually. 'Not what I was expecting.'

'Would you like another?' Those sharp eyes missed nothing.

Yes. Desperately. 'No, thank you. We'll call that an experiment satisfactorily undertaken.' She gulped at her water.

'Arthur shouldn't push you so hard. You're still getting used to farm life. You look worn out.'

Ah, that will be the sleepless nights wondering how I can get out of all of this. Wondering what I will do if I leave here without Gwen's babies. But as long as they were talking about Arthur, they weren't talking about midwifery and pickled eggs.

'It's not his fault. The heat just takes me by surprise. I can't work out how it can be so warm and so cool only a few hours apart. I love it out there with Arthur. The joeys are doing so well…'

Bel effectively steered the conversation onto matters less contentious as she gnawed on the dried meat strip and sipped her water. The chewy protein wasn't her first since arriving and it was fast becoming a favourite. Alice chatted about what she was preserving this week and cleaned up after the last of her onions.

'All done?' the older woman asked when Bel brought the half-empty plate to the kitchen island.

'Yes. I don't want to spoil dinner.'

Alice glanced at the remaining contents as she scraped them into the scraps bin. For no good reason Bel was reminded of the wacky tea leaf reading woman at her local tea-house back home.

'I…um…might just go and find Flynn. Thank you for the break and the snacks. I feel much recovered.'

Alice smiled. 'Good. Remind that boy he's eating with us tonight. He's worked through enough dinners lately.'

'I will. Thank you, Alice.'

It was hard not to demurely respond when Alice turned her

full matriarchal powers onto her. She reminded Bel so much of her own missed grandmother. The one adult she'd really adored as a child.

She quietly left the kitchen and went in search of Flynn.

He'd been on and off with her for the past three weeks, in her face one minute and then keeping a healthy distance the next. For a man who was fighting so hard for the little lives inside her he really didn't seem that happy when the pregnancy confirmation came in. About the only time she enjoyed being around him was when they sat together on the bank of the stream and watched the platypus. He taught her all about their biology, about their behaviours, the threats they faced. The very specialist conditions they needed to thrive.

He was particularly resistant to any discussion about Drew and Gwen. As if he'd simply decided they were no longer worthy of his mind space. Of course this only drove her to discuss them more and, short of walking away, there was not a lot he could do to stop her speaking her mind.

But she'd grown weary of even that game the few times they were alone together and she found herself wanting to get to know more about him *from him*. Flynn the man, not Flynn the brother or son.

But first things first.

'I think your grandmother is onto us,' she said the moment she walked in his back door, puffing from the hike across the gully.

CHAPTER SIX

FLYNN looked up from his paperwork. 'What did you do?'

Bel skidded to a halt, outraged that he could have such accusation in his tone when he'd done little enough to dissuade
any of them that things weren't odd between them. 'Nothing.
But she was asking questions today, and talking about deliv-
ering babies.'

He let his focus fall back to his papers. 'She was a midwife.
She's bound to talk about it at some point.'

'It was in the way she looked at me. Like the pickled egg
was some kind of sign—'

His head snapped up. 'What pickled egg?'

'The one I tried at afternoon tea. I had a little…rest…'

He got to his feet. 'Why did you eat it?'

Her brows closed in on each other. 'Because she served it
to me on a plate. I didn't want to be rude. And besides, I felt
like an egg. What's the big deal?'

'My mother hates those eggs.'

'Understandable. They're not the prettiest to look at.' *Or to
swallow.*

'But she went crazy for them when she was pregnant with
Drew.'

Oh. 'Truly?'

'Don't eat them again.'

The seriousness of his tone infected her. 'I won't.'

But would she? She'd not meant to eat the first one, just examine it. The next thing she knew, it was in her mouth.

'You're expected for dinner tonight,' she said, changing subject rapidly.

'I'm busy—'

'No. You're not leaving me for another dinner with your own family. It's been three weeks since I sat across the table from you. *How* are they going to believe we're a couple if you treat me like I have some foul disease?'

'They know me.'

'What's that supposed to mean?'

His eyes bored into hers. 'I mean it won't surprise them at all that I've gone AWOL. I've been doing it my whole life.'

She blinked at him, unsure which was more surprising—that her need to learn more about him was being unexpectedly addressed or that he'd volunteered something personal. Flynn. Mr Uncommunicative. 'Really? Even while you're home?'

'Just because we share property doesn't mean we have to share every waking moment. I love my family but there are limits.'

Not for me. These days and nights of unconditional acceptance were some of the best days of her life. Which was a bit sad, really. Not that *unconditional* necessarily meant totally without complications. There was clearly a lot that different members of the Bradley clan were wanting to ask but they were—for the most part—restraining themselves. But how many nights of Flynn being a no-show would they tolerate?

'The longer you leave me with them, the harder it's going to be to not get into difficult territory.' She bent a little to catch his eyes when he tried to avoid her gaze. 'They're going to start asking questions I'm not equipped to answer. It's not normal that a *couple*—' she put that in finger quotes for good measure '—would spend this much time apart.'

The moment she found his eyes, he held them. She almost

regretted searching them out. 'Fine,' he growled. 'You eat with me from now on.'

Her stomach dropped. 'Here?'

'That should buy us some time.'

Time until they had definitive proof that one of the embryos had stuck well-and-truly and formed a tiny Rochester— she glanced back at him—Rochester-*Bradley*. Because until that was the case then he wasn't telling his family anything about their supposed wedding plans. And, by rights, a chance to spend some time away from the need to lie continuously to them should have been a blessing.

But still she hedged. 'What if they want to see you at dinner?'

'They see me during the day. I'm sure they'll survive.'

'But I'm expected.'

He shrugged. 'Then go. You were the one concerned about their questions.'

Frustration hissed out of her. 'It's not very fair that you've left me to deal with all of this. You've just…opted out of the whole thing.'

'Again. They're used to it.'

'But I'm not. I'm feeling the pressure. What if I say something wrong?'

'Then have dinner here tonight. With me.'

Dinner with Flynn, alone here in his house. The earthy, masculine decor suited him down to the ground and here he was very clearly the lord of his domain. The whole place even smelled like him, that distinctive *eau de Flynn* that tripped her pulse in ways it really shouldn't.

Coming down here during the mornings and pretending to spend time with him was one thing. Sitting down for a whole lonely meal with the man who'd made it all too clear how he felt about her family and—by association—her…

She'd take the Bradley inquisition any day.

She straightened and turned for the door. 'I'll see you in the morning.'

He was up in a second and caught her just as she pushed the screen door open. Two opportunistic flies buzzed in through the gap. 'Belinda...'

She stopped and turned.

'Stay.'

He said it in the same low tone he used when he worked with the Reach's two golden retrievers—mild and low. As if they'd be doing him a favour rather than obeying a command. And somehow the timbre of his voice reminded her of the way he'd taken his mother's phone call back in the café on that first day they'd driven into Oberon. Gentle. Intimate.

Which was not possible. Not with her.

And, sure enough, he followed it with, 'I think you could be right. We should start limiting how much alone time you have with them. Especially Nan, if she's growing suspicious.'

The mini-pleasure of Flynn finally admitting she was right about something only lasted a nanosecond as the reality of being stuck with his dubious company struck home. But still she couldn't help the snark. 'Will you actually be here or will you go find a wombat burrow somewhere to hole up in while I eat alone?'

His thick lashes dropped for a moment, then lifted. 'I'll be here. We should talk.'

Oh.

And suddenly talking seemed so much worse than not talking. Except that she did have a few things she wanted to say. She turned for the big house. 'I'll let your mother know...'

'No, I'll do that. Make yourself comfortable.' And, with a quick snatch of his battered akubra off the hook by the entrance to protect him from the late afternoon sun, he squeezed past her in the doorway and was gone.

Comfortable. Uh-huh. Not going to happen. Not in Flynn's company.

In order of comfortableness, Arthur came first with those quiet, companionable hours with the rehab animals—no questions about the past or the future or her home—then Bill and Denise, the parents who echoed so many of Drew's traits it was impossible not to like them. Then, despite how much she reminded Bel of her own long-gone Gran, Flynn's nan, Alice, who saw too much to be truly relaxed around...

And finally Flynn, way down the bottom of the list. The man who made her angry and nervous and self-conscious...

...and breathless and acutely aware of what every part of her body was doing at any given moment. As he had just now as he'd pressed past her in the doorway, brushing his hard frame against hers.

She crossed her arms across her front and hugged them to her.

He had his brother's charisma but it was packaged differently. Drew had channelled his into an easy charm and sharp wit that made him a joy to be around. To care for. Flynn's was all about sexy, silent, understated intelligence. Not easy to be around but, boy, did she know she was alive when she was near him.

She pushed away from the door and drifted back into the small open-plan house. The back half was blue corrugated steel and charcoal window frames, standing on timber stumps a half-metre off the rich green earth. But the front half—her favourite part of the house—was floor to ceiling tinted windows all around and it jutted out on tall stilts where the ground beneath dropped away in a sharp slope.

She crossed to the corner closest to the magnificent view down the long gully of interconnecting forested spurs. If you followed the meandering trail long enough, Flynn had told her, you would stumble out into a cave network and you could be lost for ever in the famous Blue Mountains.

She was just as happy to look from a safe distance.

But what an amazing place for two young boys to grow up.

What adventures Drew and Flynn must have had. Her hand slipped to her still-flat belly. If custody went her way would she be welcome back so that Drew's child could experience some of what he must have?

When. *When* custody went her way…

'Looking for Bunyips?' Flynn's voice sounded behind her, deep and warm. Either his accent was easing off or she was acclimatising to the Aussie twang because he practically purred the next words. 'You'll have to go deeper into the bush for that.'

Wow. Had she been lost in thought all that time or had he made the fastest return trip ever up to the main homestead? No. He wouldn't be looking forward to this any more than she was.

'I was just imagining you and your brother growing up here. How idyllic it must have been.'

Flynn snorted. 'Now I *know* Drew really didn't speak about us.'

That brought her around. 'You thought I lied about that?'

He shrugged and tossed his hat with the ease of practice onto its peg. 'Nothing would surprise me.'

She let go her natural instinct to take offence at yet another unfounded prejudice from Flynn. He was speaking to her: progress number one for a man who could go days without saying more than a handful of words. And he was speaking about Drew: progress number two. She wasn't going to mess up the chance to learn more about what had happened between them. 'You two didn't play together here?'

He looked at her strangely. 'No. We're from Sydney originally. I'm surprised my folks haven't filled you in on our background.'

No. Which only brought it more to her attention. Why would the family who would talk about anything *not* talk about that?

'All of us lived there until I was fourteen and Drew was sixteen,' he said.

'Why did you move?' En masse…

His expression grew tense. 'Lots of reasons.'

Bel sank down onto one of his broad blue fabric sofas and studied him. 'Any you care to share?'

His eyes hardened. 'With you? No.'

Okay. Her lips tightened. 'My mistake. I assumed dinner would come with conversation.'

'My misspent youth isn't really an entrée.'

'What makes you think it's yours I'm interested in?'

His eyes flared and then darkened. 'Ah, Drew again. I should have known.'

'Maybe I'm curious about what shaped the man my sister married.'

True, yet only half the truth. What she really wanted to know was how did the same geological forces that shaped the valley stretching out before them create two such different brothers. One made of air and water, the other of earth and fire.

Flynn moved to the kitchen and pulled open the pantry to examine its contents.

'Drew was more of a city boy at heart,' he said, rummaging for ingredients and then setting a pot of water to fast boil.

'And you weren't?'

'I thought this wasn't about me.'

'Of course. Carry on.'

He looked a little flummoxed, as if he didn't quite know how he'd just committed himself to continuing the discussion. 'Not much to tell. He wasn't a country boy.'

'No. I can't imagine it, really. The Drew I knew only liked to get his feet dirty on the rugby field.' But she forgave him his aversion to nature for all of his other worthy qualities. His brilliant mind. His loyal heart. His fierce focus. That dogged competitiveness was something she'd admired about him, his ability to block out distractions and just go for his goals.

But maybe it had a flipside when you were one of those distractions.

Flynn snipped open a packet of ready-made gnocchi and

tipped it into the simmering pot. He turned back to her with carefully neutral eyes. Pain leaked out despite his best efforts. 'What did he tell you?'

Bel's heart squeezed. She stood and crossed to the opposite side of the kitchen island, hedging. 'About you?'

'About all of us. Where did he say he was from, if not here?'

'Sydney. The suburbs'

Flynn grunted and tossed a tin of whole tomatoes into a bowl. He punished the tomatoes with a masher. 'And he never mentioned…'

Having a brother? Bel chose her words carefully. 'Did Gwen seem surprised when she met you?'

Talking about her sister as though she was alive pulled painfully on Bel's barely healed heartstrings.

'Not particularly.'

'Then he must have told Gwen. But never me, no.'

'And never to your parents?'

What did they have to do with anything? 'Not as far as I know. Why is that?'

He wielded the large kitchen knife he used to slice up some fresh herbs a little bit *too well*. 'Search me.'

He knew exactly why—his taut body language screamed it—but he wasn't sharing. Interesting. And the fact that he was possibly more uncomfortable than she was in this conversation made him seem that bit more approachable.

It was an evening for firsts.

She didn't need to understand his sudden tension to recognise it. But she did her bit to relieve it, and made light. 'Anything I can do towards dinner?'

'Sure, want to cut up some bread and butter it? Nice and thick between the slices.'

'Your arteries may never forgive me,' she said, smiling.

'My arteries are in perfect shape.'

Her eyes took that statement to its logical conclusion and drifted to his rear end. As she dragged them back somewhere more appropriate she met his in the reflective windows at the far end of the kitchen and the breath evacuated from her lungs. Heat surged up her throat.

Busted.

She carefully regulated her choppy respiration while she sliced the bread and levered wedges of village-made butter between the thick slices, and then took extra, *extra* care not to brush against him as they worked together in the country kitchen.

'So what did you want to talk about?' she eventually asked when the silence unnerved her more than whatever it was he wanted to say to her. When he didn't immediately answer she tried again. 'You said you wanted to talk.'

Flynn turned his back on the simmering pot of pasta and crossed his arms over his chest. 'I wanted to get some more ground rules sorted. If you're going to stay.'

'You're assuming I am.'

'The embryos took, against the odds. My money is on you going full-term.'

Her whole body tightened. She hadn't really been letting herself hope, just in case. And he'd treated her as if she were either impaired or incapable since the day she'd arrived, so to hear Flynn had faith in her... Or at least in her ability to incubate...

'What if the lawyers get things sorted in record time? I could be out of here within weeks.'

'The courts never do anything fast in my experience.'

'Oh, had a lot to do with the legal system, have you?' She meant it to be flippant, but that wasn't how he took it. Again with the heavily shuttered look.

And again, *interesting.*

'We've got legal teams on two continents sifting their way through two separate judicial systems and rewriting the book on family law,' he said. 'It's not going to be quick.'

No. Probably not. Still, they were already three weeks into

the twelve she imagined she'd be staying. 'So what were you thinking?'

'I'm thinking that Nan is definitely onto us. She's way too perceptive. The look she threw me when I nicked up to the house…' He took a moment to strain the steaming gnocchi in a large colander. 'So, we may need to ramp up the appearance of us being…a couple.'

That brought her eyes around to his. 'Ramp it up how?'

'Start planting wedding bell seeds. But nothing we can't back out of if necessary.'

Suddenly the sauce's tantalising smell seemed a whole lot less aromatic. Had she really believed he'd gone off the marriage idea just because he hadn't mentioned it in a couple of weeks? Her signature on a marriage certificate was part of their deal. The one thing that equalised them in the eyes of the law. Even his lawyers thought it was a good idea. They'd be going through with it whether either of them wanted to or not.

And the answer, for both of them, was *not*.

'What exactly are you suggesting?'

'I know we had an agreement—'

'Which I suspect you're about to welch out on.'

'They're never going to buy we're a couple if we don't touch each other, Bel. But I gave you my word. So we need to talk about it, to amend our agreement. Mutually.'

I'll break any part of you that so much as touches me. It burned her even more that one part of her actually appreciated his honesty. Despite everything else going on between them, he had at least been upfront with her on most things.

'You want to start—' *Oh, my God, could this be any more awkward?* '—touching?'

'This is not just about the touching. There's things we can both do better.'

That got her blood racing. As far as she was concerned, she'd done everything he'd told her to. And more. Once started,

Belinda Rochester liked to do things well. 'Really? And how have I been lacking, in your estimation?'

'This is sport to you. You're not taking it seriously enough.' He slid a small white bowl filled to the brim with hot, plump potato and flour morsels and drizzled in Napolitana sauce across the island bench to her. Then he dumped a chunk of farm-fresh bread on top.

She didn't even look at it. Her eyes were too busy being outraged. 'This is not sport. I am not having fun. I am doing my best to honour the conditions that you set in this ridiculous plan.' She clenched both fists on the table. 'I hate lying to your family.'

He tucked into the dinner as if they were discussing the weather, not lining up a quickie wedding that would only end in a quickie divorce and heartbreak for whichever of them went home empty-handed. 'All the more reason to get a move on with appearing crazy for each other so that a sudden wedding announcement isn't going to be suspicious.'

'In the way turning up out of the blue with a strange girl and abandoning her with your family wasn't at all suspicious?'

'I have not abandoned you.'

'You know you have. Everyone has noticed, I'm just amazed no one's mentioned it openly.' Yet.

'They wouldn't intrude on my business.'

How she wished that had been the same in her upbringing. 'They're family, Flynn. That's what families do.'

'Not with me.'

Bel stared. What was that, the fourth mention about his background? 'Okay, I'll bite. How come you get away with the whole brooding Heathcliff thing? What makes you so special?'

He forked two more loads of pasta into his mouth before deigning to answer. A single shoulder shrugged. 'My family respect my privacy.'

'Rubbish. No families are respectful of each other's privacy.'

Especially not the concentrated, intimate Bradleys. 'What's really going on? Or should I ask your nan?'

He shot her a dark glare as he soaked up the last of his sauce in the thick bread. 'I imagine they'll tell you eventually, anyway.'

'Tell me what?'

He pushed back in his seat and took a moment to wipe at his mouth with the clean brown serviette. 'I got in some trouble when I was younger.'

She picked at her gnocchi and waited for him to continue.

'You don't look very surprised,' he said, offended.

'The most surly and closed-in man I've ever met has a shady past. What a shocker!'

His glare only intensified.

She scraped off half the butter from her bread. 'Drugs?'

'Why would you assume drugs straight up?'

Was it because that was the rebellion of choice in her social circle? Or was it because it was the last thing in the world Drew would have become involved with and Flynn was fast becoming the yang to Drew's yin in her mind. 'You seem like an ideal candidate for chemical escapism.'

'Actually chemicals were about the only thing I wasn't into.'

That got her attention. 'When you said *trouble* I assumed you meant of the suspended-from-school-for-shaving-your-head variety. What are we talking about?'

His eyes dropped away. 'The only time I shaved my head it was a requirement of the…institution I spent some time in.'

Bel blinked. 'You were in prison?'

'Juvenile Detention. Three months. When I was fourteen.'

She pushed her plate away. 'What did you do?'

'It's more a question of what I got caught for. I had a slow start at school, had some trouble reading, struggled with grades. Eventually I got in with the wrong crowd, tried to keep up with the ringleaders and did too good a job of it. Got busted joyriding and took the heat for my friends.'

She spluttered. 'Did Drew know?'

His eyes hardened. 'It was Drew that dobbed me in to the police. I gather my...exploits were reflecting badly on him.'

'Drew reported you?' She couldn't imagine that of the man she'd known. Not *her* Drew.

'He thought it would be character-building.'

Wow. 'That must have been tough to get past. As brothers.'

His eyes dropped for a moment. 'In those early weeks in detention I really felt it.'

'Did you ever resolve it with him?'

He shook his head after a long pause.

'You two never even spoke about it?'

He frowned. 'What was there to say? He ratted me out. And he wasn't all that interested in making up for lost time when I came out of Rangeview. While I was in there my whole family upped sticks and moved to Oberon and they brought me here the day I was released.'

'Far away from all your shady friends?'

He shook his head. 'Away from everyone's friends.'

Bel vividly remembered the day she'd dropped out of the school she'd never fitted in, moved out of her parents' world and into a grown-up flat, alone. How cut off from everything she'd felt until she started building her own life. And that had been her choice. In Flynn and Drew's case... 'That must have been really hard on everyone.'

Tiny crescent creases formed at the corners of his tight lips.

'That wasn't a criticism, just an observation. You didn't ask to be moved away.' She tipped her head. 'Is that why your parents tiptoe around you? Because of how they ripped you from your world?'

His eyes came up, blazing. 'They traded their lives for mine. I always understood it. I never judged them.' And just like that, his great affection and loyalty to his family made perfect sense. Except for one thing.

'Unlike your brother.'

He sighed and pushed his dinner away. 'Drew was never happy here. He loved the city. He knew our whole lives were revolving around me at that time.'

'Did he blame you?'

'He didn't need to.' That was Flynn-speak for *yes*. 'He toughed it out here for two years, then got the Oxford scholarship. Everyone was so flat-out proud of him. No one from Oberon had done anything like that.'

'That's when he lost touch with you all?'

His eyes drifted out to the rapidly darkening skies. 'The truth is he started losing touch from the moment we drove through the property's gates.'

Understanding began to dawn. 'Until he came to us.'

'A shiny new family across the ocean.'

Bel clamped her hands together under the table. 'They're not so shiny, let me tell you.'

'Regardless, they were a clean slate. He could be anyone he wanted with them. Tell them anything.'

Or not tell them. Bel took a deep breath. 'You missed him.'

'He did what he needed to survive. I was in no position to challenge that, given the lengths my family went to to make sure I did.'

'Meanwhile, I would have given anything to get out of my family and into one like Drew's. Like yours. A family who loved each other enough to move the earth for one another.'

'You loved your sister,' he pointed out.

'Yes, and my Gran. But they were highlights in an otherwise unremarkable set of relationships. And I lost Gran early.'

'You didn't get on with your parents?'

'Gwen and I...We were very different. She fitted and I didn't—it was that simple.'

His eyes were steady and cautious. 'It's never that simple.'

She shrugged.

'You two sisters were physically very different...' he started.

She knew what he was saying. Or not saying. Lots of people had *not said it* in the past. Someone else's egg in the nest.

The room was darkening as rapidly as the skies outside. Flynn reached behind him for the box of matches that sat next to the stove and lit the fat warped candle that sat on the timber table top between them. It meant he didn't leave the table. It meant he was still listening. It meant his face suddenly became all sharp angles and flickering shadows caused by the single light source, and it only made her breath catch more.

So ridiculous.

'I longed to be adopted,' she went on. 'I even had my DNA checked.'

He paused, the still-burning match in his fingers. 'You're kidding.'

'When I was thirteen. I faked my mother's consent and had a bunch of hair samples analysed.'

Betcha thought you were the only bad kid on the block...

'And?'

'Sadly, no. I wasn't illegitimate either, no matter what the glitterati hinted. I wouldn't for a moment think my mother was above cheating on my father but...no...the truth is a lot less glamorous.'

'Just a regular black sheep?'

'A red sheep.' With her grandfather's ginger colouring in an otherwise all-blonde family.

His eyes creased.

'It took me years to work out why I felt so out of place there, and then years more to accept the truth.'

'Which was?'

She shrugged and hoped the candlelight would disguise a whole lifetime of hurt. 'My parents wanted a little girl, and they got Gwen.' She took a breath and straightened. 'And then they got me.'

Realisation hit. 'You were unplanned?'

'Mother blamed a dodgy IUD back in the days of shonky

contraception. She didn't like anything about the pregnancy process the first time. She didn't like getting sick, she didn't like getting fat once the novelty of the whole pregnant-glow wore off. She wasn't interested in doing it again. I felt about as welcome as an STD.' If conception could be called a disease.

Flynn stared at her long and hard. 'Is that why you were so eager to have the embryos implanted?'

'I knew they'd be loved and valued by whoever they went to. I knew how desperate the recipients would be for children. But I didn't want them ever feeling the way I had. Not fitting. Not while they had biological family who would love them.'

'Two families in this case.'

She lifted her eyes to his across the golden flicker. 'I thought you weren't going to tell your family if your suit wasn't successful?' And if he could change his mind about that…She leaned forward. 'Why can't we just tell them? They're good people, they'd understand.'

'I won't do that to them. Build their hopes up. Give them back Drew, only to possibly lose him again…'

He shook his head. 'Explain something to me. How does a twenty-three-year-old woman give up her own life for unborn children?'

She stared at him, at a loss. 'The future seems such an abstract thing. Whereas their needs were immediate.'

'They were on ice. They could have waited years.'

Bel frowned and couldn't answer that. All she'd been aware of was the urgency of her court petition and, once it was granted, the pressing instinct to act before anyone took it away from her. Rightly, as it turned out.

She hedged. 'It's not that different to what your parents did. Detoured their own lives to save yours.'

'You didn't have anyone to consult with? No one that was affected?'

Was he asking if she had a boyfriend? 'You think I would

have just blown someone off to follow you here, if I was in a relationship?'

'You thought as much of me.'

Painfully good point. 'I didn't know you then.'

He crossed his arms and rested them on the table in front of him, bringing his face closer to the soft light of the candle. Much closer to hers. 'You think you know me now?'

She didn't pull back. 'A bit. You're not quite what I thought.'

'And what did you think?'

'That you just didn't like being told what to do…' This close she could see the machinations of his mind behind his stormy eyes. And her unsteady breath practically made the candle flame dance.

'I don't.'

'…and that you were doing this for your mother.'

'I'm doing this for my whole family.'

'I don't think it's that simple.'

'Really?' His raised eyebrows said *go on* but the darkened eyes beneath them glittered *dare you*. Bel had always appreciated a good dare.

But then, just as she opened her mouth to speak, he lifted one of his large hands off the table and reached up to drag the backs of his fingers along her jaw. The unexpected caress stole the air out from under her and made it impossible to speak. Not that she could remember what she'd been about to say.

All she knew was the feel of those work-roughened fingers brushing along her skin. The riotous tingles it caused. The strength in his hand as she leaned her face just slightly into him on instinct.

She pulled back, blinking. Flushing. 'What are you doing?'

Flynn curled his fingers tightly into his palm and cleared his throat. 'Experimental touching. They're not going to buy it if you jerk away whenever I get close.'

More heat flooded her cheeks. The way she'd pressed her cheek into him at first…Though she knew he was right. His family were perpetually on the edge of asking uncomfortable questions now. 'A little warning next time, huh?'

'Maybe we could use a coded signal.' His lips twisted. 'What say I quack like a duck when I'm about to touch you.'

Despite the baffling sensations still rippling through her, despite the tense conversation they'd just been having, Bel found it hard not to smile at the image of a man like Flynn imitating a duck. The widening of her lips caused fissures to open up in the serious mask she often wore around him and tiny chunks broke free and fell away. Her skin hauled in a relieved breath for the first time since she'd arrived here.

'And what if I'm about to touch you?' she asked.

'Are you planning on it?'

'Well, it's going to look a little strange if I don't ever reciprocate...'

'Just go ahead and touch. I don't need a code.'

'I was thinking more along the lines of a subtle glance five seconds out.'

'So you can get all tense in those five seconds? Maybe better that we just get all the touching out of the way now so the ice is well and truly broken.'

'Yeah,' she muttered. 'Because that's not weird at all.'

He pushed his chair back from the table and Bel flinched. What was he going to do, embrace her?

'Let's go check on the platypus.'

Her eyes flew immediately to the clock. Where had those hours gone? They were nearly an hour late for prime platy-viewing time. *Damn*...

Bel was up in a heartbeat and Flynn could feel her presence following close behind him, out onto his back deck. As she went to skip down the steps ahead of him he reached out and stalled her with gentle fingers around her forearm. She paused and glanced back up at him.

'Quack,' he said, far too late, and then his fingers slid down the bare skin of her wrist, across her palm and interlaced with her shock-stiffened ones. 'Relax. It's just in case anyone watches us crossing the lower paddock.'

She lifted an eyebrow. 'You think they'll be sitting by the window with binoculars waiting for signs of us being cosy?'

'I wouldn't put it past Nan.'

'Holding hands isn't exactly caught-in-the-act material.'

'Holding hands is as good a place to start as any.'

She was as stiff as the freshly starched sheets they used in the chalets, walking beside him, her careful hold limper than a dead fish in his. That wasn't going to fool anyone.

'Now who's got the plague?' he said in a low voice.

She responded a moment later by resettling her fingers more comfortably in his and taking a deep fortifying breath. It was a start. The two of them were going to have to do much more before the month was out if his family were going to believe they'd been intimate enough to create a new life. Somehow he had to infuse his casual touches with enough subtext to convince his wily nan that touching was a poor substitute for what he really wanted to be doing to the woman who was supposed to be his girlfriend.

Soon-to-be fiancée…

And she was going to have to get used to having his hands on her.

Which made him smile. Unaccountably.

Flynn took the lead on the darkened pathway and kept Bel's hand tucked in close to his thigh, his fingers tangled firmly in hers. They were slim and warm and neatly manicured and they fitted his perfectly. She wasn't a jewellery wearer, unlike her bling-happy sister, and so it was skin on unbroken skin wherever they touched.

The cheek thing had been an impulse. Nothing at all to do with ice-breaking and everything to do with being drawn to the fiery challenge in her eyes and the flush of colour their spirited discussion had caused. He wanted to touch the place in her skin that the colour came so richly to life. The place she bled her emotion.

And he was a man used to acting on his impulses. Even the bad ones.

Her footsteps fell into line with his own as they wandered down towards the spring, ending the push-pull of being out of step. It made their whole movement more easy, less like a tug-of-war and more synchronised. Fluid. Like good sex.

And they were only walking.

That boded well for some casual contact over the next few weeks. It was the show that counted, but some visceral enjoyment was pure bonus. Perhaps not surprising; regardless of everything else he'd thought about up-herself Gwen Rochester, he had always understood what Drew saw in her physically. Petite and stacked and blonde.

His fingers tightened around Bel's. Maybe the chemistry between the Rochesters and the Bradleys was universal, regardless of what sister it came in? Chemistry wasn't something he would have expected to discover with Bel.

Any more than her genuinely meshing with his family.

He'd seen enough of her interactions with them to know her protestations that first night were true. She *did* enjoy their company. And though she wasn't enjoying the deceit that was necessary for the moment, she wasn't *hating* it here in Oberon and she wasn't looking down her nose at them all the way her sister had. Small mercies. But, despite her apparent bad fit in her own family, this apple wouldn't have fallen too much further from the Rochester tree than her older sister.

Different, but the same.

He glanced behind them to make sure the line-of-sight from the house was interrupted by the trees along the banks of the spring and then loosened his fingers and let hers fall free. She shifted away immediately.

'Have we missed them?' she asked, disappointment staining her voice.

Despite growing up in a cosmopolitan megalopolis, she did get appealingly excited by small moments of simple pleasure. The platypus foraging. Releasing a hand-reared joey into the juvenile roo paddock. Sunrises. He had to remind himself that while her grandmother's money meant she could lie around and do nothing all day if she wanted to, she chose to work with injured wildlife back home rather than party with the beautiful people by night and sleep by day.

Just like she chose to have herself implanted with her sister's babies.

She was a whole mass of contradictions wrapped up in a tall, lean, flaming package.

'Let's give it a few minutes. Sometimes they wait for the moon to get higher.'

She sank down onto the bank below a eucalypt tree and stared at the water as if her focus would make the platypus materialise through sheer perseverance.

'So...' she finally said, not looking at him. 'About this touching...'

Here we go...

'I agree we need some ground rules. Boundaries really. What kind of touching are you talking about?'

Her voice was a low, husky whisper to keep from disturbing the platypus but it did a mighty job of disturbing him. He shook the thought free. 'You want me to spell it out?'

'Yes. Please. So I know what to expect.'

And what to slap him for, probably.

She took a deep breath. 'Hand-holding, obviously.'

'Obviously.'

She turned to stare at him expectantly. She seriously wanted him to list it. Okay... 'Ah, my hand on your lower back, maybe. Or your shoulder.'

'All right...'

Okay, this was good. Weird but manageable. 'I might... brush your thigh.'

'Really?'

'Not saying it's guaranteed.'

'Thigh-brushing. Check.' The husk in her voice seemed a hint tighter.

Which matched the tautness of his body perfectly. He pushed to his feet and moved next to her and sank down, sliding his glance sideways at her. 'Chances are I'd lean into you at some point. Just briefly.'

Bel nodded. And swallowed. Her enormous eyes seemed extra blue in the moonlight. 'Uh-huh…? Would I lean back?'

'You might. If the situation warrants it.' His eyes fell to her hair, where tiny loose strands clung defiantly to her cheek. They seemed to multiply as he watched. 'I'd probably stroke your hair away from your face.' His eyes dropped lower and he swallowed hard. 'Or your throat.'

The stream burbled in the silence and when she finally spoke it was softer than he'd ever heard it. 'Sounds convincing…'

Her gaze slid lower to where his hands hung between his knees, itching to enact his thoughts. 'That's the idea.'

She lifted her eyes and locked with his. 'What else?'

She wanted more? *Careful what you wish for, sweetheart…*

'If I thought we had an audience, I might sit behind you on the bank here, pull you back against me…' the more he said, the more the words thickened in his throat; her lips fell open, just a hint, and his eyes leapt straight to them '…and rest my chin on your head.'

'Really?' Breathless this time. 'Why?'

'Just to be close.' He frowned. 'Just to *seem* close.'

'What would I do? To seem close?'

What he wished in that moment she'd do and what he thought in a million years she'd allow were very different things. 'You'd probably hook your arms around my knees and pull them close. Just to complete the circle.'

Her eyes were like black full moons as she stared at him. 'Okay.'

He forced air through his tight chest.

'And when they think we don't know they're watching I'd almost certainly graze my thumb across your lips. As though I was about to kiss you.'

Hell, he could feel it now. The fullness of her bottom lip, spongy and sweet against his rough thumb. His mouth dried.

'Which you wouldn't.' Her blink was slow motion but there was definite wariness behind it.

'Never in front of my family.'

'Why not?'

He leaned closer. Murmured, 'Because a kiss is something personal, between two people. Something intimate. Not something to be aired in public.'

'People kiss in public all the time.'

'Not my kind of kisses.'

Her tongue stole out to wet her lips and she stared at him long and hard. Was her body reacting like his was? As if they'd actually done every one of those things?

She blew a puff of air out between tight lips. 'Wow. I'm glad I checked. That's quite a performance.'

Performance. Right.

Her meaning couldn't have been clearer if she'd shoved him headlong into the frigid stream tumbling past their feet. 'That's the plan. We'll give a new definition to the term *faking it.*'

She almost winced. But then those plump lips split in a broad smile. 'Well, there's nothing too untoward there.'

'You're comfortable with all of that?'

'I'm…' she groped around for the right word and sat up straighter, breaking the filaments of attraction that had formed between them '…as eager as you are to end the suspicion in your family's eyes. So yes. All of that will be acceptable.'

Acceptable. It was a term straight out of the Gwen Rochester dictionary and a healthy reminder that no matter how brightly her eyes sparkled as the sun set, or the platypus splashed, or the candle flickered, Belinda was still a Rochester deep down.

And she was a temporary necessity. A diversion. An incubator.

Nothing more.

CHAPTER SEVEN

'Only twenty minutes now.' Flynn shot her a tight smile—
the *in private* one, the one not full of artificial promise—then
turned his eyes back to the endless expanse of Australian high-
way stretching out ahead.

Twenty minutes before they rumbled back over Bunyip's
Reach's rickety stock grid and drove the long winding gravel
track to the Bradley homestead. Twenty minutes before they
faced the inevitable moment of confessing their pregnancy
to his family, and followed it up with their intent to marry
straight away. Twenty minutes before they compounded the
lies they'd already told and complicated things for both of
them tenfold...

Because they *were* still pregnant. And thanks to what her
Sydney gynaecologist called the 'healthiest young uterus' she'd
ever seen, *both* embryos had held on past the risky period and
were now surviving and thriving deep inside her.

She turned to look out of the side window and closed her
eyes.

Twins, Gwen... Two healthy children. What her sister and
Drew had only dreamed of.

She'd known multiples were possible, or even none, but in
her head and heart she'd convinced herself that one would survive. All her imaginings of her life going forward included a
single pram. A single cot. A single pair of cut sandwiches. A

single little person jogging off for their first day at primary school.

One she could manage.

But two…

She swallowed hard. *Alone*…

Two tiny young lives needing her constant care and support. Twice as scary. What if she wasn't up to it? What if she failed them like she'd failed so many others in her life? Including herself.

'Are you feeling okay, Bel?' Her tiny groan must have caught Flynn's ear.

She dragged her eyes back to his. 'I'm just—' *terrified* '—thinking.'

He nodded and turned his focus back to the road. 'A lot to think about.'

'For you, too.' Though raising twins within a supportive three-generation family with two experienced mothers, a house built for youngsters and a property most kids would only dream of wasn't quite the same as imagining them practically sleeping in drawers in her too-small London flat.

He looked at her strangely. 'Nothing a few minutes editing the documents won't fix.'

That brought her head more fully around to him. 'What documents?'

'The court documentation. I called them while you were changing. To update the petition.'

She blinked. He'd already notified his lawyers? While she hadn't even thought beyond the shock of how she was going to manage two children on her own.

'Fast work,' she said tightly.

He glanced at her, then dragged his eyes back to the road, resting his hand on the handbrake next to her thigh as they ate up the roads at a hundred kilometres per hour, and she did her best to be unobtrusive as she shrank away from it.

Had she thought for one moment that being touched so often

would turn out to be more stressful than continuing to fabricate excuses why Flynn was *not* touching her, she would have turned and walked away all those weeks ago when he'd first suggested they ramp up the faux intimacy.

They'd eased into it gradually—an indulgent look here, a gentle smile there—and worked their way up to the more serious, now commonplace, contact between the two of them. On some mad, inexperienced level Bel thought it would become easier—like stage directions in the drama club plays at school which became second nature with rehearsal.

But it hadn't, and not because she couldn't bear his touch.

Quite the opposite.

Her skin shivered every time Flynn's earth-roughened fingers brushed it, which was often. He was a good looking, charismatic man and—despite everything going on between them—she was a young, fertile and apparently healthily responsive woman. He touched, she crumbled. He brushed, she shivered. He leaned, she absorbed.

He faked...she believed.

But his family were believing, too. They were delighted and patently relieved when Flynn finally started showing some interest in their guest and the probing questions eased off almost immediately. Now their roused suspicions lay comfortably, quietly snoring.

And twin babies were only going to push the doubt out of their minds for ever.

She turned to face him. 'So how do you want to handle the marriage?'

'We'll go back into Sydney in a couple of weeks. As soon as we get our licence.'

She stared at him. 'A registery office marriage?'

He frowned at her gaping expression. 'Don't tell me you want the full white-dress catastrophe? I wouldn't have thought—'

'Not me, Flynn, your mother. From what you told me, she

already missed out on one son's wedding. You can't seriously be thinking of excluding her from this one? Poor Denise.'

The frown deepened. He turned back to the road and was silent for a long time. They turned off the main road before hitting Oberon and started heading towards Bunyip's Reach.

'Are you angry with me?' she risked after another few kilometres of stony silence.

His lips pressed together and his eyes spat sparks. 'I'm angry at myself, Bel. I should have thought of that. For Mum.'

Oh. His distress disarmed her entirely. He wasn't a man to admit to his mistakes often. And he was clearly beating himself up over it.

He looked sideways at her. 'You'd really stand up at a formal wedding ceremony with me?'

'It's still a marriage on paper only,' she cautioned past suddenly tight breath. 'Whether there's a performance to go with it or not is all the same to me. But your whole family's going to expect it.'

'There'll be vows.'

When so much of your life was lies, what were a few more? She twisted her lips. 'My parents had vows, too. They weren't terribly binding.' Love. Honour. Obey…

But Gwen and Drew's had been. Personally written and heartfelt. She'd cried buckets while they were reciting them. Somewhere deep inside she'd always wondered if she'd find a man like him to pledge himself to her so beautifully. She'd never dreamed that vows could be as fake as touching. Or that she'd wind up exchanging them with Drew's little brother. It was somehow right and so wrong at the same time.

'Leave it to me, then. I'll sort something.'

A twinge yanked deep inside. Why that irritated apathy was hurtful, after everything he'd done… Her lips twisted. 'How romantic.'

He slid those deep grey eyes her way again but didn't say a word. Then he steered the powerful car down the long turn that marked the entry to Bunyip's Reach and everything but the impending tangle of lies fled her mind.

The Bradley dinner table had not been this silent since she'd first sat in Drew's chair all those weeks ago.

Flynn cleared his throat. 'Somebody say something. Please.'

It was the first time Bel had seen him anything less than completely composed. His tension showed in the tiny crescent lines at the corners of his mouth and his white-knuckled grip on the table edge. It made her feel a whole lot better about being such a wreck herself.

Four sets of eyes around the table were wide and shocked. But not horrified—Bel was together enough to notice that. But then Denise moved and everyone else exploded into life behind her. She threw her arms around Flynn just as Arthur threw one around Bel.

'Twins!' Arthur said, chuffing and puffing and doing what one of *them* should have done back in Sydney. Being thrilled.

'A wedding,' Denise cried, 'here in Oberon.' She pushed her son away long enough to stare into his eyes. Her own were wary, preparing for another blow. Her voice lowered. 'It is here?'

Flynn flicked Bel the briefest of glances before reassuring his mother in a deep rumble, 'Yes. Here.'

She squealed and turned a delighted face to Bel, who smiled back as best she could. 'A wedding!'

'Welcome to the family, Belinda,' Arthur Bradley said quietly in her ear, and his eyes fell to her belly.

Guilt gnawed hard and vicious on her soul. She'd wanted this sort of reception her whole life but...like this? Knowing she'd have to confess everything later? 'Thank you, Arthur...'

'I knew it,' Alice said, squeezing past her husband to embrace her. 'I was burning to say something.'

'The pickled eggs?'

The older woman laughed. 'The eggs. The way your skin changed. Your hair. The way Flynn was so careful with you.'

'Oh, no...' But then she remembered not to deny it. And truthfully she was curious. 'When?'

'When you first arrived.' Alice smiled. 'Like you were extra-precious. Always hovering. Always watching. I understand now.'

Bel couldn't remember him being at all careful of her, she could only remember his absence. And his silence.

'You shouldn't be working with the wildlife—'

'No!' Her fervent plea startled Alice to silence. 'Please don't take them away from me. I...need them.' They were the only things keeping her sane.

'Need?'

Alice's lined face creased and Bel rushed in to undo her gaffe. 'Enjoy. I really enjoy working with them.'

Alice nodded but her frown didn't ease. 'Okay. But we might need some health precautions.'

'Precautions are fine.' Whatever it took.

The older woman chuckled and dropped her voice, glancing at Flynn discreetly. 'Though precautions might have been a good idea a few months ago, no?'

Oh, my God... Bel's laugh was critically tight. Was every single word out of her mouth from now on going to be deceit?

'Flynn, get over here and join your future wife. Mother of your child!' Bill's booming voice rose above the general hubbub.

'Children!' Denise cried. 'Grandchildren!'

Bel's eyes fell shut briefly, but when they opened he was moving towards her with a warning disguised in the smile he offered. His arm slipped around her middle easily and he pulled her against him, hard. Her skin did its usual tingly thing even though the message was clear.

Stay the course.

She plastered a wide smile on her face, slid one arm around

Flynn's hips and crossed the other one in front of him in a public embrace. He stiffened immediately but she held on. If she was going to burn for the lies she was telling, then she was taking him with her.

He'd be good-looking company in hell.

The ceremony was going to be brief.

That was about the only good thing Bel could think to say about it. Flynn had told her it would be fifteen minutes max, family only. And though he had friends aplenty here in Oberon, Bel didn't know any of them, and so the only 'reception' he'd planned was a family dinner back at the homestead.

Denise and Alice had fussed around her all morning, working hard to be the bridesmaids she was missing out on, being so far from home, seeing to everything so that there wasn't a thing for Bel to do. It was so kind of them but so painfully awkward, given she was repaying their kindness with deception. Plus, she'd been relying on being busy so that she wouldn't have to dwell on what was about to happen. What she was about to do.

Marrying Flynn Bradley.

She took another deep breath.

'Aren't you the slightest bit curious about where the ceremony is?' Alice said to her now, just back from doing the rehab chores they hadn't allowed her to do today because of her perfectly manicured wedding nails. Again, not her idea.

Bel gauged the women's suspicion level. A bride should be burning with curiosity, she knew, but it was too late to suddenly invent excitement she clearly wasn't displaying. 'I trust Flynn,' she improvised, infusing her voice with artificial tranquillity. 'He knows exactly what he's doing.'

In so many ways.

Denise smiled. 'That he does. He's always been such a capable boy. And so thoughtful. I'm sure he'll pick the perfect place for you.'

Actually, it would make this whole thing easier if he chose

the *least* perfect place. Like some glitzy, chrome and glass high rise in the city. Then it would be easy for her to maintain the artifice and go through the motions of yet another lie. Her only condition was that it shouldn't be a church. Not that she was overtly religious, but lying in God's House—right under His all-seeing nose—was not something she could bring herself to undertake, regardless of her denomination.

Bad enough that she was lying to a group of people who were fast feeling like a proxy family.

'We could get married in a hole in the ground for all I care—' the two older women exchanged knowing glances and Bel forced a smile to her face '—just as long as Flynn turns up.'

Denise laughed and took her hand. 'Oh, he'll come. He's very excited about all of this.'

Then he's a better actor than I am if he's fooling the people who know him best. And apparently without conscience.

'It may not be the conventional order to do things in, Bel,' Denise continued gently, 'but Flynn's never been a man to do anything he didn't want to. If he's asked you to be his then it's because he wants you to be his.'

It would be so easy to imagine both women knew exactly what was going on. About Drew and Gwen, about their babies. And tempting to imagine that—in full knowledge of everything that was happening—Denise and Bill were happy that their son would be married today to a Rochester girl. Just so that there'd be one fewer untruth lying before her like a darkened pit trap. One fewer thing to worry about stumbling into and not being able to crawl out of. Or that the girl Alice and Arthur thought they were getting was really *her*. A capable, reliable, lovable Bel Rochester.

Or that the babies she was carrying were really Flynn's.

Her body tightened immediately at the thought of carrying Flynn's babies—of *making* Flynn's babies—and heat suffused her.

She'd done her best to habituate herself to all the touching, but he was getting so good and frequent at it, it was all too easy to kid herself it might be real. Instead of being about his family and anyone who might be watching. Her mind kept trying to tell the rest of her, but it seemed her body was operating in blissful, intentional ignorance. If it didn't listen to the truth then her muscles could continue to quiver when he leaned into her as they walked. Her flesh could continue to thrill when his fingers brushed her hair, and her heart could continue to flutter when he leaned close to speak warm breath in her ear.

Only weeks ago she'd sat on the flight out of London and scrunched herself as close to the window as she could to avoid even pressing her hip against Drew's arrogant brother in the tight confines of the aircraft seating. Now she was fantasising about making babies together.

How it would feel.

How *Flynn* would feel.

Her abdomen coiled and she straightened and shifted away from the window where she'd been staring off down the same gully she could see from Flynn's place. What was wrong with her?

'That's better,' Alice murmured, approving. 'A bit of colour in those porcelain cheeks to replace the nervous blanch. Whatever you were just thinking, keep it up until the ceremony.'

The rogue thought had sneaked through in the first place; she certainly wasn't walking down a carpeted aisle with visions of strong, binding limbs and slippery, sweat-drenched muscles swilling through her mind.

Denise took her hands and warmed them between her own. The heat—and the gesture—soaked straight to Bel's soul. Kind brown eyes twinkled at her. 'Time to go, eh? Before you make yourself sick with nerves.'

Bel glanced sideways at the full-length mirror in Alice's room in the grandparents' wing of the Bradley household. Her filmy dress was simple—one she'd packed from home, expecting Australia to be sizzling hot and in case she had need of something vaguely formal. Something that could expand with her. Ironic that she'd be one of few twenty-something women these days who could genuinely wear white at their wedding, yet she'd be in a pale blush. A dress that toned unusually perfectly with her neon hair.

Alice had woven sprigs of tiny white flowers into the twisted braids that Denise had spent hours creating; it was about the prettiest she'd ever seen her hair. Both were simple in their execution and perfect in their intent, and so close to what she would have chosen for herself the sight brought a prickle of tears to her eyes.

This was all such a sham...

'No, you don't, missy. Not with all that eye make-up on...!'

Alice spun her away from the mirror and gathered her hands in front of her before letting her eyes grow unusually sombre. 'Belinda, you look like something that truly belongs in a fairy forest. Oberon himself could not have wished for a more transcendent bride. When you walk down that aisle, Flynn's heart may just stop.'

Something in the truth of Alice's words stilled Bel's breath. And in that moment she knew she wanted Flynn Bradley to look at her as if she *was* his bride—the woman his heart would stop for—even if he didn't mean it. Just for those moments she wanted to stand before him in her fairy forest wedding dress and look at the man waiting for her at the altar and pretend that they were truly, madly and irrevocably in love with each other.

Because—for the first time—the person she really wanted to lie to was herself. She'd earned a tiny moment of denial and it might just be the only wedding she was ever going to have.

She lifted her eyes and smiled at both women. 'Okay. Let's go.'

She turned and walked down the carpeted landing of the

Bradley homestead calmly and graciously—exactly as she planned on moving down the aisle towards Flynn.

As it turned out, there was not so much an *aisle* as a set of steep steel stairs that plunged like a gangplank deep into the bowels of the earth. Her dress colour changed with the artificial lighting hidden amongst the rocks of the cave system until it was impossible to know what colour it had originally been, as she moved a couple of hundred metres through a series of dramatic underground caverns flanked at the rear by Denise and Alice and at the front by a formally dressed guide.

The humidity rose and the temperature dropped as they followed the cut deeper into the primary cave system and then through and out into the secondary ones until Bel's skin almost sparkled with the zillion tiny droplets that clung to the translucent hairs on her skin.

Her breath came in tight puffs but it was awe that shoved her nerves aside, practically gaping at everything as Bel moved through one spectacular cavern and into the next. Their guide unlocked a chained-off walkway and sealed it up behind them and then drew them through a darkened low-point until they emerged on the other side into a towering maw.

'And here we are,' the guide announced quietly as Bel's eyes adjusted to the natural lighting that suddenly flooded the cavernous opening. Her breath rushed back in an unexpected gasp. She was standing in a natural fissure what had to be halfway up a cliff face, opening out onto the most stunning natural view Bel had ever seen. A lake, other-worldly in its intense blinding blue and flanked on all sides by deep, green, foreign Australian bush.

'Bel…' Someone nudged her from behind. Denise? Alice? It didn't matter. Her watering eyes flicked left, along the steel walkway until she saw an unmistakable shape silhouetted against the bright outside light.

Flynn.

And a few paces to his left two dark shapes she assumed were Bill and Arthur. Standing for their son and grandson.

She started to tremble. She'd begged Flynn not to choose a church for the ceremony so that she could look God in the eye later despite what they were about to do, and he'd chosen *this*... The closest thing to nature's birth place she could imagine.

So utterly, *awfully* perfect.

The guide nudged her onward.

Left and right of the walkway, giant ancient spurs stuck up like fangs from the gums of the earth and acted as silent sentinels for what was about to take place. Warm air rushed in the fissure opening and met the cool air of the cave system, and caused tiny eddies that blew dry the damp curls about her face.

The rock base of the cave slowly rose to meet the platform until she stepped off and trod the same granite mound that Flynn waited on.

Waiting for her.

Her pulse began to hammer in earnest.

The blue lake stretched out behind him but Bel couldn't take her eyes off the man standing before her. It wasn't a tux or even a formal wedding suit, but it was dark and imposing and all shoulders and totally suited a man one might find in the belly of the earth. His hair was neatly groomed and the collar of his crisp formal shirt gaped like the cave mouth to reveal just a hint of dark hair against a tanned throat.

And his eyes as she stepped closer... Her heart thumped. Had they always been the colour of tarnished pewter?

He brought her gently closer to him and murmured low, 'I thought you might have backed out.'

She studied his expression for disapproval but only saw caution. 'Am I late?'

His lashes dropped to look down at her. 'You're shaking. Are you okay?'

Bel knew without looking that all eyes were on them. She

forced her lips apart into a parody of a smile. 'I... It was cold, coming through...'

Great. Now she was officially lying to *everyone* here.

'Not long and we're done. Remember, try to make it convincing.'

Her nostrils flared. As if she hadn't been trying all this time...

Their guide stepped forward and picked up a folder from a small cloth-covered table Bel had only just noticed and stepped before them, his back to the amazing outlook, his kind face to them.

'You're a celebrant?' Bel croaked.

'All legal and binding,' the man said quietly. 'We do weddings all the time.'

Binding. In the real world, maybe. But two people here knew this was only for now, not for ever.

Flynn reached across her and took her hand, turning her towards him. Her pulse kicked up. This was it... The moment of no return. Once Flynn had her signature on the wedding certificate he'd have equal rights under the law. Equal family standing and equal marriage status. Equal chance of taking Gwen and Drew's children.

Her lashes fluttered shut and something shifted deep inside her. The same something that thought standing here with this man felt so right.

Flynn had every right to contest the decree. He was full uncle to these babies as she was full aunt. He was just fighting for them, too.

'Bel...?'

Whatever came, they would face it together. It might not be conventional togetherness but it was the first time in years that she felt as if she had someone to stand with her. To understand.

She opened her eyes and locked onto Flynn's and, for the first time in months, she spoke the truth. 'I'm ready.'

He turned them both back to face the celebrant-guide. The man composed himself with his folder nice and high and met both their eyes in turn.

'Please take each other's hands…'

The vows weren't traditional, a small mercy. Bel wasn't sure she could have stood straight through all that loving and honouring and sickness and health. They were untraditional, like their venue. Like their marriage. Flynn had even thought to use only first names in the ceremony so that there were no awkward Rochester/Cluney moments.

Thank God one of them was thinking.

All Bel could do was drown in the celebrant's words and cling embarrassingly to Flynn's hand. Even though it was also the hand twisting hers into this marriage. There was no one else here she could turn to for understanding, no one she wasn't already going to hurt with her lies. And so she shielded herself for brief moments in the poetry of the vows and dreamed of how it might feel to be truly standing here with a man she loved.

'…and let this sacrifice bind you…' the celebrant said, pouring a half-glass of what smelled like champagne into the earth '…and hold you, as you hold each other.'

Flynn added a second hand to the first and she struggled to ignore how secure his fingers felt wrapped around her shaking ones. He'd been watching her closely since the start of the ceremony, presumably waiting for any sign she was going to lose it.

She took another deep breath.

She would not lose it here in this underworld. The earth demanded her strength. Her eyes lifted to Flynn's and she let herself be consumed by the grey depths. Was it coincidence that the celebrant had spoken of sacrifice? They were both giving up their freedom for the children she carried.

'Let family keep you…'

She blinked with confusion. First sacrifice and now family. Was someone trying to make a point?

'*...and the earth sustain you.*'

Okay... She glared at Flynn pointedly. He just smiled, fast and tiny. The celebrant moved between them and put his hands on their joined ones.

'The rings?'

Arthur stepped forward with two white gold bands on a thread of ribbon. One delicate and fine and minutely engraved with swirls, the other larger and thicker. He'd thought of rings. For some reason, she hadn't expected a ring. Given she'd be returning it in a few months.

Flynn slid his hand around beneath her left one and lifted it. He concentrated on getting the delicate white gold band safely onto the tip of her ring-finger and then lifted his blazing eyes to hers and held them as he slowly slid the ring down the length of her finger. Until it could go no further.

As if it was never coming off.

The heat in his gaze threw her. He picked *now* to suddenly be angry with her? She searched his expression.

The celebrant cleared his throat meaningfully.

Oh... She took the remaining ring in her tremulous fingers and forced them to be steady long enough to get the ring onto Flynn's. She'd not seen his nails this clean since London. The ridiculousness of that observation made her almost giggle.

Flynn narrowed his eyes—was he waiting for her to turn hysterical?

The celebrant spoke again. 'And so, in the presence of your family and of each other, it is done. You are husband and wife.' They both stared at him and, for a moment, he looked at a loss. Denise and Alice burst into excited applause and under the screen of their excitement he quietly hinted to them, 'You may kiss.'

Kiss? Bel flicked her focus urgently between the celebrant and Flynn. 'Uh... Is it still...' she whispered. 'Can it be legal without...?'

A deep frown cut the celebrant-guide's moderate face. 'It's legal, yes...but...'

'She's kidding,' Flynn cut in, glaring at her meaningfully the moment the celebrant looked down at his folder. 'And shy.'

'Of course,' the man said. 'How about I just prepare the certificate...?'

And then he was off, leaving just the two of them perched high in the opening of the earth, with his family and all her lies on one side and a two hundred foot drop to an ancient frigid crater on the other. And a belly-full of babies, which meant there was really only one way she could go.

'It's just a kiss, Bel.'

Panic surged through her on painful pulses. 'I don't... We don't... Your family's watching...'

'Exactly. How will that look? We're supposed to have made children together and you won't even kiss me?'

I don't care how it will look. I care about how it will feel. How I will feel... Her heart hammered furiously in her chest cavity. 'You said you don't kiss in public.'

'This is going to have to be an exception.' He slipped his hands from hers and slid them up to frame her face. 'They're all waiting.'

Oh, God...

He inched closer, towering over her, and the excited chatter from his family warped into a high-pitched drone in her ears. She could feel Flynn's pulse beating as powerfully as hers into her lower lip as he dragged his thumb gently over it, learning its shape.

The tingles she usually felt on contact with him had dressed up for the occasion, too. They zinged, live and sharp as electric current down into her body and caused what little air remained in her lungs to escape on a shocked breath.

His eyes flicked down briefly as her mouth fell open, but

then he returned them to hers, studying her for the slightest reaction, his own lips parting as he lowered his head. And then their lips touched—his, warm and soft and encouraging; hers, cool and startled and non-participatory.

She physically jerked at the first touch, but the fingers curled around the base of her skull meant she couldn't go far. He lingered for a heartbeat before shuffling half a step closer and tilting her face for a better angle. They pressed more firmly against her and his breath warmed the deathly cool of her flesh while her head swam with the earthy scent of him. It felt as if he were stealing her soul through her frigid lips and he slid one hand down around her middle to keep her upright. That brought her hard up against his torso and triggered an uprising in her already struggling heartbeat. It surged so forcefully through her veins…he'd have to feel it pulsing in her lips.

She broke the contact long enough to suck in a breath and that would have been the time to step back, to end the kiss and this farce of a wedding. But those full, sweet lips were only millimetres from hers and still so warm and inviting, and the body held against hers was so intriguingly masculine, and all the rogue thoughts from Alice's bedroom came flooding back. Wondering what it would be like to touch Flynn for real, imagining him pressed down on top of her, buried in her kiss, buried in *her*…

Even though that was a bad, bad, *bad* idea.

Her fingers closed around his jacket. Escape was just a gentle push away.

But escape was in the other direction, and Bel's body stretched back up to close the distance between them. Flynn's eyes flared briefly as she pressed her mouth back against his but the shock didn't slow him for long. He forked his free hand around beneath the complicated twists of braids in her hair and realigned his mouth to fully seal them together.

A proper kiss. A killer kiss.

His lips nudged hers into movement, opening them wider

and dragging back and forth across them. And then his tongue joined the party and Bel was lost in the hot, wet, hormonal haze. Her chest squeezed for lack of air and when she finally breathed in it was mostly Flynn's exhaled breath.

He pulled her up harder against him. Hips to hips. Hard to soft. She clung to him hopelessly as the bowels of the earth spun madly around them.

Behind them, someone cleared their throat tactfully and Bel came screaming back to reality. She tore her lips from Flynn's and fought to focus her cloudy gaze on the politely averted eyes of his family.

Drew's family. He should have been here, too.

Flynn stiffened up immediately. He didn't release her far, but he tucked his lips down to her ear and whispered thickly, darkly, 'Wrong brother, Princess.'

As he pulled back, Bel stumbled at the glacial ore burning into her where, moments ago, such heat had been.

Oh, God, had she said that aloud? She glanced at the sharp line of Flynn's jaw and knew she must have. She blushed furiously at her error and Alice clapped her hands with delight, misreading the colour flooding her cheeks. The whole family joined in, celebrating the newlyweds. Bel took advantage of Flynn's firm hold and leaned into him since her knees weren't quite up to the task yet. He at least had the good grace not to drop her on her face.

Still, no one else had heard. She fumbled to make good. 'Flynn—'

The look he shot her would have stilled an earthquake but he disguised it by escorting her to the signing table and waiting while she tremulously signed. He added his own distinctive mark to the document, taking care to position one hand carefully so that neither of his parents saw Bel's true surname as they signed their witness. They were too excited and emotional to notice.

She was still not quite steady from his kiss. She tried again. 'Flynn—'

'Forget it,' he gritted, not quite meeting her eyes and pulling her closer to him as Arthur took a few photographs on his ancient camera. He released her the moment it was done. 'I'm sure you weren't the only one wishing my brother was here.'

'I wasn't…' How could she tell him he'd blown all thoughts of anyone else from her mind with that kiss? Until she'd turned and seen the Bradleys surging towards her and remembered exactly why they were here… Why she had a ring on her finger. Gwen and Drew. She couldn't. Not without sounding ridiculous. And he really didn't need any more ammunition in that regard. Besides, this was all just a ruse to him. What did it matter what she'd blurted?

She stared, her feet only now returning to steadiness. 'So, now what?'

He glanced at his family, who were moving towards them. 'Now you put that smile back on your face and pretend this isn't the worst moment of your life.'

She wiped her palms down her dress, eyes flickering at the unfamiliar feeling of a ring where one hadn't been. 'Flynn—'

Bill and Denise swept up to them, aglow with congratulations. Arthur and Alice weren't far behind.

Later, Flynn mouthed and turned with a big, fat, fake smile into the open arms of his family.

CHAPTER EIGHT

LATER turned out to be much later. The celebratory dinner went on for hours and hours and Bel saw the Bradley clan in full raucous flight. Flynn winced every time a champagne cork hit the ceiling or Denise and Bill danced noisily in the kitchen or Arthur grabbed a pregnant Bel and twirled her across the room. It was all so…country.

His wife laughed and clapped and appeared to genuinely enjoy being the centre of the universe tonight, although always with the hint of shadow that perpetually clung to her.

His wife.

Freaky.

He'd felt very connected to her standing in that cave listening to the celebrant's words. He'd certainly felt *for* her and done his best to still her trembling. This whole thing had been a whirlwind for both of them but at least he was at home, in his element, surrounded by people who loved him.

Bel had no one.

But then she'd murmured his brother's name, almost under her breath. He'd swear she didn't even know she'd done it. And in truth he had no right to expect any different, given Drew was the reason they were all here, but it really wasn't the first word he'd hoped to hear from her after *you may kiss the bride*.

And what a kiss it had been.

She spun past in Pop's embrace, her gauzy dress floating in a cloud around her and wafting upwards to reveal even more of those endless porcelain legs. Long enough to wrap around him twice. As she came to a stop, the dress clung to her curves in a way that accentuated rather than disguised the body beneath it. His eyes raked over her. She claimed her midsection was thickening with the babies but he couldn't really see much evidence of it anywhere else on her body.

'Dance with your wife, Flynn,' his nan called from her seat across the room, a knowing smile on her face. 'Don't just stare at her.'

He held his drink up in salute and she matched it and then turned her eyes happily back to the celebrating family. Flynn's followed.

She moved like a dancer, not like a pregnant woman. Bending, flowing, twisting…

His whole body tightened and he shifted uncomfortably in his seat. Before long, the music slowed and Arthur released Bel and turned to search out someone a few decades closer to his own age to slow dance with.

Without even meaning to, Flynn pushed to his feet and crossed to stand before her.

She lifted wide eyes to him. 'Is it time to go?'

She hoped not—it was written all over her face. Was that the cause of the shadows under her eyes? Was she anxious about moving back to his house with him? There was no real reason—it wasn't as if it was a real wedding night. Doubly so with the spectre of his dead brother hovering all of a sudden.

He held out a single hand.

The wide eyes creased with confusion. 'Really?'

'I believe it's customary for the bride and groom to dance at some point.' Though not usually under sufferance. 'I won't bite.'

She stood and joined him in the heart of the living room where all the furniture had been pushed back against the walls, and let him draw her into his hold. The music was quiet enough to talk over, but loud enough that they could do so unheard by the others. His parents had moved into their own slow dance in the country kitchen and his grandparents spread out on the sofa.

Bel stood stiff and awkward in his arms and kept her eyes low.

He leaned closer, lower, and whispered, 'Relax. You look like I'm walking you to the guillotine.'

She was like a furnace in his arms and heat leached into him wherever they touched. She straightened her spine and pressed herself closer to him, lifting her eyes to his.

'About earlier—'

No. They were not going to talk about that now. Here. He shook her a warning look. 'How are you feeling?'

Her answer was immediate. 'Overwhelmed.'

'It's done now. You can relax'

'No. I won't be able to relax until this is all truly over.'

His lips tightened. 'When you're back in London?'

'When I'm back in the real world.'

'This is the real world.'

'Yours, maybe. For me, this is like living someone else's life. A fantasy life. Like I just warped in here one night and no one has noticed yet that I don't belong.'

He'd worried for the first few weeks that she wore her heart too clearly on her sleeve, that she wasn't as proficient in pretence as her socially skilled sister. But as time wore on he'd convinced himself she was coping. Carving a niche for herself. Perhaps she was a better performer than he thought if she was still actually feeling so disconnected. You wouldn't know it to look at her. She looked as if she'd been living here her whole life, surrounded by his family and connecting with their land.

The idea immediately resonated in its rightness. He frowned and pushed the thought away. 'You're doing fine.'

'Fine.' She sighed, exhaustion manifesting as dampness in her blue eyes. 'Such a beige word. I had hoped you'd recognise how hard I'm working. At least give me that much credit.'

He slowed to almost a standstill. It wasn't her fault he'd crossed a line at the ceremony today. Forgotten why they were really there. The swell of her abdomen low against his was the reminder he needed. He tucked her closer into him and murmured, 'I know.'

'I'm performing from sunrise until sunset. The only time I can be me is when I'm alone.' The moisture threatened to spill over.

His hands tightened on hers. 'Or with me.'

She looked at him strangely then. 'Not even then. Not with how you feel about my family.'

He glanced around to make sure their conversation was still private. 'Okay, look. I'm willing to accept that you aren't cut from the same cloth as your sister—'

'Gwen,' Bel spat, managing somehow to keep her face fairly neutral. But her eyes blazed. 'Her name was Gwen and though you didn't like her I loved her with everything I had. She deserves to be remembered by her name.'

Flynn studied her pale face and finally saw what he suspected he'd been missing all this time. It hurt her when he bagged her sister. And he did that a lot.

He picked his path carefully, still hurting from her slip-up earlier today. 'You're different to Gwen. I can see that.'

The music changed and the next song was fast and loud, giving them more cover to have this long overdue conversation. The older Bradleys all retreated to the comfort of the kitchen for a drink.

'Your family likes Belinda Cluney from London. Why wouldn't they like Belinda Rochester? Just because of her surname? Are they truly incapable of drawing a distinction?'

He frowned. 'No, they're not. But I don't think they would have given you a chance if they'd known upfront who you were.'

'Like they didn't give Gwen a chance?'

He stared at her. A feeling that wasn't quite guilt and wasn't quite shame nipped at his conscience. Could they have come to like Gwendoline Rochester if they'd met her under different circumstances? Difficult to imagine.

He tried again. 'Your world and mine are very different...'

'The difference is I don't judge you for yours.'

That uncomfortable nip again. Her eyes flicked around the room, looking for anything other than him to settle on. Suddenly he was overcome with a burning need to get her alone.

To have a long overdue discussion.

He spun her back towards him and brought them both to a halt in the centre of the room, reaching around her from behind and folding her into the care of his arms. 'I think it's time we got going,' he announced over the music. Firmly. His family wanted to protest but they saw his expression and relented.

Bel stumbled behind him through a round of goodnights and then towards the back door of the house. The air outside was frigid and she was still wearing nothing but the light dress she'd worn to the ceremony that afternoon.

He stripped off his coat and helped her into it. It hung loose and ridiculous on her slim frame but it didn't make her any less beautiful. So much of her flaming hair had come down with all the dancing she looked flushed and in disarray—as if she'd been thoroughly tumbled in a barn somewhere. The image hit him straight in the groin.

'Thank you,' she said quietly, tucking the coat firmly around her. 'My bags...'

'Dad took your luggage down earlier today. It's in your room.'

She looked so intensely relieved he had to wonder what was amongst her belongings that she valued so much. Or was it because he'd said *your* room...? Did she think he was going to force her in with him?

'Listen, about the arrangements...'

She lifted her eyes to his; how was it possible that she looked so suspicious and so trusting at the same time?

'Even though we have separate rooms, we're going to be spending a fair bit of time together,' he said. 'We'll be like… roommates. I just wanted to let you know that I'll do my best to stay out of your way.'

'It's not a big house; that could be tricky.'

'In spirit, then, if not in person.' He took a deep breath. 'You won't even know I'm there.'

Bel frowned. 'I don't think I want that. I don't want you to stay out of my way.'

Surprise stilled his feet. He turned her to look at him in the darkness halfway between the houses.

'I lived like that for most of my childhood,' she went on. 'Like a ghost in my family. I'm not in a hurry to be invisible again.'

Empathy washed through him. He knew something about feeling invisible. Although it was impossible to imagine how she could have been in a room and not been at the centre of it. 'That's how you felt?'

'Always. Except for Gwen. She saw me.' Her eyes softened. 'And then Drew.'

And they were back to his brother. *Saint Freaking Andrew.* Wasn't it enough that he'd played second fiddle to his brother his whole life? Did he have to do it on his wedding night, albeit a fake one? It was starting to be impossible to ignore the obvious. 'You really cared for him, didn't you?'

Her eyes rounded up to him. 'Your brother was the best man I ever knew. Despite what you thought of him.'

Ever. Present tense included.

Right.

The unspoken criticism rankled. 'Drew was no prince, Bel. He had a sour streak and could hold a grudge for eternity.' Literally, as it turned out. 'Not sure he deserved such a lofty position in your estimation.'

'You weren't there. He saved me when I was seventeen and going off the rails. He grounded me.'

He did? Then he'd made an exception because that sure wasn't his own experience when he'd been in need. 'How?'

'By being constant and welcoming me and letting me into his love for Gwen. He could so easily have sidelined me like my parents did, kept her to himself.'

'The Drew I knew would have.' His brother had made an art of self-absorption. Second only to his competitive streak. Probably what made him so successful in his field. 'Maybe he just liked having a leggy young sycophant feeding his ego?'

Maybe he missed the unconditional adoration of a younger sibling.

Bel squeezed and released her fists. 'Or maybe he grew in his years away from you. Changed.'

Unexplainable hurt ravaged him. That Drew had needed to leave the family to turn into a good man, that once again little brother failed to measure up.

'Your unflinching loyalty is a credit to you, Bel. Misguided as it may be.'

'That's your opinion. It's always been your opinion and I give up trying to change it. You will just have to accept that your brother and my sister were different people in England.'

'Or you'll have to accept that you were so blinkered by your fascination with Drew that you couldn't see the truth.'

Frustration almost exploded from her tight chest. Her voice lifted. 'I was not *fascinated* by him,' she gritted though she felt the heat rise in her cheeks again.

'Come on.' And it was almost a sneer. 'You clearly had an obsessive thing going on.'

'I loved him, of course. But not…' She swished her skirt angrily as she kept pace with his long strides. 'He was like my brother.'

He spun around to face her. 'He was *my* brother, not yours.' The vehemence with which those words spat from his lips seemed to surprise even Flynn. But it was so telling. The only sound other than their strained breathing was the crunch of their feet on the dry paddock as he started off again.

'I think it's you that's obsessed by him,' she called out to him when he failed to notice he'd left her behind. 'You've held onto all that resentment and hurt for years. You see echoes of Drew in everything. And now you're dragging me into it. Looking for reasons to be mad at me.'

He stalled and turned back towards her, his jaw pure granite. Frowning. And not denying it.

'Why didn't you ever try to see him, Flynn—to bring him back? To heal things?'

She thought he wasn't going to answer but then words fought their way out of his strangled throat. 'Anything I said, he did the complete opposite of. So I stopped trying.'

She smiled sadly. 'He always was determined.'

'Belligerent,' Flynn snorted.

'Single-minded.'

'Stubborn.'

'Tomato/tomahto.' She smiled softly

He glanced at her from under low lashes and took two deep breaths. 'The point is, there was a brief window where I might have been able to bring him home but that slammed shut the day he met your sister.'

Again with the Gwen-bashing. But this unhappy dynamic between them wasn't going to change if neither of them did. Maybe she'd just have to be the bigger man. 'I was there that day, Flynn. It was the closest thing to love at first sight I've ever seen. They were utterly captivated with each other. Both so…enraptured.'

His dark eyes simmered. It looked like anger.

'Why would you wish that not so?' she asked. 'Do you truly resent them both that much? They found that rare thing we all seek.'

He stared at her, eyes creased.

'Their *other*...' she went on. 'The one person that is out there for each of us.'

'You truly believe that?'

'I suppose you'd say true love doesn't exist? Despite the two thriving examples living on this property.'

He indulged her and the look made her feel all of seventeen again. 'My grandparents married because Nan got pregnant. Love was a long time coming for them but they toughed it out for my father's sake.' His lips pressed together. 'My parents... They've just always been so solid and steady. They met in school and just never parted. There's no great romance there.'

Bel stared. How sad for him that he couldn't see the truth. 'Well, your brother found it. He found it.'

Flynn snorted. 'Just one more jewel in the crown of Drew's brilliance.'

'He's dead, Flynn. How can you think of him like that?'

'I know he's dead, Belinda,' he blazed down on her. 'He died in a fetid river trying to save *your* sister.'

The scorn burned. 'Because he loved her. Gwen was the air he breathed. They had the sort of love I can only dream of.'

Flynn stared at her, thinking. 'Yet you're willing to give up your chance at that to raise their unborn children.'

Pain lanced through her. His words so closely matched her deepest fears it stole her breath. 'You assume the two are mutually exclusive.'

'It's a big sacrifice.'

'These babies had a family once and it was ripped away from them. They deserve their chance to be loved. And to love.'

'They do? Or you do?'

She winced. 'Is that so terrible? Am I not entitled to some happiness, too? Someone to love me?' *Two little someones, in fact.*

As she stared at him his own face cleared and understanding widened his eyes. 'You don't think it's there for you.'

What?

He stepped closer, looked down on her, close and warm, and her body thrilled. 'That's why you're willing to fill your body with someone else's babies. That's why you were willing to travel halfway around the world with a total stranger. Marry that stranger. A beautiful twenty-three-year-old woman.' His head tilted as he studied her. 'You don't think that kind of love is out there for you anywhere.'

Panic bubbled through her at how close he was to the truth and that her face might give her away. Or her hammering heartbeat. She faked a shrug. 'What are the odds of it happening twice in one family?'

Let alone in two families.

'I don't think it even happens once,' Flynn said flatly. 'What you saw was just the product of a child's lens—'

That brought her up cold. 'Child? I was seventeen.'

'Physically, perhaps.'

'You think I didn't know what I saw in front of my face? They were in love.'

'Would you even know what it looks like?'

She frowned at him. *It looks just like this. It feels just like this. Good and horribly fatal at the same time.* 'Of course I'd know...'

'Bel. You came from a home where affection was in short supply. You've built these two people you lost up into saints. Martyrs, practically. And you cling to these perceptions about love because they help you to justify everything you are. Everything you've done.'

Like having the babies.

'What you were seeing was attraction,' he ended. 'Pure and simple.'

'No.' Okay, *yes*...but no. 'There was more there. Complete connection. They got engaged just weeks later. They knew they'd found it.' Because if they hadn't, then what made her think she ever would?

Flynn snorted and turned for his cottage. The lights glowed

a welcome and a spiral of smoke curled from the chimney. Pop's forethought: *good man.* 'Two narcissists managed to find each other through the crowd. Alert the media!'

She shot off after him. 'Don't change the subject.'

'The subject? Of whether or not true love exists? Hell of a conversation to be having on our wedding night.'

'You know, you and your brother might have been more alike than I realised.'

He looked at her sideways.

'You have the same basic traits. Solid. Consistent. I may not always like the things you do or say but you're as dependable as the earth we're walking on.'

He skipped over her not liking things he did and zeroed straight in on him having the same basic traits as *the best man she ever knew.* Selective hearing was a wonderful thing. He swung around as they reached the cottage door to look down on her.

Really look.

This entire stubborn discussion reminded him so much of his youth. 'You know, you might be onto something…'

She frowned up at him. 'Onto what?'

'The whole Drew thing…' The creases between her eyes only deepened. 'Well, the thing with Drew and you, really…'

Her eyes fell shut and he could swear he could hear her counting to ten. 'There was no *thing* with Drew and me—'

'The thing with you *and me* and Drew, then.'

That got her attention.

'I've been racking my brain as to why you and I set off so many sparks.'

Her eyes flared. 'Apart from the obvious, you mean?'

He blinked at her.

'The way you've had your lawyers drag every single part of my personal life across their desk and sift through it looking for usable dirt. The fact we're neck-deep in a custody battle.'

He waved a hand. 'No, not that.'

'Then what?'

'I thought it was because you were like Gwen.'

'*What* was?'

He stepped closer on the crowded top step. 'The reason you get so firmly under my skin.'

Her tiny gasp was partly disguised by the wind buffeting overhead. But her lips parted and her pupils slowly grew as she twigged what he was saying. 'I was ready for you to be stylish and socially flawless and all about outward appearances,' he said. 'But you're not like that at all. You're clumsy and messy and—'

The speculation in her eyes drained. 'I think I liked you better when you were all moody and silent...'

He held a hand up to continue. 'And you're down-to-earth and warm and...natural.' The hand reached out and tucked a lock of red hair behind her ear. 'And *so* completely my type.'

Her breath froze. 'Are you drunk, Flynn?' she managed to squeeze out.

He chuckled, deep and low. 'No. But I haven't been able to work out—for the life of me—why you bother me so much. What it is about you. Why I didn't just jump your bones the second week here. But I got it just now.'

The pounding in her chest increased. 'And?'

'The way you're fighting so fiercely for custody of the babies, the way you won't accept anything but victory. The way you're so quick with a witty comeback and so damned fast on the uptake with new things. The way you've colonised my family and become like the sun around which they all revolve. The way you push every single one of my buttons. *Repeatedly.*'

She held her breath, staring at him wide-eyed.

'You're not Gwen,' he rounded off. 'You're *Drew*.'

His triumphant declaration almost echoed in the loaded silence that followed.

'Are you saying I'm the female equivalent of your brother?' Bel finally got out.

'*Just like him.* I can't believe I didn't see it sooner.'

She stared at him, her voice cooling. 'Drew the "uncompromising", "narcissistic", pedant?'

He stumbled then. 'Okay...no...not like him in all things... Obviously.'

She reached for the door handle, her face hard. 'Goodnight, Flynn.'

He quickly slipped his hand over the top of hers to still it. It took him straight back to that open cave mouth. 'Bel...I just wanted to—'

She rounded back on him. 'To what, Flynn? Get back at me? Hurt me?'

What the...? 'Hurt you? You worshipped the man.'

'But you hated him.'

He winced and then twisted his body uncomfortably. 'I didn't hate him, Bel. We were brothers. But he...we had issues.'

'That's what you wanted to tell me? That I give you issues?'

'Woman—' his voice thickened '—you have no idea.'

'Goodnight, Flynn.'

'Bel, wait...' He snaked strong fingers around her wrist and halted her progress as the door swung open.

She lifted her chin when he didn't continue. 'So was that it? I remind you of Drew. Mystery solved. Offence identified. Burden offloaded?'

'I didn't tell you to offload a burden.'

She brought her eyes back around to his. 'Then why did you tell me?'

He opened his mouth and then closed it again. Second time lucky... 'Because I wanted to explain...apologise, really...for being reactive with you sometimes.'

'Sometimes?'

The glint of challenge in her eyes got his blood racing. 'Now you *are* being a pedant.'

She stared at him. Then she pushed open the door to the house. Then she stopped. 'Oh, my…'

It looked as if Pop hadn't come down alone. In addition to a toasty blaze in the fireplace, dozens of flickering half-spent candles littered the living area, throwing the whole place into a soft glow. It was beautiful. And so horribly out of phase with the conversation they were having.

Bel swung back around to him and lifted her chin, her blue eyes sparking more than the fireplace. 'Fine. Apology accepted, if that's what it was. I have no problem being the best parts of your brother.'

His thumb traced strokes on her bare wrist where he still restrained her. He knew she'd said it to be provocative but something about the way the dozens of flickering lights played on her skin and hair robbed him of interest in carrying on that conversation. He wasn't in the mood to fight any more. 'So I'm not entirely Hades, then?'

She flicked her eyes up from next to him. 'I never thought you were.'

He turned her towards him and peeled his coat from her shoulders. 'You stood before me today like you were being sacrificed to him.'

'Today was…challenging.' She immediately crossed to the fire and warmed herself, keeping her eyes shy of his.

'You've had plenty of notice.'

She looked at him strangely. 'Time doesn't make it any easier. Didn't the irony of it strike you?'

'Irony?' Like the fact they'd entered their marital home talking about his brother?

'Standing in that exquisite place doing something so…'

'Non-exquisite?' Like marrying *him*…

'…So hollow.'

'That's what was bothering you? That it was fake?'

'No one wants their wedding day to be empty. Even you. You can't tell me you didn't think at all about what it might be like to stand there with someone who actually loved you. Who you loved. The full soft focus dream.'

The reminder that she was doing it under sufferance didn't sit well with him. Not when he knew full well he'd originally just wanted it over with as he'd stood facing the terrifying drop to the pristine lake below, waiting for the women to arrive. But then he'd turned and seen this glowing, radiant vision walking towards him—scared out of her wits but so ethereal and brave—and he'd stopped thinking about anything but getting his ring on her finger.

Making her his.

Crazy.

So, maybe he did buy into the dream just a little bit. Just like he was buying into this wedding night. The slow dancing. The close contact. Every opportunity to touch her. The firelight arcing off her hair right now.

'"The soft focus dream." Is that what the kiss was about?' he asked.

Her eyes flew to his. 'The kiss was necessary. You said so yourself.'

He leaned on the kitchen island and crossed his arms across his broad chest and asked her what he'd really wanted to know all evening. What he'd been thinking about since the cave. 'The first kiss was necessary for show. What was the second one about?'

Her eyes flew to his and her mouth parted on a silent gasp. It reminded him immediately of the way her lips had felt under his. How his tongue had slipped past her defences into the confused heat of her mouth and gone to town. How she'd kissed him back.

'I…' Heat flared in her cheeks bringing that hayloft tumbling back to mind. What he wouldn't give to have a big pile of fresh straw somewhere handy right now. To lay her back in it. To get straw in places it wasn't meant to be. He crossed his ankles to compress the sudden tingling at the other end of his legs. But he didn't rescue her. What she said next would be very telling.

'You wanted it to be convincing…' she stammered.

She looked pained but he wasn't in the mood for politely letting it go. Not if they were going to be sharing a roof. There was too much at stake. One of them had to talk about the giant *thing* simmering between them that they'd both been politely ignoring. 'We made Nan blush. That's unprecedented. Why did you really do it?'

She twisted and untwisted the fabric of her dress in her hands like she had back in that London hospital. He was sure she didn't notice, but *he* noticed because every twist momentarily flashed a hint more of long leg. He fought the surge of desire and concentrated on backing her into the emotional corner he knew would reveal the truth. Whatever it might be.

He took a breath and a risk. 'You wanted to kiss me.'

Her eyes flared. 'Get over yourself, Flynn. I was curious…'

'Curious?'

Her chin lifted defiantly. 'You've been going to town with the touching…all this time. I just wanted to see if the main attraction was worth the hype of the previews.'

Bull. She wanted to kiss him. Inexplicable warmth surged through him. He pushed slowly away from the island bench. She was such a terrible liar now he knew what to look for. The parted lips, the darting glance, the wringing hands…

'So how did I do?'

Her wild eyes swung back to him. 'It was…fine.'

'Fine?'

'Acceptable.'

Ouch. Pride dragged out his ego to defend its honour. 'You know that it wasn't even close to being the main attraction. Most people would consider kissing the preview…'

He certainly did, the way she'd opened up to his thrusting tongue… It put images in his head he'd had no business thinking in the presence of his grandparents. Or Belinda Rochester.

'Wow. You have a cast-iron ego, don't you?' she said now.

That halted his advance when his toes nearly touched hers and he simmered down on her, the heat from the fire baking even hotter parts of him that were already ablaze. Every part of his body was hyper-alert. 'Would you like references? From previous satisfied customers?'

The laugh that barked from her was more about the release of pressure than any delight she took in his words. She leaned back away from him. 'No, thank you.'

'Then you leave me no alternative but to prove it to you.'

He slid an arm around her waist and pulled her close to him, and then swooped down to take her outraged mouth with his. She held herself stiff and frozen for seconds and the small part of him that was still semi-conscious wondered if he'd misjudged her. But her struggles were half-hearted and the squirming only served to grind them closer together in some very intimate places. Places that were already on high alert.

His body responded graphically to the torturous rubbing, and her eyes flew open. She stared at him with curiosity blazing out of the sapphire depths, and her struggling ceased. His hands roamed freely across the soft exposed skin of her back and shoulders as his mouth echoed them across her lips.

Slowly, so slowly, she relaxed in his arms until her own crept up to circle his neck and she uttered a tiny little sigh. Her mouth matched his exploration and his whole body twitched as she tentatively slid her tongue in to duel with his, her delicate teeth nipping at his lips. She gasped when he returned the favour.

'Why are you smiling?' he murmured against the lips that had parted in a grin against his.

She stretched more fully against him, pressing hard nipples into his chest. The fact that his kisses had made them like that only burned him more. 'If you'd asked me this morning how you and I would be spending our wedding night,' she breathed, hot and heavy against his skin, 'this would have been the last thing I would have imagined.'

'And that's funny?'

'Only because it's the first thing most people would imagine.'

He took her mouth again, hard and hungry. In case it was the last chance he got. 'You have a point. But I say we just go with it…'

But Bel showed no signs of slowing and she led him backwards until the sofa edge hit her calves. Okay, so things were officially not going at all as he'd expected either. He took her slight weight and eased her down onto her back before sinking down on top of her, sliding sideways slightly so that he didn't press uncomfortably on her abdomen. Where two little lives nestled.

He happily pressed into her everywhere else—hard where she was soft, flesh against flesh. Her fingers speared through his hair and kept his mouth locked on hers and his own traced down the flushed heat of her skin—one resting just below the curve of a breast and the other sliding to her thigh. He bunched her skirt and dragged it upwards, desperate to feel the silken length of those long legs against his hands. He stroked the back of his hand clear up to where the thin strap of her panties crossed her hip.

Her eyes flew open again. And stayed open. She twisted her mouth free and took several deep breaths. Flynn shifted his focus to her throat, which suddenly stretched out enticingly in front of him, pale and luminous.

'Flynn…' Small hands pushed ineffectively against him.

His body on fire, he mouthed his way to the high point in her jaw, just below her earlobe, and breathed into it, 'What?'

Bel groaned deep at the back of her throat and pressed into his lips. The sound did terrible things to his self-control and he arched his desire more firmly against her. God, why hadn't they been doing this from the beginning?

'Flynn…!'

The firm tone finally got his attention. He pulled his mouth free and stared at her. She lay below him, flushed, dishevelled, undignified and utterly gorgeous. 'What's wrong?'

'I don't… um…' Her chest rose and fell enticingly with the strain of speaking. 'This can't…'

This can't happen.

He knew that. Somewhere. But his body sure hadn't got the message. Frustration screamed through him. 'You started it, Princess.' He'd only planned on kissing her; she was the one who'd moved things to the sofa.

'I know, I… Oh, God…' Her luminous eyes narrowed in a pained frown. 'Let me up. I can't think while you're…'

Harder than a dry riverbed for you?

Also not something he'd expected tonight. Though he couldn't be sorry.

He shifted his weight so that she could sit up, and carefully slid the hem of her dress back down for her. She pushed herself into a more upright position. Awkward and embarrassed and—his stomach sank—was that a flare of shame?

'I should explain…'

He slid his eyes away, not ready for what was going to come. 'Nothing to explain,' he gritted.

'No, Flynn. I should explain.' She swung her legs to the floor and pushed herself more respectably into the sofa back. Then she met his eyes. And held them. 'I'm a virgin, Flynn.'

If it was possible for all the air to get sucked out of his lungs just as a new lot rushed in, it happened, robbing him of speech.

A virgin?

The smile she gave him was unsteady. 'So all of…this…is a bit new to me.'

He mastered the air flailing around in his lungs and forced it into words. 'All of it?' His inner caveman roared and thumped the ground with his club. *His* were the first hands on her perfect flesh? She'd never even got horizontal with a man?

'Not the kissing, but…' She shrugged. The pink high in her cheeks made the blue of her raised eyes ever more startling. More beautiful.

He had air now but was still basically speechless. 'How?'

She laughed, throaty and low. 'Bad management?'

The awkwardness was still there. He pushed fully upright and turned more towards her. 'No, really. How? Why?'

Her mouth opened and closed soundlessly. But eventually she said, 'I've been waiting for Mr Right.'

He narrowed his eyes. Something niggled. A girl like her must have had a world of offers at the ready. But this was Belinda Rochester he was talking to. 'Mr Right or Mr Good Enough For You?'

She nearly managed to hide the wince. But then she locked clear, deep blue eyes on his. 'Okay. Yes. I was waiting for someone special. But not because I thought I was,' she raced on. 'I just…set a high bar.'

The best man she ever knew…

Old doubts came surging back. He waved his hands towards the sofa, his voice thick. 'So what was this? Some kind of consolation prize?'

Bel took a deep breath and watched Flynn's face streak ashen. He thought she was telling him he didn't measure up. She knew enough about old pain to recognise it when she saw it. The part of her that had lived her whole life not being good enough cried out for the sudden evidence of it in him. Somehow he was totally missing the fact that she'd just been lying spread-eagled under him with her skirt hiked high, and was focusing instead on a few simple words.

And getting them totally wrong.

She swallowed her umbrage. There was only one path through shattered feelings: honesty, carefully trodden and clearly stated. But it was a terrifying path. Her heart pounded noisily. '*This* was about us, Flynn. You and me and the way the air thickens when we're sharing it.'

The doubt in his eyes didn't dissipate. 'You don't deny it?'

'How can I? I feel it as much as you do, even if I don't quite understand it.'

He scoffed, but his eyes were wary. 'You're making the assumption that it's mutual—'

It would be easy to blush, to slip back into Bel-of-six-months-ago paradigm and let the doubt silence her. But then confidence—raw and sexual and new—surged through her. She suddenly became aware of every hidden corner of her body. 'Two minutes ago we were exchanging oxygen.' Her eyes meshed with his. 'It's mutual.'

He crossed his arms across his broad chest. 'Maybe I'm just in this for a quick—'

'With a Rochester girl?' she cut in. 'I don't think so. That's more a reason for *not* coming near me.' She noted the way he stood, chest heaving, just millimetres from her. Glaring down at her. She lifted her chin. 'Yet here we are, both panting like a pair of worn out gladiators.'

And here she was, desperate to feel that hard chest under her hands again. And desperate that he understood she was breathing heavily for *him*.

'I'll grant you there's chemistry between us,' he conceded. 'But I'm no way near worn out. I'm just getting started.'

The lascivious look in his eyes—so full of promise, so full of the dangerously unknown—chased her off. She hadn't put a halt to their heady kissing and offloaded her biggest secret only to leap straight back into his arms. She turned for the back of the house where the spare room was. 'Well, you're going to have to finish on your own then. I'm exhausted and going to bed.'

'I'll join you.'

She rounded back, laughing roughly. 'That wasn't an invitation.'

'I know.'

Was he possibly that obtuse? 'We're not having sex, Flynn.'

'I wasn't offering sex, Belinda.'

She reeled. 'Then what…?'

'You've just admitted to this fatal attraction between us. I thought it would be worth…exploring. Testing.'

'Testing?'

'The parameters. See how far it goes. What if it's just the magic of the day talking?'

Today was as far from actual magic as she could imagine being. A business transaction in the Twilight Zone. 'Then we'd be better off testing it tomorrow.' Not that she had any intention of that either. No matter what her hopeless heart wanted.

He glanced at the kitchen clock. 'It *is* tomorrow. Just.'

'Flynn, this is ridiculous…' And way too calculated. And when did he get that close?

'Is it?' His breath blew the tiny hairs on her forehead to attention. 'It wasn't ten minutes ago. It felt pretty un-ridiculous then. Like something that's been waiting to happen since we first met.'

'I'm not interested in—'

'Let's find out, shall we?'

He hauled her against his hard body and lowered his mouth to hers.

Proving a point.

Making a statement.

Marking his territory.

It was nothing like his last kiss. Or their first one. She pulled herself free and wiped her hand across lips which tingled treacherously despite his presumption. He didn't try all that hard to keep her.

'You know I can see you as the bad-boy teenager every now and again,' she panted, staring closely at the way the grey of his eyes simmered dangerously. 'But somehow, deep down, it's not quite convincing. Even now you look quite sorry to have just manhandled me.'

'Maybe I just lack commitment to my own cause?'

'Meaning?'

He stepped closer. 'Meaning first I was the good-boy-that-turned-bad, then I was the bad-boy-that-came-good. Maybe all the time I should have just been a more balanced mix of both.' He came to a halt a breath from her. 'I should have just gone for what I needed and damn the consequences instead of endlessly apologising for imagined sins.'

She stared at him, not quite making the connection. 'What do you need?'

'Right now? You.' This time his eyes backed him up.

Her pulse lurched.

'Especially now that I understand what it is about you that drives me so crazy. I can get past it. Get to more…productive… aspects.'

'Productive?'

He moved closer in the darkness. She felt the heat coming off him long before his words breathed across her ear. 'Pleasurable.'

His lips pressed hotly against her jaw and roamed their way across to her mouth. Bel forced her frozen body to move again before he felt the way it had locked up. The way *he'd* locked it up. Blood raced through her startled arteries. Exulting.

'Flynn—'

'You were right about the attraction between us. It's real. It's there. Despite everything.'

Despite her being so much like the brother that he'd had a fractured relationship with? Despite them being on opposite sides of the court case? He rested his forehead against hers and her head swam with his nearness.

'I'm not having sex with you, Flynn,' she whispered. The more she said it, the more likely it was to be true. Right?

'That's not what I'm offering,' he murmured, stroking her hair. 'I'm talking about bed. Sleeping. Together. On our wedding night.'

She lifted her face. 'You want to literally sleep…together?'

God help her but the idea was seductive. Even more so when he referred to it in terms of *offering.* That was dangerously suggestive of respect. And choice. And the ability to say no.

Which would mean robbing herself of the chance to nestle in next to him, wrapping her arms around all that masculine heat.

He started moving around the living room, extinguishing each candle with a kiss of air. 'I'm bushed, Bel. I've been up for twenty-two hours. You wouldn't be getting me at my best, anyway.'

As if...

'What?'

Her head snapped up. Had she said that aloud, too? She really had to get a muzzle for her subconscious. 'I said, I don't think it's a good idea.'

'Bel… You're a virgin and five months pregnant with twins, I'm not going to risk hurting any of you. I just want to sleep.'

He blew out the last candle, leaving the room lit only by the orange stain of the glowing fire. The low light threw a shadow, tall and ominous up along the far wall and turned Flynn into a dangerously delectable silhouette.

She swallowed as best she could. 'I can get one of the dogs down here if it's body heat you're after.'

The silhouette moved towards her and slid its strong, warm hand into her clammy one. 'Hilarious.'

'Where are we going?' He tugged her down the hall.

'My bed's bigger.'

'I haven't agreed yet.' She cringed at her own slip. *Yet...*

'You will. Your body wants to.'

She put the brakes on, way too late for her own dignity. 'My body doesn't know what it wants.' Lies. Damned lies. It was screaming for more contact with his.

'Then let's find out.'

'Flynn, this is ridiculous…'

'Just something small. Just sharing a bed. No strings.'

The idea perked up and whispered in her ear. Yes…something small. A test. Just a test. There was no harm in just sleeping, was there?

Pure delusion.

'Tell you what, if you hate it then you're welcome to sneak back into your own bed the moment I'm out cold.'

There was no way on this planet she was going to hate it. But that was the problem. 'Wouldn't a glass of warm milk be more beneficial?'

'No. I need you.'

Three simple words.

Not the ones she'd truly love to hear, but close enough. And had she really expected more? They tugged deep down in her soul. Flynn was choosing her—inexplicably, and after a lifetime of being overlooked. The man who had every reason to hate her was asking her to trust him. To test the waters of whatever this was between them. To end the hostilities.

He spun around and looked down on her. 'I'm so tired of being tired, Bel. I don't think I've slept well since the day you arrived.' He cupped his hand behind her head and traced her jaw with his thumb in the darkness. 'But if you seriously don't want to then I'll take you to your own room. And I'll lock the door myself.'

She gave it two and a half seconds' thought. Curl up alone in her cold bed while the sexiest man she'd ever known tossed and turned restlessly a thin wall away, or follow her heart and share a bed with the man she wanted so very badly! The man she wouldn't be able to sleep for thinking about anyway. The man whose wife she *wanted* to be.

Even for just one night.

Even if it was make-believe.

She slept with Flynn all night and into the morning, curled hard into the shelter and strength of his body. He'd shed his wedding suit and donned some modest and inexplicably sexy

track pants before tugging her behind him down into the pil-
lowed heaven of his enormous bed as though it were the most
normal thing in the world to do.

Never mind the fact she'd not shared a bed with someone
since she was four years old.

They'd started out careful, giving each other respectful
space. But as minutes ticked into ten she'd forced her body to
relax and let it merge with the heat of his, tucking back into
his welcome, trusted hold.

What she'd been dying to do for…who knew how long?

She'd let the smell and feel of him wash over her and when
she felt his breath on her neck morph into the half-asleep press
of his lips to her throat she didn't pull away.

She'd rolled towards him.

His lazy kisses had stirred her blood—roaming, explor-
ing—and his silent hands traced her entire body as if memo-
rising it. Worshipping it. She'd done the same, pressing into his
furnace-hot body and letting her skin discover his. But neither
of them escalated things further, too tired in body or maybe in
spirit. Or was it simply that they both knew, deep-down, that
having sex really wasn't the most productive—or moral—way
to take their minds off their troubles.

Dr Cabanallo would still have his miracle birth and Bel
would walk out of this room today with everything she'd had
when Flynn led her into it.

Except perhaps her heart.

She pulled away carefully now, and looked at the sleeping
man next to her.

His face, normally so carefully composed, was relaxed in
sleep, like the boy he must have been back when the Bradleys
first came to Bunyip's Reach. It wasn't the incensed face that
had slapped a court order onto the hospital glass, or the stern
one that had glared at her at thirty thousand feet. Or the cold
one that had given her a script of lies to recite to his family
that day in the Oberon coffee shop. It wasn't even the carefully

unreadable face she'd lifted her eyes to as she slid the white gold ring onto his finger yesterday or the tortured, pained one that had pulled her in here last night.

Her husband.

The man she'd given her emotional virginity to, if not the physical one.

Her heart tore free from her chest and tumbled, uncontrolled, into the pit of her stomach on a disorienting physical lurch and she curled her hands into fists on the cool sheets to steady the wild tilting.

Exactly when, or how, or *why* was a total mystery, but the sensations in her body and the swelling of her heart as she'd stretched up to Flynn in that cave and pressed her lips to his in a silent *I do* was evidence enough. She really didn't need the overwhelming sense of emotion and rightness last night had brought to convince her…

Another Rochester woman had fallen for another Bradley man. Every bit as deeply and irreversibly as the first.

Against all odds.

When exactly had it happened? When had she realised that he was as good a man as his brother and quite possibly better? There was no time she could remember suddenly lifting her head and realising that he was meant for her. She couldn't even pick the moment she'd stopped dreading the sound of his footfall and started anticipating it. But she never would have allowed him to sweep her into his bed if her soul hadn't recognised the mark of its *other*.

Grumpy, protective, wounded…but one hundred per cent right for her.

And so she'd let Flynn kiss her into virtual unconsciousness and then snuggled in contentedly when he had pulled her tight beneath his chin, into his hot, unsatisfied body, and gently stroked both of them into a deep, gratifying sleep.

And now it was morning.

And his eyes were going to open any moment.

And conversation would be required.

What on earth was she going to say?

'Stop thinking so loud,' a deep, rumbly voice croaked.

She flinched and then dragged her focus from the place between his pectoral muscles where she was doing her thinking back up to his. His eyes were barely open, more of a grey squint, but they were locked hard on her.

'Good morning,' she stuttered.

He twisted his head towards the wall clock and then let it fall back to the pillow. 'Actually, I think it's afternoon.'

'Oh.' She pushed to a half-sitting position, mortified at their sloth. 'What will your parents think?'

'They'll think we wore ourselves out in here last night. Not too far from the truth, just not what they'll be imagining.'

Not a conventional wedding night, by any means. But since when had they done anything conventionally?

It was impossible to know from his still half-asleep manner whether he was as uncomfortable as her. Whether he regretted what the accusations of last night had led to. One part suppressed tension, one part emotional upheaval, two parts blatant desire… A recipe for more than disaster.

'I should go back to my room…' She swung her legs over the edge of Flynn's king-sized bed.

A strong arm coiled around her waist. 'Stay.'

One word. That was all it was. But it was rich with intent and overflowing with promise. The delights of the night before rushed back to her, blazing a warm trail through her cheeks. The things they'd done… While only kisses, the idea of him doing those things with anyone else—as he must have—made her literally feel sick.

Or it could just be the babies.

She forced herself free of his hold and sprinted for the en suite bathroom. But she was at least spared the humiliation of vomiting just metres from him as the wave of morning sickness settled. She drank a glass of water and splashed the rest on her face and clutched the towel she dried it with to her chest as if it would cushion the ache there.

'Are you okay?'

She turned towards the doorway and her whole body leapt at the sight of him standing shirtless like a golden Adonis with track pants slung low on his hips and bare tanned feet curling into the bedroom carpet.

'I'm fine. These morning dashes have been getting rarer as the weeks pass. I think it might just be all the…um…activity last night. Stirring everything up.' That probably wasn't even possible. Her own inexperience screamed at her. Heat poured back into her blanched cheeks.

Flynn smiled and leaned on the door frame. 'You're beautiful when you blush.'

Her heart began to hammer. Somehow the physical intimacy they'd shared last night, even the angry moments in between, paled against the implied emotional intimacy of a statement like that. Just hours ago he'd told her that the very things that were part of her nature bothered him. Challenged him. Too much like his brother. And then he had her on her back on the sofa.

Now happy families in the bathroom.

Which is it, Flynn? A question she could rightly ask herself, too.

The coldness of the autumn day finally registered and she pushed herself back upright, shivering. Flynn dragged the rumpled quilt off the bed and threw it round his shoulders, then held it open to invite her in. It closed around her like an envelope of warm air and she was back pressed against the furnace of Flynn's chest.

Where she'd really been very happy all night.

'You're uncomfortable,' he rumbled.

On the contrary. Standing within the circle of his arms, toasty-warm from his radiated heat was about as comfortable as she'd been in years. The nausea more fully dissipated. She glanced up at him, trying to read his expression. 'This isn't weird for you?'

How often had he done this? Stood might-as-well-be naked in a bathroom with a woman in his arms. Bel was afraid of the answer.

'Not weird. Surprising, maybe.'

Very.

'This wasn't something I planned, Bel.'

'I know.'

'But I'm not going to apologise for it, if that's what you're waiting for.'

She lifted her eyes again. 'I'm not waiting for anything. I just don't know what to do now.'

That made him smile. He stroked the hair from her face. 'Now? It's easy. We dress, we eat, we go see what the rest of the world is up to.'

She nodded mutely. *We pretend none of this ever happened.* An awful sinking feeling consumed her.

'Or...' he drew her with him backwards out of the chilly bathroom '...we go back to bed and do all of that tomorrow.'

'We can't sleep all day, Flynn. We both have work to do.'

'We got married yesterday. No one is going to expect us anywhere today.'

'But...' But what? It was such a sensationally good idea. And bad. 'Should we push our luck?' Every minute they were horizontal together was a minute closer to consummating this marriage. All it would take was a momentary lack of resolve on either of their parts...

'Do I strike you as someone who doesn't like to take a few risks?' His smile was sexy enough to melt her resolve before she even hit the sheets. He raised his right hand. 'Scout's honour, Bel. I promise your virtue will be safe.'

'Why?'

He stared at her. 'Why what?'

'Why would you do that to yourself?' Or to me. 'It can't be…comfortable.'

His stare intensified and she could see his brain turning over the right response. 'There's a world of options between kissing and sex, Bel. And plenty of time to explore whatever this is we have going on between us.'

Test it, he'd said last night.

'But no actual…' Words failed her. 'Because I'm pregnant?' *Because I'm about to treble in size?*

His eyes narrowed. 'Indirectly.'

Oh.

But then he spelled it out for her. 'Annulment of our marriage is going to be conditional on it not being consummated. It's in both our best interests. If you want the marriage revoked…'

She stumbled at the bed edge. Annulment. He was still thinking about the court case. He was still thinking about *the end*. And here she was thinking about love and flowers and happy ever afters.

'Right. Yes, of course.' Her voice grew hushed. 'So this is…?'

'There's something between us, Bel. For better or worse. And we have months yet to try and work it out of our systems.'

She internalised the slap across the face that statement was. *Right. Because that always went so well in the movies…*

She shouldn't be surprised. It was a natural progression for someone like Flynn from attraction…to exploration of the feelings…to exorcism of them. A man who sought disappointment would never let himself find anything else.

'So what's it going to be?' he said, brightening. 'Bed or breakfast?'

Self-preservation finally reared its lazy head. 'I vote for eating.'

He looked surprised. And a little bit crestfallen. 'Two minutes ago you were about to throw up.'

She shrugged. 'It's a pregnancy thing. Now I'm ready to eat.'

He studied her silently, then finally released his hold on her quilted prison. 'Then breakfast it is.'

'Lunch.'

Somehow, given what had happened between them last night, they did manage to get things back on a reasonably even footing over a simple meal of grilled cheese on wholemeal toast. So much had changed since lunchtime yesterday, it felt quite surreal. Playing house with a man she'd been sparring with for so many months felt odd enough without also knowing how he looked semi-naked. How he *felt* naked. And how she felt when she was naked with him. Semi-naked.

Alive, was the answer. Amazingly, embarrassingly alive.

And she hadn't felt that for…

She frowned.

…*ever*.

Flynn tossed her a cloth and she wiped the lunch crumbs off the kitchen island. 'I was awake for a while after you fell asleep,' he said. 'Thinking. Watching you sleep.'

She stared at him. 'Oh, that's not creepy at all.'

He chuckled. 'The important thing is what I decided.' He stared at her expectantly.

Okay. 'What did you decide, Flynn?'

'I'm done bagging Gwen and Drew. The past belongs in the past. I can't change any of it, particularly now. I need to be looking to the future.'

Bold words. If he could do it. Lord knew she'd had little enough success getting her heart and body to do what her mind recommended. He had a lot of unresolved feelings about his brother, still. 'I think that's a great idea. These babies don't need the extra confusion of an uncle who didn't like their parents.'

His eyes shot up to her, wide and intense. 'Uncle? You're still assuming you'll get custody.'

She matched his stare. 'I have to assume that.' Otherwise, what did she have?

'And you're planning on telling them they're not yours? Ours?'

She reeled. 'Well, yes. Are you saying you weren't?'

'It's a lot for kids to understand.'

'That they had parents who loved them and wanted them badly enough to go through the hell of IVF for?'

'That their parents died and their aunt carried them?'

'It's the truth.'

'Truth isn't always the best option.'

'How were you planning on explaining a mother or a father who left them? One of us isn't going to be there. How is that the best option?'

The idea seemed to make him angrier. 'By surrounding them with love so that they have support when they eventually work that out.'

'Well, that's fine for you but I don't have a support network. I only have me. *They'll* only have me.' Her own words made her frown. That couldn't be good, could it? What if something happened to her?

His nostrils flared. 'Why don't we leave that discussion until we have an outcome? That's still a few months away.'

Her hand slipped low on her belly. 'Well, they'd better hurry up or these babies will be in high school.'

His eyes followed her hands and then lingered there, and then to her empty plate, taking on a speculative light. 'So, you're adequately refuelled then?'

She channelled that nurse from the hospital in London—Lord, that felt like two lifetimes ago—and crossed her arms. 'Not on your life, sunshine.'

But then, because of Flynn's comically crushed expression and because in that split second she realised she wasn't at all ready to never feel his body against hers again, she took a deep breath and modified. 'Not until sunset, at least.'

CHAPTER NINE

WINTER in Oberon was so much like winter in England Bel felt at home for the first time all year. A thick layer of snow spread across fields that were once green, and mounded up on tree limbs that had once had leaves until it overbalanced and crashed to the ground with a muted thud.

Bel lay on the sofa closest to the window in the main homestead, snuggled into a quilt woven from the fleece of one of Arthur's belligerent alpacas, a hot chocolate in hand, staring out absently at the picturesque scene.

It was possible she was just adapting, finally, to Australian life. And it was possible that she felt at home because Bunyip's Reach had started to *be* her home. Here she had new parents and grandparents who enjoyed her company and wanted her around. She had a husband who seemed to enjoy her conversation as much as her body. What parts he'd had access to. And now that he was letting himself get closer to her.

Some kind of internal switch had flicked the day Flynn finally worked out why she affected him so much—because she reminded him of his brother. From that moment—maybe from the following morning—he'd been incrementally warming to her. Letting himself laugh, letting himself learn. Letting himself…if not quite *love*, then definitely *like*.

The twins were healthy and robust at eight months and, consequently, Bel was officially enormous. Her tiny frame exploded to the front like a watermelon she'd strapped there—not too far from how it felt as her muscles twinged in sequence, ensuring she was never quite comfortable. Her belly might have made a handy shelf for her hot chocolate while reclining, but she'd offered weeks ago to move back to her own room and leave Flynn in the comfort of his bed without having to squeeze around the *HMS Belinda*, which he'd flat out refused. Which meant she still had the nightly pleasure of snuggling back against his hot frame and falling asleep to the warmth of his easy breathing against her ear, the beat of his heart against her back, and the possessive heat of his hand on her drum-tight belly.

It wasn't perfect, but it was the kind of heaven she'd never let herself imagine having. And if she squinted just the right way it almost looked like love.

Unsatisfying, unconsummated, unrequited love.

But that was as much her doing as his. While she'd never had a fastidious bone in her body when it came to her appearance, suddenly she didn't want Flynn seeing her puffing and ungainly lurching around when he was still as solid and gorgeous as ever. And for him, holding back on that one final intimacy had grown to mean something important, something beyond the preservation of the annulment that hovered on the horizon. A deep and paranoid part of her feared that—for Flynn—as long as her body remained inviolate, so did his heart. After all…despite the many joys and comforts of living as Mrs Flynn Bradley, neither one of them had said a word about love. Or the future. Or about what was going to happen when the Crown's decree finally came in. Some days it was almost possible to forget entirely that the dispute even existed and just enjoy life on the tablelands. The happy family illusion. Bel knew that day would be hard enough without obsessing over it in advance.

Flynn was a very practical man. And, apparently, a very disciplined one. There was no way in the world that a man as careful as he was would ever have impregnated a girl accidentally. The more she got to know him, the more surprised she was that his family bought that. It just wasn't him.

She frowned.

Another thing she'd almost forgotten about. All the lies. Marrying Flynn had effectively rendered everything that came before it rather void. And the lies had started to roll all too comfortably off her tongue. She actually felt like Belinda Bradley. The old Belinda and all her troubles were virtually gone from her mind.

Maybe if you said something enough times it really did start to be truth?

'Sugar.' Over in the corner Denise ranted one of her more moderate curse words.

Bel looked up from the book she was reading. For the past six weeks she'd been barred from all but the lightest of chores and was officially on wait-duty, confined to the main homestead until Flynn returned from whatever task he was doing. Going mad with boredom.

And not the best time to be without something to keep her hands and mind busy, given the custody hearing had been in court since the start of the month.

'Problem?' she asked Denise.

'Internet is down again. It's this weather. One good storm and we're out for days.'

'Something you need particularly?'

She laughed. 'Just contact with the outside world. I have a pile of emails in my outbox just waiting for a decent connection.'

Another thing she'd prefer not to think about. The outside world was so not welcome right now. Like King Oberon's mythical subjects, she had no interest in knowing what was happening outside the forest. Reality had a way of messing with fantasy. The white-out could go on for ever as far as she was concerned, just as long as she had Flynn's arms to crawl into at night and the Bradley clan to hang out with by day. And a belly-full of babies.

Yep, denial was more than comfortable enough, thanks very much.

'I'll have to send Flynn and Bill into town to see if they have better luck with signal there. You should put in an order.'

There was almost no point. Anything she needed she could get in Sydney next month when she went in to have the twins. Not that she'd have a long list. Everything she needed she had. Healthy children, a warm, welcoming home and if not the *love* of a good man then at least his affection and attention.

Denise's frustrated sigh disguised her own.

She'd spent a lifetime mining what hints of affection she could from people, surviving off them. Suppressing her emotions was virtually second nature now—not that it hurt any less in the middle of the night when the shifting babies woke her and she thought about leaving the man whose arms she lay in—but it had become an easy habit with practice. Easy and necessary. She'd long since accepted that Flynn's heart was nowhere near as deep into this temporary marriage as his body was, and that it was going to be one-sided—her side—until the day it was over.

And that day had to be coming soon. Bel did her very best to ignore it. Because ignoring it meant she could have Flynn.

And she wanted him very much.

Decision day—D-Day—hung over everything, ominous and looming. Any time now Flynn's petition would be decided and they'd have a binding outcome and she'd be leaving Australia either empty-handed or with very full hands indeed.

Scarily full hands.

Not for the first time, she reminded herself that she'd let just about everyone in her life down. Why would the twins be any different? Just because she wanted it to be? What if she wasn't cut out to be a single mother? What if she failed? This wouldn't be like bailing out of school or moving out of home, things that only impacted on her.

Her hand slid to her belly. If she failed these two little people then *they* would be at risk. And assuring their future was the point of all of this.

But what other option did she have? She knew the drill when she first came to Bunyip's Reach and, despite everything, nothing had really changed. Flynn had never once said *what if* or spoken of other ways they might proceed with this. If she stayed. How that could work…

She wrapped her arms more tightly around herself in the window seat. God, she couldn't even *think* the words…

If he wanted her to stay and be a family, he would have asked.

Just because they were sharing a bed didn't mean he'd changed his mind about anything else. They were just *working it out of their systems.*

Well, he was. She was taking whatever she could get while it lasted.

Any day now she was going to confess all to the people who loved her, hurt them, and take two children from the arms of the man she loved and leave him for ever. Or…*it was still possible*…walk away from here with nothing. Just when she thought her life couldn't get any emptier than it had been.

A chill as arctic as the wind outside rattled through her body.

She suspected there were depths of *empty* she'd not even begun to plumb.

'Nothing for me, thanks.' Bel smiled at Flynn as three generations of Bradley men piled into Bill's old utility. They'd decided it would take all three of them to retrieve the long list of supplies Alice had given them, but Bel figured a few quiet ones with mates at the Oberon tavern was probably more on the agenda.

Some time amongst friends. Away from the women-folk. She didn't begrudge them that at all. A little separation was healthy in a relationship.

She snorted inwardly at her own presumption. Since when was she the expert on relationships? She was probably the most *under*-qualified one on the whole farm to make statements like that. Just because the time she spent with Flynn after a number of hours apart were the sweetest of her day…

'Give me your phone, then,' he said. 'I'll find some signal and download your mail for you.'

Email. Outside world. There was only one particular email he was thinking about… And Bel didn't want to think about it at all. But she handed over her phone politely, every move she made these days a kind of deception, every moment she didn't tell him how she felt about him. 'Thanks, Flynn. I'll see you when you get back.'

I'll miss you while you're gone.

Flynn tucked her phone into his pocket with one hand and pulled her close with the other, planting a gentle kiss on her lips, lingering, enjoying. Reading her silent thought as clearly as if she'd spoken—which, given her history, was a distinct possibility. As always, his touch caused a riot amongst the tiny hairs along her arms, and they prickled to attention.

And as always she stood grinning like an idiot when he stepped away and slid into the crowded back seat of his father's old extra-cab utility, loaded up with ecoshopping bags and every mobile phone in the place.

All three women hurried back into the warmth of the house after losing sight of the men-folk around the Reach's long drive.

'Tea, Bel?'

'I'm English, aren't I?' she quipped, inexplicably out of sorts. Maybe her disrupted sleep was finally getting to her. Or Flynn was. Whatever, she didn't feel quite right.

Please don't let it be because Flynn's not here. Please don't let me have become that bad…

Alice lit the stove and filled the kettle with fresh rainwater from the tank. 'The last Brit we had here didn't drink tea at all. Only coffee. Short black. Was most disconcerting, culturally.'

Bel froze.

Gwen. They were talking about Gwen. After how many months? She'd truly believed they would never, ever speak of her sister and now that they had she wished they'd stop. But the opportunity to find out, first-hand, what they'd so objected to about her flesh and blood was too good to walk away from.

'Was she one of your chalet customers?' she asked casually, her voice unnaturally tight, even to her own ears.

Alice laughed. 'Far from it, love. She was our daughter-in-law.'

Daughter. In law. Just like Bel was. Unless it was possible to be a daughter-against-the-law? Because what she was didn't really count.

She knew Alice and Denise would expect her surprise so she did her best to fake it. 'Flynn's brother was married to an English girl?' It was more croak than voice. How could some lies seem so much worse than others? Was it too late to back out of the discussion?

'She was such an elegant thing. Very European. So different to everyone on the Tablelands.'

Not if you'd seen her lounging around the house in training pants and socks, shovelling pizza into her mouth. In her comfort zone. She was just a normal Chelsea girl then.

'Was?' Bel risked.

Alice's eyes grew hooded. Denise averted hers entirely. 'She died in the same accident as our Andrew.'

Pain surprised her, sharp and low. Even though she knew how this story ended. Her body reacted with a shaft of biting misery hard across her mid-section. 'Oh. I'm sorry.'

'Don't be sorry for us. It's not like we lost two of our own. Though I'm sure her own family mourned her.'

You have no idea. 'She wasn't a daughter to you?' The un-fairness of that really lodged in Bel's gut.

Alice smiled sadly. 'Not the way you are, love. We barely knew her.'

'Why not?'

'We only met her the once, face to face.' Alice glanced at Denise. Neither woman looked comfortable about it. 'She didn't…fit. She didn't belong here.'

No. She belonged at home in Chelsea with the people who loved her. Defensiveness crowded in. 'Maybe she sensed she didn't belong. Wasn't welcome.'

'Oh, don't get me wrong, Bel. She was always welcome, re-gardless. She loved our Andrew. She just wasn't happy here. Her loyalty was with Drew. Rightfully.'

Bel frowned. 'What do you mean?'

'Things were strained between our two boys,' Alice said. 'It wasn't comfortable for anyone when they were together back then. We all tried not to take sides, but Gwendoline was fiercely loyal to Drew, we could see that. Actually, I respected that even if I didn't like it.'

Denise snorted. 'We're not having this argument again.'

Alice rolled her eyes kindly and heaved the kettle off the hob to pour boiling water into three mugs. 'Andrew did not leave us because of Gwendoline Rochester, and well you know it,' she said to her daughter. She tightened her lips and then turned back to Bel and addressed the rest of the story to her. 'But I'll grant you she was the reason he stayed away. He loved that girl beyond compare.'

Beyond compare. Alice understood what her living grand-son didn't. That some loves just didn't tarnish.

'Sounds like he was lucky to have found that in life,' Bel murmured.

Alice looked at her strangely. 'You sound almost wistful. Don't tell me the newly-wed shine is wearing off already?'

A love beyond compare—with Flynn? Bel couldn't see it

happening, no matter what *she* felt. There were too many secrets and lies between them. And a honking great court case.

As if recognising the shadows in Bel's gaze, Alice rushed on past her own insensitivity. 'Well, regardless, suffice to say that despite having an identical accent to our other daughter-in-law, your character has restored our faith in the people of Britain.'

Her smile was weak. Her accent must bring Gwen to mind every day for them. She waved an imaginary flag. 'Bully for me.'

'Not to mention making Flynn the happiest I've seen him.'

Bel narrowed her eyes. While the past few weeks were most definitely the happiest *she'd* seen him, it said a lot about his usual demeanour if he was achieving some kind of lifetime personal best in the happiness stakes.

She took a deep breath and stuck her nose firmly into her husband's business, rubbing a twinge low along her hip. 'What happened between Flynn and his brother?'

'Anyone who says hell hath no fury like a *woman* scorned has clearly never met Flynn Douglas Bradley,' Alice said chuckling.

Bel frowned. 'But…didn't Drew trigger it? By leaving?'

'I'm sure Flynn would have you believe so, but no…Drew *ended* it by leaving. And not a moment too soon before they did some permanent damage to their relationship.' Her eyes grew sad. 'Although no one could have foreseen what was going to happen on his travels.'

'Can you tell me the story?'

Denise snorted. 'Oh, we'd need a white-out longer than this one to tell the whole sorry saga, Bel…'

She looked around them and shrugged. 'I've got nowhere to be.'

And so it came out. The whole hurtful mess. Flynn, the young boy with a borderline learning disability who'd idolised his older brother, who followed him around like a puppy when he was younger. Flynn, the awkward adolescent having trouble fitting into his mismatched thirteen-year-old body parts, who was never quite as bright, quite as talented or quite as popular as his big brother—the brother who hit high school two years ahead of him and whose life grew too busy to have a kid tag along. Flynn, the boy who finally found acceptance and even adulation amongst a ratbag group of boys from troubled homes in the Sydney suburbs and finally found a way of getting noticed. Getting some spotlight.

The good boy turned bad.

Immediately Flynn's words months ago made more sense. He must have felt sub-standard his whole life because of the slow start he got on his education. And Bel could most definitely relate to the self-worth issue. Flynn's troubles with Drew were not because he hated him, they were because he loved him. Too much.

'Everything he did was to get Drew's attention,' Bel whispered, her heart aching for the hurting young boy he must have been.

'Oh, he got it,' Alice murmured. 'Just not the way he'd hoped.'

Such a promising little boy had become a damaged young man, despite having the best parents a kid could want. It brought her own life journey into sharp relief. If she'd had the love of her parents, would she have chosen to resent Gwen for being the favoured child instead of clinging desperately to her love? Building a life around hers? Were her life decisions all that different from Flynn's?

Leaving home. Dropping out of school. The fashion. The sullen determination to go her own way.

Had they just been a cry to be noticed by her—heartbreakingly oblivious—family?

She lifted damp eyes. 'And they never got past it? Drew and Flynn?' She knew the answer. But was desperate for a hint of light in the dark tale.

'Drew becoming such a global success was the final nail in Flynn's emotional coffin,' Alice whispered. 'He felt he'd been left far, far behind. Like he didn't cut it.'

'But he's so good at what he does. So capable.' And his kind of capable was insanely attractive whether it was at a computer or in a paddock...

'Flynn developed a different kind of smarts to his brother,' Denise said.

'I know which brother I'd want with me in a crisis,' Bel agreed automatically. And it was true. For all Drew's brilliance and corporate smarts and talent, he'd hired in others to take care of life's more practical or unpleasant necessities.

If Flynn had been on that Thai ferry he would have saved Gwen.

The thought came out of nowhere and shook her. Hard. Her heart pulsed in her chest and started to gallop as old loyalties battled with new. She'd never in a million years imagined herself thinking something like that about Drew. She didn't blame him for Gwen's death—she didn't! So where had it come from?

You know where...

It didn't matter how important Drew had been to her before, it was Flynn who was important to her now. It was Flynn she loved. And respected. And honoured. Just like the vows they'd never said.

'You say that like you knew him,' Denise cut in, offended, and Bel realised how dangerous this whole conversation was becoming. 'But Drew was a wonderful, loving boy who never caused us a moment of grief growing up.'

Alice smiled sadly, sliding a fresh brew towards her. 'I'm glad Flynn talks to you about him. He needs to let go of some of his old feelings.'

Bel stretched across the kitchen counter to take the mug of hot tea and as she did her body crumpled in on itself as a vicious spasm hit her mid-section. It managed to be sharp, dull, heavy and laser-precise all at the same time. Her mug knocked and spilled hot tea across the kitchen benchtop.

Oh, God...

'Bel?' Denise got there first, supporting her lest she tumble from the stool she was perched on.

'Get her onto the sofa.'

Distantly she realised that all the acrimony of just moments before was lost as Alice went straight into midwife mode and Denise willingly complied. Alice glanced at her watch. Then at Denise. Bel caught the look they exchanged.

The funny moments of earlier today made sudden, awful sense. The weird offish feeling, the sharp pains low below her bump, the racing heart, the tight gut...

'No...'

'Don't panic, love,' Alice said, patting her shoulder as she sank into the sofa. 'It's probably just Braxton Hicks. Very common. But I'll keep time just in case.'

The landline was out. Their mobile phones were jostling their way towards Oberon township in Bill's utility. There was always Flynn's car but Alice didn't drive and Denise couldn't safely without her glasses, which were also in Oberon being repaired. And there was no way Bel could have squeezed her enormous belly behind a steering wheel even if she wasn't doubled over in pain. They were just going to have to make do until the men returned.

'Flynn...' she whispered under her breath. She'd never wanted someone by her side more in her life. Capable, sensible Flynn.

'He'll be home soon,' Denise crooned reassuringly. But the second glance the two older women exchanged when they thought she wasn't looking told a different story.

'It's too early,' Bel gritted as the wave of ache slowly eased off.

Alice stroked strands of hair from Bel's suddenly clammy

forehead. 'Not for twins, love. Now, you just relax and I'll make you a fresh cuppa. You may not have a single twinge more all day.'

Or not.

Bel lay stretched out on the living room rug with the now-drenched quilt from the spare room under her and a pile of sofa cushions propping her into a half sitting position, the only position she'd been able to find in five hours of labour that was vaguely comfortable.

Labour. Several weeks early but otherwise progressing quite by the book which was probably the only good news as far as she was concerned. She fell back against the pillows following another contraction and took a sip from the lukewarm water Denise offered her.

'God, I'm so glad you're both here,' she said to the women who she was lying to every minute of every day. Along with everyone else. Including Flynn, now that she had to hide her true feelings from him twenty-four-seven.

Alice clucked. 'There are much worse people to be stranded in labour with than a midwife and a woman who's birthed two healthy babies of her own.' But she still glanced at the wall clock and, though her expression didn't change much, it added another wrinkle to the corner of her carefully neutral eyes. 'And much worse places in this weather than a comfortable house with electricity and hot running water.'

Bel nodded. It was true. What if she'd been out walking or alone in Flynn's cottage? But knowing that didn't help much— she was still absolutely terrified. Not for herself—for her children. At absolute worst, if she died from the excruciating pain that had started to feel as if it would never end, then at least the babies would have two willing, warm breasts to be pressed against and a whole family to rally behind them. They'd barely even know what they were missing.

And if she didn't die…

She flexed her aching back. She'd cross that bridge if and when she came to it. Right now, surviving this just didn't seem that likely. 'Is it supposed to hurt this much?' she gritted.

Alice sank back onto her haunches and stared at her seriously. 'Honestly? You're only getting warmed up, Bel. I think it's time that I did a physical exam, not just a visual. We're getting much closer.'

Her stomach sank. Not a good time to be prudish, she knew, but she'd been uncomfortable enough adding the aged Alice Bradley to the very short list of people who'd ever *seen* down there without shortening the odds even further by having her *feel* down there. Up there, presumably. But she was going to be getting very familiar with Bel's body soon enough... She just had to start thinking of Alice as medical personnel and not family.

Not that she was, truly, family. She didn't really have any of those left. Not that counted.

Tears prickled dangerously. God, where was Flynn?

But she'd have to get through crises all on her lonesome after she went back to England. Better to start now. 'Okay,' she croaked. 'What do you need me to do?'

Alice took her through the basics of what was required, then disappeared into the kitchen briefly to wash her hands. When she returned they were bright red from the hot water and scrubbing. Denise stood by anxiously, waiting to be of more use.

Bel looked away as Alice did what she needed to do. Wow. If a few fingers were that uncomfortable going in, what were two little people going to feel like coming out...?

Alice's voice drew her eyes back. 'Relax, Bel. Remember your antenatal information. Your body is built to accommodate this process. Everything's going to loosen up and expand. Babies have been slipping down birth canals for millennia.'

Slipping. That sounded good. Slipping sounded easy. And quick.

'Liar.'

Alice chuckled and stared somewhere up towards the second storey of the house as she let her fingers do the walking. Assessing, measuring. Concentrating. The moment Bel felt the resistance of her body and saw the flare of confusion in Alice's eyes, she knew she'd forgotten something major. *Major*-major.

Hymen.

The one Dr Cabanallo had left intact out of whimsy. The one the OBGYN told her would be taken care of by her body's own natural changes when the birth process got fully underway.

The one tellingly still intact.

Which meant two awful things for Bel. First—she groaned deep down inside—that meant the birth process wasn't even fully underway yet. And second...

She and Flynn were well and truly busted.

Months of lies fluttered like dead moths down around her prostrate form on the living room floor.

'Mum?' Denise asked anxiously, seeing Alice's frozen demeanour. 'Everything okay?'

The older woman didn't take her eyes from Bel's but they narrowed slightly. 'Everything's good. We have a way to go though. No need to rush. Denise, love, I'd kill for a cup of tea, if you wouldn't mind?'

More tea. The country cure-all. Except it wasn't going to cure this. Nothing was going to undo the expression on Alice's face. As soon as Denise was out of earshot, the Bradley family matriarch leaned forward. 'Is there something you want to tell me, Bel?'

Tears rushed forward. 'I can't.'

They narrowed further until they were little more than slits. 'Why not?'

Because you'll all hate me.

Because I'm a liar wanting to steal your only great-grand-children away.

Because I've dragged your already fallen angel down even further into hell with me.

'It's not my story to tell.' Her body spasmed again briefly and she flinched. 'And it's not the right time.' No, the right time had been eight months ago, the day she'd met them for the first time. That window had well and truly slammed shut.

Alice regarded her steadily. 'Later, then. Let's get these children safely into our arms first.'

Bel sagged backwards and made no effort to hide her relief but Alice didn't give an inch. 'But make no mistake. As soon as everyone is safely recovered we will be speaking about this. *With Flynn.* There must be quite a story here.'

Oh, there was. A story of deception and collusion and fake marriage and secret love. Only she doubted Alice could even conceive how deeply Flynn was involved. They'd cling to their prejudices about the Rochester girls and no doubt speak of this day in whispered, appalled tones to the next wife that Flynn brought home.

The thought broke Bel's heart but she disguised her cry amongst the slamming agony that hit her as her body tried to force these babies into the world early.

Bill and Arthur had long since given up drawing Flynn back into their conversation, reading his expression all too accurately. Bill took the turn-off down Bunyip Reach's drive and rattled the final kilometre to the homestead. Flynn's trip to town had been effectively aborted the moment his mobile pinged to announce it was back in range and down-streamed two days' worth of emails and voicemail messages.

He'd only needed to see the subject line of one email from Sanders & Sanders to know:

Subject: FINDING RETURNED... NEXT STEPS?

You didn't ask for next steps if you'd won. And what he found inside the message was *so far* from winning...

Arthur threw him another worried look. They'd had to keep driving after discovering that all of Oberon was incommunicado, two-hours further to reach the city of Bathurst. And two hours of stony silence returning wasn't fun for anyone, least of all Flynn as his mind compensated for the silence with a flickering montage of images and memories of the past eight months.

He'd been stupid to close his eyes and ears to the reality of what was really going on with him and Bel. It had been so easy to buy into the temporary happy family fantasy and lose himself in introducing her to some of the pleasures of her body and learning what made her mind and soul tick. To let himself care. Not think about what was coming.

Or how this was going to end.

And now they were perilously close to that end. They had a verdict—albeit a wrong one—and in a few weeks they'd have the children safely delivered, too. Weeks. That was all he had to figure something out. Some way of ending this differently. So no one got hurt. Especially not the children.

The car lurched to a halt outside the homestead and Arthur looked around. 'Where is everyone?' Not even the dogs had come out to investigate the return of the prodigal Bradleys. Flynn unbuckled his back seat belt and climbed out.

He and his foul mood were a dozen steps ahead of his father and grandfather when the cry tore through the damp air—tortured and terrified.

Bel...

None of the Bradley men ran as a rule—it just wasn't *country* to do more than amble—but all three of them ran now as they realised the women they loved were in trouble. Flynn just about took the door off its hinges as he burst into the homestead and then skidded to a halt at the sight that met him.

Bel—stretched out on the floor drenched in sweat, her whole

body heaving and shaking, her torso straining forward. Legs pulled up unnaturally hard.

His mother—horribly pale, standing off to one side, staring intently at the pile of clean cloths bundled in her arms.

His grandmother—too busy between Bel's braced legs to pay any attention to the men who had just arrived.

'One more, Bel. You can do it. We're so close...' His nan's voice was firm and uncompromising, but he could see Bel clinging to that confidence like a lifeline. 'Flynn Bradley, stop gawping and get in here,' she said without looking up.

Only then did Bel notice him, her eyes sliding desperately to his. Full of fear. Full of pain and desperate relief. Her hand stretched towards him, trembling.

It was such an honest, heartfelt gesture...

His heart sucked into a tiny nugget and then exploded outwards. Every latent feeling he'd been ignoring—suppressing desperately—surged forward and tangled about his useless feet. He'd judged her, he'd used her, he'd teased her, he'd fought with her and he'd kissed her. He had so little to offer her in return.

Yet she kept that trembling hand more or less steady in his direction.

If this was what he could do for her, it was something.

He was with her in seconds, dropping down to ground level, sliding in under her to be the human equivalent of the cushions that were doing such a lousy job of supporting her. She sobbed his name between loud, pained strains but it was hard to know if it was relief or misery. She hooked her arms around his as she pushed back against him hard, her heels digging into the quilt spread out on the living room floor.

'Nearly there, Bel. Good girl...'

His father rushed immediately to his mother's side and Pop stood next to his nan and waited for instructions he knew would come. His nan smiled up at her husband with a love Flynn recognised and didn't at the same time. He knew that smile well. But how had he never seen how full of love it was?

These two people had had as unpromising a start as he could imagine, yet they'd found their way to a true and evident love.

So maybe stranger things had happened than him and Bel working it out...

His nan's voice was calm and clear when it finally came. 'My curling set, please, dear?'

Bel whimpered in Flynn's arms as Arthur hurried towards the stairs, but then he realised she was laughing, weak and pathetic. 'Is this the best time to worry about your hair, Alice?' The hint of a smile on her face was the only thing that gave him any reassurance at all that she wasn't dying in his arms.

'I need the clips,' she admonished. 'They'll do to clamp the umbilical cords until we can get them to the hospital.'

Cords. Plural? One baby was still emerging, but...

Flynn lifted his eyes to the bundle of cloth in Denise's arms—the very particular shape of it—and he crashed into his mother's own teary gaze.

'It's a boy,' she whispered, lifting the little swaddled bundle slightly. It was only then that he noticed the bruised, strangled looking cord in his mother's clenched fist. He gasped: his mother was clamping shut the baby's umbilical cord with her bare hand and had been for who knew how long. Her knuckles were white and shook from the effort of protecting the baby.

His son.

Drew's son.

Bill seemed to notice at the same time and he wrapped his larger fist around his wife's to lend her his strength.

Bel's renewed screams brought Flynn back sharply. She needed him. He couldn't do much other than brace her and be a human stress-ball for her Herculean fingers but he did that much, murmuring lame words of encouragement close to her ear that were totally drowned out by the inhuman sounds ripping from her.

They wanted—so badly—to be words of affection. Of love.

Sudden anger surged through him. This should not be Bel's

deflowering—afraid and on the floor, something this terrifying, this painful. He should have sucked it up and finished what he'd started that night of their wedding. Consummated the damn marriage. Not because it made much difference physically…but emotionally…

It shouldn't be like this for Bel.

And then it hit him in a blinding flash, how stupid he'd been. How insanely ridiculous to cling to something as transient as a piece of flesh to prove their marriage had gone unconsummated, when that same flesh would never survive a birth.

He could have been the one Bel gifted with her innocence instead of some guy she might find in the future. He could have been the one to teach her safely, gently about a woman's body. And a man's. He could have had her and she could still have had the annulment he'd promised her when they'd first embarked on this desperate deception.

No one but the two of them would ever have known otherwise.

All this time…he could have had her body, if not her heart.

Instead, *this* would be what she remembered for ever about the day she lost her virginity.

But as she flung her head back for one final surging scream he saw something else in the face almost deformed with agony. *Exultation.* The barbaric glittering of her eyes, the blazing defiance. The part of her that was determined to bring these babies into the world carefully and quickly and defend them to her last breath.

His stomach turned over. And over.

This woman was a *mother.* Regardless of where the babies originated. Or who they belonged to. Or what the law decided. In the short time he'd known her, Bel had turned from girl…to woman…to mother. She'd blossomed under the care of his family, under his own touch, she'd opened herself to him and shown herself to be cut from different cloth to her sister.

Though she had every reason in the world not to, she'd risked
her heart and let herself care for the people in his family.

He looked in turn at every member of that family and it
sliced him right through his middle.

Because he knew what he had to do...

But right now his only job was keeping her conscious and
upright as the tiny precious life slipped silently into his nan's
waiting hands.

CHAPTER TEN

THE whole blue-tinged, not-breathing thing freaked Bel out much more when the first little boy materialised from inside her, because after everything she'd gone through emotionally and psychologically—and physically—to get them this far, it would be more than a tragedy for Gwen and Drew's babies not to survive.

It would be unbearable.

But the second little boy was exactly the same bruised colour and this time *she* squeezed Flynn's arm in reassurance—as if she'd been doing this for decades rather than minutes—as Alice deftly dealt with the cord with her ruined fabric scissors, knotted it and patted his tiny lungs firmly out of his aquatic existence and into this one.

Two boys. A tiny Flynn and tiny Drew of her own. Something to remember both of them by after she was back in London. She closed her eyes over a leak of tears and shared the news with Gwen as Alice cleared the second twin's airways and cocooned him in warm towels. It was hard not to imagine the intense surge of love and warmth that coursed through her channelled straight from her sister, but it amplified overwhelmingly as Alice gently placed her little boy on her chest and then retreated to deal with the afterbirth. Denise approached with his older brother.

Both babies now had a hairdressing clamp in place to make sure the hand-tied knot in their umbilical cords stayed put.

Flynn's hands shook as he reached around her to take the baby from Denise. Bel was torn three ways between a desperate desire to look at him, the baby resting on her chest and the one now safely curled in Flynn's hands, so she focused on the babies and just leaned her head into the strength of Flynn's hold in lieu.

'Brothers...' he murmured, and she knew he'd be thinking about Drew just then. They all were. Denise's eyes shone with pain and a kind of healing and Bill tucked her against him gently. Alice's face was split in a smile wider than the gully running down to the caves, even though she had the messiest end of the whole proceedings to still deal with.

The babies were perfect. Silent and overwhelmed by the curious new world they found themselves in, but they had everything in the right quantities. And they had their father's eyes.

And their uncle's, technically.

Flynn placed the tiny firstborn on Bel's chest closer to his brother and both babies instinctively turned towards the other, fussing. She shifted them hard up against each other and they immediately settled.

'They know each other...' Flynn murmured.

'They should. They've been each other's world for eight months.' Her crooning did nothing to draw their attention back to her but their eyes closed after a moment of the soft sound.

His deep voice rumbled, 'They know their mother, too.'

Their mother. But there was no question, regardless of their genetic origins. She'd carried them, talked to them, loved them and birthed them. These children were hers.

The impossible responsibility of that washed over her in a wave of anxiety and her heart rate picked up. What did she know about being a parent? To twins? In a tiny flat in London. What had seemed so straightforward in theory—when it was just an intangible *one day*—seemed insurmountable now. These were little human beings. There was no room for mistakes. Their needs had to come first.

'They're so small…'

'Their growth was inhibited by each other and they're a little early, but they'll make up for lost time.' Alice appeared next to her, wiping her hands on the last clean towel. It was only then Bel realised what a blood-bath the Bradleys' living room had become. She owed them some serious linen. And a rug. And some dressmaking scissors.

Alice pushed damp hair from her own forehead and then looked at Flynn. 'As soon as you're ready, we need to get her to a hospital.'

All the colour drained from his face. 'Why? What's wrong?'

Her aged laugh was a bark. 'She's just given birth on the floor. Twice. That's what's wrong.' She patted his hand. 'She and the babies need a full check-up and some time in a comfortable bed, getting up to speed with all of this.'

His arms tightened. 'I'll take her myself. Now.'

'Is that the best plan, Flynn? Squeeze two newborns and a traumatised woman into your luxurious two-seater…with no one along to assist if anything happens? Would an ambulance be a better idea, dear?'

Despite the pain and the anxiety and the overwhelming-ness of everything that had happened and was yet to happen, Bel had to smile. The whole Alice good-cop-bad-cop thing took some getting used to. As tough as a military sergeant while she was in labour, but as gentle as pie on her poor, shocked grandson.

'I'll do it on the CB radio,' Arthur called from the kitchen where—bless his socks—he'd popped the kettle on for yet another restorative cup of tea before heading out to his vehicle. But, as Bel brought her eyes back towards the babies, she saw the tremor in Alice's fingers and the pallor at her hairline. She'd been through quite a trauma, too. Seventy-nine-year-old women didn't participate in marathons all that often. Bel tucked the babies tighter to her chest with one arm and reached

out with the other. 'Alice. Thank you. I could not have done
this without you. These boys are alive because of you.'

Her lips tightened but Bel knew it was to corral the tears
that threatened in her aged grey eyes. 'Rubbish. They're alive
because of you. And Flynn.' Although she hadn't lost the speculative glint. 'Though I don't mind saying I don't want to ever
do that again. Not sure my heart is up to it. And there's a reason I crawled up to this end of you, Bel. I think my knees have
gone…'

Bill helped his mother excruciatingly to her feet and supported her to the nearest sofa, where she sank gratefully into
it and tucked her trembling hands from view while her son
clucked around her. Denise collected up all the soiled linen
and disappeared upstairs before returning with a fresh quilt,
which she draped over Bel and the babies.

Bel spent the time just staring at her boys—all three of
them—and snuggling back into Flynn.

'Are you in pain?' he whispered against her ear.

You have no idea. And not all of it physical. But pain had
no place here for the next few minutes. This was for them
alone. She shook her head. 'Look at them, Flynn. They look
just like—' *too many ears in the room* '—their father.'

His eyes glittered and he smiled. 'I know.'

'Look at those Bradley foreheads,' Denise piped up from
the sofa. 'But if you ask me, they look more like Drew at birth.
Flynn was so much darker.'

Bel's whole body tightened up.

The glance Alice slid past Bel made her wonder if the wily
woman wasn't slowly piecing together the puzzle. Though,
never correctly—there was no way she possibly could. Who in
a million years could imagine what she and Flynn had done?
But she was definitely doing quiet mental maths. 'They don't
look much of anything at the moment, all squashed from the
birth.'

'I wouldn't care if they ended up looking like your legendary Bunyip,' Bel said fiercely. 'I think they're perfect.'

'Hear, hear...' Arthur said from the kitchen and suddenly the entire family began buzzing with excitement and remembering the births of their own children at great speed and volume. Bel sagged into the happy cacophony and stared at the two little people suddenly dominating her world.

Massively, overwhelmingly, entirely dominating.

Flynn kissed her sweaty head and murmured, 'Need anything?'

'Just to lie here. Just to look at them.' Just to have you close. For however long it lasts.

Baby number one pressed its face to Baby number two and began sucking his tiny chin.

'Should I try and feed them, Alice...?' Her mouth dried at the thought. The terrifying learning curve began now. She really had no clue. Everything she knew about babies she knew from books or dolls. Yet she thought she could do this alone? She'd only just grown used to Flynn seeing her breasts; now they were going to become public property...

'They feel like a feed about as much as you feel like one right now, Bel. They've been through an ordeal at least as traumatic as yours. Sleep and medical care are the most important things for the next little while. And contact with their parents. The rest will come in its own time.'

She was happy with that. Delaying the inevitable. Holding them—loving them—was the easy part. She'd willingly do that until the end of time.

The family bustle went on. Eventually Alice pulled herself to her feet and disappeared to take a well-earned shower.

Bel picked her moment and whispered to Flynn, 'Alice knows.'

He looked at her sharply. 'What do you mean?'

'She felt... She knows I was a virgin.'

His lips tightened.

'I didn't think, Flynn…'

He squeezed her hand. 'It's not your fault. We both thought this would happen in a controlled medical environment.' He glanced at his occupied parents. 'Do you think she'll believe it's just a freak of nature?'

'If I'd been quicker on my feet, maybe. She knows there's some kind of secret, just not what it is.'

Flynn nodded. Thought. Hard. 'Okay. Well, we'll think of something.'

'No. No more lies. No more half- and quarter-truths.' She kept her voice calm for the babies' sake but put all her seriousness into her eyes. 'I'm done.'

He wanted to argue. She could see it. But the dark shadows at the back of his expression coagulated into visible pain. 'I suppose it's going to be a moot point soon, anyway.'

Bel frowned. What did he mean?

'But you don't have to deal with that now. We'll talk about this more when you're fully recovered. I'll deal with any questions Nan might have.'

To spare her the humiliation? Or to control what was said? 'No. I'm not hiding behind you, Flynn. I need to face the music. Tell them personally. It's the least I owe them, especially after today.' She caught and held his gaze. 'I won't taint the start of these lives with more deception.'

She felt his body sag behind hers. 'Okay, Bel. When you get out of hospital. Just focus on getting you and these little blokes strong.'

They couldn't go on calling them *Baby number one* or the *little blokes*. 'We need to choose names, Flynn.'

Flynn's large thumb brushed some of the rapidly crusting wax residue from the baby closest to him and, after a long thoughtful pause, said what they'd both been thinking.

'Andrew?'

It was totally appropriate, given his origins, and anyone looking in from the outside would just see one brother honouring another. And he did have a kind of Andrew look about him. But knowing now how much of Flynn's emotional heart was tied up in his past with his brother…

'Are you sure?'

He thought about it some more and nodded. 'I'm sure.'

She frowned. 'But Andy for short.' She didn't think any of them could call him Drew without it hurting.

Flynn turned his eyes to the second-born baby. He was harder. There was no male equivalent of Gwendoline, at least not one he'd have a hope of getting a classroom of school mates to pronounce correctly. Bel moved on to her sister's middle name. Liana.

'Liam?'

They both stared at the babies. *Andrew and Liam Bradley.*

'Perfect,' Flynn said.

The longer she stared at the sleeping infants, the heavier her own eyes felt. And as the natural hormone high wore off and the pain spread out to an awful, full body ache, the rigours of the birth finally registered on her exhausted muscles.

A drug-free home birth had definitely not been on her must-do list.

'Sleep, Bel.' Flynn pressed the words into her temple, tucking his arms more securely around them all and flexing his own muscles in anticipation of a long stay. 'I'll be here when you wake.'

But for how long? The thought drifted in and onwards as she started to doze into exhausted slumber, her senses filled with the smell of newborn baby and the warmth of the man she loved. Though it wasn't entirely restful. Soon they'd have a verdict and one of them would be heartbroken and empty-handed.

Empty-lived.

And right up until Alice had placed Liam, hot and tiny, on her chest, she would have said it wasn't going to be her. No way. But that was before the intense weight of two tiny lives bore down on her and before she realised that what *they* needed was what mattered most.

Although right now—like their mother—they just needed sleep.

CHAPTER ELEVEN

BATHURST HOSPITAL was the nearest major centre and, because there were no serious complications with Andrew and Liam's births, they got to stay there rather than be transferred to Sydney.

Which was not to say there were no complications at all. Liam's little lungs struggled to drain as quickly as his brother's and Andrew proved himself to be an unaccomplished feeder. Bel had been secretly relying on them knowing instinctively what to do and so she was more than a bit anxious to find they had to learn what went where every bit as much as she did.

'It's the blind leading the blind, isn't it, Andy...'

She tried him again, endlessly patient but determined their breastfeeding planets would align at some point. Frustration and fear of failing him hovered permanently in the wings but she kept them at bay by remembering what a miracle it was that she had him and his brother at all and how these were moments she might have to carry in her heart for ever if things didn't go her way in the courts. Besides, for little Andy there was always what Flynn called *express-o*. Her firstborn gorged himself on the bottle full of her pumped breast milk.

Appetite was clearly not an issue.

Flynn tried to be circumspect about it but she could tell he delighted in the chance to have the bonding experience of feeding Andy. And one tiny, secret part of her knew that keeping a hint of emotional distance might be critical for when the court's verdict came in. So maybe it was a blessing in disguise…

Nutrition was more important than technical correctness or societal expectations right now. She grabbed a bottle now, left by the nurse in case things didn't go well, and negotiated the teat into Andy's mouth. He latched on and sucked harder than any of the kangaroo joeys she'd helped rear

'Maybe it's just not meant to be…' She sighed and stroked his tiny pink cheek with her fingertip, talking about a whole lot more than just their inability to get the feeding going.

'It's only been a couple of days, Bel. Give it a chance.'

Flynn walked back in from the en suite bathroom at that moment. He'd been with her every minute of those couple of days and was giving no sign of leaving soon. Not until he was driving them all back to Oberon. Together. His perpetual closeness had started to scrape on her nerves. It was humiliating enough that he was witnessing her at her incompetent worst, or seeing her fumbling around with suddenly udder-like breasts, but watching the nurses falling over themselves to catch his eye only reminded her what a fairy tale existence they'd been leading out on his property. Why would a man like Flynn tie himself to her when he could have any woman in the district? Australian women. Country women. Women who knew what to do on the land he loved so much.

And why did he feel the need to stay glued to her side like this? Did he think she'd skip town with the babies now that they were born? Was this just an extension on dragging her to Australia to keep her in his sights? Or was he trying to make a point about how plainly ill-equipped she was to look after two babies without help? Well, not everyone had family to go home to…

'Maybe if you didn't hover so much…' she snapped.

Flynn's only response was to lift one eyebrow and then lift baby Andy carefully away from her irritable fingers and take over the express-o feed, infinitely calmer. She glanced at Liam, sleeping off his full belly in the boys' joint crib, and shook her head.

Was this what being dragged back into the real world did to her relationship with Flynn? Had everything she'd felt been built on an illusion? Something fragile and false? Some kind of extended holiday romance? If so, she had no one but herself to blame. She'd chosen to lower her barriers in the first place. He hadn't made her a single promise. It was totally unreasonable to punish him for that.

She took a deep breath and let her lashes drop briefly. 'Flynn, I'm sorry…I just…'

'You're tired.'

Frustration hissed out of her. 'This is not about resting. This is about wondering, and worrying.' She lifted her eyes and hoped they weren't as bleak as his. 'What are we going to do?'

Finally, someone had said it. Acknowledged the honking great elephant in the room.

His brows drew together and he watched the last dregs of watery milk disappear from Andy's bottle. 'We don't need to talk about this now, Bel…'

'We've been not talking about it for days, Flynn. *Months.* But now it's here. Any day now, we're going to get a decree that determines whether these boys will grow up Australian or British. And I don't think I'm ready for it, whichever way it goes.'

He couldn't even meet her eyes. He shifted Andy in his arms and awkwardly patted his back. 'Bel…'

'Don't patronise me, Flynn. We need to talk about this. Rationally.' As if that was possible. 'Work out a survival strategy. Because what I thought I wanted on arriving in Australia was very different to what I want now.' The woman she now was. Everything had changed.

Having children.

Marrying Flynn.

Loving Flynn.

All in the space of a few months. No wonder she'd had her head in the sand all this time. Denial was a wonderfully safe place to spend time.

His face grew guarded. 'What do you want now?'

She'd done this her whole life…held her tongue when she should have asked for what she wanted. Found the courage. For better or worse. Well, it was time to find some courage. For her boys' sake, if not her own. 'It's more a case of what I don't want…'

His eyes automatically followed hers to the twins.

'I don't think I can raise them alone, Flynn.' Her voice cracked on that and she swallowed twice to clear it. 'What if I'm not good enough?'

His face hardened. 'You'll be a great mother.'

'When?' she despaired. 'Everything is so hard.'

'Everyone has to learn some time. You can't leave them behind without trying. You'll hate yourself.'

Bel stared at him, mouth open. 'I'm not saying I'll leave them behind. I'm saying I want to stay here…with them.' She took a deep breath and found his eyes. 'With you.'

Tension locked his expression into a shield. He didn't speak, though she could see his mind working feverishly in the depths of his grey eyes and his voice box lurching up and down. Her heart pounded painfully. 'Boys should grow up on the land, not in a crowded inner city suburb. And we've been… You and I… Things have been good between us.' Though her confidence slipped at his continuing silence. 'Okay, anyway…'

If you could define 'okay' as companionable days and exciting, exploratory nights. 'We can call the lawyers off. Work something else out…'

God, Flynn, *speak!*

But, when he did, his voice was so cautious. She recognised the tone immediately. 'You're talking about forever, Bel.' He didn't trust her. He didn't believe her. Or did he just not want her? 'Not just a year, not just short-term. *Forever.* With me.'

But there was no going back now. She met his eyes. 'I know.'

'What if you meet someone later on? Fall in love.' A muscle pulsed, high in his jaw. 'You'll be stuck with me.'

'I won't.' Not now that she knew what love should feel like. She wouldn't find this…rightness…again. 'I know what I'm asking.'

His face lost some of its colour. 'Do you, Bel? Or are you just panicking about being a single parent and this seems the path of least resistance?'

'You think it wouldn't be easier for me to just take the babies and get on a plane than to risk… Telling you…' She took a deep breath. 'We've had this discussion before. I know what I'm asking.' She stared at him intently. 'But do you know what I'm saying?'

He didn't want to. It was written clearly in his expression. Discomfort. Dread. 'You're saying you want to live on Bunyip's Reach. You're saying you want to make our marriage real. Permanent. For the boys.'

'I do.' So help me God. 'And for me.'

'Because…?'

He needed to hear it. Almost as much as she feared saying it. God, how she wanted to say it. To finally tell *someone.* To shout it from the hospital rooftop. 'Because I want you. Because I love you.'

His nostrils flared and his jaw clenched. But he didn't move. Not one inch. 'How do you know?'

That threw her. She wasn't naïve enough to hope for immediate reciprocation but she certainly wasn't expecting to have to qualify her feelings.

'I'm sleeping with you.' In a manner of speaking.

'Not that big a deal these days.'

'It is for me. A huge deal.' It was everything.

'My point exactly. You could be confusing lust with love.'

'I'm not.'

'How would you know? You have no point of reference. Unless you count Drew.'

Suddenly the insinuation and inquisition grew too much and her throat tightened. 'If you don't want me to stay, just say it. Don't drag this out. And don't cower behind your brother.'

She sat, as composed as a woman in a hospital gown with two ballooning breasts beneath it could, on the edge of the bed, stiff with misery.

He stared at her, assessing. 'You understand what staying would mean? We'd be husband and wife...in every sense of the word.'

'Matching towels. I get it.'

He stepped in close to her thighs. 'No more annulment to protect...'

'Are you saying chivalry is now dead?' She stared up at him, throwing provocation into the very short list of tools she had at her disposal. Necessity was the mother of invention.

His left hand came up to brush away the stray hairs from her face. The cool of his wedding band kissed along her skin. He seemed almost as surprised by the move as she was. 'Chivalry might have to be banished to the barn.'

Her pulse skyrocketed. 'Shame,' she whispered. 'I was hoping to do it in the barn at some point.'

His head literally reeled back and he let out a hiss. 'This isn't a game, Bel. It's life-changing. For both of us. What if we just have the mother of all chemistry going on?'

Why? Was that all he felt? Serious doubt bit for the first time.

'I can't speak for your feelings.' Or lack of. 'I can only speak for mine.'

'Maybe you'd say anything to guarantee you get to keep the babies. Or do anything.'

Like sleep with him? That stung but, in fairness, she'd given him plenty of reason to make that presumption. Every decision she'd made since he'd met her was linked to the unborn children. 'Do you believe that?'

Yes, he did. It was written in the twisted angle of his frown.

'I think you'd even believe it,' he murmured.

Deep sorrow washed through her. 'You don't feel it.' It wasn't a question.

Oh, God...

His nostrils flared. 'Bel, my feelings for you are...' He shook his head. 'I'm thirty-five years old, and I barely understand how I feel when I'm with you. Can you appreciate why I might question yours? A twenty-three-year-old with very little life experience.'

'Are you saying you want me to go out and get some...experience...first? With someone else?'

His eyes darkened. 'I'm saying you don't have to commit to forever to explore the rest of what it is between us. Physically. I'd be open to continuing our...'

'Our what, Flynn?' Her chest clenched into a fist. She sucked in a tight breath. 'Exactly what is it that you've been doing while I've been falling in love with you? Enjoying the free and convenient—'

His lips thinned. 'I made you no promises, Bel.'

'I'm *so* aware of that, Flynn. I guess I really am that naïve twenty-three-year-old, after all. I thought that maybe you'd be willing to explore an unconventional marriage for the sake of the children. That maybe love could grow between us like it did with your grandparents. But you have your heart too tightly tethered down to even do that, haven't you?'

'This isn't about me...'

'No. Of course not,' she ranted. 'I'd fall in love with any passing man if I thought it would guarantee me custody of these boys. I'm surprised I didn't fall for the magistrates...'

He hissed, 'Can you look me in the eye and tell me the boys are not a factor? That if they didn't exist you would still be sitting here pouring your heart out?'

The dismissal in his tone bit almost as hard as the fact that she knew, deep down, that the children were part of the complicated mass of feelings she had for him. 'If they didn't exist I wouldn't even have met you.' That seemed so inconceivable now. She sighed past the tight wad of reality balling in her sternum. 'What do you want to do? Wait for the decree to come in and then have this conversation again? Is that what it will take for you to believe my feelings—for me to get custody and still tell you I love you?'

His eyes sparkled dangerously and he shrugged his arm free of her. He found her focus and held it, uncertainty in their grey depths. But then his shoulders rose and fell again and the doubt hardened to grief. And then to…nothing. A flat kind of resignation.

'The decree is in.'

She stared at him, a block of fear wedging in her gut. 'What? When?'

'The day the boys were born.'

'How did they know—?'

'It had nothing to do with the birth. That was when the emails and voice messages came through. When I went to town.'

Her mouth dried up completely and her sharp mind raced ahead. He'd kept the findings to himself. Which meant he didn't want to hurt her. Which meant…

All but the tiniest shard of air sucked out of the room. Her eyes darted frantically between Andrew and Liam. Her babies. She'd lost them. And she'd only had them such a short time. The panic of being out of time and options descended and her breathing grew choppy. 'No—'

The hardness in Flynn's eyes wavered and he took a half-step towards her before stilling his feet. 'Breathe, Bel. You haven't lost them.'

That brought her desperate gaze back to his. Her head spun as her emotional bungee yanked her back from the depths of despair and flung her up into the blue, blue sky of relief. But then she slowed and tipped and started to free fall again. If she'd won, that meant Flynn had lost. She was going to take the twins from Bunyip's Reach and leave him with nothing. Nothing but a heartbroken family that had already been through so much. Her happiness meant desolation for him and all the people who'd shown her such love and kindness since she'd arrived.

Hurting him generated physical pain in her own body. She wrapped her arms around her torso to keep it contained. 'Oh, Flynn…'

Both his hands shot up between them. 'The decree was clear that in the event of only one of the two babies surviving, that custody was to go to you.'

God, just the thought of one of the boys not making it made her wince. But she supposed the court had to cover their bases. *Wait…* Something about the look in his eyes. The hint of reservation amidst the hate. She took a shallow breath.

'But…?'

His eyes held hers steadily. Almost like two hands supporting her. 'But if both survived, then custody was to be split.'

She blinked at him, trying to make sense of the words. 'The courts want us to ship the boys back and forth across the globe?'

'No, Bel, not shared. *Split.*'

The room swirled around her as every drop of blood pooled instantly in her vital organs. Flynn's voice, when it came, was distorted and choked.

'We've been granted one child each.'

'No…'

Bel shook her pale, pinched face and lurched off her tilt-up bed, crossing to the crib where the boys slept peacefully. She turned her eyes back to him. 'Flynn, no… How could they?'

She looked exactly as he'd felt on the drive home from

Bathurst. Incredulous. Appalled. Dead inside. He cleared his thick throat. 'I gather they reached a legal stalemate. This was the most expedient solution.'

'Expedient?' she croaked. 'They're children. Not a DVD collection!'

He shook his head. 'It has something to do with the embryos being authorised for donation by Drew and Gwen. It opened the door for the embryos to be treated as property under the law, not…'

Not people.

Bel sagged back onto her bed and her words when they came were like a lance deep into his chest cavity. A mini moment of history repeating itself. 'But they're not embryos now, they're brothers. All they've known is each other.'

What could he say? His solicitors had already talked him through the complex web of negotiations and legislation that had tangled things up so badly. He barely understood it but he knew they'd tried all options. 'This case has challenged the course of family law—'

'Off-course! Horribly, horribly off-course, Flynn. This whole thing was to keep the family together…' She shook her head numbly, then lifted agonised eyes. 'Even knowing this—' she looked at him desperately, going impossibly paler '—you would still let them be separated rather than be tied to me for real?'

He pushed his fingers through his hair painfully, watching her tormented eyes fill with tears.

'Do you despise me that much, Flynn?'

Compassion clawed its way out of the dark place inside him. The place that didn't trust. Didn't believe. 'Bel—'

'How are the happy parents?'

Both their heads snapped around towards the door, where Alice and Arthur stood with a matching pair of furry blue teddy bears, Denise and Bill behind them, oblivious to the raging tension in the room.

Bel took one look at the cheerful matching bears and burst into floods of tears, rushing into the en suite bathroom.

Everyone froze. But, as always, it was his nan who greased the awkward social situation. 'Hormones,' she announced simply and turned to the others. 'How about we give her some space and go grab a bite to eat in the hospital cafeteria?'

The men vacated gratefully but Denise took a little prodding, her eyes stretching wistfully towards the sleeping babies. Eventually, though, she backed out of the door.

'Aren't you coming?' she said to her mother-in-law.

'I'll be right along. Order me a soup, there's a dear.'

The door closed under her heavy hand and Flynn braced himself for his nan's inquisition. But she turned, leaned on the door and looked at him with such compassion and understanding *he* felt like bursting into tears.

'Give her a moment,' she said quietly, 'and then the two of you are going to tell me what on earth is going on.'

His heart sank. He couldn't lie to his nan.

And so that meant it was over.

All of it.

CHAPTER TWELVE

EITHER you agree to tell them under your own speed or I'll ask you outright at the very next family dinner.

Short of never attending another meal with the people who loved him, Bel knew Flynn really didn't have a lot of choice. There was no question Alice would be as good as her threat and, given what the courts had decreed, Bel really couldn't see how things could get any worse, anyway. What was worse than breaking up a family?

None of it mattered now. Not the lies. Not the false name. Not what she wanted, least of all what she needed. Only one thing mattered. The future of their boys.

Because they were *theirs*. Every single person in the room had a stake in them.

Both older women fussed around the babies now—Alice most particularly—and saw that they were settled into the old-fashioned crib that Arthur had pulled out of storage and re-stored while Bel was in hospital. They knew that Flynn had called a family meeting, but not much more. Though all of them threw concerned glances in the direction of Bel and her ashen face.

She felt like death; she couldn't imagine she looked any better.

This day had always been coming. Regardless of what Flynn had asked her to tell them, there was never any way she was going to whisk their grandchildren back to England with them believing she'd just...*changed her mind* about her marriage to Flynn. That would have been too low a blow. Too much a betrayal of her own feelings for him. But she'd never let herself fully imagine what it would be like to sit across the table and confess everything—*everything*—to the people who'd been so good to her.

The eldest Bradley most especially. Arthur and his quiet acceptance, his unconditional, non-judgemental support of her. Watching his disappointment was going to hurt almost as much as betraying Flynn.

She pulled the sleeves of her jumper down over her icy fingers and swallowed past the lump that had been resident low in her throat since she'd emerged from the en suite bathroom at the hospital and seen two pairs of Bradley eyes staring back at her.

Now all eyes flicked nervously between her and Flynn. His own were fixed firmly on a spot on the far wall.

She pressed her fingers hard into her palms and focused on the bite of her nails. The tiny pain. It didn't centre her the way it always had; it barely registered through the thick fog of agony she'd been living with since Flynn had thrown her love back in her face. Since he'd told her about the verdict. She braved a glance at him. Impotent seconds ticked by as he impaled her with his dead regard.

Finally he nodded, almost imperceptibly.

Bel shifted her eyes to Arthur. Cowardice, perhaps, but she couldn't face either of Drew's parents as she started her story. She knew what she was going to see there.

'My name—' She cut herself off, having started far too loud in the silent, silent room. She took a breath and tried again. 'My name is not Belinda Cluney.' Three sets of eyebrows folded around the table. 'It's Belinda Rochester. I'm Gwendoline Rochester's younger sister.'

Denise paled instantly. Bill froze. Arthur's face filled with something she'd never seen.

'I didn't tell you who I was because we…' She paused. No, this was her sword to fall on. She'd made her own choices. And she was already hurting Flynn enough without destroying his relationship with his family even more. 'Because *I* knew how you felt about my sister and I believed I would not be welcome here if you knew.'

Denise opened her mouth, twisted with hurt, to say something, but her husband silenced her with one hand on hers.

'I understand why you had difficulties with Gwen. But the fact remains, I am a Rochester.'

'You are a Bradley,' Denise cried. 'You married our son!' She turned her hurt to her husband, who was trying to silence her.

'Is the marriage legal?' Arthur asked.

'It's legal,' Flynn interjected flatly. 'But technically…unconsummated.' His Adams apple worked up and down hard with the effort of not saying more. How lucky that was now. It would take nothing to end the marriage between them.

End her life. Her dreams.

That brought Denise's swimming eyes back around. 'But—'

But you've been sleeping together every night.

Denise did the mental maths and her focus shot straight to the sleeping twins. And then to her son. 'They're not yours, Flynn? They're not ours?' she croaked.

Bel pressed her lips together to hold back a sob. Denise's pain was so raw, and what they were about to say was only going to stick a scorching blade into the open wound. For so long she'd been intently focused on making sure that Gwen and Drew's babies made it into the world. Into the family. Now she'd give anything for them to be Flynn's.

'They…they're…'

But courage failed her just when she needed it most and Flynn intervened. Quietly. Coldly. 'They're Drew's.'

Even Arthur paled then, and the tiniest glimmer of moisture flooded into eyes that had never before looked at her with anything but affection. He thought she'd slept with Drew. Just when she thought there was not enough of her heart left to fracture, a tiny shard further sheared off at the accusation in his eyes.

She took a shaky breath and forced her spine straighter against the chair back.

'And *Gwen's*,' Alice intervened. She looked at Bel and nodded encouragement.

Bel took another breath. 'Drew and my sister were on IVF when they died.'

She persevered over the top of the collective gasp. 'Liam and Andrew were the product of that and I…I couldn't bear them to go to strangers, to be…' The tiniest amount of acid crept up her throat. 'To be separated from each other. I applied to the courts for permission to raise them as my own.'

Of all the people, Denise was the one whose head tilted. Whose eyes softened. Just momentarily.

'Without notifying us?' Bill said.

'The courts tried…' But in that breath Bel realised she'd been no less judgemental than the Bradleys had. She'd always blamed Drew's parents and grandparents for ostracizing her sister but she'd made no effort to contact them personally because of how Gwen had felt about them. Because of a bunch of stories. One-sided stories. She had been all too ready to believe that his family wouldn't want the babies.

'I should have tried harder,' she admitted. 'I should have got in touch personally rather than just letting my lawyers send a—'

'There was a mistake,' Flynn hedged, still eager to protect his mother from realising how close they had come to never knowing about these children at all because of her own inability to deal with Drew's loss. 'But I was able to rectify it. While custody was determined.'

'But you *married* her?' This from his grandfather. She'd

been *Belly* last week, now she was *her*. 'We stood in that damned cave and witnessed your vows.'

Flynn held his eyes. 'For legal reasons. To improve my chances in the custody case. That's the only reason.'

The careful words traced a series of lethal cuts across her soul. She'd let herself forget why she was here in the first place. She'd let the magic of this place, these people, of *Flynn's kisses* rob her of her good judgement. Her survival instinct.

She'd been so in love with the idea of being in love…

But Flynn was here to remind her.

'Are you expecting that your magnanimous gesture should be enough reason for us to tolerate your continued presence here?' Denise grated. 'Your lies?'

'Mum—'

'I have nothing to say to you,' she lashed at Flynn, her voice rich with agony. 'You have betrayed us infinitely worse than your brother. He left in the first place because of you and then you have the nerve to bring…' She turned her streaming eyes on Bel but couldn't finish.

Flynn paled at his mother's cutting words. 'That's exactly why we didn't use her name. You never would have given her a chance. You *liked* Belinda Cluney.'

'I *loved* Belinda Cluney,' she broke in, angry and hurt. Bel's own heart haemorrhaged. 'But that was all lies. Has any one thing about the past eight months been true?'

Damn you, Flynn Bradley. This could all have been avoided.

'It's true that those little boys are your grandsons,' Bel croaked above the din. 'You have living, breathing reminders of Drew in your living room because of what Flynn and I have done.'

'Would you like a medal?' Denise scoffed, but misery saturated her words. 'It doesn't bring my son back.'

'We all lost someone that day, Denise, but you have a son right here. Alive and healthy. You should be holding onto him with everything you've got, not dismissing him because he had the audacity to try and do something that would protect you.'

'Bel…' Flynn's own voice was tight but he found her eyes for the first time in hours. Crazy how they still impacted deep down in her soul.

His mother dragged her eyes to her son. 'What does she mean?'

Eight months of tension leached out of her in an unstoppable torrent. 'This was all about you, Denise. Everything Flynn's done, every lie I've told, was because he feared that you couldn't deal with the truth. That it would push you too far. Because you never dealt with Drew's loss. The son you favoured moved away from you while the other one is working himself to the bone trying to compare.'

Flynn stood and turned half-on to her to block her from his mother's view as though that would be enough to silence her. 'Bel, enough.'

'That's not true,' Denise protested, leaning around him. 'It nearly killed me to lose my firstborn but I've made myself accept it.'

'That's true, Bel,' Alice murmured. 'We all have.'

Her mind roiled. What? But everything they'd done… Why? 'Then who…?'

All eyes shifted to the youngest man in the room. The one with the wildly lurching throat standing like a referee between the woman who raised him and the woman who married him.

'Is that true, Flynn?' she whispered.

Flynn clenched his jaw, failing to still the twitch pulsing wildly near his ear. His eyes looked haunted and bleak.

'Were mine not the only lies being told?' she asked gently.

His face creased as he began, 'I didn't…' But his gaze clouded and his lips tightened and he turned his confusion to his mother as if he was only just seeing her now.

Denise's own face mirrored his as understanding finally hit her. Hit them all. How much he'd been suffering. 'Oh, love…'

Flynn's chest rose and fell and Bel felt the pain of every tight breath. *He hadn't realised.* He'd been projecting it all onto his mother…

'In it or out of it, my brother was integral to the fabric of this family,' he gritted, still struggling with the truth. 'His loss has changed it for ever.'

Empathy washed through her. This whole thing—all the lying—was about Flynn trying to put his family back together. Trying to undo the damage he had caused when he was fourteen. And about his inability to deal with the loss of the brother he'd idolised.

'And you thought raising his babies would change it back?'

His lips tightened. 'He left us.'

'He *died*, Flynn.'

'He abandoned us long before that.'

She softened her voice. 'Abandoned *you*, you mean?'

He froze.

'He was your big brother. You loved him and yet he let old resentments come between you time and time again. And then he was gone and it was too late.'

Pain tightened his features, flared his nostrils. Glinted dangerously in his eyes.

She stood to face him and whispered, '*You* need these babies. They keep him alive for you. Don't they?' They healed him. How had she not seen it earlier? 'You've never really let him go.'

His voice, thin and raw. 'He was my big brother…'

'I know,' she whispered. She knew all too well what it was to be sidelined by people who were supposed to love you. 'But you need to say goodbye.'

His eyes dropped to hers, desperate and pleading.

'Forgive him,' she whispered.

They stood there for moments, eye-locked, intensely private in a room full of people.

But then Denise spoke, standing as well. 'Nothing you've

said changes the fact that you have lied to us since the moment you set foot in this house. And now you're using two little boys, dangling them under our noses as bait to keep you here. Tied to our son.'

'She's not dangling anything, Denise,' Alice cut in. 'Tell her, Belinda.'

Tell her that you'll be leaving one baby behind when you fly back to Old Blighty. Tell her that some faceless, nameless bureaucrats have made an obscene decision that undermines everything you and Flynn worked for. Everything that is right.

She stared at Alice. Then at her boys. Then at Flynn who needed them so very badly.

Then she shook her head.

'No.' But as Flynn opened his mouth to do it for her she sped on. 'I have not used them as bait. But I have used them for something else.'

She looked at Flynn, begging him with her eyes to understand. 'I've been so broken, Flynn. I was lost and lonely and ostracised from my parents, who made me feel worthless. My own life might as well have ended when that ferry sank in Thailand. Those babies were the only thing worth living for, and fighting for the embryos gave me the first bit of hope in my meaningless existence. I became more and more obsessed with them every time some*one* or some *law* told me I couldn't have them.'

Flynn frowned, deep and hard.

'And then my petition was granted. And by then the embryos were the centre of my hollow, vacant world, and preparing my body for them became my entire purpose. And I somehow convinced myself that being with family—being together—was the most important thing for them. I ignored how ill-prepared I was to be a mother. How inappropriate my flat was. How little support I had without my sister. How I was going to support them, long-term. None of that mattered as long as I kept them in the family. In my family. It was such a *grand* purpose. And *that* was the urgency,' she said, answering a question from weeks ago. 'The urgency was in me.'

Her chest heaved with the enormity of what she was about to do and her hands shook from the terror. 'But I was selfish. I was doing it for me, not for them. I think I lost sight of what really matters in my grief. Their health. Their happiness. But I remain resolute on one point... These boys will *not* be separated. Not while I breathe.'

Flynn stared at her. 'You're going to keep fighting for them?'

Tears filled her eyes. 'No, Flynn. I'm finished fighting. I'm giving them to you.'

'Bel—' Alice gasped. Denise echoed her shocked intake of air.

'But you're their mother! They need you,' Flynn said.

She spun on him. 'And I'm *being* a mother. How I feel can't matter. Those boys will not grow up separated, only hearing about each other online.' She took a deep breath. 'You, of all people, should understand the importance of keeping their family together.'

Panic was written loud and clear on his face. 'Then stay. Raise your boys here.'

Pain sliced deep into her. Asking her to stay was his clear and desperate last resort. And it would kill them both. 'You know that's not going to work, Flynn.'

'We'll make it work.'

'A marriage based on lies will only hurt the children it's meant to protect.'

'We'll make it work,' he repeated roughly.

'Without love?' God, how it hurt to say that out loud.

'I—' He couldn't hold her eyes.

'She's not welcome to stay,' Denise chimed in, her voice thick. 'She's disrespected our whole family.'

Flynn snarled towards his mother. 'She did that for me.'

Bel pushed to her feet. 'It doesn't matter, Flynn. I won't stay where I'm not welcome. I won't be treated the way Gwen was.'

Arthur dropped his gaze to his feet.

'Then we'll leave together,' Flynn improvised. 'Raise the boys together. Away from here.'

'No!' Alice's voice this time.

'I will not be responsible for breaking up your family,' Bel cried, hoarse and heartsore. *And I will not live with you, loving you, without your love.* It was going to be hard enough continuing to breathe away from him.

Flynn's face was granite. His voice dropped. 'But you'll have no one, Bel…'

Hearing it said out loud hurt almost as much as realising he couldn't love her. She forced the lump blocking her throat aside long enough to swallow the pain. 'I've got me. And it's about time I started believing in myself.'

'Bel, this is ridiculous. You can't leave.' Arthur finally spoke. He turned to Alice. 'This can be worked out.'

'No,' Denise said firmly. The woman who'd helped bring her children into the world just a week ago now wanted her gone. Long, long gone.

Bel swung towards Flynn urgently and spoke to him as though they were alone in the room, blinking past the tears fast gathering behind her lashes. As though none of the distance or pain of the past few days existed. She spoke to him as she might have if they'd been lying in each other's arms, determinedly *not* sleeping together. 'Flynn, I lived seventeen years in enemy territory and it nearly broke me. It was unhealthy and intolerable. I cannot do that again—'

He said under his breath, 'Then I'll—'

'No. You already hold yourself responsible for the fragmentation of your family. I won't let you do what Drew did. Isolate yourself from them. For me.'

He looked to the babies.

She fought back the ache. 'They will grow up surrounded by love and nature and wide blue open skies. They'll run and hide and fall into the stream and track mud into the house and

Alice will growl at them. They'll be good and they'll be bad
and even when they are they'll have three generations of family
to support them and guide them—' Despite what they might
have unconsciously absorbed here today '—and a world of opportunity as Bradleys.

'Forget what's happened between us,' she begged. 'Just let
me go. And love those boys twice as hard for me.'

He stared at her, his chest heaving, his dark eyes pained.

'Flynn. You said to make it count.' She wrung her hands
together, twisting her fingers.

A deep frown folded down between his eyes.

'That first day in Oberon I said I'd let you know when I
knew what I wanted in return for everything we've done. You
told me to make it count. Well, this does.' She curled her fingers around his and his eyes dropped to the white gold ring
she returned. 'I need to go, Flynn.'

His whole family held their breath and Bel knew she'd already torn a fissure as wide as a valley in their fabric. But then
he spoke, low and choked, and her heart ripped completely free

'I'll drive you to the airport when you're ready.'

She burst from the house, her eyes locked forward as she
tripped down the porch steps to go and pack, heart breaking
not even pausing to say goodbye to her little men. She'd done
that a hundred times since discovering the Crown's decree
since recognising that she couldn't bring herself to part them
from each other. Every look, every touch, every kiss was a
farewell. She'd stockpiled her memories and a fridge full of
expressed milk and once that was gone they were on their own
Lots of babies grew up healthy and strong on formula. Alice
would see them right.

'Bel…!'

She stumbled in the snow and struggled to right herself, to
keep moving. It was stupid to run from Flynn when he'd have
hours with her in the car heading for the airport but, right

now, she couldn't face him. She'd never get that image out of her head. The awkwardness of his demeanour as she laid her pulpy heart out on the examination table. The dread.

That was what she'd remember most from her magical time here.

'Bel.' This time his hand snagged her arm and yanked her to a halt, but her furious forward momentum spun her and sent her sprawling into the freshly fallen snow. She scrabbled away from him and desperately tried to right herself but the tears streaming from her eyes made it impossible to see.

'Bel, don't,' Flynn groaned, lurching headlong into the snow, snagging her foot and using it to get a better hold on her. In a heartbeat she was under him, both of them prostrate in the icy drift.

'Don't touch me, Flynn!' She couldn't bear it. To smell him. To feel him. Knowing she'd never do either again. She sobbed and shoved weakly against his weight.

'Bel, listen…'

She struggled under him, screeching her frustration at being trapped. So very apt.

'You can't do this.' He forced her face around to his. 'Not his. It will kill you.'

Very probably. He shimmered and swam in the tears filling her eyes. 'What else can I do? I can't stay.'

'We'll get our own place, in Oberon. That's not leaving my family.'

'You don't love me, Flynn.' Her words were like blood, pumping from her fractured heart. 'You can't love me.'

'Bel…'

The defeat in his voice hurt her most of all. 'Is that what you want for me, Flynn? To live forever surrounded by people who only tolerate me?'

'You'll have the boys.' It was desperate and he knew it.

'And what kind of men will they grow up into, seeing that? What kind of lesson will that teach them?'

His frustration puffed as mist from his lips. 'It's something.'

'It's not enough. I've finally realised that I'm worth more
I'm worth someone's *beyond compare* love, no matter how
I grew up or what mistakes I made along the way. And that
makes me stronger.' Because God knew she'd had to grow
strong this past year.

'Enough to do something this unthinkable?'

No. Probably not. 'Enough to survive it.'

'How will you put them out of your heart?'

'I won't,' she said fiercely. 'Not any of you. But as much as
remembering will hurt, it isn't a patch on how much staying
would hurt.' She found his eyes and snared them with hers.
'You accused me of not knowing what love looked like, of having no point of reference.' Her chest heaved. She swiped at the
tears that tumbled out. '*You're* my point of reference, Flynn.'

And he always would be. No matter what happened today.

'Bel—'

'I understand, Flynn. You made me no promises. I built ice
castles around a bunch of feelings I thought were there but really weren't.'

'Bel...'

She laughed emptily. 'Seems to be a habit of mine. I may
know what love feels like but I clearly have no idea what it
looks like coming back at—'

'Bel, will you shut up and listen?'

Her teeth clacked shut.

'I need to know something.' He breathed down on her, frost
puffing out with his words. 'When you look at me, what do
you see?'

She swiped at the tears blurring her vision and stared at
him, uncomprehending. 'I see you.'

'Look deeper. Who do you really see?'

The fear in his gaze was evident. Bracing himself for hurt.

'I see a boy who worshipped the ground his brother walked
on and never got over being sidelined by him. I see a man

who's lived his life expecting the same kind of disappointment and who unconsciously hunts for evidence he's been let down. Because it's all he knows.'

Flynn frowned and then his lips tightened. 'Why the hell would you love that man? An emotional train-wreck.'

She shrugged. 'Even wrecks deserve their chance at love, don't they?' She was building her whole life on that hope. 'But you're so much more as well. Bright and focused and loving. Loyal and strong and enduring. And, to be honest, I'm no prize.'

'Do you really think that?' he said when she finally ran out of steam, his brow flat and furrowed. 'That you're worthless?'

She sagged, emotionally spent. 'My whole life, I've lived in fear of disappointing people. Of seeing expressions like your mother's tonight on people's faces. I make mistakes, Flynn, a lot of them. I'm not a good fit for a man who's scrying disappointment out wherever he goes.'

'Yet you were willing to bind yourself to me for ever?'

She didn't miss his use of the past tense and her chest compressed even further. She shifted uncomfortably under him, soaked to the skin on her lower side and toasty and warm on the upper. It was the perfect metaphor for how she'd been feeling all year. 'I didn't mean for it to happen. Poor decisions have a way of finding me.' She sighed. 'You're better off being on the other side of the world from me.'

'Who are you trying to convince?' He smiled. 'Me or yourself?'

She shivered.

His face sobered. 'Are you cold, Bel?'

'I will always be cold.' *If you're not there.* She pressed her lips together to stop their tremble.

He adjusted himself more comfortably on her, taking his weight on his elbows and stroking wet hair back from her face.

'You're not letting me up?' She squinted.

He smiled again. Two in thirty seconds: world record. 'I

told you chivalry was locked in the barn for the next year.' She frowned her confusion and he took pity on her.

He took a deep bracing breath. 'I was looking for a reason not to love you, Bel.'

She blinked, her eyes widening.

'My feelings were so easy to keep corralled on a day-to-day basis, but then you asked to stay and I…I panicked. I overreacted. I shoved you away.'

She sucked in a tight breath. All she could manage under his warm weight.

'I've had a few days to think about what you said, about what it means. For me.'

She blinked up at him.

'I was desperate for something to fail you on, Bel. The spoiled princess who stole my brother from me. But you came here and were *so* not what I expected. You fitted in immediately, you worked hard, you did all the right things with the pregnancy. You were beautiful and sexy and one hundred and ten per cent the wrong person for me, yet I still found myself totally entranced.'

She forgot all about the ice numbing her bottom.

'Even while I was taking you in my arms at night—in fact, particularly because I was—I was always watching for a reason we couldn't be together and kept finding none. Nothing reasonable. So I started fabricating reasons to keep my feelings at arm's length. Your sister. Your relationship with Drew. I was just waiting for that other shoe to drop and for life to deliver the blow I knew was coming.' He stared at her. 'And then it finally did. In the worst imaginable way.'

The tears prickled back and threatened to freeze where they pooled.

'The woman I loved only wanted me to keep the babies. I can't tell you how that felt. How many old hurts and fears it fed off. I was destroyed. I wasn't listening and I certainly wasn't hearing you, Bel. I'm sorry.'

She just shook her head fractionally.

'And then I used the custody declaration to destroy you right back. Apparently, that's the man I now am.'

Desire to protect him—defend him—surged through her. 'You were angry. Upset.'

'I was a jerk. A-class.'

'Well…yes… But no one's perfect.' Except he was perfect for her.

His eyes clouded over. 'Perfection is hard to live up to.'

The urge to protect him from any more hurt swamped her. From the lofty vantage point of a woman in love with the better man—the best of men—it only served to show her how deep her love for Flynn truly ran. And how *visible* she'd felt since stepping onto that flight with him.

'You were right when you said Drew wasn't perfect, Flynn. He made mistakes, lots of them. But he tried to learn from them.' She tilted her head and wished her arms were more free to wrap around him because what she was going to say might hurt. 'I think him being so loving and warm and inclusive of me was his way of…making up…for how wrong he got it with you.' She touched his face. 'I think he might really have regretted how badly he handled himself when he was younger. And he was determined to get it right the second time around.' She took a breath. 'I think maybe you two could have found a better place again if he'd had a bit more time.'

Flynn stared at her, wide-eyed. Still cautious. Still protecting himself. 'You believe that?'

'I do.'

Bad choice of words, it only brought their wedding back into crashing focus. But, as she said the words, something shifted in him visibly. He filled his lungs with frigid mountain air and squeezed her hand. 'As far as I'm concerned, Golden Boy stuffed up at least once, big-time.'

'When?'

His warmth rained down on her from eyes so like the twins', bored right down into her soul. 'He picked the wrong sister.'

Bel gasped, the sudden hope doing laps in her system immediately warring with her instinctive need to protect herself. Her heart.

His eyes grew soft. 'I should thank him,' Flynn murmured. 'For keeping you safe for all those years. For making you feel valued. Until I could find you.'

Her eyes swam with tears again. 'I didn't think you felt—'

'I saw it happening, Bel. I was right there with you, experiencing the *thing* between us taking shape. Growing out of control. I fought it, every single day.' He tucked her freezing hands into his woollen shirt. 'Yet still I talked you into my bed and convinced myself I could have my cake and eat it: have you in my bed but not in my heart.'

He blew on her hands, then lifted his eyes to hers. 'I was wrong. Your image is engraved on my heart. Your smile is what keeps it beating and your kisses stop it cold.'

Love swelled up and threatened to choke the air right out of her. 'Then why...?'

'I couldn't conceive of a woman like you picking a man like me to love. An ex-felon. A man who drove his family apart with resentment. I was so certain you'd wake up one morning and realise the inexplicable attraction between us had run its course, that you'd tire of second best.'

'Never.'

'I believe that. Now.'

'And the attraction hasn't waned.' She glanced down his body where it pressed so close to hers. One particularly firm place. She smiled. 'For either of us, it seems.'

His eyes never left hers. 'Really? I have no idea. I've been numb from the chest down for the past ten minutes...'

Bel had never imagined in her wildest dreams that she would laugh today. But one burbled out of her and spilled into the air, melting the frost in its path. Flynn took the opportunity to capture her smiling lips in a searing kiss which went some way to heating her icy body. She slid her hands up behind his neck, his head, and kissed him back on a half-sob.

Another thing she'd thought she'd never get to do again.

'I love you, Flynn,' she risked. 'But I don't know if I have the stamina to keep proving it to you.'

His eyes met hers seriously. 'You don't need to prove anything, you just need to be you.'

She wept, deep down inside. How long had she secretly wished for someone to love her just the way she was? Not who they wanted her to be, not who they thought she should be with time and attention. Her—Bel Rochester. The woman she already was.

'Besides, it's me who has something to prove. So that you'll believe how much I love you back.'

Love—present tense.

Relief and joy and passion and laughter all scrambled for pole position, racing through her bloodstream, exciting her senses as Flynn lowered his mouth to hers again. They kissed as though it was the first time, as though they weren't both half-frozen from exposure. As though their world hadn't imploded just minutes before.

That thought slowly dragged Bel from the drugged heaven of his lips.

'What about your family? They don't want me here,' she whispered close to his mouth.

'It's been a day of shocks all round; they didn't handle themselves the best. But then neither did I.'

He dragged his icy nose back and forth across hers.

'What are you doing?'

'The Bunyip's Reach mating ritual. I'm marking you as mine.'

Her lips cracked in a chilly approximation of a smile at the ridiculous act. 'Mmm...sexy.'

His eyes grew serious. 'You are the wife of their son and the mother of their grandchildren. We will work through whatever issues my parents have with how this whole thing has evolved.'

'And if we don't?'

'If we don't, we'll leave. Start our own place.'

'I don't want to rip your family apart, Flynn.'

'You wouldn't be, they would be. Besides, we have our own family to start worrying about. Twin boys are not going to be a piece of cake to raise. Not with Bradley genes thrown in.'

An iridescent heat spread through her. 'They'll be fantastic boys. And they'll love and protect their younger brothers and sisters.'

'More children—already?'

'Just planning ahead. Someone has to help us run the property.' She kissed his frosty lips. 'Or it could just be an excuse to get you into bed. I assumed you'd be dead keen on that part.'

'Gaggingly keen, believe me. After eighty-seven nights of chivalry, I'm ready for a little debauchery.'

'You counted?'

His eyes grew sombre. 'To the minute.'

'Well, do you think we should get out of this snow before anything we'll need gets frostbite?'

'God, yes. I think there are some sleeping boys who'll be happy to have their mum back, too.'

He shuffled inelegantly backwards and pushed himself onto numb haunches, before pulling Bel carefully onto her feet. Behind them the door to the homestead opened, warm orange light pouring out, and Alice emerged onto the porch holding Bel's favourite alpaca quilt open in wide arms.

Welcoming arms.

Forgiving arms.

And in that moment Bel knew that there was nothing she couldn't face with this man at her side, those babies in her arms, and the fiercest nan she'd ever known at her back.

* * * * *

A sneaky peek at next month...

Cherish™

ROMANCE TO MELT THE HEART EVERY TIME

My wish list for next month's titles...

In stores from 20th January 2012:

❏ Back in the Soldier's Arms – Soraya Lane

& Here Comes the Groom – Karina Bliss

❏ A Match for the Doctor – Marie Ferrarella

& What the Single Dad Wants... – Marie Ferrarella

❏ The Chief Ranger – Rebecca Winters

In stores from 3rd February 2012:

❏ Invitation to the Prince's Palace – Jennie Adams

& The Prince's Second Chance – Brenda Harlen

❏ Miss Prim and the Billionaire – Lucy Gordon

Available at WHSmith, Tesco, Asda, Eason, Amazon and Apple

Just can't wait?

Visit us Online

You can buy our books online a month before they hit the shops! **www.millsandboon.co.uk**

0112/23

2 Free Books!

Join the Mills & Boon Book Club

Want to read more **Cherish**™ books? We're offering you **2 more** absolutely **FREE!**

We'll also treat you to these fabulous extras:

- 🌹 Books up to 2 months ahead of shops

- 🌹 FREE home delivery

- 🌹 Bonus books with our special rewards scheme

- 🌹 Exclusive offers and much more!

Get your free books now!

Visit us Online

Find out more at
www.millsandboon.co.uk/freebookoffer

SUBS/ONLINE/S

Don't miss Pink Tuesday
One day. 10 hours. 10 deals.

PINK TUESDAY IS COMING!

10 hours...10 unmissable deals!

This Valentine's Day we will be bringing you fantastic offers across a range of our titles—each hour, on the hour!

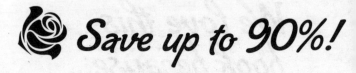

Save up to 90%!

Pink Tuesday starts
9am Tuesday 14th February